PURE SACRIFICE

A MYTHOS LEGACY

NOVEL

Also By Jami Gold

Unintended Guardian (A Mythos Legacy Short Story)
Treasured Claim (A Mythos Legacy Novel, Book One)
Ironclad Devotion (A Mythos Legacy Novel, Book Three)
Stone-Cold Heart (A Mythos Legacy Novel, Book Four)

PURE SACRIFICE

A MYTHOS LEGACY

NOVEL

JAMI GOLD

BLUE
PHOENIX
PRESS

PHOENIX, ARIZONA

Cover Design by Laird Sapir and Melinda VanLone
Content Editing by Jessa Slade and Marcy Kennedy
Line Editing by Erynn Newman of A Little Red
Copy Editing by Julie Glover
Author Photo by Mark Oxley/Studio 16

Blue Phoenix Press
18337 E San Tan Boulevard, #9435
Queen Creek, Arizona 85142
Visit our website at bluephoenixpress.com

This is a work of fiction. Names, characters, places, and incidents are a product of the author's imagination or are used fictitiously. Any resemblance to actual events, locales, or persons, living or dead, is coincidental.

The author acknowledges the trademark status and trademark owners of various products or copyright material mentioned throughout this work of fiction, including the following: Conan the Barbarian, Captain Jack Sparrow, Ferrari, and Ford Mustang. The publication and use of these trademarks is not authorized, associated with, or sponsored by the trademark owners.

Ordering Information:
Quantity sales. Special discounts are available on quantity purchases by corporations, associations, and others. For details, contact the Publisher at the address or website above.

Pure Sacrifice / Jami Gold. -- 1st ed.

Publisher's Cataloging-in-Publication Data
provided by Five Rainbows Services

Gold, Jami.
   Pure sacrifice : a mythos legacy novel / Jami Gold.
      pages cm. – (Mythos legacy, bk. 2)
   ISBN: 978-1-942928-04-1 (pbk.)
   ISBN: 978-1-942928-03-4 (e-book)
   1. Shapeshifting—Fiction. 2. Unicorns—Fiction. 3. Virginity—Fiction. 4. Magic—Fiction.
5. Love stories.   I. Title.
PS3607.O436 P87 2015
813`.6—dc23

                                                            2015909605

To join the author's mailing list and take advantage of **pre-order-only sale prices** for new releases, visit *jamigold.com/mail*

For the outsiders —
May you discover magic in your life...

Chapter One

THE STRANGER'S EYES STARED BACK AT CELIA FROM THE sketchpad. Finally. Apparently, the hundred-and-fifty-seventh time was the charm.

She leaned against the bus seat and flicked eraser bits off the paper. That was a damn good likeness if she said so herself.

Her gaze stole across the bus aisle to check out her subject. As usual, dark sunglasses hid his pools-of-warm-honey eyes. No matter. Months ago, an unsteady passenger had knocked off those shades, and she'd gotten enough of a glimpse to cement the image into her memory. Eyes like that would make puppies jealous.

In contrast, the rest of him oozed guy-you-didn't-bring-home-to-Momma. His Conan the Barbarian build added to the Captain Jack Sparrow beaded dreadlocks and leather clothes to rank him high on the *not safe* meter.

But those eyes... They fascinated her. Maybe he wore sunglasses to hide their secret.

What secret his eyes might reveal if they were exposed she had no idea. Yet she couldn't help spending an unhealthy amount of time thinking about the intimidating—and sexy—stranger.

Heat crept up her cheeks. Not that he'd turned in her direction, or even twitched. Regardless, her face burned as though behind his shades, he'd focused on her.

Impossible. No one ever noticed her.

Even now, when the bus held only one lily-white ass—hers—everyone ignored her. As usual.

The familiar taste of bitterness rose in her throat, and she buried the sensation with a swallow. The ability to live in the ninety-five-percent black neighborhood of West End without drawing attention meant she could afford another year at Washington University in St. Louis. Her scholarship was great but didn't cover housing costs.

And the world had made it perfectly clear she didn't deserve more.

The bus rounded the corner onto Hamilton Avenue, and she packed up her sketchbook and colored pencils. The stranger across the aisle stood as well.

Somehow, no matter what her class and lab schedule was each day, he always ended up on her bus. Any other person would suspect him of being a stalker. Right. He'd have to be aware of her existence first.

Her weight shifted as the bus groaned to a halt, and she let Mr. Scary-Hotpants pass by in the aisle before following him to the door. A grumble from her stomach sent heat to her face again. Hopefully she could grab some supper from her landlady, "Auntie" Harriet.

Crap! The prescription she'd promised to pick up.

Just in time, Celia yanked her foot back from stepping off the bus. Another passenger behind her on the stairs barreled forward as if she were invisible. She flattened herself against the stair railing and let the woman pass. The bus started again, and Celia scooted into a seat.

Movement outside the window caught her eye. The leather-clad stranger strode alongside the bus, his head turned toward her far enough that a blue-beaded dreadlock slid over his shoulder and swung freely. Furrows formed above the sharply angled brows peeking above his sunglasses.

Chill bumps rose on her arms despite her jacket.

The bus sped up, leaving his figure to fade in the distance. Once she lost sight of him, she twisted forward in the bench and rubbed her arms. She'd imagined that, right? He wasn't *really* a stalker and upset she hadn't gotten off the bus with him. Was he?

Well, if he was a stalker, he was a piss-poor one. They'd been riding the same bus for a year and a half—ever since her required freshman-year stint in the dorms—and other than a few times when he *might* have looked at her from behind those sunglasses, he'd fallen firmly into the you-don't-deserve-my-attention camp. And he'd never followed her home, even though she rented a room from an elderly woman more defenseless than herself.

No, the stalker thing didn't make sense. It must have just been a coincidence that his head had swiveled in her direction.

Several stops later, she used her fast stride, honed from scurrying to reach classes on time, to make it to the pharmacy while she still had some daylight. People might ignore her, but she wasn't so stupid as to rely on that fact for safety.

Not in this neighborhood.

The address from Auntie Harriet matched a little hole-in-the-wall liquor market stuck between a rundown building and a darkened community center. An electronic door chime buzzed at her arrival, and the stench of smoke and body odor inside choked her throat. The man behind the counter thumped his cigarette pack repeatedly.

Predictably, he didn't look up at her approach. Unless she spoke, she might as well not exist to the world. And sometimes not even then.

"Excuse me, I'm Celia Hawkins, here to pick up a prescription for Harriet Williams."

She'd have grumbled—not actually out loud, of course, as that never ended well for her—about Auntie Harriet sending her prescriptions to a pharmacy in this neighborhood, but conveniences like supermarkets and chain restaurants were rare in the north section of St. Louis proper. The only other pharmacies in the area were even farther away.

In a way, the lack of shopping options reminded her of the small-town life at home. As if the local violent crime was simply the big city version of cow-tipping.

After the cashier rang up the purchase, Celia stuffed the prescription bag into her backpack and slung the strap over her left shoulder. "Thanks."

The guy thumped his cigarette carton, signaling he'd already forgotten she existed. Just as bad as her professors, her classmates...

And her family.

Damn people were all the same. Someday she might just snap and decide the consequences of demanding more from the world weren't as horrible as living like this.

She snorted. Right. And someday she'd have a boyfriend too.

During the few minutes she'd been inside the store, dusk had fallen, and she zipped her jacket against the chill. Crap, she'd miss the next southbound bus for home if she didn't hustle the half mile to the bus stop.

A few blocks down, busted-out streetlights loomed overhead, and two tall, boarded-up buildings hulked over the sidewalk, darkening the area even more. She quickened her already hurried steps.

Something skimmed her hand, and she jumped, interrupting her stride. At her elbow, a bush growing through the broken pavement between the abandoned structures reached over the sidewalk.

A weak laugh burst from her. "Just a branch, Celia."

An arm shot out from beside the bush and yanked her into the darkness. A hand covered her mouth from behind, and the thumb blocked her nose. Adrenaline clawed through her body so fast she broke out in a cold sweat under her jacket.

She struggled against the strong grasp, thrashing her head and trying to pry the fingers away. But the hand stuck to her face like duct tape, and she couldn't get in a breath to do anything, much less scream. Her heartbeat filled the space of her empty lungs, pounding through her chest.

Visions of her maybe-stalker flickered in her mind. She'd have no chance at besting a goliath like him, but she swung her elbows anyway, fighting for air.

Her attacker pulled her tight to his ribs, pinning her arms. He was about her height and scraggly in build.

Not her stranger from the bus.

Her relief didn't last as this unknown stranger dragged her away from the road.

"Who's your pimp?" The scent of alcohol and sweat tainted the tiny amount of air creeping around his thumb. "Why he bringing white pussy to this 'hood?"

She twisted in his hold.

A sharp point jabbed under her jaw. "Uh-uh, no fighting, ho."

She scanned the area for anything to use as a weapon. How could she escape?

He heaved her into a narrow alley behind the buildings. Thick trees and crumbling homes, dark and vacant, framed them in from the other side. The truth settled heavily in her gut.

There was no one around to help her.

No one.

The blade pressed on her neck, and grimy fingers shoved oily fabric into her mouth, gagging her. "You cross into my territory, I get a freebie. Them's the rules."

Icy tendrils trailed the adrenaline in her limbs. God, why had she spoken and announced her presence? Of all the times to *not* let herself be overlooked. Stupid.

Think, dammit. Panic bubbled up in her chest, and her throat tightened against the too-deep-to-spit-out gag. This was definitely *not* how she'd wanted to lose her virginity.

The knife's pressure let up for a second, and she jammed her elbow back into his ribs. She hopped, moving in the only direction she could, and threw her left shoulder up. Her off-kilter backpack caught his chin. She stooped and lunged under the now-outstretched blade.

One step away. Two steps away.

Her backpack heaved in his grasp and jerked her sideways. Solid knuckles crashed into the side of her face. Fire burst through her jaw, and she stumbled.

"Bitch!" He tossed her to the blacktop.

She hit the ground hard, jarring her wrists. Glass fragments cut into her palms and stabbed through her jeans at her knees. Stings burned at every point. He straddled her from behind, grabbed a fistful of hair, and slammed the side of her head into the pavement.

Crack.

Light blasted in her eyes. Pinpricks of heat erupted across her cheek from the remnants of broken bottles slicing her skin.

"I warned you not to fight me, ho. Your pimp oughta thank me for teaching you your place." He smashed her skull into the ground again.

Warm, wet liquid met her face. Pressure built at her temple, and the horizon tilted. A metallic scent filled her nose with each sucked-in breath. She pushed up on her arms, but they didn't want to move. Red flashes speckled her vision.

He yanked her wrists behind her back and shoved her right hand through the other strap of her backpack. He twisted the pack, and the straps cut across her biceps, effectively tying her arms behind her.

Her arms, her shoulders, her muscles—everything screamed. Wrenched out of place and too weak to help. The weight of her bag added to his mass and pinned her to the ground.

She tried to lift her head and work the gag forward to spit the fabric out. Instead, the red spots in front of her eyes turned black, and the alley swirled around her. Oh God, she was going to die.

Here.

Now.

Her attacker sawed through her jeans with his blade. "That's right... Good little whore... Or I'll fuck you with my knife..."

The pounding in her skull drowned out most of the words. Or was she passing out?

Cool air drifted over her bare bottom, and pain broke through her haze. He carved into the skin of her butt cheek and chuckled like a madman. "I. Was. Here."

A scream ground its way up her throat only to be muffled by the gag. He was going to torture her until she died.

Please, no. Please, no. Please, no.

The hammering in her head deepened into a rhythmic thunder echoing her plea. In sync with the rumble, vibrations shook the asphalt under her cheek.

The thunder rolled down the alley past her. The weight of her attacker disappeared, and a shriek reverberated off the surrounding brick walls.

What...? Pressure in her temples spread into blackness. She blinked. Dark—so dark. White flashing. Moving.

A–a horse? White and glistening like freshly fallen snow. Snow. She was cold. So cold.

Dark liquid streaked down from something on the horse's

forehead as it galloped away.

Come here, horsey. But the horse wouldn't come. She didn't have any sugar cubes.

Only darkness.

Chapter Two

MARKOS DIDN'T DARE TOUCH THE VIRGIN.

By the Maker, that had been too close. He crouched down in front of her. Blood crawled across the pavement from under her head, and mottled splotches spread over her face. The sight of his near-failure turned his stomach.

What the *skoro* had she been thinking? His magic could do only so much. Keeping her pure—and alive—in a place like this made his job a thousand times harder.

"Wake up."

She didn't move.

The gag. Maybe she couldn't breathe. He took off his sunglasses and poked at the rag with its plastic arm. The tip slipped behind the fabric, and he pried the gag from her mouth.

He slapped the ground so hard the gust of air blew her blonde hair. "Wake up!"

Still nothing.

Mule's piss. He couldn't leave her here. He had to get her home and off the street. And that meant he'd have to touch her.

He stuck his sunglasses in a pocket, tugged his leather jacket over his hands to minimize contact, and slid his arms under her body. As he stood, holding her away from his chest, her head lolled to the side and revealed her injuries.

Blood poured from an open wound at her temple, cuts covered

her face, and her narrow jaw hung loosely, probably broken. She was so fragile. Too fragile.

The Virgin would die if he left her at home bleeding and unconscious.

Ass, ass, and more ass. He needed to heal her, but not here. Not in public.

New to-do list. Get her home—quickly. But how?

Her bedroom at the old woman's house was too far away for a direct transport, his magic unable to connect two distant Earthen points. No, the only way to get her home was to take her through the Mythos plane.

Piss. By the time the Council of Elders was done with him for all these transgressions, he wouldn't be worth a gelding's balls.

He mentally reached through the veil between planes and held the image of his quarters in his mind. With a swirl of his fingers, a vaporous doorway to the spartan white room formed in front of him, and he stepped into the mist. No one else was around. Thank the Maker he didn't have any unscheduled visitors asking questions he hadn't come up with answers for yet.

He half-expected her to wake as her body recognized its destiny in the Mythos plane. She didn't.

Not a good sign.

If he couldn't heal her, they were all headed straight to Hades's crows.

Mist swirled in front of him as he brought to mind her attic bedroom at the old woman's house. The vapor coalesced as his magic slipped through vents and cracked-open windows to enter the room. He carried her back into the Earthen plane and laid her on her side on the bed.

Twilight filled the room with shadows, hiding her injuries, and he switched on the table lamp beside the bed. Her backpack still bound her arms, and he slid the straps down, releasing her.

He was about to turn her onto her back when her bare rounded behind caught his eye. Heat galloped through him. He sucked in a breath through his teeth and shot back, bumping his head on the sloping ceiling. The opposite corner wasn't far enough in the small room.

This was wrong. All wrong.

He wasn't supposed to touch her. He wasn't supposed to see her like this. He wasn't even supposed to get this close to her until he'd prepared for the ritual. He couldn't do this.

Couldn't? If he didn't heal her, there wouldn't *be* a ritual.

Suck it up, jackass.

He set his jaw and returned to her side. Letter-shaped gashes bled onto her bedsheet. Too bad the son of a mule who'd attacked her couldn't die a second time. He'd gladly kill the man several times over.

The only way to heal her was to touch her, skin-to-skin. The Maker must have a sick sense of humor.

He swallowed and placed his hand over the deep graffiti cuts. His hand covered her behind, his fingers following the curves. The urge to stroke the yielding flesh twitched along his arm. He shook his head, banishing the enticing image.

He was the last of the Guardians. He would resist. He would remain pure—pure in thought and pure in action.

Warmth passed from his palm into her skin. Her body would knit itself together, and by morning, only a slight reddish mark would give evidence of the injuries. He closed his eyes and let his magic go to work. He *could* do this.

He relaxed, lulled by the softness under his fingertips. How could anything be so supple? His thumb absently circled.

Mugarok! He yanked his hand back. Caressing her? He should be the last one to make that mistake. The danger of getting too close to the Virgin hadn't been exaggerated.

His vow came out in a low rumble. "I will not be tempted."

He rolled her onto her back and tugged the bedsheet up to her neck, covering her allure. Her battered head desperately needed attention, so he forced himself to touch her again, but he dug his fingernails into the palm of his other hand. He wouldn't let impure thoughts take hold within him again.

One by one, the cuts on her face sealed shut, and shattered bones re-formed. After the last injury healed, the Virgin opened her eyes.

He froze. *Skoro* and ass. Maybe she'd be incoherent.

She reached up and stroked his dreadlocks. "I always knew you were a good guy."

Her eyelids closed again. Sleep tugged her fingers through his hair, and her arm flopped down the side of the bed. A soft *tap* sounded as her hand fell to the wood flooring.

Curse the Maker. Hopefully that "good guy" nonsense meant she *was* incoherent. He scanned her room. If she wasn't delirious, would she remember that he'd been here?

He sat back on his heels. Maybe cloaking magic would make her forget. The stories implied that type of magic wouldn't work on the Virgin, but what choice did he have? Hopefully, the stories were wrong, and it would affect her the same way it affected other humans.

Blood glistened on her dangling palm. He stood, ignoring the minor injury. Those cuts would heal on their own, and there was no pissing way he'd risk touching her again.

He drew a pattern in the air above her, calling on the threads tying the two planes together. A woven square of mist took shape from the intricate motions of his fingers, born of his intention to hide the past hour from her awareness.

He released his creation with a flick of his fingertips. "Forget."

The shroud of vapor fluttered over her head and sank into her skin. With luck, she'd think she'd overestimated her injuries and stumbled home on her own.

He switched off her light and stepped into the Mythos plane.

Time to face the Council of Elders.

Chapter Three

THE SUMMONS WAS WAITING FOR MARKOS WHEN HE ARRIVED at his quarters. Other than removing the leather jacket that had been exposed to the Virgin, he didn't bother changing before heading out. Nothing could remove the contamination inside him.

The white-marbled columns and buildings of his homeland glowed in the moonlight. The soft illumination turned the paths to Council Hall into silvery rivers winding through the trees. Burbles and sloshes from the nearby brook accompanied the smells of an eternal springtime. Green, growing, pure.

The serene evening didn't calm him. His muscles ached, still shuddering with tension from the slip with his thumb—and his thoughts.

Hoof falls shadowed him, quiet on the grass along the path.

He stopped. "Show yourself. I'm in no mood for games tonight."

Hipdemos approached and tossed his head, bouncing his white mane across his neck. Light glinted off his golden horn as he emerged from the shadows. "I hope you're not planning on entering the council chamber looking like that."

Markos surveyed his appearance. Boots, worn leather pants, Henley shirt, leather vest, wide leather wrist cuffs, and buckles everywhere. With as many mistakes as he'd made tonight, he couldn't care about breaking such an insignificant rule. He continued along the path.

Hipdemos trotted beside him and snorted. "Markos. You know as well as I do that if you appear before the priestesses in human form, they'll think you're challenging them."

For a moment, the darkness swallowed everything but the *clomps* of their feet.

Hipdemos arched his long neck closer. "Are you?"

"I've never approved of the way Alkipsia rules with an iron hoof. That's no secret. But no, I'm not challenging them."

Broad white withers blocked the path. "Then she'll find a way to punish you."

Markos pulled up short and peered toward the horizon. "I don't know if I care."

"What happened to you?"

He couldn't explain his dark mood to himself, much less to anyone else.

He shoved against Hipdemos's flank. "Move."

Hipdemos bowed his head and shuffled back. "Yes, my prince."

Markos took two steps and then stopped. By the Maker, he couldn't deal with this tonight. "I wasn't giving an order."

"It sounded like one." Hipdemos's ears pivoted forward. "Maybe you should try it more often."

"Hipdemos." He didn't restrain the warning in his tone.

"You're the last of the royal line and—"

"*And* I'm not female. I cannot rule the tribe."

Not to mention that he'd proved his unworthiness too many times over the centuries with every Virgin he'd failed to save during the ritual. And his impure thoughts tonight had been his worst mistake yet. He was going to get his whole tribe killed.

"Plenty would follow you."

"That's not the point." He started toward Council Hall again. "A tribe divided is no tribe at all."

Markos left Hipdemos at the edge of the trees and lifted his head toward the next confrontation. Council Hall stood above him on the hill at the center of his homeland.

Unlike the rest of their land, which showed signs of his tribe's fading magic, the massive columned building had been continuously maintained during the four-and-a-half centuries of Alkipsia's reign—another indication of her conceit. Familiar bitterness burned through his chest, and he tamped down the feeling.

His mother was no longer alive to rule as queen and high priestess, so thoughts like that were a dead end. Especially under Alkipsia's rule.

Faceted lanterns lit the way from the front entrance to the drapes marking the doorway to the council chamber at the end of the hall. An attendant trotted out, his ears pulled back and his lips parted, baring his teeth.

"I'm not changing." Markos kept his tone calm, almost bored. He had a feeling he should have recognized this male, but with his failures to heal their land over the centuries, he didn't deserve connections with his kind anymore.

The attendant's tail swished, and he flared his nostrils.

Maybe Hipdemos was partially right about giving more orders. He met the male's eye. "Open the curtain. Now."

Swish. Swish. Swish. Pity that flies didn't exist on the Mythos plane to give that tail something real to do.

The attendant finally lowered his head and clacked his teeth. "As you wish, my prince." He poked his golden horn through the overlap of the hanging fabric and pushed the drapes aside.

Markos entered the council chamber and faced the three priestesses huddled behind the half-wall separating the council thrones from commoners. Of course *they* were in their human form. *They* were allowed.

"I have come." He didn't acknowledge their summons, but he did perform an elaborate human bow, complete with several flourishes of his hand for added irony.

Silence fell over the group of females. Their gaze roved his appearance, and as one, their jaws dropped. Recovering first, Alkipsia gathered her gauzy dress and swept to the center throne of the high priestess, elevated above the commoners' floor even more than the other two thrones. The lower priestesses followed suit and took their seats on either side of her.

Alkipsia gave him a tight smile under her wild halo of spiraling black hair. "The council recognizes Markos Ambrostead, who has come in answer to our summons." She raised one brow. "We have rules for a reason, Markos. Requiring those who wish an audience with us to appear in their natural form ensures that no one is scorned, even those who have lost the ability to shift. We want all who appear before us to be equal."

"With you being more equal than others, of course."

Her hand waved away the obvious. "Of course."

May the Maker grant him patience. He sighed. Forget it. Lost cause.

"Remind me to bring you a book from the Earthen plane. Called *Animal Farm*."

Her eyes narrowed, and she leaned forward. "I do hope you are not comparing me to an animal, Markos."

He tilted his chin, feigning innocence. "Would I do that?"

She slapped the arms of her throne and stood. "Our kind are not *animals*. We are not simply *horses* with a horn." Her light brown skin flushed with a grimace at the epithet—*horses*.

He stomped closer to her perch. "*I* know that. We are proud, mighty, and magnificent, not merely servants of one who mistakenly believes herself more powerful..."

He closed his mouth before the words "you stupid donkey tit" emerged.

Forget about dying during the next few months. His mood was well on its way to getting him gored through the heart. Tonight.

He hadn't intended on challenging Alkipsia's rule when he'd walked into the council chamber, but somehow his frustration had gotten the better of him.

No, not *somehow*. He knew exactly where this anger was coming from. Anger at himself. Anger at his mistakes. Anger at endangering all their lives. His tribe deserved better than his failures.

Silence replaced the echoes of his words, and her stare turned cold. Finally, she retook her seat and spent a moment arranging the nearly see-through gray dress around her form. Although she was the eldest female, she didn't look a day older than a human in her twenties, and she had the vanity to go with that fact.

When she looked up again, her voice dripped with compassion. "Markos, you have served our kind well for 440 years, and we are grateful. We summoned you here to explain how we were able to smell the Virgin in our land, as we wish to understand your dilemma."

He struggled to keep his face blank. Since when did she show him respect? Even though she was undoubtedly insincere, he couldn't help wanting sympathy.

"I'm going to fail again."

His stomach lurched, and the admission that he might get them all killed even before the ceremony on the Spring Equinox stalled in his chest.

"Despite the fact that I'm the sole Guardian of our kind, the last one able to take on human form in the Earthen plane and shield the chosen Virgin of each generation, and the only one with the inborn magic to salvage even the failed rituals, I've never been qualified for this job. Worse, the Earthen plane is changing, making the task impossible for anyone."

His gaze fell, and he visually traced the maze of inlaid gold lines in the marble floor, as if they could show him where things had gone so wrong.

"This generation's Virgin is not content to stay home and await some man to pay attention to her. She has gone out into the world, and she is..." He struggled to find the right word.

Alluring. Enticing. Tempting...

"Assertive."

"Assertive? Your magic is supposed to prevent that." Alkipsia's tone dropped into a sneer, implying additional failures on his part. *That* was the Alkipsia he knew.

"No, my magic is intended only to make it easier for the Virgins to choose to join us during the ceremony. The spell creates an emotional distance by making humans, especially men, uninterested in her—unless she makes herself known in some way. As a side effect, the weaker bonds typically cause the Virgins to be shy and withdrawn, but this generation's Virgin is chafing at her situation more than usual." He glanced away. "And she is aware of my presence."

A soft gasp resounded from all three females.

Charisia, one of the lower priestesses, touched Alkipsia's forearm. "Maybe this is a sign. Maybe this Virgin will accept Markos at the ritual and heal our magic."

His twenty failures had destroyed any hope those words might have engendered.

Alkipsia froze, and deep creases formed above her stony gaze. "Tell me more."

"As she is active in the world, I have had to keep a closer watch on her than usual. She places herself in countless dangerous predicaments every day. She spends hours in assemblies with men who might become aware of her every time she speaks. She travels in a conveyance surrounded by men who are intoxicated enough to lessen the effect of my magic. I have had to follow her everywhere to ensure the preservation of her purity." He indicated his attire. "This style of clothing is intimidating to human females. Yet she goes out of her way to notice me."

"Perhaps she is merely being watchful of you as a possible threat."

"Perhaps."

He didn't bring up that she'd called him a "good guy." He stifled a snort. Delirious.

"Regardless, she is very much aware of my existence." He crossed his arms. "Tonight, a chemically altered man attacked her with the intention to defile or murder her. I killed him before he had the chance."

"Naturally."

"But she was severely wounded. To prevent her death, I had to bring her through the Mythos plane so I could return her home and begin the healing process. That is why you smelled her scent here."

Alkipsia fell back against her throne, her jaw slack. "You–you touched her?"

The answer burned his gut, and he spit out the word. "Yes."

"This disturbed you. That's why you believe you will fail again."

He didn't deny her insight. Especially as it meant he didn't have to reveal just how much weakness he'd shown in the Virgin's room. How deep his impure thoughts had led him into temptation.

"She will survive, however?" Alkipsia quietly tapped her nails on the arm of her throne. "Purity intact?"

"Yes."

She glanced at the other priestesses and then faced him again. "Wait outside until we call you. We have much to discuss."

He bowed his head and retreated from the room. They might not see eye to eye on how to rule the tribe, but Alkipsia was the only one with enough insight into the Maker's commandments to help him avoid another failure. Another needless Virgin death.

The attendant met him in the hall and neighed. "You're still alive. Glad to see it."

Markos patted his withers as he passed by. Good to know the male's earlier behavior was driven by protectiveness rather than kowtowing to the council.

He stood at the Council Hall entrance and let the cool night air wash over him. The stars overhead danced, like fireflies flickering in rhythm to a secret song. A glowing stellar disc swathed the land in a brilliant ribbon despite the moon's glow. Humans had never seen a night sky that could compare, even in the most remote corners of the planet.

He reattached a loose buckle on his vest. Although truth be told, he spent so much time on the Earthen plane these clothes felt like part of him now. Yet another reason his kind kept their distance from him.

The attendant returned sooner than expected. "The council is ready for you."

The three females sat in their thrones, and Alkipsia inclined her head to him. "You have performed a great service for our kind tonight, and I wish we could protect you from the trials yet to come. However, the Virgin must be protected, no matter the risk, and tonight's events have shown us the potential threats are greater than we imagined. Therefore, we have decided you must reside full-time on the Earthen plane—"

"*What?*"

"—where you will keep constant watch over the Virgin."

"I can't *do* that."

"You must remain strong and pure if we are to survive."

"But you're telling me to get *closer* to her."

"We regret the situation. Perhaps this Virgin will be the one, and you will finally be rewarded for your efforts." Alkipsia's grimace and flat tone didn't offer hope for that possibility.

The priestesses stood as one and left him alone in the council chamber. His limbs grew heavy and thick, the finality of their departure upsetting his balance.

He remained there—how long he didn't know—and tried to grasp the enormity of their decree. Rather than finding a solution so he wouldn't fail again, the council had dismissed the danger the Virgin posed to him. To all of them.

Physically resisting her would be difficult enough, but he'd already proven he couldn't keep his thoughts pure. He'd have to remove part of his brain to manage that feat. Yet the Maker's commandment demanded nothing less than purity, in actions *and* in thoughts.

Impossible. He might very well go insane before the Spring Equinox freed him.

Chapter Four

SOMEHOW, HE MADE IT BACK TO HIS QUARTERS DESPITE HIS stunned daze. The council's attendant, now in human form, waited for him. The male's appearance shook him from his stupor. Parimenos.

No wonder the attendant had seemed familiar. Centuries ago, Parimenos's sister was intended to be Markos's mate. His mother had arranged the pairing back when she was still alive—and matings were legal.

Parimenos's family had suffered greatly for their defense of the royal line during the Civil War—including the loss of his sister. In a show of respect for what could have been, Markos gave the male a deep bow.

"Forgive me for not recognizing you earlier. I spend far too much time away from home."

His stomach hollowed. It was only going to be worse for the near future.

"Think nothing of it, my prince." Parimenos indicated a two-foot-square stack of gold kilobars in the corner. "The council anticipated that you might need additional funds to set up a permanent domicile for you and the Virgin. These have been purified and minted to your specifications. Will this be adequate for your needs?"

Living under the same roof as the Virgin? Markos shuddered

and dismissed the idea by picking up a bar from the top of the pile. This much gold would be worth over twenty million dollars once he placed it on the market through the private Unicore Mint he'd set up on the Earthen plane.

"Yes, that will be plenty."

He had no intention of speaking with the Virgin, much less sharing a house. But he *did* need a location close enough to use for direct transport. His magic could create an Earth-bound portal only within a mile or so radius, so his lakeside castle in Ireland was unquestionably too far away. Thank the Maker the council had no way to check up on *how* he fulfilled their edicts.

Parimenos started for the door, but Markos stopped him. "I'll be importing several hundred kilos of iron bars to offset this export. Make sure the council informs the faeries. I don't want to come home to a war."

Parimenos grinned and dipped his head. "I'll ensure everyone is notified."

After the male left, Markos transported the gold bars to Unicore Mint's vault in London and wrote instructions for his executor to handle the gold and iron exchanges. The Mythos plane had plenty of gold, but non-living matter had to equalize between the planes or throw both worlds off-balance. Iron was the perfect replacement, as it wasn't naturally occurring in Mythos due to the fae, and its import allowed his tribe to craft with steel.

While at the London office, he fumbled through a computer search for real estate near the old woman's house. Once he'd printed the listings for several possibilities, he headed home. Whether the council would agree with his decision or not, he needed one last night in his quarters.

The last night in his own bed. The last night he'd get a respite from the Virgin's temptations. The last night to gather strength for his resistance.

CELIA WOKE AND SHOT UP IN BED, ADRENALINE SURGING THROUGH her veins. Everything felt off. As she stretched for the switch of her bedside table lamp, her shoulder burned and her palm stung.

Hell, her whole body ached.

The clock on the nightstand displayed nearly eight-thirty a.m. Was she running late for anything?

Her brows pulled low. What day was it?

She glanced at the small desk in the corner. Her backpack with her cell phone wasn't there. She swung one leg off the bed to get up. Wait, she was still in her jeans?

Pinpricks of red at her knee drew her eye. Something...

She examined her palm. Dozens of bloody scratches covered her skin. On her other hand too.

And her backpack sat beside the bed.

Her body became numb as her blood abandoned her. A remembered nightmare tickled her thoughts, and she slowly stood. Part of her jeans and underwear flopped down, and her ass hung out in the breeze.

It hadn't been a bad dream. It had been real.

The buzz of adrenaline strengthened, as if her attacker might still be within reach. Oh God, she'd been violated. How seriously? Her muscles tensed, torn between wanting to strike out at someone, something, anything, and wanting to run away before the situation got worse, before her head was bashed in again, before she died.

Her head... She touched her face, expecting pain. Nothing.

She twisted and checked her bottom. Despite the blood all over her jeans—and oh crap, her bed—no gashes marred her skin.

What. The. Hell.

She unzipped her backpack. The prescription bag for Auntie Harriet still lay on top.

Her legs gave out, and she plopped onto her bed. Okay, there had to be an explanation for this. The steps of the scientific method scrolled through her mind.

She'd been attacked. That much was clear, and that much she remembered. But then what had happened?

She'd gotten away. How? And how did every wound match her memory, yet several injuries were missing?

Ugh. All she had was questions and not enough information to come up with a hypothesis.

"Celia, honey, you here?" Auntie Harriet's voice carried up the stairs. "I'm cooking up some flapjacks if you want 'em."

Food. Her stomach rumbled. Last night's planned raid of her landlady's dinner spread had never happened.

"I'll be down in a minute, Auntie. Thanks."

She stripped off her bloodied clothes and threw on a robe. Maybe she'd think clearer when she wasn't starving and gross anymore. She grabbed the prescription bag and started down to the bathroom to wash up.

The vanilla smell of pancakes wafted up the stairs, and Auntie Harriet waited at the bottom. So much for cleaning up before the woman saw her.

"A robe, child? What time did you get in last night?"

"Uh..." Not a clue. She held out the bag. "Your prescription."

A true southern black woman, Auntie Harriet embodied the spirit of her home. Despite being on the "wrong" side of the Delmar Boulevard north-south dividing line, this block of well-maintained houses from the early 1900s boasted cozy details like wood flooring and arched doorways. Likewise, Auntie never left her bedroom without being perfectly put together, and she seemed to have a hat to match every Sunday church outfit.

This morning, her bright flower-print shirt clashed with the frown pulling across her face. She took the package. "Thank you, honey, I forgot all about that."

Was Auntie having another memory episode? Celia dropped her mission to stop at the bathroom first and followed the woman into the kitchen.

Auntie nodded to the small old-style TV on the counter. "I'm glad I didn't remember you were heading up to that neighborhood. The news is all a-chatter about a big murder on MLK Drive last night."

Something tugged at her memory. Something white.

"A murder? Why is that big news?"

"Because the guy"—she slipped a spatula under the edge of a pancake and peeked—"some low-life type from the looks of him, had a softball-sized hole clean through him. Not a gunshot or nothin'. The cops said it looked like he'd been impaled by a pole. They haven't found a murder weapon, and of course no one up there is talking." She flipped several pancakes onto a plate and held the dish out to Celia. "You didn't see anything, did you?"

"Not that I can remember." That was the truth.

She reached for the food, but Auntie gasped and set down the plate. "What happened to your hand, child?"

She grabbed Celia's wrist and towed her to the sink. Water rinsed away the dried blood creased in her palm print.

"I'm not sure." Celia put her other hand under the faucet as well. She needed a story that wouldn't panic the woman. "I think I fell on the sidewalk, but everything's a bit fuzzy."

Auntie grasped Celia's chin and tilted her head from side to side, squinting. "You have *blood* in your hair. You hit your head and don't remember it?" She *tsked*. "They have a clinic at that school of yours, don't they? You might have a concussion. Promise me you'll make an appointment."

"I promise."

The woman paid more attention to her than her own mother ever had. It was a pleasant change. Most of the time.

Eating didn't help Celia feel better. Instead, her confusion increased the more she thought about the news report. Did the murder have something to do with her attack? Her mind turned over the mystery while she washed the dishes and griddle.

The last thing she remembered clearly was the attacker slicing into her skin. After that, things became less distinct. Cold. Tired. A flash of white. A streak of dark liquid. Her stranger from the bus.

What? The plate she was drying nearly slipped from her grasp.

Before the memory floated away, she set down the dish and closed her eyes. An image solidified of the stranger peering down at her, a ceiling above him.

Her bedroom's sloping ceiling.

That couldn't be right. Did people with concussions suffer from hallucinations? Or maybe that part was a dream.

Her cheeks heated. She'd dreamed about him? In her bedroom?

She shook her head. Whatever. She should probably go to the police and make a report about her attack in case it was related to the murder.

She hung up the dishtowel and added "visit police station" to her mental list of things to do. Assuming she hadn't lost a day in her befuddled state, today was Thursday, and she had a break between her morning plant biology class and her ecology lab late in the afternoon.

Auntie Harriet came into the room with one of her fancy hats perched on her head.

"Where are you going all dressed up, Auntie?"

"To Sunday services, of course." The woman took a mint from a kitchen drawer and stuffed it into her purse.

"Auntie...?" Celia hesitated.

Which of them was wrong? Normally, she'd chalk this up to the woman's declining mental health, but she wasn't as sure of herself today.

The day's paper wasn't sitting in its usual spot on the table. Celia opened the front door and grabbed the newspaper from the porch. Thursday. A sigh left her muscles relaxed but her stomach tense.

"No, today is Thursday."

"Certainly not. How hard did you hit your head, child?"

"But look. I just brought this in, and it says today is Thursday."

The woman's dark eyes scanned the newspaper, and she checked her medication calendar. "Oh dear. That means I took the wrong pills this morning too." She sat heavily in a chair at the table and removed her hat. "I've done it again, haven't I?"

Celia sat beside her and patted the woman's hand until it loosened around the now-crumpled hat brim. "It's okay. I'm feeling all out of sorts today too. It happens sometimes."

"I remember the doctor telling me to expect things like that, but..."

"But it doesn't make it easier. I know."

"Could you call Roger for me? He'd want to know about the medication mix-up."

"Of course." After the woman left to put away her hat, Celia lifted the old rotary phone from its hook and dialed the long-distance number written on the notepad on the wall.

"Williams Dentistry. How may I help you?"

"This is Celia Hawkins. Is Dr. Williams available? It's about his mother."

A few minutes later, the man's deep voice sounded over the phone. "Celia? What's wrong?"

"Hi, Dr. Williams, your mother's fine, but she had another episode this morning."

The line remained silent for a moment. "How serious?"

She shared the details and then paused, listening to ensure Auntie was still back in her room. How far should she stick her nose into business that wasn't her own? "Maybe you could fly out next week for Thanksgiv—?"

"Thank you for the call, Celia, and thank you for being there with her. I'll touch base with her doctor and see if her medication should be adjusted."

"But—"

Click.

Her shoulders tensed. She knew all too well what it felt like to be shunted to the side by family. A nobody. Her usual good manners slipped, and she slammed the handset onto the wall.

Fine. Lots of people couldn't deal with the failing health of their parents. But right *now* was when Dr. Williams should visit his mother, while her Alzheimer's was still in the early stages. Her episodes were rare, and she still remembered her son, her face beaming with pride that her only child had grown up to be a well-respected dentist in North Carolina.

Sure, his desire to remain hands off was what gave Celia a cheap place to live. By letting her stay here, keeping an eye out for changes, he could delay the argument with his mother about moving her into assisted living. In exchange, Celia paid a paltry ten dollars a week for her rent, which didn't even cover food expenses for all the times Auntie Harriet treated her like a family member. But she'd gladly give that all up if it meant he wouldn't blow off his own mother.

"It's okay, child. I'll be fine." Auntie's voice shook Celia. How much had she overheard?

Celia schooled her expression into a façade of graciousness and faced the woman. "I know you will."

Auntie waved her hand. "Now go on. If today's Thursday, you have classes to get to." When Celia inhaled, ready to protest, the woman added, "Yes, I have your cell number there on the notepad if there are any problems. I remember."

A smile tugged at Celia's lips, and she squeezed Auntie's

shoulder as she passed. "Of course you do."

One quick shower later, and Celia was feeling better. Still confused, battered, and traumatized, but clean at least. A shocking amount of blood had washed out of her hair. If Auntie Harriet's eyesight were better, the woman would have marched her off to the hospital at the mess around Celia's head.

After getting dressed, she grabbed her backpack to repack it for the day's classes. A quiet rolling noise sounded from the wood floor. She bent down to check what she'd kicked with her toe.

A blue bead.

No... It couldn't be.

She held her breath and picked up the bead, certain it would vanish before her fingers closed around it. Shimmers like the sparkle of a bright blue Caribbean lagoon leapt over its surface despite the curtained dimness of her room. Her heart couldn't decide whether it was going to stop or beat a thousand times a second.

Even though the bead's unusual appearance had drawn her eye hundreds of times, she still wanted—needed—to double check. She fetched her sketchbook from her backpack. Her hands trembled with each turned page.

There. In the drawing she'd completed last week.

The face of the stranger from the bus was penciled in full color, all except his eyes, which the fuzzed paper revealed she'd failed several times to get right. But everything else was there. His eyebrows with the sharp point at the arch. His mustache and goatee. And his beaded dreadlocks—with a blue bead just to the side of his face. This blue bead.

Had that memory of him from last night *not* been a dream? Had he really been here? In her bedroom? She shivered.

The question of *how* she'd made it home suddenly seemed less of a mystery. But what—if anything—did he have to do with her lack of injuries? Or the murder?

Ugh. She shoved the bead into her pocket. She was already running late and didn't have time for all these unknowns that didn't get her closer to a hypothesis. Years of being ignored had taught her patience, so she mentally filed the mystery under "to be continued"—at least until she had time to dig deeper.

Her first opportunity to investigate presented itself just a few minutes later, when the stranger climbed onto the bus behind her. As always, he didn't look in her direction. Out of the corner of her eye, she checked.

The blue bead was missing from his dreadlocks.

Chills prickled up her arms. She rubbed warmth into her limbs. What to do, what to say? A thousand scenarios ran through her head during the bus ride.

He still looked as scary and intimidating as ever. But she *knew* he wasn't the one who'd attacked her. She *knew* someone must have rescued her from her attacker because she sure as hell hadn't been in any shape to save herself. And she *knew* he'd been in her bedroom.

Doing what though? Her unbroken bra, the closed safety pin securing her jeans, and the lack of soreness from injuries other than the attack had told her that her virginity was intact. But did he have something to do with her missing wounds? She scoffed. What—like he'd healed her? Not scientifically possible.

The bus approached Brookings Hall at the university. He stood but let her lead the way to the exit stairs. While they waited for the doors to open, she gathered her courage and spun toward him.

She focused on a buckle of his leather vest, avoiding her reflection in his sunglasses. "Thank you for making sure I made it home safely last night."

His jaw loosened, and she hurried down the steps as soon as the *swoosh* announced the door had opened. She hitched her backpack over her shoulder, and a rumble sounded as the bus pulled away. Only then did she glance back.

He'd never descended the stairs to follow her off the bus. That was a good thing, right?

Chapter Five

DEEP MID-AFTERNOON SHADOWS CONCEALED MARKOS FROM the view of the police station entrance. He checked the time on his new phone again. What was the Virgin doing in there? Giving the police a description of him?

Mule's piss. His magic hadn't worked on her, and she remembered too much. The situation was spiraling out of control.

He'd tried hanging out in the building, but even with his ability to cloak his presence, there was no way to loiter in a police station close enough to hear her conversation. Instead, he'd had to lurk here, in the shadow of the building next door, and watch for her exit.

His phone buzzed with a call, and his irritable mood leeched into his voice. "What?"

"Mark Ambrose?" The woman's anglicization of his name clued him in to the identity of the caller. "You left a message asking about the listing on Lindell Boulevard?"

After confirming that the listing was accurate about the large lot and dozens of mature trees, he made a generous no-contingency cash offer for the house and all furnishings, with a bonus if the owners closed immediately. Luckily, the owners had already moved out and left the furniture in place for showings. He threw in a raise for the housekeeper-cook and gardener to remain on staff too. Anything to avoid hassle.

"Call me when the deal requires my signature."

He disconnected the call just as the willowy form of the Virgin left the police station, and he pressed against the building's façade to stay in the dark shade. After she passed on the sidewalk, he trailed behind, slipping from one building's shadows to the next.

The open gravel field ahead posed a problem, however. He let her reach the far side before he followed in the bright fall sunshine.

As soon as he emerged from the shadows and began crossing the empty lot, she stopped. He silenced his steps on the loose rocks. Her shoulders lifted with a deep inhalation. Dread unfurled in his gut.

She spun around and glared at him, her voice carrying over the distance between them. "You know, it's rude to stalk someone after they just survived an attack."

Donkey's balls. By stopping at the same time she had, his intentions were obvious. He was a *skoro* of the first order.

Tension vibrated through his muscles. "Is that what you told the police? That I'm a stalker?"

Not what he'd planned his first words to the Virgin to be. Then again, he hadn't planned on talking to her at all.

"I didn't mention anything about you." Her shoulders dropped. "Please don't make me sorry about that."

Earlier, she'd thanked him, then she chastised him, and now she managed to reassure and threaten him at the same time. How was he supposed to respond to all that?

He approached her in case the police were listening to them yell across the open field. "I'm not a stalker."

As he stopped outside of touching distance, she stood her ground. "Right. You just follow me around and let yourself into my bedroom. Perfectly normal behavior..." She tightened her grip on the strap of her backpack. "For a stalker."

She remembered that he was in her room? His fingers curled into a fist.

"You're imagining things. I wasn't in your bedroom." He lifted his chin and looked away, as if he could hardly be bothered with her. However, he couldn't help grumbling, "And it's not my fault you get yourself into dangerous situations and need someone to keep an eye on you."

She laughed, drawing his gaze. Rosy lips and flushed cheeks colored her face like a blooming rose he wanted to explore with the lightest of caresses. The idea punched him in the stomach.

Her mirth faded into an eye roll. "A... I can't believe you just spouted that lame 'I have to stalk you to protect you' excuse. Stalking isn't sexy. It's creepy and something I can and *will* report to the police." Her hand dropped to her jeans pocket. "And B... Yes, you *were* in my bedroom last night. Don't bother lying to me."

His mouth opened, but he had no idea how to reply. She was nothing like the demure Virgins he'd watched from afar in the past. All he could think of was repeating his claim.

"I was *not* in your room."

"I really wish you hadn't lied to me again." She tugged her hand from her pocket and held up something in her fingertips. "Recognize this?"

Mugarok. He swallowed. A blue bead. *His* blue bead. The bead of his family line.

By the Maker, how had he not noticed it was missing? He'd even appeared before the council without it.

If he'd reported to his summons in his natural form, everyone would have noted its absence from his forelock. The council might have even taken that as a sign of him relinquishing his noble birthright. His decision to answer the summons in human form, for which they didn't know how he displayed the symbol of his family status, was the only thing that had saved him from political suicide.

Trembles weakened his legs, and he stiffened his spine to stay upright. The bead must have slipped off when her fingers had dragged sleepily through his hair last night. Now, the iridescence of the curved surface glittered in the sunlight, looking out of place among this block of warehouses in St. Louis. The tiny sphere, an irreplaceable gift to his ancestors from the Nyx water spirits, was unlike any substance on the Earthen plane.

Unable to help himself, he reached out for the bead.

She snatched her hand back. "Nuh-uh. Are you admitting this is yours?"

His teeth ground together. "Yes."

Her brows arched, and she considered the object held firmly in her grasp. "This thing? This thing I found in my *bedroom* this morning—this is yours?" Her faux-innocent sarcasm made her point, slicing through his false claims like a blade.

"Yes." He didn't dare move close enough to the Virgin to forcibly take the bead from her. "Now return my property."

She closed her hand around it. "Oh, but we still have to discuss how this could *possibly* have ended up in my room, since you've never been there."

Son of a mule. She had him by the balls, and she knew it.

She checked her watch. "Gee, look at the time. I have to catch the bus so the doctors at the health center can check me for a concussion. I remember injuring my head last night, and the blood I rinsed off in the shower this morning backs me up on that, yet I can't seem to find a wound. Same with my other injuries. You wouldn't happen to know anything about that, would you?"

Piss. She knew too much about what had happened last night. No answer came to mind to give her.

"No? Okay, see you later, Mr. Not-a-stalker. You know where to find me if you decide to talk." She stomped off toward the bus stop up the block.

Curse the Maker and all her creation, the situation had surpassed his worst nightmare and gone straight to Hades. Without a choice, Markos followed the Virgin to the bus stop.

OH MY GOD, OH MY GOD, OH MY GOD. WHAT THE HELL HAD SHE JUST done? Confronted a scary-ass maybe-stalker—not to mention a maybe-murderer—who could break her into tiny pieces with his pinkie finger, that's what.

What she wouldn't give to wake up and find out the whole damn day had simply been a nightmare. *Normal* people would curl into a ball and suffer from PTSD after an attack. But oh no, not her. She had to get ornery. Really ornery.

A few minutes ago, she'd defended herself from the cop's accusation that *she*—the victim—might have been responsible for the murder in the same alleyway as her attack, and that had been dangerous enough. The last time she'd spoken out like that to her family, they hadn't acknowledged her for six months. Not even to answer her direct questions.

The world didn't like it when she demanded more, and she needed to accept that. The price was too high. The last thing she could afford was for her professors to ignore her even more. How could she pass her classes if they actively pretended she didn't exist?

The diesel rumble from a bus at the intersection pulled Celia from her thoughts, and she rushed across the street before the light changed. As she boarded the bus, she took several deep breaths.

Thank God people ignored her. Today she was grateful for that fact. Now that she wasn't in Stalker Man's face anymore, he was sure to go back to dismissing her.

She slinked into an empty bench, away from the other passengers, and closed her eyes. The drama was over and done. She'd done her duty in reporting the attack to the police, and she'd thanked the stranger for keeping her safe.

Time to go back to normal. Compared to the last twenty-four hours, normal was the safe kind of boring.

A deep growling voice sounded in front of her. "You're right. I was in your room."

Her eyes popped open, and she stared at the first man who had ever approached her. The first man who had ever started a conversation with her. The first man who had ever noticed her before she'd made herself known.

So much for normal.

Chapter Six

FROM THE BUS SEAT IN FRONT OF HER, THE STRANGER HAD TWISTED around to face her. His sunglasses centered on Celia's eyes, proving beyond a doubt that he was speaking to her.

She'd never seen him this close before—close enough to see his nostrils flare. Why, oh why, did her outburst with him have to be the experiment that disproved all her conclusions?

"Oh, um, okay." She belatedly processed his words. He'd admitted he'd been in her bedroom. Holy hell. "Why?"

"I saw you were in trouble, and I ensured you made it home safely." The point of an eyebrow rose over the top of his sunglasses, and he held out a large hand. "My property."

"Did my landlady see you? Did she let you in?"

"No." A buckle on the leather band around his forearm clanged against the metal seat frame as he extended his hand farther.

Auntie Harriet forgot to lock the door half the time, so that wasn't a surprise. But still, she couldn't drop the issue. No scientific reason could explain her missing injuries, and curiosity itched under her skin.

"When you brought me home, did anything else happen?"

He recoiled, his lips curling like he'd sniffed rotten meat. "I have no desire to touch you."

Her ribs squeezed tight. "Oh, right... I mean, I didn't think you did." She shook her head. "Forget I asked."

She dropped the bead into his palm, careful not to brush his skin and trigger his revulsion again. "Thank you again for helping me."

He promptly moved to a different row across the aisle and ignored her for the rest of the journey. Whether he was a stalker or not, there was definitely nothing caring behind his actions. Even beyond the whole *impossible* thing, he had no reason to give *her* special healing attention.

She sat back against her seat, his reaction still burning in her chest. She wanted to put all thoughts of him behind her.

She tried. And failed.

For as bizarre as their conversation had been, it was more interaction with a guy than she'd ever experienced before. Pathetic, she knew, but that couldn't be helped.

Maybe she could justify her interest with a desire to uncover the truth. He was obviously hiding something—probably several somethings—and she'd gotten too flustered to ask whether he'd murdered her attacker. She should be freaked out about that possibility, right? Or had his rescue excused that crime in her mind?

Ugh. No matter how logical it was for her to feel freaked out, scared, or PTSD-style traumatized, she couldn't stop thinking about the stranger as someone she *didn't* have to fear.

Maybe that was the ultimate sign of how messed up her head was.

She *really* needed to get herself checked out. Maybe concussions caused a complete lack of common sense.

THE NEXT DAY, MARKOS SETTLED INTO HIS USUAL SEAT ON THE BUS— across the aisle and back several rows from the Virgin. Currently, she was scribbling in a notebook and stealing occasional glances at him. Like normal.

After ensuring she made it home safely today, he was due to close on his new house. Then all that remained was waiting for the owners to remove a few personal items tomorrow. Cash offers made things so much easier.

The sooner he could have a bed again, the better. The lack of sleep from last night's campout in the tree behind the Virgin's room was taking its toll.

The Virgin ripped a page from her notebook and packed up her materials as the bus turned the corner for her stop. The ordinariness of her behavior was amazing, quite honestly. Most humans would be fearful or traumatized after an attack.

The most she'd done was mention to him—angrily—that his following her was *rude*. What kind of person reacted to an attempted rape with a caustic remark about rude behavior?

He grunted and yanked the buckle around his armband tighter. Given that his impure thoughts would surely doom her even more than the other Virgins, her mental state was not something he should care about. The end of this torture couldn't come soon enough.

At the bus stop, the Virgin descended the stairs and halted on the sidewalk. After he exited behind her, she held out the ripped page. "This is for you."

Her hand extended closer, and the paper shook with her urging. He grabbed the corner of the sheet before she could come in contact with him, and he walked away.

She chased after him. "You're supposed to look at it."

He began counting to ten, delaying so she'd leave him alone. He made it to three. "Go home."

"Look at it." Her head tilted. "Please? I made it for you."

Not what he wanted to hear.

His attempt to escape her had now carried them half a block in the opposite direction of her home. He didn't even know where he was going. And still, she trailed at his side.

He stopped. "Why are you following me? Go home."

"Oh, the stalker doesn't like being stalked? Just look at it. Please."

His breath huffed through his teeth, and he lifted the paper. A stunningly detailed colored pencil drawing of his face filled the page.

His gut clenched. He couldn't decide which was more worrisome. That she'd drawn him without sunglasses and knew exactly what his not-quite-human eyes looked like. Or the message she'd written across the page in looping script:

To my hero, thank you! Celia

Hero? Him? The one who wasn't virtuous enough, pure enough, to be worthy of the Virgins? He was going to be sick.

The whole reason he wore sunglasses was to prevent her from noticing his eyes. His cloaking magic kept others from noticing their unusual color—the one way he didn't pass for human—but he'd used the glasses because the stories hinted his magic wouldn't work on the Virgin. Now, over the past two days, both his cloaking magic and his sunglasses had failed him.

The paper crinkled in his grip. "How did you know?"

Had she been more conscious two nights ago than he'd realized? The Maker help him if she'd witnessed his slip with his thumb. He caught his fingertips rubbing his thumb at the reminder of her softness and curled his hand into a fist.

She gazed at him quizzically. "What?"

"My eyes. How did you know what they look like?"

A smile sneaked across her face. "You probably don't remember it, but last spring a guy in the seat behind you knocked into your head with his backpack. Your sunglasses fell to the floor of the bus, and I got a quick glimpse."

"You have a good memory." Too good.

She shrugged. "It took me a long time to get them right. I finally figured out they needed streaks of gold."

He couldn't help admitting the truth. "You're very talented."

Her ability to capture details rivaled the best artists in the Mythos plane. In her gifted hands, a depiction of a sunrise would probably become a spiritual icon. Too bad it was never going to happen.

He pinched his eyelids closed and ground his teeth. Where had *that* regret come from?

The arms of his sunglasses slid forward over his ears. He opened his eyes and jerked back. The Virgin held his glasses in her hand.

She stepped closer and met his gaze. "Why do you wear them all the time?"

His mouth opened, but no sound came out.

Her blue-tinged hazel eyes captured all the thoughts in his head and seduced them to do her bidding. From the soft waves of her blonde hair to the narrow nose on her face, she exuded purity and elegance. She was temptation personified.

Her long, thin fingers rolled the arm of his glasses. Even the spinning motion in his peripheral vision couldn't break the spell of her gaze.

Pink crept into her cheeks as the silent moment dragged on. Evening sunlight fell on her upturned face, kissing it with color like a beautiful flower.

He was helpless. Stories told of the Virgin's own magic—the ability to ensnare his kind—but in all his years as Guardian, he'd never witnessed it. Until now.

His heart lurched in his chest, urging him closer. His fist opened, his fingers trembling with the need to reach out to her. His boot slid forward a fraction on the sidewalk.

Her hand lifted to touch his temple. A last grasp at resistance kicked in, and he pulled back.

Creases formed in the corners of her eyes, and her face dipped toward the pavement. "I'm sorry. I forgot. I promise I won't try to touch you again."

Released from their eye contact, he sucked in a gulp of air, shocking his lungs with her alluring scent, like a rose-filled meadow. Mission. Must remember his mission. He had to hold out until the Spring Equinox. Failure equaled death.

She gave him a sheepish smile. "I just think your eyes are beautiful, and it's a shame you hide them all the time."

Her honeyed voice melted over him. Prickles spread across his scalp at the sweet sound.

"That's not your concern." The shakiness of his speech nullified the determination of his words. He was even more tainted than he thought.

He opened his hand between them, demanding the return of his glasses. Focus. Focus on anything but her.

"No, of course not." Lines creased her forehead. "Okay, I'm confused. Most stalkers are obsessed with a person for a reason, but you obviously don't want anything to do with me. So what gives?"

"I told you. I'm not a stalker."

"But unwanted or obsessive attention *is* stalking. It's harassment and intimidation. Yeah, I have no friends and have never even been kissed, but screw you if you think that means I should be so desperate for any kind of attention that I'm flattered to have a stalker."

His shoulders tightened. The modern world on the Earthen plane would be the death of his tribe. How was he supposed to complete his assignment without creating an impression of stalking? Even if he succeeded with this Virgin, what about the next generation? And the next?

The frustration of his impossible situation burst from him. "I'm just trying to do my job."

Mule's piss. As soon as he'd said it, he knew he should have controlled himself better.

He started heading back toward her home. If she continued following him, at least he'd be that much closer to getting rid of her. She matched his pace and then pulled ahead to catch his gaze.

"Your job? It's your *job* to follow me around?" Despite his silence, she didn't let the question go. "Yes or no—is it your job to follow me?"

She already knew the answer, so confirming it shouldn't hurt the matter. "Yes."

"Why?"

She wouldn't get the specifics from him under any circumstances. "To keep you safe."

"Safe from what?"

"I can't tell you."

"And let me guess, you can't tell me *who* gave you this job either?"

"Correct."

"Can you tell me if my family is in danger? Or anyone I care about, like my landlady?"

"They are not."

He quickened their pace. Almost to the corner.

Her voice flattened, seeming relieved. "It's just me?"

"Just you."

"Okay." She nodded in time with their steps and gazed off to the distance. "Okay, I'll allow you to follow me around and do your job, and I won't report you to the police as a stalker, if..." She cleared her throat. "*If* you agree we can be friends."

He stopped mid-stride. "*What?*"

The idea was preposterous. He couldn't be *friends* with the Virgin. Any shreds of purity he had remaining would disintegrate.

His impure thoughts had likely already condemned her like the other Virgins, but if he became so impure as to lose his magic, every member of his tribe would die.

She shrugged. "You have a choice. Either you continue being all stalkery and intimidating, in which case, I'll report you to get rid of you. Or we become friends, and you can hang around as much as you want without me feeling harassed."

That was his choice? Keep his tribe safe from complete failure and be hassled by the police, or fulfill his mission and risk immediate death?

At whatever expression he had, she stepped back and balled her hands into fists.

"God, what is the world's problem with me? My longest conversations in the last few years have been with my not-all-there landlady and you, whoever you are. Oh yeah, and a cop who accused me of murder. No one wants to be friends with me. Why? Hell if I know. No one wants to touch me except for my landlady and a drugged-up rapist. Not even my parents, for Christ's sake. Why? Do I have leprosy or something and everyone forgot to tell me? What the hell is so horrible about the idea of being friends with me?"

Puffing sounds leaked through her lips after the outburst. Her face tightened, as though she was willing herself not to cry.

He straightened, stunned. His magic wasn't supposed to harm the Virgin, but she'd noted how only those with diminished brain function, whether medically or chemically caused, weren't affected, which might indicate that his magic was a factor. On some level, she recognized that everyone's treatment of her wasn't her fault.

For a second, he felt sorry for her. He knew all too well what it felt like to be unwelcome, to be treated as an outsider in his home.

"I agree to your proposal." The words popped out before he realized what he was saying.

Her eyes brightened. "You mean we can be friends?"

His mouth opened, ready to take back his statement, but then he'd still have the same impossible situation. He sighed like his breath was his last. He'd just have to work extra hard at maintaining the purity he had left.

"Yes, we can be friends."

She smiled and took a step toward him. The Maker help him if she pressed her body against his for an embrace.

Tingles ran through his limbs at the thought. Bad thought. Very bad thought.

He twisted away and continued walking toward her home. "But no touching."

"Got it." She followed alongside him. "No touching." Her head tilted. "So you probably already know who I am, but I feel like I should introduce myself anyway." She did a little wave. "Hi. I'm Celia Hawkins."

He gave her a curt nod and led them across the main street to where her block was on the other side. "I'm Markos—Mark—you can call me Mark."

"You don't look like a Mark. Markos fits you better. And your last name is?" When he didn't answer, she *tsked*. "I should know my friend's last name."

He already regretted his decision. Not that he'd had a choice.

"Ambrostead."

Ass. The Virgin had his real name. But without coming up with something new that he'd probably forget, his only other choice was the anglicized version. And if she had that, an internet search might come back with links to Unicore Mint or Markorn Manufacturing.

"I'm pleased to meet you, Markos Ambrostead."

The sound of his name from her lips lifted the hairs on his arms, and the tingles that had been zinging through his limbs coalesced into a warm embrace in his chest.

She fluttered her hand, indicating the neighborhood. "And where do *you* live?"

"I'm buying a house. Near your school."

"Well, isn't that convenient? I'm so glad we're friends. Otherwise I'd worry about the stalking potential with that."

He couldn't help it—his lips curved at her teasing.

She grinned. "Why, I do believe that's a smile on your face, Markos. So tell me, when are you moving in?"

"Tomorrow. I'm closing in a half hour."

"Exciting. Do you need any help moving your things?"

He shuddered at the thought of the Virgin inside his house. "No."

By this time, they'd reached the old woman's house. The Virgin walked up the path, a skip in her step. When she reached the front porch, she stopped and tossed his sunglasses to him.

"Thanks." He'd forgotten all about them.

"Bye, Markos." She waved. "See you tomorrow."

He waited for her to turn around and enter the house so he could transport away, but she rolled her hand in front of her, prompting him.

After a moment of his silence, she sighed. "Try something like, 'Bye, Celia. Not if I see you first.' You know, because you probably will see me before I see you—even though you're not a stalker." Her shoulders jiggled at her joke.

Another smile cracked his expression. "Bye, Celia. Not if I see you first."

A grin broke across her face and stole every gasp of air or logic inside him. His knees shook under him, threatening to force him to kneel and offer himself to her now—not even waiting for the ceremony.

He was so thoroughly tainted he'd never succeed. Yet the warmth flowing through his limbs wouldn't let him wish the situation were different.

His seduction was complete. He was now friends with the Virgin.

Son of a mule. He couldn't think like that, or he'd be insane by the Spring Equinox for certain.

He wasn't friends with *the* Virgin.

Celia. He was friends with Celia.

He couldn't let himself think about how he'd fail her like all the others. They could just be friends.

Until the time came for her death.

Chapter Seven

CELIA OPENED THE FRONT DOOR, HARDLY ABLE TO CONTAIN HER giddiness. She had a friend. An honest-to-God friend.

She spun around to give him another smile.

He wasn't there.

The front walkway, the sidewalk, the yard—hell, the whole block—were all empty. Only the chattering of squirrels, completing a last-minute food gathering expedition before winter, and the honks and diesel engines up the block proved the world was behaving normally.

All except for Markos's instant vanishing act.

A shiver tingled up her spine, and she closed the front door behind her harder than necessary. Here she was feeling all happy, and he had to go ruin it with another creepy mystery.

Honestly, though, what did she expect when trying to make a bodyguard, or whatever he was, into a friend? All his disappearance meant was that he excelled at his job, and that was supposed to be a good thing.

Of course, that brought up the questions he'd refused to answer about why she needed to be kept safe. From what? And who'd decided *she* was worth protecting?

Ugh. Not again. She ignored the issues that she couldn't get answers to and poked her head into the kitchen. "Auntie, I'm home."

Casserole dishes covered every surface, and Auntie Harriet

bustled around the small kitchen. "Can you grab the sack of potatoes from the pantry for me, honey?"

"Sure." She ducked into the pantry and then handed her the bag. "What's going on? Did someone from your church pass?"

"Heavens no, dearie. But I checked the calendar and saw that next week is Thanksgiving. I need to get ready for Roger and his family."

"You heard from your son today? That's wonderful that they're coming out."

"No, I didn't hear from him—"

"But—"

"—but why wouldn't he come?" Auntie gave her a scolding look. "It's Thanksgiving." She washed a handful of potatoes in the sink. "The little ones must be getting so big. I wonder if the baby is walking now."

Celia sank into a chair at the kitchen table. Auntie Harriet's grandkids were all full-grown, and the "baby" was the same age as her.

She danced around the issue. Disappointment sucked. She knew that too well.

"Did you want me to call Roger and make sure he knows what time to get here?"

"No, they only have to walk down the block."

Of course. In Auntie's memory, her son and his family hadn't yet moved away.

"Okay. Is there anything I can do to help you?" Maybe she could hang on to the last shreds of her happy mood by joining Auntie's version of reality.

"Do you know how to peel potatoes?"

Celia laughed. "I grew up on a farm, so I should hope so."

The next hour passed with Auntie sharing tales of Roger's childhood, including the embarrassing ones. After they'd finished the prep work for the dishes that could be made ahead of time, Celia bowed out to finish her homework. Soon, snippets of TV dialogue floated up the stairs. She pulled out her cell phone and dialed Dr. Williams's home number.

A minute later, he accepted the phone from his wife. "Celia, what happened?"

"I'm sorry to call so late, but when I came home from school today, your mother had started preparing a big Thanksgiving dinner for you and your family. Have you talked to her about coming out?"

"No."

"I didn't think so, especially when she was talking about getting to see your *young* kids and thinking you still lived in the neighborhood." She took a deep breath for confidence. "But maybe you should come out next week—since she's expecting you."

"That's..." He sighed. "That's just not possible."

Accusations threatened to burst from her, but she forced herself to stick to logic. "She's made all this food already. It'll go to waste."

"See if a shelter wants it."

"A *shelter*?" The high pitch of her answer would send dogs cowering.

A tiny voice at the back of her mind suggested she stop holding back her thoughts. After all, she'd gotten what she wanted with Markos only after confronting him.

No... She couldn't do that. Could she? That's not how she'd learned to survive through life. She could have all the sharp, cutting thoughts she wanted in her head, but expressing them? What if her ability to spar with Markos was a special case and speaking up here meant she'd have to endure another six months of people not speaking to her—under any circumstances? What if her punishment lasted even longer?

The tiny voice pointed out that if she didn't stand up for Harriet, no one else would.

"Dr. Williams, you might be the best dentist in North Carolina, but you're a crappy son. I'm happy to live here and help your mother, but her only child should be here. It's Thanksgiving, for cripes' sake, the holiday for expressing your thanks for what you've been given. Like a mother who loves you. You don't even know how lucky you are."

A thump sounded over the phone, as though he'd closed a door. "Listen, Celia, I appreciate everything that you're doing there, but my wife is acting as the caretaker for her own mother. We can't just take off halfway across the country."

She touched her cheek, expecting her skin to catch fire at the contact. Oh Lordy, there was more than one reason she should keep her mouth shut.

At her silence, he offered, "I *am* planning on coming out over the Christmas break. My office is closing down for two weeks, so I'll have time to visit for several days and still make it back in time for Christmas here."

Was the man really dealing with declining parents on both sides? He hadn't *seemed* heartless the few times she'd met him in person. Maybe not every setback in her life was a sign the world had it out for her personally. A part of her wanted to believe him, wanted to sympathize, but she'd witnessed family members turning their backs—and then pretending they hadn't—too many times.

"So what should I tell her? She *is* expecting you."

"I can't fix that. She'll think what she thinks."

"You don't care that she'll think you abandoned her?"

"I'm being practical. When I talked to her doctor yesterday, he said this was all normal behavior—for her—and it's what we should expect. If she's not a danger to herself or anyone else, he said she'd do better in her own home for as long as possible. The familiar helps her brain hold on a little longer."

His blunt words killed the last of her uncharacteristic desire to mouth off. She didn't want to think about Auntie going further downhill. The boundaries of compliance enclosed her again.

"Of course, Dr. Williams. I'm sorry. I'll watch for anything dangerous."

"Thank you, Celia. Goodnight."

The line clicked off, and she sat back in her desk chair. Squeaks sounded with her shifting weight. The news about his Christmas visit was reassuring, but that didn't help with next week. Auntie would be so disappointed when she realized the truth.

Whether she was truly unloved or just abandoned to other priorities, the woman would be alone for Thanksgiving either way. And that was no way to celebrate a holiday.

Although...

Celia opened the calendar app on her phone. She'd marked off Thanksgiving break with the vague words: GO HOME. Not that she had the means, or even a plan, for the weekend trip.

Her gaze skimmed the entry again. Home. The word didn't

have the meaning for her that it should. Although she loved the green fields of Iowa in summertime, winter held no draw for her. All she'd find there were barren fields to go with her family's cold hearts.

In fact, she *should* stay here and keep Auntie company. It's not like her family would notice if she didn't show, much less feel hurt or disappointed by her absence. Why should she scrounge the money for a bus ticket and be ignored there when she could instead spend the holiday here with the one person who *did* care about her?

She stood and peered out the small window at the end of her room. A streetlamp in the alley beyond the backyard flickered, casting strobe-lit shadows across the lawn. Echoing the chaotic illumination, ideas swirled in her head.

Maybe she could see if any of the woman's friends were in similar situations and in need of a place to go. Or others from her church. Or...

Her finger sought a lock of her hair and curled it around the tip. What about Markos? Did he have a family? She couldn't picture that—or much of what his normal life was like for that matter. For all she knew, his job required him to watch her under all circumstances, even during a holiday.

There was only one way to get an answer.

Chapter Eight

CELIA HAD STARED AT THE FLICKERING SHADOWS ON THE
ceiling for much of the night. Given her worries and all the
weirdness in her life lately, she wasn't surprised. Besides,
not sleeping was a good way to avoid the nightmares that invaded
her mind in the dark. Apparently, she wasn't as immune to the
traumas of her attack as she pretended, but at least she managed to
keep them at bay while she was awake.

As soon as the sun brightened the horizon, she decided to go
for a walk and clear her head. Air tinged with the chill of approaching winter bit her cheeks, and she shoved her hands deep
into her jacket pockets as she strode down the sidewalk.

She'd made it past only two houses before heavy footsteps
sounded on the pavement behind her. Her hands curled into fists,
and she straightened, ready to defend herself.

A musky, warm smell enveloped her, driving away fear of
another attack. She hadn't previously noticed Markos's scent, like
corralled sunshine, but now she'd recognize it anywhere.

"Celia." His voice rumbled low and paradoxically sent her heart
rate soaring. "What are you doing?"

She stopped and faced him. "Looking for you."

Not quite what she had in mind, but lying was better than
seeming like an idiot. Especially as she remembered too late that if
she was supposedly in danger, wandering around by herself in a

still-sleeping neighborhood with iffy crime statistics might not be the smartest idea.

He removed his sunglasses and rubbed his eyes. Even in the dim light, they appeared more tired than they had yesterday. "Do you know what time it is?"

"Time to milk the cows?" When his brows pulled low, she moved closer, faking a plan. "I have a question for you, and I don't have any way to get a hold of you. So I figured I'd head out and see if you'd show up."

Muscles stood out along his neck. Yeah, so not happy.

She covered up her embarrassment by giving him a grin. A compliment couldn't hurt either.

"I'm impressed, actually, that you caught up so quickly. You're really good at your job."

He growled. "I don't have time for these games today. You're not making it easy to be friends with you."

Her shoulders curled inward. Even the frosty morning breeze couldn't cool off her cheeks. He was right. She didn't deserve to have a friend. Talk about clingy.

Her gaze fell to the sidewalk. "I'm sorry."

She turned to go back to Auntie's house. Back to where she could crawl under the covers and hope she woke up to discover this had been a terrible dream.

Before she took a step, a heavy sigh sent a cloud of condensed breath over the top of her head. "I'm sorry. I shouldn't have said that."

The brittleness in his tone didn't make her feel better. She kept her face downcast.

"No, you're right. It's just—I don't know what this whole 'threat' thing means for me. I've been on my own for so long. And I've never had a friend before. I'm *not* any good at it."

She strode away before she could dig the hole any deeper. He grabbed the back of her coat.

Her feet froze mid-stride. He was *touching* her. Well, her jacket anyway.

She half-expected a choir to break out with the "Hallelujah Chorus" on the front lawn of the house beside them, but the world was disturbingly silent. Even the birds weren't chipper yet.

She twisted and searched his face for an explanation. His mouth had fallen open, and creases around his eyes almost made him look pained.

He dropped his grasp and stared at his hand like it had acted without his permission. Reinforcing the "Celia has girl cooties" idea, he wiped his palm on his leather jacket and returned his attention to her.

"I've rarely had a friend before either. You've taken early morning walks your whole life, and I have no reason to expect that to change now. I'm just frustrated with my work, and I took it out on you." He inclined his head in a strangely formal bow. "I am sorry."

He'd revealed so much in his little speech she didn't know what to respond to first. Finally, she decided repairing whatever kind of odd friendship they had took priority.

"You have a hard time with friendships too?"

He replaced his sunglasses, shielding his eyes. "My work leaves no time for friends."

"I'm sorry for that." She nibbled at her lip. "And if I'm your job right now, I guess in a way, that makes this my fault."

"If it wasn't you, I'd be watching someone else."

Small comfort.

She took a deep breath, wishing the cold air could give her strength. Instead, his scent filled her lungs, warming her from the inside out.

"Then if I'm going to be a good friend to you, the least I can do is make your job easier. Tell me what the risks are and how I can lessen them, and you'll get a break in your work too. What do I need to do? Carry a weapon? Watch out for certain people or behaviors?"

Creases formed over his glasses. "You're serious?"

"Yes, that's what friends do for each other, right? Try to help each other. So tell me."

His arms crossed in front of his chest, and he widened his stance until his presence dominated her awareness. "The only way my job gets easier is if you quit school, move back home, and stay in your parents' house all the time."

Was *he* serious? She couldn't do that. If she took so much as a semester off, she'd lose her scholarship, and then goodbye, college degree and all her dreams. At that point, she wouldn't be living her life anymore, and that didn't even count the whole issue of becoming a prisoner in her parents' house.

She swallowed. "For how long?"

"Until your life here is over."

A laugh burst from her. "Funny." For a second, she'd almost thought he was being sincere. "No, come on. I'm serious. Should I take self-defense classes or something?"

His brows rearranged into an expression she couldn't read behind his sunglasses. "That would *not* help."

She rolled her eyes at his patronizing tone. "You could have said there wasn't anything I could do without taking that attitude. I just asked because I hate feeling completely helpless."

He uncrossed his arms. The dreadlock with the blue bead slid in front of his shoulder. "I've offended you. I did not intend to." He cleared his throat. "If you avoid chemically altered individuals, you will lessen the risk to yourself."

Chemically altered individuals? "You mean, like drunks and drug users?" She couldn't get over how someone who looked like him spoke so formally sometimes. Maybe he worked for an uptight government agency.

"Yes."

"Deal. I have no desire to hang out with those types anyway, and if it makes your job easier, that's a bonus. Anything else?"

His lips twitched. "Stay away from men."

"Any specific description for this bad guy? Or just men in general?" She could play along with his teasing.

"Men in general."

"Ah, yes, I know this one particularly shady guy. I should probably report him to the police, but he makes me laugh." She struggled to keep a straight face.

His mouth turned down for a second, as though confused by her joke. He *had* been kidding, right?

Then a grin broke across his features. "Don't worry. I'll keep an eye on him."

Her muscles relaxed, and she jumped onto the next landmine. "Well, I was going to invite him to Thanksgiving dinner with me and Auntie—er, my landlady. And if he's going to be there, maybe you should be too. You know, keeping me safe from such a scary guy."

His expression slid into serious mode again. "Thanksgiving dinner?"

She stepped back so fast her heel slipped off the sidewalk edge. Crap, she'd backed him into a corner again.

"Sorry, I didn't mean to spring that on you like that."

She waved her hand in front of her, erasing her mistake, and started over. "My landlady's son isn't coming in for Thanksgiving this year. And rather than leave her alone for the holiday, I'm staying here with her. I'm going to invite her neighbors and church friends who might be alone too." Her hands lifted in a helpless gesture for forgiveness. "Anyway, if you don't already have plans with your family, you're welcome to join us."

"I have no family." His chin angled, aiming his focus down the street. "I've never been to a Thanksgiving dinner. What would be expected of me?"

Questions about his revelations begged to be voiced, but common sense won out. If they remained friends, she'd eventually get her answers without resorting to the interrogation technique.

"You don't need to bring anything. Believe me, Auntie will have *plenty* of food. Other than that, it's just a big dinner with family and friends. Expect to leave stuffed."

"It's just a *meal*?" His question ended on an incredulous note.

"Wow. You have no idea what Thanksgiving is? Where did you grow up?"

"Not here. Not in the United States."

"Oh." Sure, she'd noticed that he used words oddly sometimes, but he had less of an accent than many of her classmates and professors.

Now that she thought about it though, his looks exactly didn't blend in either. Not only were his clothes a bit over the top, but his unusual eye color would stand out on anyone, much less on someone with his skin tone, which was like the ochre color of a fallow field. His genetic history was probably fascinating.

"Okay, don't worry. I'd make sure you're not uncomfortable. Yes, it's a meal, but it's more than that. It's about celebrating the things we're thankful for. Like my landlady, who really *is* family to me. Or you, my very first friend. So I'd like you to be there, but I'll understand if you don't want to come."

His Adam's apple bobbed. Then he bent at his waist, giving her a real bow this time. "I would be honored to join your celebration of family and friends."

She couldn't help it—she giggled. "Thank you, my friend."

"That was the question you came out here to ask of me?"

"Yes, so I'll go back to Auntie's house, and you can go back to— oh! Aren't you moving into your new house today?"

"Yes."

No wonder he'd been tired and cranky. "I know you already said you didn't need any help, but are you sure there isn't anything I can do?"

"You can stay home today, so I don't have to interrupt my day to come out here."

Theoretically, she could put off the other Thanksgiving invitations until tomorrow. It would be easier to catch Auntie Harriet's church friends on Sunday too. And that would give her time to make sure Auntie was okay with the whole plan.

"Okay." She cupped a hand to her ear and exaggeratedly leaned toward Auntie's house. "I think I hear my homework calling anyway. But tomorrow, I have to head out."

She pulled out her cell phone and brought up the contacts app. "What's your number? I can text you before I leave the house tomorrow."

"Text?"

"Yeah, text message." Her arms lowered to her side. "You *do* have a cell phone, don't you?"

He answered by sliding a phone from the inside of his leather jacket. She wished she could touch his clothes. The form-fitting leather looked so soft. Would clothes like that be comfortable to wear? He made them look damn good, with that broad chest and...

He held his phone out to her, pulling her attention from his body. Oops.

"Show me how."

She entered her number into his contacts list. The first and only contact on his phone, in fact. Then she pivoted so he could watch over her shoulder while she sent herself a message from his phone.

Her phone chirped, and she showed him the result from the other end. After saving his number, she sent a reply so he could see the whole process.

"And you promise to *text* me before leaving tomorrow?" If his tone was any indication, he didn't trust the technology—or her.

"Yes, I promise. And if I don't get a reply, I'll call too. Okay? Even though you're not telling me what I'm up against, I won't be stupid about it."

His brows arched high over his sunglasses.

She ignored his obvious disbelief. "Okay, go. Do your thing. This is me heading home." She waved and walked half-backward, the better to keep an eye on his disappearing act.

Other than a wave in return, he didn't move. She even climbed the stairs to Auntie's porch backward too. Her hand fumbled with the key over the doorknob, and she checked back to unlock the door. It took her only a second. But when she glanced up again, he was gone.

One of these times, she'd catch him.

Chapter Nine

CELIA PICKED UP THE PEARLS FROM THE DINING TABLE AND fastened them around Auntie's neck. "Are you sure you're okay?"

The woman swiveled and gave her a level stare, even though she was quite a bit shorter than Celia. "I need you to stop asking me that question, child." She shook her head. "Roger already called to wish me a happy Thanksgiving and promised to visit in a couple of weeks. And you and I are going to have a lovely meal with friends. What could I possibly be upset about?"

True. Two neighbors and three widows from church would be arriving any minute, so assuming Markos showed up, they'd have a full table of eight, which was more than enough to feel like a real Thanksgiving gathering.

Celia smoothed the satiny cornflower blue of her dress. The outfit seemed like overkill, but Auntie Harriet had insisted. Even though Celia had explained that she and Markos were just friends, the woman claimed that was simply a temporary setback.

Not that the two had even met yet, considering that he usually kept his distance and acted like he and Celia were strangers who just happened to ride the same bus. Each step of progress in their friendship had resulted from her making the first move.

She supposed she couldn't blame him, as he'd admitted he wasn't good at the friend thing either. The key was for her to keep her expectations low. That way she couldn't be disappointed. Simple, right?

The doorbell rang exactly at the time she'd asked him to come by. She opened the door and stumbled back from the near-invasion. Markos didn't so much stand outside the door as block the entire doorway. Other than on the bus, she'd always seen him outside. Here, he dwarfed the scale of Auntie's house.

She swept her arm. "Please, come in. I want to introduce you to Auntie before everyone else arrives."

She led him to the kitchen, where Auntie was managing the final dance of heating up dishes so they'd all be ready at the same time. The woman stood from poking her head in the oven and looked up. And up and up. Celia pinched her lips together to prevent a grin at Auntie's *oh my word* expression.

"Auntie, this is Markos Ambrostead. Markos, this is my land-lady, Harriet Williams."

After he inclined his head in that little bow thing he did, Auntie gave him a broad smile. "I hope you brought your appetite. You're just the man I need to help make sure this food doesn't go to waste."

"I would be happy to help. However, I do not partake of the meat of hoofed animals."

No touching *and* food restrictions? Maybe it was a religious thing.

At Auntie's confused look, Celia clarified. "Hoofed animals, like cows." She assured Markos, "We're not having any beef, just turkey."

Auntie laid her hand on his arm. *Crap!* She'd forgotten to give a *no touching* warning.

But he didn't react in the slightest as the woman patted his forearm. No twitch of his lips, no flaring of his nostrils. Nothing.

Tightness constricted Celia's chest and spread up her throat. Her arms pressed close, but nothing could protect her from the truth before her eyes.

It wasn't touch in general he detested. It was *her* touch. And only her touch.

Auntie's strong, reedy voice shook her from that realization. "For a minute there, I worried you were a vegetarian. Almost all

Pure Sacrifice

my dishes have broth or cheese or eggs or something in them, and I couldn't possibly let you leave hungry."

"That's vegan you're thinking of." Celia pasted a smile on her face, burying the hurt deep inside. She'd keep her expectations in line if it killed her. "Most vegetarians are fine with non-meat animal products. In fact, I went through a vegetarian phase when I learned the little chicks I raised would one day be food."

Auntie looked askance at her, as though she'd suddenly grown a second head. "You eat meat all the time."

"Yeah. Now."

Markos bent toward Auntie and chuckled. "I suppose eight year olds have a hard time preparing their own vegetarian meals."

Celia sucked in a breath and stiffened. That seemed too specific—and random—to be a simple lucky guess.

Heck, until he'd mentioned it, she might not have even been able to remember the exact year she'd had those arguments with her parents. In retrospect, the way they'd ignored her pleas was just the beginning of her awareness of how much they dismissed her compared to her big brother and baby sister.

But if it wasn't a lucky guess, how the hell would he know *why* she'd given up her protest? Or how old she'd been? She hadn't mentioned her age—she was sure of it.

She scrutinized the hulking man seemingly taking up half the kitchen. He and Auntie, oblivious to Celia's shock, joked about some comment she'd missed. Every new piece of information shot her predictions and theories to hell.

The doorbell rang, interrupting her unspoken questions. Once again, she'd have to be patient.

The activity and conversation of Thanksgiving dinner distracted her for the next several hours. Markos sat quietly among the crowd, speaking only to answer direct inquiries. And those answers were as vague as ever. At least that particular quirk remained the same.

After the rest of their guests left later that evening, Auntie cornered Celia at the kitchen sink. "That Markos is some man you have there."

Celia bounced her hand in a signal to lower the volume. "Shh. He's just in the next room." When Auntie stared pointedly at her, she draped the damp kitchen towel over her shoulder. "Yes, he's something all right, but I told you, he's not my man."

"He's so well-mannered. And did you see the size of his biceps when I insisted he take off his jacket for dinner?"

"Auntie!" Honestly, she'd very much noticed those biceps—along with the rest of his well-muscled chest under his snug shirt—but she wasn't going to admit that and encourage the woman.

The woman raised her hands in a guilty gesture. "Just don't count him out, child. That's all I'm saying."

Right. As if the no-touching rule wasn't enough of a clue to his *non*-interest, there was also the whole issue of him hanging around only because it was his *job*. She didn't need more disappointment in her life.

Markos entered the kitchen with an armload of dishes. "This is the last stack from the table."

Auntie's overly large smile flashed like a warning light. "Thank you, dear."

Celia groaned and grabbed a dirty plate so she could face the suds and ignore whatever schemes the woman had. If only the scrubbing sounds from the sponge as she attacked the stack of dishes and platters could drown out their conversation.

"I'm so glad Celia has a friend to call on now." Auntie's voice trailed across the kitchen behind her, approaching Markos no doubt. "I worry about her safety all the time. Riding buses after dark. Traveling into unsafe neighborhoods."

"I worry about her as well." Given his growling tone, he was probably glaring at her back.

Celia ignored both of them and concentrated on a stubborn spot in the casserole dish. Scrubbing, scrubbing, scrubbing. They could just pretend she wasn't here.

"Why, last week she even insisted on picking up my prescription in the Wells-Goodfellow neighborhood. Can you imagine that? A little thing like her, all alone in that area near nightfall?"

"I know. In fact, you could say that's how we met—when I brought her home after rescuing her."

"*Rescuing* her?" Auntie's high-pitched shriek shredded the last hope for an enjoyable evening. "From *what*?"

Celia hunched over the sink. Not this conversation. Please.

Thuds sounded on the floor behind her at Markos's approach. A *clunk* accompanied his armload of plates being set on the counter beside her. "You didn't tell her?"

His rumbled whisper was probably too low for Auntie to hear, but Celia didn't look up to confirm. Some things were definitely easier when no one cared about her. Like dealing with her life her own way.

"Celia, honey." Auntie's no-nonsense tone would freeze kids with their hands in the cookie jar. "This is about when you showed up to breakfast with *blood* in your hair, isn't it? Fell on the sidewalk?" She *tsked*, and her voice twisted like the wrung-out dishtowel over Celia's shoulder. "You lied to me."

The Thanksgiving meal protested in Celia's stomach, churning with a sickening lurch. After everything Auntie had done for her, this was her thanks?

"I'm sorry. I didn't want you to worry." Every syllable was a plea for forgiveness.

Markos stepped away from the counter toward Auntie Harriet. "Celia was fine. I addressed her injuries, so they weren't serious."

Addressed her—? Several pieces of the Markos-puzzle snapped together into a theory-shaped idea, and Celia threw the sponge into the sink and whirled around. "You. Me. Outside. Now."

She flung the kitchen towel to the counter and stomped to the back door. His heavy booted footsteps followed behind, but she didn't look, or she might risk not making it to the yard before bursting. On the back stoop, she swung her arm out, indicating he should join her in the backyard, and then she closed the door firmly, so they might have a chance at privacy.

He motioned like a referee signaling an incomplete play. "I will not apologize for sharing my worry with her. You *do* need to be more careful."

She crowded closer and held up her hand. "That's *not* what this is about."

He took a step back. Whether from avoiding her nearness or from the vehemence of her tone, she didn't know. Didn't care.

"Then what—?"

"You told Auntie that you 'addressed my injuries,' which means you *did* do something to heal me. My bloodied face. The gashes on

Jami Gold

my bottom. They were nowhere to be seen the next morning, and no science in the world can explain their disappearance."

His eyes widened, and he took another step back.

She followed, keeping him close. "So what I want to know is, who the hell are you, that you know my life history? And how the hell did you heal my injuries without a trace?"

Her days of being patient? She was so done with that.

Chapter Ten

EVERY MUSCLE IN MARKOS'S BODY TIGHTENED FOR BATTLE. HER questions battered him harder than the worst of any warrior's deadly thrusts.

He was a fool, and she was anything but. When Harriet's accusations had cornered Celia, an overwhelming need to defend her had stampeded into his thoughts. He'd blurted the first thing he could think of that would shield Celia and reassure the old woman, and now he'd revealed far more than he'd intended by exhibiting the brains of an ass.

The easy excuse would be that he'd fallen under her spell. No one would blame him, especially if they saw her graceful body in the flowing dress that accentuated the blue tinges of her eyes.

On cue, the breeze caught her long, wavy hair and the hem of her dress. The fabric whispered over the curves of her shapely thighs, and sudden dryness clamped his mouth shut. The material teased and taunted him, enjoying the motions he couldn't allow himself to want. Low clouds reflected the light of sunset, tinting the fabric of her dress to match the unique shade of his blue bead.

He walked away from the entrancing vision. "I refuse to have this conversation."

"You refuse?" She strode in front of him and planted herself in his path. "Well, I *refuse* to take *no answer* for an answer when it comes to *my* life."

Her hands moved to her hips, emphasizing her figure. His fingers could probably stretch a fair distance around her waist.

He growled and pivoted away again. Thoughts of what he would do if she were in his arms tumbled through his imagination. His throat tightened to the point of pain. Those ideas alone forever condemned him—and her.

She appeared in front of him once more. "You know, I keep trying *not* to be suspicious of you. Not to think about how you might have killed that guy who attacked me. How just because I don't know of any way I could be in danger doesn't mean it's impossible. But it's hard. It's hard to be friends with you."

He crossed his arms, the chill in the air competing with the cold of her words.

Before he had a chance to decide if he should protest that no part of this friendship was his idea, she climbed the porch steps and opened the back door. She reached through the gap and grabbed his jacket off the row of hooks in the hallway.

Two thoughts warred in his head as she held his coat out to him. One, that she was touching his jacket, and two, that even in the midst of this confrontation, she still paid attention to his needs.

He shook his head. "I'm fine, thank you."

If she could stand out here in her thin dress, then his three-quarter sleeve knit shirt and leather vest should be more than sufficient.

She shrugged. "Well, *I'm* cold."

A piercing sensation seized his heart, as if the arms she slipped into the sleeves of his jacket punctured his chest. A flip of her hair sent waves of light gold past the collar, and she tugged the leather across her shoulders. The material hung loosely on her small body, covering half her hands and behind. She buried her nose in the leather, and a tiny smile crept over her features.

Piss. He'd really liked that jacket. He'd broken it in perfectly to fit him, and now he'd have to burn it to avoid her tempting scent.

"Time to spill." She fixed her gaze on him. "So far, all I have is your word that I'm in danger and it's your job to protect me. And since no one has ever cared about me before, I have a hard time believing that someone wants to hurt me or wants me dead or whatever kind of danger I'm in. Or that anyone cares enough to hire a bodyguard to protect me. So let's start with those details. Is someone after me?"

Once again, she'd left him with no options. Would she report him to the police if he didn't cooperate? Or had she already pieced things together and was just testing his honesty, like she'd done with the bead?

"As far as I know, there is no one specifically after you." There had better not be.

"Then what's the danger?"

"Everything. I have to protect you from anything that might cause you harm."

"That's ridiculous." She walked toward the tree and bent over.

Her rounded behind curved the dress beneath the edge of his jacket. He looked away, breathing hard. Memories of soft skin and the mistake he'd made burned his lungs. He was constantly one second away from making an even worse slip-up. How could he resist her? How could he resist even the thought?

Leaves crunched under her feet as she neared again. She held up a pointy stick. "Does *everything* include this stick? It could scratch me. It could poke me in the eye. It could stab me."

"What you do with a stick is no concern of mine."

"Ah, so you don't mean that you have to protect me from *anything*. So let me ask you again, what kind of danger are you talking about?"

He set his jaw. This *conversation* was dangerous.

The safest words he could use to explain the situation tasted dirty on his tongue, and he spit them out. "Rape or murder."

Her eyes widened, and she stepped back. "Your job is specifically to prevent that, and yet..."

He inhaled sharply. Yes, and yet he'd almost failed. She didn't need to give voice to the accusation. He felt his flaws deep into his bones.

She searched his face. "And yet someone almost succeeded—until you killed him?"

"I apologize. He never should have gotten that close. I'd gotten complacent about your schedule, which I should never do with you. There is no excuse."

She leaned closer, scrutinizing his expression for an unknown sign. "You admit you killed that man? Just like that." She straightened away from him. "I think I knew, but I hadn't really wanted to figure it out. Like if I knew, I'd have to decide whether to tell the police."

He stiffened, his muscles freezing into place for reasons that had nothing to do with the temperature. Human morals were unpredictable. The case was simple to his mind, but humans had complicated laws and expectations. The fate of his entire tribe rested in her hands now—in more ways than one.

She gazed into the darkening evening. "I think I blocked it out because I didn't see you there. I thought I saw..."

He held his breath, but she didn't finish her sentence.

Her eyes locked on his again. "I know the only thing that prevented him from raping and torturing me until I died was your action. You saved me, and I owe you my life." She nibbled her lip. "I also know the police might not see things so black and white. If I tell the police, they might see you as a vigilante, or if they're racists, as something even worse. They might try to..." She frowned. "Have you killed someone like that before?"

"No." Not in the way she meant anyway.

"Right. But they might try to link you to other crimes." She sighed. "This probably means I'm a horrible person, but I just can't see what benefit would come out of me going to the police." She raised the stick, warning him. "But I reserve the right to change my mind if you do anything that makes me think you're a bigger threat."

His chest unwound, releasing his breath, and he bowed his head. "Understood."

"So here's what I don't understand—why me? Why aren't you out there saving other women from rapes and murders? If it's just me, someone must have hired you. Who? Why?"

Her questions sent the conversation off a deadly cliff. How could he answer that without revealing her fate?

"You are important."

"Why? I haven't done anything. I'm, quite literally, a nobody who barely exists as far as the rest of the world is concerned. Sure, I plan on changing that big fat zero next to my name—that's the whole point of my biology degree and doctorate plans after all—

but none of my grand ideas have become reality yet."

He kept his face a mask. He couldn't afford any more slip-ups.

At his silence, she leaned forward and whispered conspiratorially, "Is that it? Is this about protecting me for the future?"

Perhaps her tendency to leap to conclusions on her own would prove helpful. He allowed himself a sharp nod.

Her face brightened despite the now-dim light in the yard. "Are you *from* the future?"

A scowl scrunched his features before he could prevent it. Her ridiculous assumption might be the misunderstanding he needed to avoid questions too close to the truth.

"Right. Even if you were, you probably wouldn't be allowed to tell me." She tossed the stick toward the tree and paced in a circle, trailing her fingertips over the plants at the edge of the lawn. "Okay, here's a question you should be able to answer. Is the explanation for how you know I'm important in the future the same explanation for how you know details about my life?"

She was right. That question was safe. "Yes."

"And the same explanation for how you were able to heal me?"

If her mind was going in the direction he thought it was, he might escape this conversation relatively unscathed. He met her gaze for added sincerity. "Yes."

She stopped her circling, and her lips parted. For some reason, he was still staring at those lips when her tongue darted out, wetting them. Longing ached through his body. Longing for something he wasn't allowed to want, much less do.

Her voice was soft and pleading. "Do I do something good in the future? Something helpful?"

What answer would satisfy her? Before he could stop himself, the truth poured from his mouth. "You save a race from extinction."

Her eyes rounded just as he pinched his lids closed. By the Maker, what had gotten into him? Next he'd be spilling all his secrets. At least he hadn't revealed *how* she saved this race or *who* they were. He hoped he could hold out that much.

He opened his eyes and attempted to judge her reaction. Her hands had risen to cover her mouth. Light glistened and wavered on the surface of her eyes. A drop gathered in the corner, hung for a second, and then rolled down her cheek.

Movement in his peripheral vision drew his attention. His finger had automatically extended to wipe away her tear, and he barely caught himself in time. "I'm sorry. I shouldn't have said anything."

She blinked, sending more drops down her cheeks. "No. Thank you." She swallowed and shook her head. "Thank you. That's the best gift anyone has ever given me."

Piss. What the *skoro* had he just done?

Chapter Eleven

ELIA WRAPPED HER ARMS AROUND HER RIBS AND HUGGED herself tight. If she didn't restrain herself, she'd throw herself at Markos and squeeze him for delivering that news.

He wouldn't like that. At all.

Her legs were as unsteady as a newborn calf's, and she sat on Auntie Harriet's back porch before they buckled. The chilly concrete stoop made her shivering worse. She wiped her face and took a deep breath to calm down.

Right. Like *that* was going to happen.

Not when this news made everything—from the issues with her family to the long hours of studying—worth it. Not when this meant everything she'd worked for, everything she'd dreamed of, everything that gave her life meaning for the last several years...

Her goals *were* within reach.

"Are you all right?" Markos had removed his sunglasses, apparently concerned enough to want to see her better in the dimming light of the backyard.

She nodded her head, but it probably looked like more shivers.

She took a deep, steadying breath and tested her voice. "My whole life, I've wanted to make a difference—a positive difference—in the world. That's impossible to do when people ignore you. Others in my situation might have acted out, become a rowdy teenager, pushed the envelope to see how much they could get away with before people *stopped* ignoring them. But none of that would have been *positive*."

Passion for her life's path smoothed the trembles of her body. She sat up straighter, and her voice strengthened.

"That's why I decided to become a scientist. Someone who could change the world even if no one noticed me." She shook her head. "Art matters only if people pay attention, but plants sat still while I sketched, so that led to botany drawings, and then plant biology and genetic engineering. And I realized that's how I could make a difference."

She stood and began pacing between the tree and the porch. "With the right genetic engineering, famine could be wiped out across the globe. Higher yields would bring costs down and still provide profit to farmers. Packing nutrients into everyday grains would allow people to lead healthy lives on limited food supplies." She grasped at the air in front of her. "It's the answer to everything."

If the tightness around Markos's eyes was any indication, he wasn't convinced that he'd done the right thing by telling her the truth.

She stopped and dropped her arms. "I'm sorry. This must all be history to you."

Leaves crunched under her shoe as she spun and started pacing again.

"It's just that... Well, I won't lie. It's been harder than I expected. When I first got here"—she waved in the direction of Washington University—"I couldn't even pronounce half the words in my classes." She halted her steps. "So to hear that my work hasn't been a waste, that I *will* be successful..." A mixture of pride and embarrassment tingled through her limbs at the less-than-humble words. "It makes all this effort worth it. It's a *gift*."

She reached toward his hands but didn't try to touch him.

"Thank you. Truly." She emphasized each word. "Thank. You."

In the flickers from the alley streetlight, his eyes shimmered, the gold streaks in his eyes seemingly reflecting light. She leaned closer, angling for a better look.

He shoved his sunglasses onto his face and stepped back. "I

have to go." He looked toward the back door, and she followed his gaze to the house. "Please express my gratitude to Harriet for the meal."

"Of—" She glanced back at him.

But he was gone.

"Course..."

Her ecstatic mood shrank into nothingness, hollowing her chest until it felt empty. She shivered inside the jacket he'd left behind.

What had she done wrong this time?

MARKOS STOMPED THROUGH HIS NEW HOUSE, HIS BOOTS ECHOING IN the massive spaces, and out to the backyard. Just as he'd surmised, the backyard made the home worth its purchase price.

Tall trees and thick vegetation formed a solid wall along the fences and dotted the center lawn. The yard wasn't as secluded as the remote forests of the lakeside estate in Ireland, but it would suffice for a local home base where he could directly transport back and forth to Celia's location.

A fountain burbled on the back patio, and as he stepped onto the soft and silent grass, he could almost imagine himself at home on the Mythos plane, surrounded by woodlands and babbling streams. From under one of the large trees on the lawn, he could even pretend the dearth of stars in the sky was due to them hiding behind the leaves and not because the heavens of the Earthen plane paled in comparison.

He lay on his back and dug his fingertips between the blades of damp grass. If the Maker was feeling generous, the contact with nature would calm his mind the same way a hard run through the trees could do.

No such luck. His mind whirled with the events of the evening.

At first, he'd thought Celia's assumptions about him being from the future would make his job easier. How wrong he'd been.

Her heartfelt explanation of what she wanted to do with her life filled his gut with sour acid. He hadn't felt that passionate about anything in years. Maybe ever.

She was right to pursue her goals. And his tribe was selfish for wanting to take them from her.

No wonder his race had been weakening for centuries. Why would any Virgin want to abandon *her* life to live among his kind?

For generations—even before the Civil War—no Virgin had chosen to stay with a Guardian. The denials had accumulated for so long that his tribe's magic had faded to a mere shadow. He couldn't blame so many of his tribe for choosing Alkipsia's side in the war—not when she offered a method to sustain them even when a Virgin rejected the invitation.

All Alkipsia asked of her followers was to accept the death of the Virgin if the Guardian didn't measure up—if *he* didn't measure up. It was an easy choice for a desperate tribe who didn't have to live with the guilt that destroyed his soul.

Despite the impossibility, he wished Celia could see the future of her dreams. He wished she could somehow help both her people and his own. He wished she could truly live.

A rumble started in his core and built in power. A bellow ripped from his throat like a beast beyond his control. The roar swept across the lawn and caused dogs to bark in the distance.

He was failing. In every way possible, he'd botched this mission from here to Hades. Her passion tempted him to feel hope, and that wasn't an emotion he could afford.

Here he was, thinking of her like a person with wants and needs and desires beyond her destiny for his kind. The Virgins had never been *people* before. He'd always kept them distant—for the sake of his purity, for the sake of his sanity, for the sake of avoiding the agony when the ritual resulted in their death.

Then came Celia.

He'd known she was unlike any other Virgin. He hadn't known how much he'd respect the person he finally recognized her to be. A small part of him even wished she'd still choose to be friends with him if she knew the truth behind his lies.

That thought alone was proof he'd slipped under her spell and—

A cold, wet *thing* touched his arm, and he sat up. A dog stood next to him and nosed his arm. Again.

Markos looked toward the gate next to the carriage house. Closed.

"Where did you come from?"

The dog tilted its head.

"Go home. I don't do pets."

The creature sat down next to him.

Markos commanded the dog to go home in every human language he'd picked up in his 400-plus years. When he ran out of possibilities, the dog shoved its head between Markos's arm and body. The dog didn't have a collar—and had twigs caught in its fur.

"Did you hop the fence and crawl through the bushes to get here?"

A short yip was his answer.

"I don't care if you came here because you heard my yell. I still don't do pets."

The dog laid its head in his lap.

"You're as annoying and insistent as she is. You know that, don't you?"

As if to prove his point, the creature rolled into Markos's forearm and exposed its belly, which conveniently ended up right beside his hand. In the darkness, it was hard to tell the dog's colors, but he'd guess it was a mix of black and white fur over a small collie-type body.

While the animal was on its back, Markos was able to confirm that it was a female dog.

"I should have known. Females are trouble."

At least, all the ones he'd had to deal with lately fell into that category. Alkipsia. This creature. Celia.

Especially Celia.

As soon as he thought of her, his mind tangled into a jumble again.

"Sorry, dog. I don't need a pet. What I need to do is go for a run and clear my head."

The dog scrambled upright and made several circles. Apparently he'd said the magic words.

He stood and brushed himself clean of dirt—and a stray twig. "I'm not going running anywhere around here. So unless you feel like a quick trip to Ireland, you should find someone else to pester."

Another sharp yip answered that question.

"Fine. But I'll leave you there if you get in my way." He bent down and held out his arms. "If you're coming with me, I have to carry you."

The dog jumped into his hold without hesitation.

Unlike some of the fae, unicorns had no ability to speak to animals, yet this dog—which *was* a dog and not a shapeshifter tied to the magic of Mythos—acted like she knew what he was saying. Odd, but he had enough other questions to puzzle over right now.

His magic formed a misty rectangle to his Mythos quarters, the extra hop required by the distance to his lakeside estate in Ireland. He tightened his grip on the animal, lest she become upset at the journey.

On the other side of the second doorway, near-freezing wind blasted through his shirt. He set the dog down and waited to see how she would react to the sudden change in temperature, sights, and smells. The dog hunkered down, her nose wildly sniffing in the direction of the lake, the mountains, and then finally, the trees.

Not a soul was around, which was exactly why he'd bought this place years ago. Satisfied by the lack of threats in the darkness, she looked up at him and wagged her tail.

"You haven't seen anything yet."

With that, swirls of mist surrounded him, and he took his beastly shape. The ground receded as he grew even taller, broader, heavier. His vision changed as his eyes took their new position. He toppled forward, his balance shifting to four legs. Fine, silky white hair feathered the lower section of his legs, and similar hair fell halfway down his body from along his neck. The blue bead of his royal heritage hung on his forelock, which dangled to the side of his golden horn.

The dog backed up several steps, taking in his size. Then she spun in circles again and gave a yip.

If only the human world were so accepting. His kind was nothing like the delicate animals humans imagined for unicorns.

In reality, they were giant and powerful, larger than horses, with hefty muscles to match their height. They could crush with their weight, shatter with a kick from their massive legs, and stab with their sharp horns. They were warrior beasts.

And he was the biggest and strongest of them all.

He snorted and tossed his mane. "Ready?"

The dog took off, gaining a head start.

Markos nickered under his breath. "Cheater."

His long strides closed the distance in no time. Wind whistled past his ears. Soft dirt gave way under his hooves. Trees zoomed by as silent sentinels to their race.

The dog scampered admirably fast, keeping up with his pace over stretches of woodland. Markos lost track of time and distance, focused only on their run. *Thup-da-lup thup-da-lup thup-da-lup.* Acres of ground passed under their hooves and paws.

His trance-like state stumbled as he nearly tripped over the dog for the third time. "Watch where you're going."

Again, the dog edged closer, causing him to veer to the side. Just as he was about to snap at the creature, they entered a clearing among the trees. Fog weaved between the tree trunks and danced in the open center, reminding him of the Mythos plane.

Markos pulled up and skidded across the damp grass. The dog trotted to a small pool in the clearing and slurped several mouthfuls of water.

Belatedly, Markos recognized the dog's behavior. "You herded me here."

He wanted to be insulted, but as the fog wrapped itself around him, swirling amidst his legs, he relaxed. This glade seemed so much like the Mythos plane he wouldn't be surprised to see dryads emerge from the trees. He felt more at home than he had in years. All because this creature had risked being trampled and killed.

Brave dog.

The animal looked up from lapping water, inviting him to join her at the pond. He ambled over and lowered his head to the surface. Already, he felt a kinship to the creature, and maybe that was the answer he needed. The desperate loneliness of his life had turned his insistence that he didn't want a pet into a lie.

A faint gray light filled the sky and gave the fog and the steam rising from his flanks a ghostly glow. If it was pre-dawn here, it was past midnight in St. Louis. Time to head back.

Just as he'd hoped, his mind had cleared with the exertion, and the dog's appearance had clarified the problem: Loneliness ate at his soul like a disease.

For centuries, he'd been a failure, an outcast, a focus of war and bloodshed. The others had to accept him as a Guardian because no other options remained, but he wasn't actually virtuous enough to succeed. He didn't fit in on Mythos, and he certainly didn't fit in on Earth.

Then Celia had come along and showed him what he was missing. He *did* need companionship, and she offered the best gift he could imagine. The gift of a few months of her friendship, her goodness filling the void of his soul, and her presence offering a sanctuary where he was wanted.

For the time she had left, he would enjoy what they had, in whatever way he could within the bounds of his tribe's commandments. He would be a true friend to the best of his ability.

Pain gathered in his chest and climbed up his throat. The rest of the truth refused to stay silent, and he let the thoughts surface. She deserved that much.

Because the truth was that at the Spring Equinox ceremony, to save his kind from extinction, he would steal her from her future dreams. He would allow Alkipsia to force the choice upon her. He would watch as her life bled out when he failed to remain pure enough for the ritual.

And if he survived that torture, he would deal with the guilt later.

Chapter Twelve

AT THE RING OF THE DOORBELL, CELIA SET HER LAPTOP BESIDE her on the couch and got up to answer the door. She peeked out the peephole and then stepped back. Markos.

What was he doing here? Her arms enfolded her chest, holding in the sudden tightness. Last night's hurt at how the evening had ended churned in her gut anew, and she didn't need to add the disappointment of hoping this was his first-ever social visit.

She shoved the questions away. He was probably just here for his jacket.

She smoothed her hair and opened the door, ensuring her lips curved into a friendly smile. "Good morning."

He inclined his head. "Good morning. I hope I'm not disturbing you too early."

She laughed and waved him inside. "Farm girl, remember? I've already been up and working on homework for a couple of hours."

He entered and surveyed the house. "Where is Harriet?"

"She went Black Friday shopping with a friend from church."

He grunted some level of understanding and then indicated the living room behind him. "Do you think she'll mind if a dog comes in?"

"A dog?"

Sure enough, a black and white border collie sat on the front porch, waiting for the A-okay.

"I didn't know you had a dog."

"I don't. She adopted me last night, and we've since come to an understanding."

Celia crouched in the doorway and held out her hand for the dog to sniff. "Hi. I'm Celia. What's your name?"

"She doesn't have a name as far as I'm aware. No collar."

She stared up at Markos. "So what have you been calling her? *Dog?*"

Furrows formed above his sunglasses. "What else would I call her?"

Celia turned back to the dog. A white stripe streaked down her forehead and broadened to encircle her snout. The rest of her was black except for white at the tip of her tail, the stockings of her feet, and the fluff of her chest.

"She's a cutie."

The dog licked her hand and then thrust its head closer so Celia could scratch behind her ears.

She chuckled. "And smart." She considered the animal. "I think she looks like a Molly. What do you think?"

The dog gave a quick yip and spun in a circle.

Markos stepped behind her. "Molly, you say?" Another bark. "Then Molly it is."

Celia stood and tried not to notice that Markos's approach into the doorway to talk to Molly had left him close enough to touch. He glanced down at her and didn't recoil at their proximity.

"So do you think Harriet will mind if Molly comes in?"

This close, it was freaky to look up at him and not be able to see his eyes behind his sunglasses. Only her own dim reflection met her gaze.

"I don't think so, but let's keep her in the front room, just in case."

Markos didn't change position to create an opening for the dog. And Celia certainly wasn't going to make the first move and lose whatever ground she'd gained by his decision to let her get within touching distance. Molly didn't mind. She wound her way through their legs and let herself into the living room.

Markos focused on Celia for another moment from behind his shades, and then he cleared his throat and followed Molly into the room. The breath Celia had been holding escaped in a slow exhale. Her lungs gulped air, as if the intensity of his presence had frozen her chest.

She covered up her gasps by heading down the hall. "Hang on, let me get your jacket."

She unhooked his coat from the back hall area and brought the leather to her nose one last time. Markos's aroma filled her with warmth. For some reason, his scent felt like happy memories, the sort that belonged to another life, one where she hadn't been ignored by her family and everyone else.

She'd never admit it to him, but she'd slept in his jacket last night, letting his aroma wrap around her like the hug he'd never give her. That sleep had been the best she'd gotten since the attack, his scent making her feel safe and protected.

Even though his sudden abandonment last evening had hurt, she still trusted that he'd make sure nothing dangerous happened to her. She just had to do a better job of restraining her expectations when it came to him. That's all.

Wishing for him to be a real friend didn't make it so. He was a bodyguard first, and any other possibilities came in a distant second. A far distant second.

She reentered the living room and held out his jacket. His mouth tightened before he took it from her. His arm hung limp at his side, and he made no move to put on the coat.

When he didn't thank her for returning it, she broke the awkward silence. "Thank you for letting me borrow it yesterday."

He grunted an acknowledgment. More silence.

What was he waiting for? He had his jacket. Was she supposed to apologize for whatever she'd done to upset him last night? She couldn't very well do that when she didn't know what she'd done wrong.

He indicated the couch. "Do you mind if I sit?"

"Uh, no. I mean, make yourself at home." What game was he playing now?

He took a seat on the couch next to her laptop. Even sitting, he was still a giant. She mentally uttered a quick prayer that Auntie's furniture would survive.

He laid his jacket over his lap and then sniffed. His face pulled into a grimace, and he lifted the leather to his nose. He deeply inhaled and focused his attention on her.

"You had a nightmare?"

"*What?*" How could he know that? The craziness of his knowledge invaded her privacy. "No, that's not—"

He held the coat out to Molly. She took one sniff and crouched low, staring at Celia like a predator ready to pounce.

What the heck? Celia backed up, heels thumping the edge of the couch. Molly inched forward, her eyes locked on Celia in a hypnotic gaze. Unable to retreat any more, Celia braced herself on the arm of the couch and plopped onto the other side of her laptop from Markos.

Only then did Molly sit up and break the staring contest.

Markos gave an approving nod. "She chose me. And now she's choosing you too."

Celia's defensiveness broke into a laugh. "She herded *you* too?"

One pointy brow rose over the top rim of his sunglasses. "Yes."

"Wow." She looked at Molly with new respect. "You go, girl."

Markos shook the jacket. "Explain. I know you wore my jacket to bed and had nightmares last night, and Molly knows it too. Scents reveal everything." As if confirming his words, Molly laid her head in Celia's lap and gave a sympathetic whimper.

A flicker of an echo repeated his words in her mind. *Scents reveal everything.* Like how his smell made her warm and happy inside and how she wanted him closer.

She dismissed the thought before expectations followed. "Why do you care? Nightmares don't fall into any of your *dangerous* categories that require your protection."

His expression scrunched tight. "I..."

But he didn't have an answer.

"Look, I appreciate your concern, but I have a ton of homework to do, and I returned your jacket. I promise I'll be here all day, so you don't have to stay."

He perched his elbows on his knees and squinted toward the front window. "You want me to go."

Crap. She'd messed things up again.

"No, I didn't mean it like that. It's just..." She sighed, debating what to admit. "Well, you came here to pick up your coat, right?

And then you started with all these questions, and I don't know why." She ran her fingers over Molly's head. "I don't *want* you to go."

"I didn't come here for my jacket." He twisted toward her, his knee sliding up onto the couch cushion. "I wanted to introduce Molly to..." He swallowed. "To my friend."

Oh no. She was a jerk. And an idiot. An idiotic jerk.

"I'm sorry. I didn't realize..." She shrugged. "It's not like you've ever just dropped by before." Before he could take her words the wrong way, she added, "But I'm glad you did."

His head dipped, acknowledging her apology. "Does that mean you'll tell me about your nightmare?"

Her breath escaped in a slow exhale, and the meaning behind his question sank past her defenses. He cared about her. Not just as part of his job, but as a friend. She threaded her fingers into Molly's fur to ground herself from the onslaught of emotions.

She couldn't let this revelation change her expectations. This didn't mean Auntie was right about the potential for anything more.

No matter what her heart might think about this intimidating-as-hell and hadn't-denied-that-he-might-be-from-the-future bodyguard, she had to keep her head. No matter that she couldn't tear her eyes away from his chest, his shoulders, and, Lordy, his biceps.

This was about *friendship*. That's all.

She peered down at Molly. The dog looked up at her with eyes filled with too much understanding. She'd heard border collies could be near-prescient due to their intense watchfulness and intuition, but this was ridiculous. She didn't know which was worse—Molly's all-seeing eyes or Markos's sunglasses.

Her gaze slid up to him through her lashes. "Can you take off your sunglasses?" She turned to face him on the couch, matching his pose. "It's hard to have a conversation with you when all I see is my own reflection."

His lips pressed together. Regardless, he removed the shades and tucked them into a pocket of his vest.

Now that she saw his warm, golden eyes across from her, though, her nerve fled. She busied herself with grabbing her laptop from the cushion between them and setting it on the floor. Once that was out of the way, she brought her sock-covered feet onto the sofa and hugged her knees.

Molly leaned against her and pressed her weight in a comforting gesture of security. Celia draped her wrist around Molly's head. Thus prepared, she forced herself to open up to Markos.

"I've had nightmares *every* night since the attack."

He jerked back but let her continue.

"I know he's dead and can't hurt me anymore. I know the chances of something like that happening again—especially with you around—are astronomical. I know it could have been much worse. But in my nightmares, it always *is* worse. He's not really dead, he follows me home, he's not alone..." She nibbled on her lip. "You're not there to stop him."

Lines formed around his eyes, tightening.

She sighed. "Anyway, you name a way it could have been worse, and I've dreamed it. Last night was actually the *best* sleep I've gotten in the week and a half since it happened. But yes, I still had some nightmares."

"I apologize." He stretched his fingers from their clenched shape. "You've seemed so"—his mouth thinned—"strong every time we spoke I didn't realize you hadn't fully recovered from the attack."

"It's not your fault. I've been on my own for so long that I learned to deal with my problems my own way. I've never needed to be a sharing kind of person."

His hands formed a fist again. "It *is* my fault. He never should have been able to get close to you, much less hurt you in any way."

She released her knees and stretched her arm along the back of the couch toward him. "No, I *don't* blame you. Please don't blame yourself. I didn't even know you were around to save me. So I certainly shouldn't have put myself in a situation where I needed saving."

Markos lay his hand along the back of the couch too. Only an inch separated their fingers.

"You shouldn't blame yourself either. You should be able to travel freely without worrying about such things."

"On that, we can agree."

"I..." His mouth closed, opened, and then closed again. "I don't want you to suffer from nightmares." His other hand rubbed the back of his neck. "There must be some way to stop them."

Her throat grew thick, and she itched to lean forward and clasp their fingers together. She resisted the urge and moistened her lips.

That had to be the sweetest thing anyone ever said to her. Auntie cared about her, sure, but that was mostly about the woman's motherly instinct. Not about liking her as a person.

Not like a friend.

The tension in her legs loosened, and she tipped over and leaned against the back of the couch, letting her feet slide off the cushion. She laid her cheek on her extended arm.

"I don't know of any way to stop nightmares." She winked at him and confessed in a low voice. "I mean, last night I slept in the jacket of the biggest and best protector I know, and that still didn't keep the nightmares away."

He leaned against the back of the couch, mimicking her position. A slow smile built on his face. "If it would help, I'm sure he'd let you keep the jacket. Going around cold would be a small price to pay for you to feel safe."

She inhaled, ready to continue their banter, but closed her mouth in the nick of time. She'd almost admitted that she'd feel safer with *him*, rather than just his jacket, and there was no way for that to come out in any way close to appropriate.

Instead, she left her response vague. "I'd like that. Thank you."

The smile dropped from his face. His fingers slid closer, only a centimeter from hers on the back of the couch. "I promise you, I *will* keep you safe. And I will do whatever necessary to earn your trust in that fact."

His vow struck her in the chest and left her breathless. "Markos…" Her voice came out weak and fluttery. She took a deep breath and tried again. "This *isn't* about me not trusting you to keep me safe."

Their fingertips were now just a few millimeters apart. She could feel the heat radiating off his skin. Her fingers tingled with the desire to close the gap between them. To comfort him. To console him.

He leaned forward. "Then what *are* you afraid of?"

Everything.

She was scared that he'd discover whatever it was that caused others to avoid her. That she'd place too many expectations on this friendship and open herself to emotional pain. That she'd mess up the future.

Between finally gaining a friend and learning of her future, she should have been ecstatic. Instead, she didn't trust that any of it would last. Maybe this was all part of a cosmic joke meant to break her.

She straightened and drew her arm in to her chest. Keeping her distance and her expectations low was the best protection. "You're welcome to stay, but I really need to finish my homework."

His mouth opened, but he seemed to think better of whatever he was going to say. He glanced at Molly, who came to his side, and then he nodded at Celia. "We'll wait in the front yard for Harriet to return. I'd like Molly to meet her too."

She opened her laptop. "It might be a while. Today's paper is on the kitchen table if you want to entertain yourself."

When he tossed his jacket aside and strode into the kitchen, she sank into the cushions and let her hair fall forward. Ugh. That was just wonderful. She'd succeeded in pushing him away. These fears weren't his fault.

She set her laptop down again and jogged into the kitchen. "Can I get you something to drink?" She poked her head in the fridge. "I think we have sweet tea, juice, Coke, water."

"Thank you. I'll take some water."

She grabbed the water pitcher and took down two glasses from the cabinet. His gaze followed her around the room, making her feel like an awkward puppet in her own skin.

Was it her imagination, or was he watching her more closely today? Or maybe he'd always stared at her, and she never realized it before because of his sunglasses.

After filling the first glass, she reached for the second. Her arm swung more uncoordinatedly than usual, and she knocked into the cup, sending it skittering across the counter. Markos appeared at her side and caught the glass before it crashed to the floor.

A nervous laugh bubbled up from her lungs, and she set down the water pitcher. "Thank you."

She accepted the glass from him without meeting his gaze and placed it on the counter, being extra careful to withdraw her fingers slowly.

Markos lifted his hand and hesitated, holding it a fraction above her shoulder. "Are you all right?"

She didn't have an answer for that question. In every way, she should be better than all right. But she couldn't shake the feeling that the other shoe was hovering, just out of sight, waiting for her to let down her guard so it could crush her under its heel.

At her silence, he lowered his hand. "I'm sorry. I upset you by forcing you to speak of the attack. I shouldn't have insisted."

She shook her head at his assumption. "No, it's okay."

Then she made the mistake of looking up into his eyes. So close, so intense, so beautiful. Once again, they reminded her of a pool of warm honey, and she couldn't help diving in, allowing herself to be helpless and stuck in his gaze. Her breaths quickened, and she drowned in the golden depths.

His warmth flooded through her body. They were close enough that she could see his pulse at the corner of his eye, beating fast and strong like hers. She lifted her hand—oh so tempted to touch him—but let her fingers rest on her lips instead.

He closed his eyes, breaking the spell, and pivoted away from her, leaning against the counter. She gulped in a large breath and exhaled slowly, quietly—willing her heartbeat to settle.

As soon as she trusted her muscles, she poured the other water and handed the glass to him. "Here you go, unbroken and everything." For some reason, her voice sounded low and sultry. She cleared her throat and tried again. "Let me grab my laptop, and I'll join you in the front yard. We should all enjoy this sunny weather while we can."

He opened his eyes and accepted the glass without comment. Her steps back to the living room were stiff and ungraceful with her attempt to *not* flee the kitchen. She collapsed onto the couch and buried her head in her palms.

What was she *doing*? Hadn't she just been thinking about how she needed to keep her distance? Keep her guard up? Keep her expectations low?

But no… One look into his eyes, and she was ready to throw herself at him, heedless of the hurt and disappointment she knew waited for her on the other side.

She'd known she was curious about him. Fascinated even. But her utter captivation was beyond either of those. And it wasn't just about his broad chest or thick biceps either.

This was a deeper connection. Almost primal. Almost like destiny.

Molly licked her chin, and Celia lifted her head. Markos stood in the doorway.

Heat spread up her face. How long had he been standing there, watching her?

He slid his sunglasses over his eyes and headed to the door, newspaper and glass of water in hand. She clutched her laptop to her chest, grabbed her water from the kitchen, and set out to follow him.

Tomorrow she'd work on rebuilding her defenses. Today...

Today she'd just enjoy the warm weather with her friend.

Right. Nothing to it.

Chapter Thirteen

MARKOS STOOD IN THE DARKENED ROOM AND WATCHED Celia sleep. She would hate for him to be here, calling it stalkerish behavior, but the threat of her chastisement didn't matter. Even the threat to his sanity from being in the same room as her—being able to stare at her peaceful and lovely face all he wanted—didn't matter.

He would prevent her nightmares. That's what mattered.

Only now, when she was asleep, did he take off his sunglasses again. He'd learned his lesson earlier that afternoon. More than just a shield to prevent Celia from seeing what his eyes looked like—which, now that she'd seen them plenty of times, was irrelevant—the shades also seemed to add a layer of protection.

Every time he'd taken off his sunglasses, he'd gotten lost in her eyes, her face, her purity. If he wasn't careful, one of these times he'd lose his common sense and let her touch him. Or worse, he'd fail to prevent *himself* from touching her.

He'd lost count of how many times he'd almost touched her that afternoon. He'd wanted to clasp her hand on the couch, hold her shoulder for comfort in the kitchen. He was hopelessly under her spell, thinking forbidden thoughts, and all he could do now was ensure he didn't *act* on any of those thoughts.

She rolled over and hugged her pillow. Her luscious hair spilled over his old leather jacket and nearly glowed in the flickering light leaking through the curtains. Even asleep, her danger was apparent.

His nerves tingled at her nearness, and her fresh, sweet scent lured him closer. The urge to stroke her face, her hair, her hand ached in his fingers. They twitched, begging him for just one caress. Just one.

But he was a Guardian. Strong and focused. He would resist.

He'd prepared for her temptations before coming here. He'd tightened the buckles of the bands on his forearms until the leather bit into his skin. He'd removed his vest and rolled his shirtsleeves up to allow the cold night air keep him alert. And he'd done something he hadn't done since childhood. He'd knelt in the moonlight and prayed to the Maker that he'd have the strength to do what was right, what was necessary.

A soft moan slipped from her lips. His weight shifted to the balls of his feet, ready to step forward if this was a sign the nightmares were starting.

Regardless of what she'd said that morning, they *were* his fault. He was supposed to be there to protect her.

If he'd done his job, she wouldn't have had to face that ordeal. If he'd done his job, she wouldn't have memories of an attack to cause these awful dreams. That was the truth that mattered.

Her arm thrashed against the covers. In an instant, he was at her bedside, weaving a misty cloth of calm and peace. The shroud drifted over her head.

He breathed, "I will keep you safe."

The ethereal substance sank into her skin with his vow. Her movements calmed, and he hoped that would be the end of it, despite the uncertain effect of his magic.

But a moment later, her quiet whimper brought him to his knees. Her body trembled under the bedspread. Her hand jerked, clutching the sheet to her chest. A light sheen of sweat glistened on her forehead.

His throat tightened at the grimace on her face, and his jaw clenched at the terrified sobs on her lips. What torture was she enduring in this dream? How was he failing her this time?

She flinched and whimpered, "No," in her sleep.

Acting on its own, his hand reached out and settled on her

back. He left it there.

Layers of leather, sheets, blankets, and bedspreads separated his palm from her skin. He wasn't *actually* touching her. He could ignore the feel of her body beneath the covers. He *would* ignore her curves, her softness, her perfection.

Her eyes popped open, and he froze. Her face was blank and unseeing, like she was in a half-awake and half-asleep state.

"You're here." Her voice was thick and groggy.

He swallowed a profanity. Would speaking wake her more or help her sleep?

He decided to risk it, for the sake of chasing away the nightmares. "I'm here to keep you safe."

"You'll stay?"

"Yes."

Her eyes closed again and then fluttered open, wide with panic. "Promise me." Her gaze darted across his face, searching his expression. "Promise you'll always keep me safe."

"Always." He lied.

Her eyelids grew heavy once more, and she stretched her arm and touched a finger to his lips. "I trust you."

His lips parted, longing to kiss her fingertip, longing to press her palm against his cheek. He resisted the temptation, but the thought alone would earn him banishment from his tribe if they knew. He couldn't make himself care. Right now, he cared only about her.

As her eyes closed, and remained closed this time, his heart twisted in his chest until he felt nauseated. Self-hatred rose in his throat, ready to burn him in Hades for his sins. He tried to swallow, but his muscles choked on the sensation.

Her hand drooped back to the mattress, and her breathing settled into a deep, steady pattern.

He lifted his hand from her back and stumbled to the far corner of the room. His knees refused to hold his weight, and he sank to the floor. His lips still tingled from her touch, and he brought his own fingers to the spot.

Never before had a Virgin known him, trusted him, believed him. Celia did. And that would affect his approach for the Spring Equinox ceremony.

Her trust would make her abduction easier.
And the ritual itself so, *so* much harder.
He'd chased away the nightmares, but at the cost of his soul.
If it improved her remaining months, it was worth it.
Of that, he was certain.

Chapter Fourteen

EVER SINCE FINDING OUT ABOUT HIS JOB, CELIA HAD SUSPECTED that Markos must shadow her throughout the day, but he'd always disappeared as soon as she reached campus. Now, for the past week since Thanksgiving, he sat with her on the bus and accompanied her from class to class, slipping away only when the professor started the lecture or lab. He brought Molly to the house every evening while Celia did homework and never said no when Auntie invited him to stay for dinner.

They talked and laughed and acted like the friendship was real. Just like she'd wished for.

And every day, she found it harder to keep her emotional distance.

This evening, they sat together in the living room to give Auntie privacy while she talked to her son on the kitchen phone. Molly lay in the center of the couch, enforcing a comfortable distance between them, her head in Markos's lap. He'd taken up the habit of pretending to read the newspaper every night, but she'd caught him napping behind the cover of his sunglasses several times when he didn't respond to her questions.

She almost hoped he was tired because her dreams about him being in her bedroom were true. And not just because those dreams had chased away most of the nightmares.

Celia rubbed her temples. She *needed* to stop thinking about

Jami Gold

this, about him, and focus on her fast-approaching final exams. The letters on her laptop, especially all the Latin-based words, swam before her eyes. She pressed harder on her skull—if only that could force the information into her brain.

Before she could refocus, Auntie entered the room, clutching a piece of paper like it was a winning lottery ticket. "It's all settled. Roger gave me his flight number and everything."

Celia closed her laptop at the excuse for a distraction. "He's coming out for Christmas?"

The woman settled into her usual overstuffed seat in the corner and pulled out her quilting supplies from the basket beside her chair. "For the week before Christmas."

"He won't be here Christmas Day though?"

"No, he won't." Auntie laid the note with Dr. Williams's flight information on the side table and set her quilting squares on her lap, fixing Celia with her gaze. "But don't you dare think about skipping your own Christmas to stay here with me."

Celia gave a half-shrug. "You can't be alone on Christmas."

"I didn't protest at Thanksgiving because you were right about that being too long of a trip for such a short break. But you haven't seen your folks since summer, child. And if you don't go now, you won't see them until *next* summer."

Markos jerked his head up, no longer pretending to pay attention to the newspaper.

Auntie stabbed the air with her needle. "Your family needs to see you more than I do."

"They don't *need* to see me." Celia scratched Molly's ears. "Do you know they never called for Thanksgiving? Never called to see if I was coming in. Never called to see if I was alone for the holiday. I finally called them late Thanksgiving night, and they hadn't even noticed I wasn't there."

Auntie's expression slipped into one of pity. Celia closed her eyes at the sight. Pity was the *last* thing she wanted from anyone.

"I'm sorry for that, child. But when you've lived as long as I have, you learn that you have to give people another chance. When you stop trying, any hope of fixing the problem dies."

Celia opened her eyes. "And just how many chances am I

supposed to give them before I decide it hurts too much?" She gave Molly a kiss on the top of her head. "I have no reason to go."

Markos closed the newspaper. "If you don't see them for Christmas, when would your next visit be?"

"Spring break falls mid-term, so I usually have tons of home-work to catch up on." She rolled her shoulders in a drawn-out shrug. "I probably wouldn't see them until next summer."

"You have to visit them for Christmas."

Her jaw loosened. "I *have* to? I don't have to do anything."

The pointy arch of his brow rose over his sunglasses. "It is *important* that you go."

"Important?" She glanced at Auntie and bit back the questions he couldn't answer in front of an audience. "I don't have the money for the bus trip."

"I'll drive you."

"Drive me?" She rolled her eyes. "You don't have a car either, Mr. Bus-riding Man, so how the heck could you drive me?"

"I'll buy a car and learn."

"*Learn?*" She squinted at Molly. "Are you listening to this insanity?" She tugged her earlobe, wondering if she was hearing him right. "In the next two weeks, you're going to learn how to drive, buy a car, and then make a day-long trip along roads you've never driven before—all so I can be ignored by my family in person?"

"Yes."

His mouth didn't twitch with amusement. His lips didn't stretch into a smile. His body didn't soften into a casual pose. He was serious.

Her gaze sought out Auntie for assistance, but the woman was no help. Instead, she nodded her head, as if to say, *see, I told you.*

Celia inhaled and tried to come up with a way to talk some sense into Markos. But nothing came to her. Finally, she settled on the only question that mattered.

"Why?"

He gave Molly a pat, all calm and casual-like, acting like this wasn't the craziest idea ever. "You need to see your family, and where you go, I go."

Where you go, I go? The extent of his offer sank past her shock and crushed her lungs, knocking the breath out of her. This wasn't just about giving her a ride.

She leaned over Molly and nailed Markos with her gaze. "You're planning on staying at my family's house *with* me, and we're all going to act like one big, happy family?"

He gave her a look with no room for argument. "Yes."

She closed her eyes and moaned, falling against the back of the couch. Any visit to her family was always nerve-wracking, just because of their attitude toward her.

But now add in that she'd be bringing a *guy* home with her? And that guy was black? And that her father was not the most open-minded person on the planet?

And none of that even touched on the worry about how Markos might change how he treated her after meeting her family and seeing that she was nobody special.

This was the first sign of the apocalypse.

That's all there was to it.

MARKOS HELD HIS STIFF POSE. HE WOULDN'T LET HER TALK HIM OUT of this.

This trip would be the last time she'd get to see her family, and the Maker help him, he was going to make sure she brought back some happy memories. He couldn't change her destiny, but he could change what experiences she had in these last few months, make sure they were enjoyable.

She lifted her head off the back of the couch and eyed him. "You know this is going to be a disaster, right?"

"It won't be. Trust me." His stomach turned over for using those words with her. He should be the last person she'd trust.

Clapping from the corner interrupted their dispute. A broad grin stretched Harriet's face. "Good. It's all settled. Thank you, dear, for talking some sense into her."

Celia glared at her landlady, and then she shifted away from him and reopened her laptop, obviously intent on ignoring them.

Markos stifled a chuckle and opened the newspaper. Somewhere in here, he'd seen a *Cars* section.

Pure Sacrifice

He paged through the advertisements for inspiration on how to create better memories for Celia. One headline caught his eye:

Best-Selling Pony Cars of the Year.

Pony cars? His lips twitched. That was all the inspiration he needed.

Chapter Fifteen

TWO WEEKS LATER, CELIA LUGGED HER SUITCASE DOWN THE stairs. The solid ball in her stomach felt even heavier than her luggage.

As she'd expected, her mom had been uninterested in the details of her visit when she'd called. Even the warning that she was bringing a guy friend—a *black* guy friend—home with her didn't trigger a reaction. If her parents didn't care enough to freak out about that, maybe that was one less thing to worry about.

Markos let himself in the front door right as she reached the bottom of the stairs. She could only manage a half-smile in greeting. He'd never told her why this trip was so important, and she still hadn't forgiven him for pressuring her into this disaster-to-be. At her stagger, he caught the suitcase from her as if it were empty.

That bit of gallantry earned him a genuine smile. "Thanks." She tried catching a glimpse of the infamous car out the kitchen window, but his broad chest blocked the view. "I'm glad to see you made it here in one piece. Are you sure you're ready for this?"

"You're not going to talk me out of this trip."

She grabbed the bag of Christmas presents from under the tree in the living room and set it beside the door. Her hand waved with faux-innocence. "Oh, I wouldn't *dream* of it."

He deadpanned, "Good."

"Let me say goodbye to Auntie before we go." She headed down the back hallway to Auntie Harriet's room, where the woman was getting ready for her son's arrival later that afternoon.

Celia knocked. "Auntie?" The door was open several inches, and she peeked in. "Auntie?"

The room was torn up beyond recognition. She pushed the door open the rest of the way. Every drawer, every purse's contents, and every item from the closet had all been dumped onto the floor and the bed.

She rushed forward. "Auntie? Are you okay?"

Her landlady emerged from the small washroom. Her wild eyes lit on Celia, and she lurched across the room. She seized Celia's shoulders and shook her.

"What have you done with them?"

Celia's thoughts froze, and her hands protectively jumped to her chest. "Done with what? Tell me what you're looking for, and I'll help you find them."

"Liar! You've been stealing from me behind my back." The woman slapped her hard across the cheek.

Adrenaline shot through Celia, making the impact sting even harder, and she squeaked and stumbled back into the hallway. Like a rescuer on a white steed, Markos was at her side in an instant, waving his fingers in front of him like a bizarre kind of martial artist.

He spread his arms in front of Auntie and murmured, "Remember."

She staggered toward them, and he caught her before she fell. When she next looked up, her eyes were clear.

"Oh... Oh dear."

Without a word, Markos helped Auntie Harriet down the hall and settled her into a chair at the kitchen table. Celia stood in the doorway, a fist pressed to her lips, unable to stop herself from shaking. Markos glanced up at her, and she nodded, encouraging him to deal with Auntie first.

Thank goodness he was here to handle the situation. However he'd managed to overcome the woman's episode, she was grateful. If she'd been here alone with Auntie...

She didn't want to think about that.

He sat in the chair beside the woman. She didn't meet his stare.

"Harriet, I need you to talk to me. I need to know if you're all right."

"I'm so sorry." She clutched his arm. "I didn't mean that. You have to believe me, I didn't mean that." She half-turned over her shoulder toward Celia. "I'm so sorry, child."

Celia swallowed and concentrated on making her voice steady. "It's okay. I know you didn't mean it."

"Harriet." Markos demanded her attention again. "Do you know what happened?"

"I've been so anxious about Roger's arrival..." She shook her head. "That's no excuse, I know. I—" She broke into a nervous laugh. "I was thinking I needed to find my car keys to pick him up from the airport."

Celia leaned against the doorframe, her limbs weak. With all the talk of cars lately, it made sense that Auntie would have fixated on the idea, forgetting that her son had sold her car last year after her first serious episode.

Markos pressed, ensuring the woman had fully recovered. "You know where those keys are, don't you?"

She looked down and folded her hands together. "With a nice young family in Affton."

Markos peered up at Celia. "What do you think?"

Unsure of her voice, she just nodded. But then she remembered the bigger issue. "I can't leave her like this. Her room is a mess, and Dr. Williams isn't going to be here until later."

Her landlady rose from the chair, strong and determined once more. "Nonsense. You have a long trip ahead of you, and I won't keep you from it. Besides, cleaning that mess will give me something to do before Roger comes."

She held up a hand as soon as Celia opened her mouth to protest.

"I'm serious, child." Her eyes softened, and her chin quivered. "I feel horrible enough as it is. Don't add to my guilt by making yourself late."

Those were the magic words. *Don't add guilt* was the one thing Auntie Harriet could mention to make leaving feel in any way acceptable.

Celia strode forward and wrapped her arms around the woman.

"I just wish there was more I could do. I feel so helpless."

Auntie patted her back. "I know. And you try so hard. But right now, I need you to get going on your trip."

"Are you sure?" Celia pulled back to check her reaction. "Maybe we should exchange presents now, before I go, just to end on a happier note."

"We're going to stick to the plan. I'm going to leave that beautifully wrapped present from you under the tree until you come back." Auntie winked. "That'll give me something to look forward to."

Celia hugged her tight, putting all the angst twisting her stomach into the embrace. "I love you, Auntie. You have a wonderful visit with your son, and have a Merry Christmas."

"Merry Christmas to you too, child." The woman gave her a kiss on the cheek and then thrust her toward Markos. "Take her out of here while you can."

Markos squeezed Auntie Harriet's shoulder and then picked up Celia's suitcase and the bag of Christmas presents by the door. "Come on, Molly's out in the car and probably wondering what's taking us so long."

The car. She'd forgotten all about that aspect of this journey. Celia grasped Auntie's hand for a final goodbye, claimed her jacket from the hall, and then let Markos lead her outside. She stopped halfway down the front porch stairs, her fingers still in the process of zipping up her coat.

The car was nothing like what she'd expected. Even after learning of the secret behind his job, she'd naively assumed that Markos took the bus all the time because he was poor like her and thought his car would be a used rust-bucket. But no...

Apparently, he rode the bus every day only because she did.

A shiny new sports car with custom detailing sat in the driveway. An extra air intake jutted above the slope of the hood, so he'd probably upgraded to the top-of-the-line engine too. A glossy black body with white swirls along the side, which reminded her of a horse's mane flowing in the wind, all added to the impression that this was a true muscle car.

"Wow."

Molly sat in the front seat and barked a greeting through the window. Celia resumed her steps and circled the car.

"Nice. What is it?"

"A pony car." He chuckled as though he'd made a joke. "A Mustang Shelby GT."

Markos popped the trunk and set the bag of presents and her suitcase inside while she moved to the passenger door. But then she saw Auntie waving goodbye from the front porch, and the smile slipped off her face.

Markos opened her door and caged her against the car. "Get in."

Any other time, she'd have shuddered from the nearness of his body and the deep rumble of his command. Instead, she shook her head and whispered, "I don't know if I can do this."

"You can call her son from the road. Let him know what happened."

She looked up at him gratefully and gathered strength from his presence. She gave Auntie a final wave before getting into the car. Molly licked her chin from the driver's seat and then hopped into the back.

Markos opened his door and eased himself inside. His head came in just a couple of inches below the roof, and his legs filled the area below the steering wheel.

She peeked down at the pedals. "Huh, you *do* fit."

He flicked over a switch and adjusted the steering wheel. "I did have to add an after-market telescoping steering wheel."

"Why not buy a bigger car?"

He started the car and revved the engine, which gave a loud growl. "I liked *this* one."

His tone was the closest she'd ever heard him get to saying *duh* at the end of a sentence. Add that to seeing him behind the wheel of this beast of a car and using words like *after-market*, and he seemed more like a stereotypical guy than ever before. Damn if that didn't add to his attractiveness.

He tossed his replacement leather jacket in back with Molly and put the car in gear. As he turned onto Hamilton Avenue and smoothly maneuvered through traffic, he glanced over, and lines on his face formed a frown. "Weren't you going to call Roger?"

Her mouth opened, but she snapped it shut. Her throat closed up in denial, maybe even shock, at the thought of having to say what had happened, what Auntie had done.

"Would you like me to call him for you?"

At whatever expression she had on her face, Markos claimed her phone—which she hadn't even realized she'd been holding in a vise grip this whole time.

A sour taste on her tongue increased her sense of failure about keeping herself together. Once again, Markos was coming to her rescue.

At least Auntie had mentioned him to her son several times—near constantly in fact—so it wasn't like the men were complete strangers.

A few minutes later, he hung up the call. "All taken care of. I caught him just before he left for the airport."

"What did he say?" Not that she really wanted to know. "I mean, did he blame me?"

"Blame you?" He faced her, his lips tight. "You did nothing wrong."

Then why did she feel like such a failure? "Thank you. For everything, I mean. For inside the house and for calling him too."

"You're welcome." He gave her a heart-warming smile.

Sometimes he was amazingly sensitive and thoughtful.

His thumb tapped the steering wheel. "Roger did want to know if you planned on moving out."

"*What?* No." She shook her head, emphasizing her words.

Markos shifted in his seat. "It *is* something to consider."

"No. It's not." She twisted toward him. "If I move out, they'll have a big argument about moving her into an assisted living place. She's not ready for that yet. Yes, she has these episodes, but they're still the exception, not the norm."

She wrestled to take her coat off, all the stress of the last several minutes making her feel hot and antsy. Her right arm didn't want to slip from its sleeve, and she leaned to the left with her tugs.

In the tight fit of the car, her shoulder bumped his. She sat up and glanced at his face, ready for the look of disgust. It didn't come.

That oddity made her even more agitated, and her whole chest tightened. She finished getting her jacket off and threw it into the back seat, and then she sat up straight, pretending nothing had happened. Because it hadn't. Just because he forgave her for that accidental slip didn't mean touching was suddenly okay.

She cleared her throat. "Besides, I can't afford any place else."

"I could—"

"So help me, if you're going to tell me that you have enough money to pay for a place for me, just shut it right now. I don't want to hear it. It's better for her if I stay—for now. And that's all there is to it."

There was a limit to how much she could handle him being her rescuer. Especially if she wanted to have any control over her heart.

His arms stiffened. "Understood."

After that, they fell into silence. The only noise was the roar of the engine as exit numbers dropped, the miles passing on their way north to Iowa. The silence gained in power until it was deafening.

The awkward situation didn't help the tightness in her stomach. How much of what they seemed to have in common was like the issue of him riding the bus? That their commonalities were only because he mimicked what she did as part of his job?

If that was the case, that meant she was bringing a stranger she didn't really know into her parents' home, and unless her mother's non-interest held, they were somewhere between *likely* and *certain* to freak out. And somehow they all had to survive two weeks together.

Oh joy. It had all the makings of a perfect Christmas.

Chapter Sixteen

MARKOS PUSHED HIS TENSION ABOUT THE SITUATION WITH Harriet into the accelerator pedal. The thought that Celia would stay in a potentially dangerous environment left his mouth so dry it had glued shut. What would happen next time? What if he wasn't there?

Thank the Maker his magic had worked to stop Harriet's episode. However, the further she slipped into the disease, the more her brain's damage would decrease the chances of his magic working again. He liked the woman, but she was reaching the point of being a danger to herself and others faster than Celia would admit.

His muscles tensed with the effort of holding in his protests. Unless he had an answer to the dilemma of Celia's living arrangements—that she'd accept—anything he said would be meaningless. He'd actually planned on offering to pay for a caretaker for the woman, but Celia had made it perfectly clear that she was uncomfortable with him spending money anywhere near her.

The only solution that didn't require him spending money would be to invite Celia to stay with him—and that was out of the question. But which was worse? Going insane with worry about what could happen at Harriet's? Or going insane with temptation if Celia was even closer—without a chaperone?

In his peripheral vision, she twisted a lock of her hair around her finger. "So do I need to give you a primer on my family? Or does the fact that you knew about the vegetarian thing from when I was a kid mean you're like an uber-stalker who already knows all the details of my life?"

Her questions veered into dangerous territory again. He ran his hand down his mustache and goatee and kept his gaze on the pavement ahead.

"I never saw you as anything but a job until recently, so most of your history didn't make an impression on me. The vegetarian thing was just a random detail I happened to remember."

For the most part, that was true. For his sanity, she *had* been merely a means to an end in his mind—before their friendship. But as the vegetarian memory proved, he might have taken a stronger interest in her over the years than he'd realized.

Her lips twitched. "So I shouldn't worry about that hideous haircut I had in eighth grade tainting your image of me?"

He burst out with a belly laugh. "No, but now that you mention it, short hair wasn't a good look for you."

"So glad I was able to remind you."

His chest warmed as her eyes lit with humor once more. He wanted to enjoy the sight, but he forced his attention back to the road. "The strength and determination I've seen in you every day have made a far bigger impression than anything in your past. That's the woman I'm proud to call my friend."

She inhaled deeply. "How did you know the perfect thing to say? That was so good you almost made me stop worrying about this trip."

"Almost?"

"I still have to deal with my family."

"We'll deal with them."

She bit her lip. "*You're* going to deal with my family?"

"All of us together. Right, Molly?" Through the rearview mirror, he glanced into the back seat, where she gave a sleepy yip.

Celia giggled. "Oh, in that case, forgive me for not being more optimistic."

"Tell me your biggest fears about this visit, and I'll see what I can do."

Over the next couple of hours of their drive, his heart sank so deep his throat felt stretched to the point of pain. For most of her life, Celia had acted like the typical shy and quiet Virgin, so he'd stayed in the background as usual and hadn't paid attention to whether the magic he'd woven at her birth was working as expected.

Now the tragedy of her childhood laid out like a path lined with guilt-tinged flames. The forgotten birthdays, the lack of Christmas gifts, the months at a time when they'd refused to pick her up from school and insisted all their children were already home when the administration called. Her family had never physically abused her, but the severe neglect qualified as emotional and mental abuse.

Were her parents simply abusive? Or had it been because of his magic?

His magic *shouldn't* have worked like that. It should have just weakened the emotional bonds and kept others uninterested unless she did something to garner attention. It wasn't supposed to cause harm.

But he feared that for whatever reason, in her case, his magic had ruined her life. He said a fervent prayer to the Maker that his fear was unfounded.

He watched the road through narrow slits and pinched the bridge of his nose. Regardless of the cause of her horrible childhood, he wished he really *could* time travel. Then he could go back and try to undo some of the damage.

By the time they pulled onto the country road leading to her family's farmhouse, dusk had already settled over the barn and farm fields, and lights glowed from several rooms of the two-and-a-half-story house. He turned off the car engine and prepared for what was to come.

Celia gave him a half-smile. "Too bad you got us here safely. I was almost hoping for a fiery crash to keep us away."

He got out and grabbed their things from the back. "Don't say that." He watched Molly make a beeline to the nearest tree. "You said they're okay with dogs, right?"

"Oh, Molly will be fine. It's you I'm worried about."

He shrugged, faking a confidence he no longer felt. "We'll all be fine."

After Molly caught up to them, Celia opened the front door. "I'm home."

Jami Gold

Her brows lifted at the lack of a reaction, as if to say, *I told you so.* Sounds floated to them from down the hall. He set the suitcases against the wall and left the bag of presents next to the tree in the front room before following her to the source. Her younger sister and older brother were watching television in the family room.

She lifted her hand in a nervous wave. "Hi. Merry Christmas."

Her brother, an athletic type—Celia had mentioned he'd gone to, and barely graduated from, college on a football scholarship—glanced over. "Hey." He did a double take. "What's up with the giant?"

"Chris, this giant is my *friend*, Markos. Markos, this is my brother, Chris, who's upset that you're even bigger than he is."

"Your friend, huh? Didn't know you had any." He returned his attention to the television. "Dad's going to *love* that, by the way. Don't you think you're taking the black-sheep-of-the-family thing too far?" He laughed. "Get it? Black sheep?"

Celia's jaw tightened. "Markos, my sister there who can't even be bothered to say hi is Lisa."

Her sister, a spoiled teenager from what he remembered, waved without looking away from the screen.

Celia pulled back and then released her hair in a gesture of frustration. "See? Can you handle their excitement at seeing me for the first time in months?"

Neither of her siblings responded.

She groaned. "Let's go find my parents and get the rest of this out of the way."

Lisa finally focused in their direction, but her gaze never lifted to their faces. "Cool dog. What's his name?"

Markos threw as much booming intimidation into his voice as possible. "*Her* name is Molly."

He stood as tall as he could and crossed his arms to glare at the child. His earlier guilt lessened with his dislike of her siblings. Their smug and self-indulgent behavior went beyond what his magic could be responsible for. He was sure of it.

At least he hoped to Hades and back that was the case. If not, the price to his soul for his sins might kill him.

Lisa's eyes locked on his, fear flickering in her expression. "Holy crap, Cece. Are you trying to cause World War III?"

"Sure." Celia folded her arms across her chest, mimicking

Markos's posture. "I thought it would be fun."

"Your death." Her sister patted her knees. "Come here, Molly. Come here, girl."

Molly, to her eternal credit, sneezed and walked off down the hall. Celia released her arms and led Markos behind Molly toward the kitchen. She paused in the doorway and squared her shoulders.

Celia approached the side of her mother, who stood at the counter putting together a salad, and gave her a kiss on the cheek. "Hi, Mom. Merry Christmas."

Her mother startled and turned, a smile on her face. Her lips flattened when she saw who stood beside her. "Oh, I wasn't expecting you."

"Remember, Mom?" Celia used the same tone as when Harriet experienced an episode, and her patience with that situation suddenly made more sense—as did her horror when Harriet had turned against her. "I called and told you I was coming."

"Did you? I must have…" For the first time, her gaze roamed to the doorway where Markos stood. "Who is *he*?"

"This is my friend, Markos. I told you about him on the phone too."

"You did not say any such thing." Her mother glanced to the back door, strands falling from the hair gathered at the back of her head. "You need to get him out of here. Quickly."

"No, Mom. He's my friend. The *one* friend I have. He's staying."

"I won't have you upsetting your—"

The back door opened, and Celia's father, a bear of a man, walked into the kitchen. Celia and her mother both froze, eyes wide. He tossed his keys into the basket on the counter and looked up, noticing Markos. The skin around his eyes tightened so much his cheeks rose.

"Who the hell let one of *them* into my house?"

"Dad!" Celia's hands clenched into fists. "Markos is my *friend.*" She stormed up to him, a stick figure in the shadow of a behemoth. "I *demand* that you treat him with respect."

His expression wiped clear, like a snow pile disintegrating in the rain. He approached his wife as if nothing had happened and gave her a kiss.

"Everything good on the home front?"

Adding to the outlandish scene, her mother had similarly transformed from tense to relaxed. "Quiet evening. The kids are in watching TV. Why don't you call them for dinner?"

He headed down the hall without a look to Celia or Markos. "Hey, kids, come help your mother with dinner."

What the *skoro* was going on in this family? Ignoring her was one thing; pretending she literally didn't exist—had never existed—was something far beyond the bounds of his magic.

His pulse quickened, and his muscles readied for a fight. Markos turned to Celia for insight into the bizarre exchange. Someone needed to explain it to him before he started ripping into people for their disrespect.

Her features had crumpled into a horrified expression. Her chin trembled, and she backed up a step, her arms hanging limp at her sides.

When she noticed his gaze, her lips thinned, and tears gathered at the corners of her eyes. She broke eye contact and begged in a low whisper, "Can we go now? Please?"

She didn't wait for an answer, walking past him and out the front door. He followed, pausing to hold the door open for Molly.

Celia was crossing the yard toward the car.

He jogged after her. "Wait. We can't leave."

She focused on a tire swing hanging from an immense tree in the front yard. "We can't stay. You saw what happened."

"I saw, but I don't understand." Something had happened in that kitchen. Something that left his blood cold. "What just happened?"

A cloud of condensation was left behind at her sigh, and she walked away. She maneuvered her legs through the center of the swing and hugged the tire against her chest.

"It's my fault." Her blinks quickened. "I couldn't just stand there and let them treat you so poorly."

He rubbed his forehead. "Me? I thought this was about the horrible, revolting, abhorrent way they treated you."

Her lips twitched at his description, and then she shook her head. "No, remember how I warned you about my father? He's usually one of the quiet racists, the ones who get away with their views because they expose them only to their buddies. Together with the way my parents don't care about me, I'd hoped that *not caring* meant he wouldn't disrespect you to your face. But that *not caring* worked only to the point that you were just as ignored as I was after I dared *demand* anything from them."

She finally looked up and met his eyes. "I should have known my father's racism was too destructive to ignore. I'm so sorry for all that."

The first piece of the puzzle of that confrontation snapped into place. He seized the swing's chain above her head.

"Racism is cruel and has no place in decent society, but it's meaningless to me personally." With his ability to cloak his presence if he desired, most humans never had an opportunity to disrespect him. "It's not part of my heritage, so only bad behavior offends me."

"That *was* bad behavior."

"I'm more concerned about what happened after that."

She rested her cheek against the side of the tire. "I don't know what it is, honestly. I know that people have ignored me my whole life unless I stand up for myself in some way. And I know that if I'm too assertive, too aggressive, too demanding, whatever, then I go from being ignored but tolerated to being wiped off the face of the earth."

She kicked off the ground and set the swing in a slow rocking motion.

"If the last time this happened is any indication, I will, for all intents and purposes, be invisible to them—like they can't even hear me, like they don't even *remember* they have an older daughter—for about six months. I no longer exist."

His breath stopped, and the hair rose on his arms for reasons that had nothing to do with the scattered snow flurries floating around them. An iron ball gathered in his stomach, twisting this way and that as it tried to escape the truth.

She shrugged. "It's like everyone wants to teach me a lesson. I shouldn't speak up. I shouldn't have my own opinions. I should just be quiet and meek and go along with whatever happens."

He'd done this.

He'd suspected a month ago that his magic might have had more of an effect on her than intended, but he never would have guessed it had gone this far. His magic had intensified to counter-act her internal strength. He'd never seen it before because he'd never encountered a Virgin like her before. But it made sense. If she demanded that people pay attention to her, his magic would have to respond.

Have to make others ignore her on a deeper level.

Have to erase her existence.

His stomach roiled. The iron ball crashed through his chest and smashed his lungs, taking away his breath. He sank to his knees, unable to hold up the weight of his guilt.

Molly cocked her head at him, and he swore he could see dis-appointment and pity in the dog's eyes.

His hand had slipped off the chain and onto his lap. He now reached up to Celia.

The purity of her expression—her concern for *him* as he col-lapsed to the ground—made her glow in the moonlight peeking between the snow clouds. The kindest Virgin he'd ever known, and he'd destroyed her life.

Yet still, he took her trust. Let her believe in him.

His palm landed on the tire next to her leg. "I'm sorry."

She straightened. "Markos, it's not your fault."

But it was.

She surveyed the yard and shook her head. A few snowflakes shed from her hair.

"Honestly, I'm just glad it didn't affect you. I don't know what I would do if you suddenly didn't remember I existed. I couldn't..." She bit her lip. "I couldn't handle that."

And he didn't know how to handle her trust in him. How could he repay that?

He wanted to, needed to, make this better somehow.

A thought floated at the edge of his mind. The iron ball in his stomach grew into iron determination. It would break every rule of the council by risking the survival of his race, but the rules could hang out in Hades with the crows.

He would create a bubble around the house to protect her from the effects of his spell for as long as they stayed here.

He would grant her a normal life for two weeks.

He *would* fix things with her family.

Chapter Seventeen

CELIA STOPPED THE ROCKING OF THE TIRE SWING. MARKOS'S expression had turned hard. Had she said the wrong thing? He stood, his face chiseled with determination. "We're going back in there." He cut her off before she could protest. "I'm going to make this better."

Her heart lifted at his concern for her. The strength in his statement almost made her believe it possible, at least enough that she disentangled herself from the swing.

He led her to the front door of her childhood home. "And don't concern yourself with any racist comments from your father. They may as well be in a foreign language for as much as they mean to me."

She nodded and longed for a world where skin color truly didn't matter. He opened the door for her and Molly, and they went to the dining room, where the rest of the family had started setting the table. Markos caught her eye and indicated the stack of dishes in the serving cupboard and then the table.

She stifled a groan. Yes, how well she remembered these days. Back when she'd have to add a place setting to the table for herself. Or when she'd do the dishes for the whole family to try to get out of whatever trouble she *must* have caused, and they'd acted like the dishes were still dirty and washed them all again.

He directed her to set their two place settings along one length of the table. Without recognizing their presence in the room, her siblings rearranged themselves to sit on the opposite side. Like they didn't want to get too close to the black hole around her.

Markos pulled out her chair. "Sit. Let me take care of this."

She sat but didn't hold out much hope.

When her parents and siblings had taken their seats, Markos moved to stand behind her. In her peripheral vision, he seemed to be fidgeting with his hands above her head. Maybe he was nervous now that he could see and understand how awful it was. She didn't blame him.

And then he did something he'd never done before.

He *touched* her.

On purpose.

He set his palms on her shoulders, and even though she thought she might tense up at this development, a profound sense of peace and belonging flowed through her, relaxing her body. She'd never have guessed that his touch—no matter how unexpected—would have had such an effect on her. A blanket of energy enveloped her and sank into the core of her being.

Just as surprising were his words. "I want you all to welcome Celia, your daughter, your sister."

Her family looked up at his voice, and then they turned to her. And they didn't just look at her, but they really focused on her, as though seeing her for the first time.

"She's someone you all should be proud to know. She excels in school, earning a full scholarship to a competitive college and getting top grades in her classes. She's studying biology with an emphasis on the chemistry and potential of genetic engineering in plants, an extremely difficult major."

Her cheeks bloomed with heat, but he wasn't done yet.

"In addition to keeping up with her demanding classwork, she occasionally does artwork for the Missouri Botanical Garden. Between the scholarship and that freelance work, she's supported herself at college. She's also the kindest and most patient person I've ever known. She lives with and cares for an elderly woman suffering from Alzheimer's. Now, she's home for two weeks to celebrate Christmas with you. And while she's in this house, you should enjoy your time with her."

His hands had sat like unmoving bricks on her shoulders through all that, but now they lightly squeezed her.

"She is someone you want to know, support, and love."

He removed his hands and stepped back. She sat, completely stunned. No one had ever spoken positively about her to others, especially not in such glowing terms.

Her family hadn't moved, not even to blink, through his whole speech. Now they all shifted, as if waking from a trance, and dozens of emotions flickered across their faces at once. Confusion, surprise, remorse.

Eventually, they all settled on the same expression. Excitement.

They bounced up from their chairs and quickly surrounded her. She was hauled from her chair and into a jumble of hugs. Their voices overlapped in their rush to welcome her.

"Celia, you're home!"

"Hey, sis, great to see you."

"Glad to see you're putting your brains to good use."

"You look wonderful, honey. So beautiful."

The attention caught her in a spotlight, and she wanted to crawl inside her skin and hide. Could a person experience a fear of crowds among only four others? Her own family members no less? She supposed it would have been enjoyable and gratifying if it wasn't so...

Hugely, enormously, extremely...

Odd.

She twisted in someone's hold—she couldn't even tell whose—and stared at Markos, her brows stretching high on her forehead. She mouthed, *What. Just. Happened?*

His jaw was tight, and if she wasn't mistaken, it might have even trembled a bit. He cleared his throat. "I can be very persuasive." He bowed his head. "Enjoy."

Her family still peppered her with exclamations, and she pivoted back to them.

"How are classes going?"

"How were your finals?"

"Uh, decent. I think I did well."

"Are you getting enough to eat there?"

"What's it like in the city?"

"Um, yeah. My landlady is a great cook. I don't live in the downtown area, so it's not as glamorous as it sounds."

"Who's the hunk?"

Her sister's question landed like a boulder in the middle of the hubbub. Suddenly, everyone's attention shifted from her to Markos. Her father stiffened, and his face hardened into a grimace. She knew this acceptance couldn't last.

"Everyone, this is my friend, Markos." That seemed inadequate to cover what he really meant to her. "He's my best friend actually. He's been there for me every time I needed him."

Her father's expression opened a touch. Would he listen to her enough to be convinced?

"In fact, back before Thanksgiving, he saved my life when a drug addict attacked me on the street."

Her mother gasped and tightened her arms around Celia and then turned to her father. "Did you hear that, Jerry? He saved our precious girl's life." She released Celia and gave Markos a hug. "Thank you."

Celia kept her gaze on her father. His jaw worked back and forth several times. Finally, he held out a hand to Markos. "Thanks."

That, more than anything, forced tears to her eyes. She hugged her father. "Thank you, Daddy."

Her brother gave her a light punch on the arm. "All right, can we continue this during dinner? I'm starving."

A laugh rippled across the group, and everyone retook their chairs. Molly curled up in the corner, smart enough not to beg at the table. The conversation flowed around Celia and through her, not just past her like usual. They caught her up in the happenings of their lives and continued being polite to Markos.

For the first time, she felt like part of the family. A real family.

Her heart warred with the idea. This couldn't possibly be real. People didn't suddenly start showing love and affection to some-one after almost twenty-one years simply because of a few pretty words.

She wanted to believe this would be the new normal, but a man she didn't know as well as she should sat by her side. And the only thing that made this Norman Rockwell scene make sense was if he'd done...

Something.

Somehow—along with his ability to travel through time and heal her critical injuries—he also had the ability to create an alternate history for her family. One where they didn't ignore her.

Neat trick, but still a trick. This wasn't real.

He caught her staring at him, and her skepticism was probably written on her face. He sighed a whisper. "Can't you just enjoy this? Please?"

She swallowed. His answer confirmed her hypothesis that he was responsible for the changes, but maybe this was his plan and why he'd wanted her to come home for Christmas all along.

"Celia, are you okay? I've asked you three times if you wanted seconds."

She jerked out of her analysis at the sound of her mother's voice. "I'm sorry. I think I'm just tired after the long drive today."

"Of course, sweetie. I didn't even think about that. You can turn in after dinner if you want. You even have your old bedroom all to yourself now because your father fixed up the big attic room for Lisa." Her mother eyed Markos. "It'll take me just a few minutes to get the guest bedroom ready for you."

Celia had to stifle a laugh. She recognized that tone in her mother's voice. It was the tone she'd used with Lisa's boyfriends to warn them that they shouldn't try anything funny. But she'd never had to use that tone in regards to Celia before.

For a second, she was tempted to let her mother go on assuming that she and Markos were together, just for the amusement factor. That might make Markos uncomfortable though. A shame.

"Mom, it's fine. Markos and I are just friends."

"Oh." Her mom straightened. "Of course, honey."

Lisa leaned forward, ensuring her chest was front and center. "So, Markos, tell us all about *you*. What do you do? Are you a student too?"

Celia rolled her eyes and sat back in her chair. Good Lord, couldn't her sister let her have *one* special thing in her life?

In a way, it was comforting to see that Lisa had changed her behavior least of all among her family. Up until her sister had reached the age of five or so, they'd been somewhat close, like normal sisters who were four years apart in age. But as Lisa had gotten older, she'd started treating Celia the same as everyone else. And now, seeing that her sister was still the same flirtatious party girl as before gave Celia something solid to recognize.

These weren't just random strangers who happened to look like her family after all. They *were* acting normally—and including her in that normal for the first time in her life.

Markos extended his arm onto the back of her chair, only an inch behind her shoulders. "I work in personal security."

Her father chimed in, starting the interrogation she'd been expecting. "Personal security? Like a bodyguard?"

"Essentially, yes."

"Where are you from? Your accent doesn't match your folks' usual way of speaking."

Celia coughed and slid a finger over her eyebrow. Translation: Her father had expected Markos to sound like a rapper.

For his part, Markos didn't seem to take offense, just as he'd said he wouldn't. "I've worked all over the world, and I speak over twenty different languages. I'm sure that's made my accent unique."

Celia did a double take. He'd never revealed those details before. Had his time traveling given him a way to live in all those places and learn all those languages in between watching her?

Lisa leaned even further forward and rested her forearms on the table, plumping her breasts over them. "Wow. That's *so* amazing."

Her mother cleared her throat, but Lisa didn't react.

Chris stretched his limbs and threw an arm over the back of his chair, no doubt trying to make himself look bigger. Celia had never seen her brother intimidated before, and it was...

Interesting.

He twirled his fork between the fingers of his other hand. "So why the hell are you *here*? In podunk Iowa?"

Markos's focus landed on Celia, and her cheeks heated in response. "Where Celia goes, I go."

Her family exchanged glances. Yeah, *that* sounded like a perfectly reasonable explanation. Not.

She almost dropped her head back in exasperation, but she

remembered at the last second that Markos's arm was still behind her on the chair. Her expression seemed to be enough for him to catch on to his slip.

"Celia knows I have no family, and she's my best friend as well, so when the opportunity arose to spend Christmas with her and her family, it made sense to come and meet all of you."

Nice recovery. The smile she gave him, however, might have reflected a bit more of her internal glee than she intended. He'd called her his best friend. Her shoulders lifted with the urge to hug the words and hold them close.

Lisa ran her tongue over her lips, peeked up through her lashes, and purred, "And we're *so* glad you decided to come."

Her mother loudly settled her silverware over her plate, now that they'd all finished eating. Lisa still didn't lean back from the table. Was it bad manners to think of her little sister as a wanna-be tramp?

Chris scoffed at their sister, obviously aligned with Celia's thinking, and pointed his fork toward Markos. "What's with the shades? Indoors *and* at night? Dude, that's trying too hard."

Lisa tossed her hair toward her brother. "Well, *I* think he looks cool."

Markos's lips curled down in a snarl. "They are required for my work. I do not wear them to look *cool.*"

Celia sat up, attuned to his moods. He was angry about something. He seemed to slip into more formal speech patterns—specifically his avoidance of contractions—when he was upset.

She was about to interrupt her brother's twenty questions when Lisa squealed. "Ooh, are those recording everything you see?" She nearly thrust herself halfway across the table, chest first, and preened her hair.

Oh Lord. *Seriously?*

Markos stood up. "I'll clear the dishes from the table."

Her mother brightened. "Thank you, Markos."

But he took only his place setting as he fled the room. Celia was about to follow and check on him when Chris slugged Lisa in her arm.

"Ow! What was that for?"

"You don't hit on your sister's guy. That's low class, even for you."

"Cece said they were just friends." Lisa rubbed her shoulder. "He's fair game."

"Cut the porno queen act, or I'll give you more where that came from. Can't you see Celia likes him?"

Everyone's gaze landed on Celia. She shrank down in her chair. *Crap.* Was it that obvious? When her lunkhead of a brother noticed, that wasn't a good sign.

She looked down at her lap where Molly had laid her head. "Well, he's not interested in me."

"See?" Lisa poked Chris. "You keep your fists to yourself. I'm not your punching bag."

"Lisa." Their mother gave her the *mom* glare. "Regardless, he's too old for you."

Markos called from the doorway to the kitchen. "Celia, may I see you a moment?"

"Sure." She grabbed her plate and nodded to her parents. "Excuse me."

Hopefully he hadn't heard that conversation. Heat crept up her neck in preparation for the embarrassment she suspected was coming.

She set her plate in the sink and faced him. "What's up?"

"I am at a loss for how I can avoid your sister in these close quarters." He gripped the counter, his muscles bunching in a display of anger beyond any she'd seen from him. "I can't explain the details of why, but her behavior toward me is deeply offensive."

Er, that wasn't quite the reaction she'd expected. "Offensive?"

Racism wasn't offensive to him, but flirting was? If that was the case, maybe she should feel grateful she was so terrible at flirting that she'd never tried it with him.

A low growl rumbled from his chest. He removed his sunglasses and tossed them on the counter, and then he pressed on his eyes, rubbing them firmly. "Think of it like a religious belief and that her behavior disrespects my beliefs."

Her brows pulled tight. He had a religious belief against flirting?

He turned and caught her in his gaze. "If you were still a vegetarian, wouldn't it be offensive if someone tried to shove meat down your throat? And didn't care that you weren't interested in trying it, or that you hated it, or that the thought of eating meat made you feel sick?"

"Uh, sure."

"That is one benefit of how I normally stay hidden from others. I do not wish to be the target of that type of behavior."

"Of course."

That she could understand. Like the feeling of being seen only as a sexual object. Not that she'd had any experience with that problem, but it couldn't be comfortable.

She shifted her weight, facing him more directly. "Have I ever made you feel like that? Done anything to offend you?"

His eyes softened, their honey color flowing to wrap her in his world. His hand lifted and skimmed the air an inch from her face. He licked his lips, drawing her gaze from one dangerous body part to another.

His voice lowered, raising the temperature in the room by several degrees. "My Celia."

Just when she thought he might touch her—thought he might express real affection—he straightened and jerked his arm back. He cleared his throat and replaced his sunglasses. "You have never sought to offend me." His tone was crisp and formal again.

Her hand rested on her heart. What did that mean? Had she offended him, but he forgave her because he knew she was too clueless to mean it?

A *clink* of silverware brought their attention to the doorway. Lisa stood there, mouth slightly agape.

"Uh, I didn't mean to interrupt. I was just helping clear the table."

Markos took a step back, letting Celia stand in front of him. Great. He saw her as the *safe* girl. The one who could protect him from flirting because she herself was incapable of it.

Lisa caught Celia's eye and then lowered her gaze. "I'm sorry. I won't do it again."

Uh... "Okay."

What had brought that on? Had their parents been chewing her out in the other room?

Between Markos's revelation and Lisa's abrupt turnaround—not to mention the fact that her family was relating to her at all—Celia felt unbalanced. Maybe she sucked at reading people more than she thought. She'd already lost count of how many times events seemed over her head tonight.

She shrugged to herself. If understanding the nuances of what happened was important, she'd eventually figure it out.

She always did.

Chapter Eighteen

ARKOS SAT ON THE COUCH IN THE FRONT ROOM AND TRIED to ignore the fact that Celia's body was squeezed next his. The whole family had gathered to open Christmas presents, and that meant he, Celia, and Chris were together on the long sofa with Molly at their feet. Her parents were on the loveseat, and Lisa was on the big chair by the wood stove. To her credit, Celia tried to avoid touching him as best she could, but when only an inch separated them, bumps and brushes were bound to happen.

The previous week had passed calmly. Whatever had triggered Lisa's change of heart in regard to her behavior had stuck. Thank the Maker. The thought of that child trying to tempt him elicited disgust on more levels than he could count.

Nothing like the emotions Celia brought forth in him.

If only he *could* control his reaction toward Celia. Disgust would make everything so much easier. But such was not the case.

The fact that the child had taken every opportunity to throw him and Celia in close proximity made him fear Lisa had witnessed them in the kitchen together when he'd been stupid enough to take off his glasses again. Had witnessed him nearly touch Celia. Had witnessed him call her "his."

Was there no end to his weakness? He could never have anyone. And neither could Celia. Or anyone else of his kind for that matter.

The centuries of Virgin rejections had dangerously weakened his tribe, and while the Maker had given them a way to survive the drought, no one in his tribe could mate until a Virgin fully healed their magic. Any mating would be impure and spread their damaged genetics. That sacrifice was the Maker's commandment to ensure his tribe's survival.

Margaret, Celia's mother, unwrapped a present on her lap, her words pulling him back into the moment. "This one is from Celia and Markos."

Before they'd left St. Louis, Celia had added his name to all her presents so he wouldn't feel odd about showing up to their Christmas celebration empty-handed. At the time, it had sounded like a reasonable tactic. Now, though, every time their names were read together, his stomach clenched. The joining of their names was a mockery of what his body wanted but would never have.

Margaret opened the box and made *oh* noises at the contents. Until she held it up, he didn't have a clue what "they'd" given to her. She turned a large platter to face the gathering.

A colorful and realistic painting of a Christmas scene decorated the front. He recognized Celia's artistic talents.

"Celia did the painting."

Celia shot a sharp glance his way. "You weren't supposed to tell her that."

"Why not?" At her embarrassed expression, he added, "Your skills are something to be proud of, not hidden."

Margaret set down the platter. "He's right, honey. This is beautiful, and it means so much more knowing that you made it."

Celia let her hair fall in front of her face. "I didn't want you to think I hadn't spent enough."

"Oh, sweetie, the time and love you put into this are more valuable than anything money could buy." Her mother approached. Molly edged out of the way so Margaret could kneel in front of Celia. "You haven't let the fact that your daddy and I haven't been able to contribute to your education hold you back, and I know things have to be tight for you. So I'm doubly proud of you right now."

Celia pushed her hair behind her ear. "Really?"

"Really." Her mother gave her a smile. "You're kind and

generous, supporting yourself, doing well in school, and you have a good head on your shoulders. Plus you have amazing talent and"—she winked at Markos—"excellent taste in friends."

She lifted Celia's chin and stared, demanding her daughter's attention. "Never doubt yourself. You are special."

Celia's lips pressed together, but he could see her chin quiver regardless. Her hands tangled together on her lap, her fingers pulling and twisting along with her emotions.

Finally, no longer willing—or able—to hold herself back, she pried her hands apart and flung her arms around Margaret. Trembles shook her shoulders, and she clung to her mother.

"Shh..." Margaret drew her close and rocked them together. "I'm here, honey. I'm here." She stroked Celia's hair and let her daughter soak up twenty years worth of delayed love and affection.

Markos crossed his arms and covered his mouth with his fist. He squeezed his elbows against his ribs, savoring the warmth flowing from his heart.

This was the gift he'd wished to give her. *This* would bring her happiness, at least for the moment. *This* made his efforts here worthwhile.

After several minutes, Celia pulled back and gave a sniffly laugh. "Sorry. Tears and snot. How's that for Christmas spirit?"

Everyone joined in the laughter, the tension of the emotional moment broken.

Chris bumped her shoulder. "You're such a girl."

She managed not to crash into Markos on her other side and pushed back. "Hey, you brute."

Lisa threw a wadded-up ball of wrapping paper at her brother. "See? I've been telling you."

Chris grinned and caught Markos's gaze, his eyes twinkling. "Hold Cece still while I get her."

Markos and Celia had enough time to both get out a "*What?*" before Chris tickled her waist. She squealed and squirmed away, which landed her half in Markos's lap. Her limbs flailed in defense, kicking and swatting at her brother.

Hades's crows! Markos held his breath and his body utterly still. The Maker wanted to kill him. That was the only explanation.

Either that, or he'd died, and this was the Afterlife. He didn't want to admit how much he wished for that to be the case.

His arms ached to hold her, feel her soft curves against his chest. And the more she wiggled on his lap, the more he longed to do even more. Longed to do things that proved how far he'd fallen into impurity.

He didn't care. He wanted to do them anyway.

Visions of what he could do to her flashed in his mind. Her sweet, flowery aroma filled his senses and made him insane with desire. He wanted to smell their scents mingled together and mixed with the sweat of passion. He swallowed most of a growl.

Celia shot a glance to Markos, her eyes wide, and slid back onto the cushions despite her brother's ongoing teasing. "Stop." She shoved against his arms. "Chris, I'm serious. Stop."

Markos breathed through gritted teeth and willed himself to regain control. Thankfully, her mother announced the next present, this one for Lisa. While the family's attention turned to the younger daughter, he focused on slowing his heartbeat, releasing his clenched fists, and maintaining a steady breath so no one would hear his gasping.

Celia kept her gaze on her sister, but whispered to him. "I'm sorry. I didn't—"

"I will live." Most likely.

She looked up at him, her flushed face recalling his mind's imaginings of how she would appear if he had his way with her. "Thank you, by the way. No matter whether this is real or all going to disappear tomorrow, today is perfect."

"Enjoy the here and now."

"Exactly." Her smile blossomed, full and pure, without the bittersweet tinge visible the rest of the week. "I *do* wish I could hug you or squeeze your hand or lean on your shoulder or something to show my gratitude and share my happiness."

He was weak still. Oh so weak.

"You may lean on my shoulder." Son of a mule, he was an idiot, but he couldn't help himself. He tried to salvage the situation by adding, "Just this once."

Her lips curved in the most tempting way. "Just this once."

She rested her head on his shoulder and relaxed into a sigh.

Even though she carefully kept the rest of her body distant, her presence filled him with warmth. It took all his self-control not to wrap his arm around her and encourage her to snuggle closer.

Margaret leaned forward and held out a present. "This one's for you, Celia. From Markos. It's something heavy."

He might have forgotten himself and reached out to grab the box, letting his biceps brush the side of Celia's breast. Or he might have done it on purpose.

He didn't even know anymore. Insanity had claimed him.

Celia sat up and took the present he passed to her. "Wow, that *is* heavy. Oh, can you find my gift to Markos in the pile too?" While her mother sorted through the gifts under the tree, Celia gave him a teasing smile. "What part of 'you don't have to get me anything' did you not understand?"

"I could say the same to you."

Chris made a big show of clearing his throat and leaning away from them on the couch. "Should we leave the room when you two open your presents to each other? Give you some privacy."

She poked him. "Don't be ridiculous."

Margaret handed over a flat rectangular gift. "Here it is, Markos."

Celia grinned. "You first."

"I thought the saying was *ladies first.*"

When she pointed insistently at the gift on his lap, he slid his finger under the tape and carefully unwrapped the present as requested. His efforts revealed the back of something, and he flipped it over.

The framed image in his grasp tugged his lips into a broad curve. He sat back, stunned by the gift's perfection.

A series of colored drawings depicted the growth of a rose from a seedling to a young plant, then to flower bud, and finally to a beautifully formed rose. The images looked so real, complete with a misting of dew on the petals, that he sniffed the cotton fiber, expecting to smell a rose. Instead, he detected Celia's own flowery bouquet along with the scent of the colored pencils she favored.

Even better. *That* was Celia.

"You drew him some *flowers*?" Chris's disbelief interrupted his pleasure. "Sheesh. It's bad enough that girls are buying guys flowers now, thinking they'll care, but to give him a *drawing* of some?"

He sat back from leaning over his sister, where he'd been stealing a glimpse. "Sorry, sis, but that's the lamest—"

"Most perfect gift ever."

Celia jerked her head and stared up at him. "Perfect? And here I was just aiming for a 'that's nice.'"

Markos held out the frame so the rest of the family could see Celia's talent. Her family showed polite interest but didn't grasp the significance of the images. To his mind, it was a self-portrait, as she grew from nothing into a pure and flawless bloom. He spun the picture around and sniffed the paper again.

"No drawing you make is merely *nice*." He enjoyed watching the pink climb into her cheeks.

"So you don't think it's lame?"

"Not at all." He bowed his head. "It will have a place of honor in my home."

Maybe on the ceiling over his bed, in fact, so he could think of her as he went to sleep. Luckily, he managed to restrain himself from mentioning that part.

"Now it's your turn." He nodded to the gift in her hands.

Chris gave an exaggerated sigh. "I just know I'm going to be disappointed. There's a distinct lack of scandal going on here."

Lisa threw another ball of used wrapping paper at him. "Shut up. I think it's sweet."

"Yeah, you're a girl. You would."

Celia elbowed her brother. "So am I, you nitwit."

She set upon the present, ripping through the paper. Markos stroked his mustache and goatee, covering his mouth so he couldn't give anything away.

During one of his quick trips through the Mythos plane on the way to his driving classes, he'd contacted Hipdemos, giving specifications—and a strict request for secrecy, especially from the council—for the gift. Markos had picked it up and sent the replacement iron bars to the Mythos plane just last night. According to Hipdemos, their greatest historian, Archimedes—who wasn't sympathetic to the council either—had helped with the design.

Under the wrapping paper, Markos had used layers of newspaper for more protection, and Celia now rotated the package in her hands, searching for the edge. Finally, she unfolded the paper and revealed the gold-lidded, carved wooden box.

She gave a sharp intake of breath, and Chris swore softly beside her. Her fingertip traced the silver relief sculptures on the lid. A beautiful Virgin held the muzzle of a unicorn, mesmerizing him, enchanting him, ensnaring him.

And most importantly, the Virgin still lived after facing the unicorn in his natural form.

The surrounding relief carvings of forest and flowers on the lid were all gold. It had been Archimedes's idea to put the figures in silver so they'd stand out more. The next time Markos went home, he'd have to thank the ancient male along with Hipdemos and the artisans.

"Dude." Chris leaned forward. "Is that real gold?"

Celia whispered, "Please tell me it's not." When he didn't deny it, she closed her eyes. "I was stunned by the beauty of the artistry, the carvings, but this..." She gazed at him again, her eyes glistening. "Markos, it's too much."

His skin tightened. He hadn't anticipated the extent of her issue with money.

Maybe he could mislead her. "Consider this a thank you from those I work with."

She touched her fingers to her lips and blinked back tears. "Thank you. It's beautiful."

As he hoped, she seemed to think a group present from the future was less problematic than a gift from him alone.

"I was thinking you could use it to store your drawing pencils." He lifted the lid and showed off the velvet-lined interior. "Maybe not the ones you keep in your backpack, but the ones at home."

She laughed. "Yes, definitely not for carrying around in my backpack."

"Well," Margaret piped up, "do the rest of us get to see this present?"

The folds of newspaper had blocked the view for the rest of the family.

"I think I'll pass this one around." Celia checked with him. "If that's okay?"

"Of course. It's your gift to do with as you wish."

She handed the box to her brother, who hefted its weight in his hands. "Yep, that's real gold all right." Chris passed the case on to Lisa and then eyed Markos. "You know you're making the rest of us look like slackers, right?"

"That was not my intention, I assure you." He stretched his arm out on the couch behind Celia. "I wished merely to give her a gift that felt appropriate."

Every day proved how impure he was, so he couldn't allow himself to hope for a happy ending to her ritual to match the scene on the case. But he could acknowledge that was what she deserved.

"Wow." Lisa admired the box. "I thought you all were kidding. Markos, you don't happen to have a younger brother, do you?"

Celia groaned and flopped back against the cushion. Her head hit below where his hand lay, but her hair trailed over his fingers. He didn't move his arm. Her hair was no threat.

"I have no family."

"Too bad." She gave the wooden box to Margaret.

Celia's parents continued their appreciation of his gift. His fingers stroked the locks of her hair, careful not to tug so she wouldn't know what he was doing. So soft. He wished he could slide his fingers into her hair as he held her head, fell into her gaze, and lost himself inside her.

He shook himself. If he allowed that wish to come true, he and his tribe would die.

He glanced along the couch so he could gently extract his hand from her hair. Chris caught his eye and stared pointedly down at Markos's hand, where he'd swirled her hair around his index finger to rub with his thumb.

Mugarok. That was no accidental-looking sight, and her brother had witnessed his weakness. Chris thumped his fist to his chest twice and then made a motion like he was zipping his lips.

Markos nodded his thanks and untangled himself from her hair just before she leaned forward to reclaim the box from her parents.

She gave him a wry smile and held up the gold-topped case. "*Now* will you admit that the gift I gave you is lame?"

"Not at all. Any gift that will be treasured cannot possibly be lame."

She *tsked.* "You know you're saying the perfect thing again."

He placed his hand on his heart. "That is because I speak the truth."

Her face lit up brighter than the Christmas tree, promising a lifetime of happy memories wrapped in her purity and goodness. He swallowed the lump of his emotions as they marched to his brain where they planned to stage a coup d'état and overthrow his logic.

He wished he could die, this very moment, and have her expression be the last thing he saw. And then he'd never need to fail his tribe. Or fail her.

Lost in that thought, he drifted through the remainder of Christmas Day in blurry impressions. Later that night, he sat in the rocking chair of her childhood bedroom, and still, he struggled to make sense of his conflicting emotions.

No matter how much he wished for an escape from his obligation and her destiny, none existed. They both had roles to fulfill, and fulfill them they would. They must.

He found himself watching her in sleep, as he still did for a fair portion of most nights, more out of habit and the sum of his weaknesses than for her now-vanquished nightmares. The more he saw of her, learned who she was as a person, the more he appreciated the goodness inside her. But he had stayed strong and resistant for weeks now, and strong he would remain. That was his duty.

"Dude," Chris whispered from the doorway.

Markos startled and stood from the rocking chair, the wood creaking in his haste. Piss. He'd been too wrapped in his thoughts to hear the door click open.

Chris motioned to the hallway. Too late to disappear, Markos held in a sigh and followed him down the hall. Chris led him into his bedroom, closed the door, and indicated he should sit in the chair at his desk. Markos took the seat and tried not to look too guilty at being caught in Celia's room. He wasn't doing anything wrong. Not really.

"Okay, I'd ask what the hell you were doing hanging out in my sister's bedroom, but I have a pretty good idea. And more importantly, I know what you *weren't* doing there." Chris sat on the bed and tossed a football in the air, catching and releasing it in a slow rhythm. "Because of that, I'm giving you the heads up that I heard my parents talking tonight about you two. They're 'concerned.' My dad's going to be poking his head into Celia's bedroom sometime tonight, and it wouldn't be pretty if he caught you in there."

Markos couldn't protest that Jerry wouldn't catch him, as Chris had succeeded at doing just that. "Thank you for the warning."

"Don't thank me. If I'd caught you boning my sister in my parents' house, I'd have beat you to hell and back myself."

"That is not an issue. Celia is a virgin, and I intend for her to stay that way."

Chris caught the football and stopped. "Now *that* surprises me. That sounds kinda..." He judged Markos's expression. "Final."

When Markos didn't deny it, Chris pointed the football at him, his gaze steady.

"I want to see my sister happy, so I'll give you another warning. Don't screw with Celia's heart. She thinks you're not interested in her, but you and I both know that's a lie. If you lead her on, I'll hunt you down, string you up as a scarecrow in the middle of a field, and feed your entrails to the crows. You feel me?"

Markos held in his smile. That settled it. He liked this young man.

"I give you my promise, I will not hurt your sister for as long as she resides on Earth."

That was true enough. What happened after that point was best left unsaid.

For that matter, what would happen in a week when the spell reactivated as they left the house was best left in the back of his mind as well. He'd risked his tribe's survival by leaving her unprotected by the magic he'd woven over her crib years ago. He'd let her experience the love and affection of her family. He'd given her the happiness she deserved.

He should feel satisfied with his efforts. Proud about what he'd been able to do for her. That should have been the end of the issue. Alkipsia would say he shouldn't feel guilty at all, much less guilty that Celia's family would be taken away from her next week.

But he did.

Chapter Nineteen

CELIA PACKED AND REPACKED HER CLOTHES IN THE SUITCASE. How had she gotten everything to fit before? For the first time in her life, she'd received plenty of Christmas presents from her family, and those gift bags were already lined up by the door, ready to go. Just this stupid suitcase remained. She sat on the lid, squishing everything down, and tugged on the zipper.

Lisa knocked on the open door. "Hey."

"Hey, come on in, and give me a hand with this stupid thing." She shifted to put her full weight on the suitcase, folding her legs onto the lid and out of the way. With Lisa's help, she finally got the zipper to behave. "Thanks."

"Sure." Lisa closed the door and then sat on the corner of the bed. "Can I ask you something before you go?"

"Uh..." Her sister's tone of voice sounded like trouble, but she didn't want to leave on a bad note. "Okay, I guess."

"Your first night here, you said Markos wasn't interested in you. Why do you think that?"

She shrugged, not wanting to get into the complicated nature of their friendship. "I just know."

Lisa slid her leg onto the bed, spinning to face Celia. "See, I think you're wrong. I think he likes you. A lot."

"Well, we're good friends. Friends like each other."

"No, I saw the way he looked at you in the kitchen that first night. He was looking at you like more than 'just a friend.' It was more like he *really* likes you. Like he thinks about touching you all the time. Like he can't keep his eyes off you."

Celia laughed and tossed a throw pillow at her sister. "Now I *know* you're delusional. Other than that one time, you haven't seen his eyes to know if they're on me or not."

Lisa smacked the pillow away and didn't crack a smile. "I can tell. His expression changes when he's watching you."

"No, but he..."

Celia stopped and swallowed. Did she really want to admit this? Maybe saying it aloud would force her brain to accept the truth and stop holding out for something that was never going to happen.

"He refuses to let me touch him." She held her palms up, helpless to explain the issue. "I don't know if you've noticed, because we've accidentally touched more during these past two weeks than we had in total before, but he was pretty darn disgusted at the thought of touching me not that long ago."

"Disgusted?" Lisa leaned forward. "Or freaked out about how much your touch affects him?" Lisa jiggled her shoulders in a show of attitude that reminded Celia just how much more experience her sister had when it came to guys despite being four years younger. "I mean, think back to kindergarten. The boys who liked you *hit* you. So it's not unheard of for a guy to do the opposite of how he feels."

Wow. Was it her imagination, or did her sister's theory actually sound plausible?

"I suppose it could be possible. But how would I tell?"

Lisa crossed her legs. "You said you've accidentally touched him a few times on this trip, right? And no disgust—I definitely would have noticed that. So the question is, is the lack of disgust because of the audience or because he's really not disgusted?" She held her hands out, offering the answer on an imaginary silver platter. "You should continue to accidentally touch him when you're back at school and there's no audience around. If there's still no disgust, that means he's just terrified of liking you too much."

"Markos? Terrified?" Celia scoffed. "Sorry, I can't imagine that being the case."

Lisa stood and headed to the door. "I could be wrong, but I bet you anything I'm not. What do you have to lose by trying?"

On that note, Lisa opened the door and dramatically swept into the hallway. Her blonde hair flounced behind her like a cape to go with her supposed love-life-fixing superpowers.

Yeah, her sister was crazy. That explained everything.

Lisa's voice carried from down the hall. "Oh hey, Markos, Cece and I were just talking about you."

Great. She was crazy *and* meddlesome.

Markos entered her room. "Talking about me?"

"Yep, Lisa helped me with the zipper on my suitcase, so I'm ready to go."

"I could have helped you."

"I don't know. You might have been *too* strong and broken the zipper instead."

He laughed, just as she'd hoped, so any thoughts of what else Lisa and she might have been discussing would be forgotten. He picked up the overstuffed suitcase and all the gift bags like they were full of air.

"I'll take these out to the car while you're telling your family goodbye." His voice deadened at the end of his sentence, the word *goodbye* sad and final.

She found her family gathered in the front room, where they were taking the ornaments off the tree. Christmas trees always looked so pathetic when they were bare again, the high point of their life behind them.

Her mother removed one of the ornaments Celia had hand-painted as a kid. "I remember you giving this to me, but I don't think I ever noticed until this moment how beautiful it is, how much talent you had at such a young age. I'll admit I'm surprised you didn't decide to make art your career."

"I wanted to do more to help people." Well, that and the fact that far too often people didn't notice her art because *she* was the one who had made it.

Her mother carefully wrapped the ornament and placed it in the storage box. "St. Louis is too far away. When will you be able to visit again? Spring break?"

"I don't know. I'll tell you when I figure it out." Were Markos's changes permanent? She hadn't wanted to think that far. "I'll miss you though." She gave her mom a hug. "That much I know."

Her mom returned her hug, squeezing her tight. "Oh, I love you so much, honey. You keep yourself safe, okay?"

"Promise."

Her mom gave her a kiss and then pulled back, blinking hard. She fanned herself. "Don't mind me. I just hate goodbyes."

Chris came up behind Celia and wrapped her in a near-tackle. "Geeze, Mom, you never got that weepy over me."

Lisa piped in beside him. "She can't miss you if you're still here, dumbass."

"Hey, I *tried* leaving. It's not my fault my rotator cuff injury kept me from going pro."

Celia leaned into Chris, soaking up the last of her family's camaraderie. She *would* miss them, including all the teasing and sparring—things that other people took for granted about their families.

Chris clutched her head and made like he was ruffling her hair, but he tugged her ear to his lips and whispered, "I like Markos, but you let me know if he does anything to hurt you, okay? I don't care how huge he is. Your big bro wants to see you happy. You deserve it."

She stiffened. His comment seemed so out-of-place, yet a lump formed in her throat at his concern. She nodded against him.

When he released her, she saw Markos standing in the door-way. Her brother thumped his chest with a fist twice, as if he were part-gorilla and making a display of guy-ness.

He shook Markos's hand. "Don't worry. I kept my promise. Now you keep yours."

She had no idea what they were talking about, and she missed Markos's reply because Lisa gave her a hug and squealed in her ear. "You're going to try it, right? You have to. And then you have to tell me how it goes." Her sister stepped back and squeezed her hands. "Good luck."

"Thanks. And yes, I'll give it a try or two." If for no other reason than simple curiosity.

Only her father remained. He hadn't warmed up to her or

Markos as much as the others had, but now he caught her eye and opened his arms wide.

Her knees wobbled at the sight, and her voice came out weak. "Daddy..."

Unable to resist his offer of acceptance, she rushed to him. He enfolded her in his bear hug, lifting her off the ground and squishing a giggle out of her. After he set her down, he gave her a fauxserious look.

"For as long as I can do that, you're still my little girl." He didn't break eye contact with her, but he raised his voice, directing his words to Markos, who had come up beside her. "I heard about a promise you made, son. If you keep it, you'll be okay in my book."

"Understood." With that cryptic agreement, the two men shook hands.

At the door, she soaked up one last vision of her family, all happy and loving. This was how she wanted to remember them, just in case whatever trick Markos had used to change things faded eventually.

He watched her, obviously letting her lead for when she was done with her goodbyes. She closed her eyes for a moment to hold onto the vision and then gave him a nod.

"Time to go, Molly." He patted the side of his leg. Molly gave a lick to Lisa, who had been granting her a belly rubbing, and trotted over to join them at the door.

A final chorus of goodbyes rang through the room as Markos opened the front door. She waved and blew kisses before following him outside. The cold wind drove her deep into her jacket, and she hunkered down for the trudge to the car. Markos jogged ahead and let Molly into the backseat. He'd already started the car so it could warm up, but she was in no rush to run across the yard and leave her happy mood.

As she passed the tire swing, a weight settled over her.

Crushed her.

Broke her.

She stopped mid-stride, unable to breathe. Her chest ached with emptiness, and she bent over, her hands propped on legs that were barely holding her up. She lifted her head, tried to draw air, but the sight around her didn't help.

Gray loneliness covered everything, like watercolors dripping down a canvas. She was alone, utterly alone, and the world had no place for her.

She had lost her family. Of that, she was certain.

Her strength gave out, and she crumpled to the ground. Her eyes stung with unshed tears. Pain radiated from her heart and made her limbs too heavy to move.

She couldn't explain how she knew she'd lost them, but the truth was unavoidable in the depths of her soul. *Something* had shifted in the world and taken them away.

Now her need to grieve their loss was just as strong as if they had all died. In a way, the family she had known these past two weeks *had* died. The people left in the house now were strangers to her, and she was a stranger to them.

She became aware of Markos's approach only because he blocked the wind for her. "I'm sorry."

She had no voice yet. No breath, no air, no words to express.

"I was never sure if I did the right thing. Giving that to you when I knew it would be taken away. I'd hoped the benefits would outweigh the costs. I judged wrong. I'm sorry."

She shook her head and struggled to find her voice among the wreckage. "No. Don't be sorry. You were right. The memories I have..." She peered up at him, where his expression reflected her own agony. "I wouldn't want to give them up for anything. Not even to avoid this. I'm still thankful for the past two weeks. My memories were worth this. It was all worth it."

Whether to convince Markos or herself, she didn't know, but she repeated her statement as she staggered to her feet.

"It was all worth it."

She looked back at her childhood home, her fingertips trembling against her lips. The wind swirled around her, dried her tears, and carried them away.

Never to return.

The family she'd longed for, the family she'd loved, was gone. Her real family cheered for her, loved her, cherished her. The beings inside who looked like her family would foul her memories of her real family. So the only solution was to avoid going home ever again.

Never to return.

She shoved her hands in her pockets. "I'm never coming back here."

Markos jerked and focused on her, his mouth falling open. "How did you...?"

"I know who my real family is now." Without another glance at the house, she headed to the car. "And my family is dead."

Never to return.

Chapter Twenty

CELIA DOODLED IN THE CORNER OF HER NOTEBOOK WHILE SHE waited for class to start. The rose she'd drawn was far from perfect, and a tear-shaped petal hung down from the flower's base. Not exactly subtle, but it matched her mood.

The last month and a half had passed in a blur of suppressed grief. Auntie wouldn't understand, and Markos understood all too well. He'd withdrawn upon seeing her sorrow, feeling guilty she was sure. Testing the possibility of a relationship with Markos had taken a backseat to her depression.

Two female classmates settled into chairs on either side of her, talking over her like she wasn't there. One obnoxiously leaned over Celia's desk to whisper to the other girl about their weekend plans.

The pushy one scanned for eavesdroppers, taking no notice of Celia sitting between them, mere inches away. "Sigma's having an unregistered off-campus party tonight. The Heart Day Hookup Party."

She slid her phone across Celia's desk. The address of the party glowed on the screen.

The other girl glanced at the address and left the phone beside Celia's doodles. "I'm not exactly what frat guys look for."

Celia's brow stretched up her forehead. Not that she had a clue what frat guys liked, but surely some of them would appreciate the pretty girl beside her, even if, like Celia, she lacked the voluptuous curves of Miss Obnoxious.

"Oh please." The insistent one pointed to her phone. "Do you know how much alcohol they're going to have? The guys will be trashed enough to hook up with that fatso over there." She waved to a classmate several rows down, who was hopefully out of earshot and deserved better than a beer-goggled frat guy anyway.

The professor stood at the lectern. Thank goodness. The pushy girl finally sat back in her chair, removing herself from Celia's personal space.

Celia stifled a laugh at the ridiculousness of the situation. It was that or cry at the reminder of how she was once again invisible. But as the class wore on, bitter anger rose up her throat instead.

The Christmas trip had given her a taste of a normal life, and she wanted more. She wanted all the normal things. Like a boyfriend. Like a date for Valentine's Day. Hell, at this point, she might even take a hookup just to get a kiss. At least then she wouldn't still be completely inexperienced when she turned twenty-one next month.

Being nonexistent sucked, and she was sick of it. Scribbled pencil marks took shape over her drawing of the rose. Wild, unrestrained lines covered the bloom.

She wanted to be more assertive, to demand that others pay attention to her, but Christmas had proved her earlier problems with that approach were no accident. For reasons that escaped her, beyond a hypothesis that his time travel inoculated him, the only one she could be bolder with—at least without repercussions—was Markos.

Markos.

The one person she wanted to be close to more than anyone else, but she'd lost the ability to talk to him. And it was her own fault for withdrawing.

Yet maybe that meant she could fix the situation.

She stopped scribbling. Flames now licked out from the petals, engulfing the rose in a fiery energy.

Before she could feel nervous, she planned her attack. And

thanks to a Christmas gift from Lisa, the *real* Lisa, she had the perfect outfit for tonight.

MARKOS ESCORTED CELIA HOME JUST LIKE HE DID EVERY DAY AFTER her classes, but when he reached for the doorknob of Harriet's front door, Celia spun toward him. The look on her face was somehow both eager and pensive—and very different from the expression she'd worn since Christmas.

"You know what? I'm sick of being sad and depressed. I want to do something fun. Let's go out."

"Fun?"

"Yeah, you know. A little dinner. Maybe catch a movie. Fun."

He tilted his head, considering her. Her wide eyes reflected more liveliness than he'd seen from her in weeks. It was a pleasant change. Although it had been easier to keep his distance, he'd hated seeing her depressed. Yet he'd been at a loss for what he could do to fix the situation. Especially as he'd been the cause.

"Sure. We can do something fun."

"Like, maybe a *nice* dinner?" Her voice was hopeful, but tinged with nervousness.

His chin dropped to his chest. He was an ass. With the car and his Christmas gift, he'd exposed the fact that he wasn't poor like she was, and yet he'd continued living in her world, taking the bus with her every day rather than driving her to classes or doing anything special for her.

"Yes, in fact I'll go home and get the car, so we can go anywhere you wish." He gave her a sheepish grin. "No matter how far off the bus routes."

Her face burst into a smile so wide his resistance stumbled. "Perfect. Can you give me an hour before you pick me up? I want to get ready."

Since when did she need an hour to get ready? "All right."

"Okay, see you then." She waved and disappeared into the house.

A ball of uncertainty landed in his gut. What had he just agreed to?

Precisely an hour later, he knocked on Harriet's door. He'd changed into his least broken-in leathers and wore a collared shirt underneath his jacket. For his usual Earthen plane clothes, this was dressed up.

Harriet let him in and gave him a hug. "I'm so glad you're taking her out. This date might be just the thing to shake her out of her funk."

Date? His spine stiffened.

No. He shook his head. That couldn't be what Harriet had meant. Or if she had meant it, she was in one of her confused moods.

"I just want to see her happy again."

"Well, if a Valentine's dinner date with you doesn't accomplish that, I don't know what will."

The distressed feeling in his gut intensified. Valentine's Day? A nice dinner? The signs didn't look good. He offered a silent prayer to the Maker that Harriet was wrong.

She put her hand to her forehead and then shuffled to the kitchen.

"Harriet? Are you limping?"

"Hmm?" She rubbed her temple. "Was I? I was just in..." She looked toward the living room and waved. "In there. Working on..." Her eyes scrunched, and she made a sewing motion with her hands. "My leg must have fallen asleep." She opened the refrigerator. "Did you want anything? I'm going to heat up some milk and turn in early. See if I can sleep off this headache."

"I'm fine, thank you. Do you want me to do it for you?"

"No, no, you stay there and watch for your girl coming downstairs."

At that reminder, the floorboard creaked at the top of the stairs. Celia slowly walked down the steps in heels that created he-was-going-to-die-of-a-heart-attack curves on her legs. His gaze traveled up her calves and kept going. Past her knees. Paused at her thighs.

She was not only *not* wearing jeans for one of the few times since they'd been close, but she was also wearing a dangerously short skirt. Not short compared to the clothes of her peers, but plenty dangerous to him.

His gaze remained paused long enough to watch those bare

thighs swish past each other as she descended the stairs. His mouth watered, and his fingers twitched, desperate to touch, caress, slide even higher.

He forced his eyes to refocus on the rest of her. It didn't help.

On top, she wore a silky, thin-strapped blouse that exposed acres of bare skin across her arms and shoulders. The fabric draped around and between her breasts in folds that framed her perfect shape. A groan threatened to escape from his throat, so he cleared it instead and lifted his gaze to her face.

Hades's crows. He stumbled back, his hand reaching for the doorknob. He wasn't going to survive the evening.

She'd pulled back some of the hair from around her face, and if anything, this hairstyle accentuated the bloom of her cheeks, her lips. May the Maker grant him strength. Her lips. He couldn't tear his eyes away. So lush and full and pink, like a fresh bud opening. On cue, her lips parted, and he licked his.

He leaned against the door, struggling to keep his balance against the wild thumping of his heartbeat. His sunglasses wouldn't protect him from her spell tonight.

She stopped in front of him, too close. Her scent more intoxicating than ever.

"Hi."

His body melted at the sound. He couldn't speak.

Harriet came to his rescue, appearing in the doorway to the kitchen. "You look lovely, dear. Do you have something to wear over that? Spring may have come early this year, but it's still chilly at night."

Celia held up a jacket she'd hooked over her elbow. "I'll be fine."

She started putting on the extra layer, which would thankfully cover some of that distracting skin, when Harriet gave him a pointed look. "Tut tut. A *gentleman* would help a lady on with her coat."

"Auntie," Celia protested, "I'm fine."

The woman continued to glare at him until he nudged his feet forward and held up the jacket for Celia. Her arms slid into the sleeves without incident, but as he lifted the coat's collar above her shoulders, she freed her hair and he found his hands once again buried in her long, soft locks. His fingers withdrew at his command, and if he ignored the fact that they'd stroked her hair along the way, he could almost be proud of his control.

Celia grabbed her purse and gave Harriet a hug. "I'm not sure what time we'll be back, so you have a good night."

Markos opened the front door and walked out. Maybe fresh air would clear his head. Celia followed him onto the front walk and waved.

Harriet returned her wave from the doorway. "Have a fun time, kids. You be a good boy, Roger."

The door closed, and Celia stared at the house and then at him. "*Roger?* You look nothing like her son."

"She said something about being tired and having a headache."

The thought occurred to him that Celia might want to cancel their plans out of worry for Harriet. He tried to keep the hopefulness out of his voice so he wouldn't sound happy about Harriet's condition. "We can reschedule if you wish to stay with her."

Celia hooked a stray hair over her ear and shifted her weight on her heels. "Just a headache, she said?"

"Yes, she was going to warm some milk and then head to bed."

"I guess it would be ridiculous to cancel just so I can hang around while she sleeps." She sighed and glanced at the car. "And would you believe I've never been to a nice restaurant?"

He knew what she was going to decide before she said it. What he didn't know was how her words would affect him.

She stepped closer and gazed up at him. "I want to spend tonight with you."

Son of a mule. His blood pressure spiked and locked his muscles. Her words—her perfectly innocent words about wanting to spend time with her friend—shot through him with fantasies of an entirely different way to spend the evening. His body flashed with heat despite the cool night air.

He again found himself unable to speak. He nodded instead. That was safer than whatever he might say right now anyway.

He took a deep breath, hoping the cold would chill his inappropriate thoughts, and opened her door. Standing above her, he had a scandalous view of her thighs as she sat and adjusted her skirt. Before he entered his side of the car, he inhaled the crisp air several more times.

Celia was an innocent. Even now, with his worries about Harriet's references to a *date*, she'd done nothing wrong. Nothing like the tasteless flirting of her sister. Nothing like the unseemly clothing of her classmates.

The only impure things were his thoughts.

He started the car and refused to let himself peek in her direction. During the drive, he repeated his mantra. *Stay pure.*

After several minutes, she swiveled toward him, her skirt shifting further up her thigh. Not that he noticed.

"Did you have a plan for where we're going for dinner?"

Dinner. He'd completely forgotten the point of the evening. "No."

"Oh." Her eyes twinkled in the passing streetlights. "I figured since we hadn't talked about it, and you just started driving, that you *must* have a plan."

He scanned the vicinity. Where *had* he been driving to?

The university sat off to the right, and his house lay down the street to the left. He let himself believe that he'd been heading to her school out of habit. He drove several more blocks and then pulled over to the curb on a side street.

"Sorry. No plan. We should come up with one."

She twisted toward him, her closer leg sliding up onto the seat. Separating her legs. Showing him the way.

He tried swallowing, but his throat mutinied halfway through. His pants suddenly felt uncomfortably small.

She pulled out her phone and touched the screen. "Let's see what restaurants they recommend. What kind of food are you in the mood for?"

"You choose." His voice was thick.

"Come on, you have to help me with this. I've never been to a nice restaurant, remember?" She leaned over the center console and held the phone between them. "Come here and help me narrow this down."

Her brows lifted as she waited for him to browse the contents on the screen. He clenched his jaw and scooted closer. But when he looked down, the phone's screen was important only for being in the way of his view of her thighs.

He refocused his gaze. The screen. He couldn't make the letters stop dancing long enough to read the words, but his near-focus discovered something else. He could see down the front of her blouse and make out the lacy edge of her bra, a creamy curve of skin.

Son of a mule! He shot back in his chair and gripped the leather seat. An ache burned in his chest, and his breaths came fast and shallow. His hair itched all over his body, tingling at the ends of his nerves.

"Markos? Are you okay?"

He was most definitely *not* all right. He was in danger of throwing away his tribe's only chance for survival. All because...

"Markos, you're scaring me. Is there something I can do? Something I *should* do?"

He should tell her to leave. Stay far away from him.

"Markos, you're hyperventilating. You have to stop breathing so fast."

He couldn't stop. Besides, his light-headedness was all due to her. His breaths continued short and quick.

"I'm sorry. But you're freaking me out, so I have to do this."

She knelt on her seat, seized either side of his face, and turned his head to focus on her. "Look at me. Breathe. Deep and slow."

Her touch sent a shudder through his body like an electric shock. Together with her words, *deep and slow*, he could imagine taking her. Could imagine condemning his tribe.

Could imagine it being worth it.

Just to have her.

Even once.

Chapter Twenty-One

"NO!" MARKOS TUMBLED OUT OF THE CAR AND STOOD IN the middle of the street.

Maybe a car would hit him. No, that wouldn't be big enough to kill him. A semi-truck. He needed a semi-truck. He scanned up and down the street.

Celia scrambled to the front of the car. "I'm sorry! I was worried about you. I know my touch disgusts you, but..."

He whirled around. Her lips were pressed together, like she was attempting to hold back tears. Her rush from the car had shoved her jacket behind her shoulder, exposing all that bare skin again.

"You don't *disgust* me. That's the *problem*."

Piss. That made it sound like this was her fault. And it wasn't.

Her face scrunched, and she stood straighter. "I don't understand."

A car laid on its horn and swerved around him. "Get out of the road, you stupid drunk."

"I'm a failure."

She inched closer to the front corner of the car. "No, your job is to keep me alive, right? Guess what? I'm still alive, so you're not a failure. And we can talk about this after you get out of the road."

He ignored her and continued watching for a semi-truck. Another car curved around him, its horn blaring. The blood rushing through his veins spiked his body temperature. He ripped off his leather jacket and threw it into his car through his still-open door.

"Markos, get out of the road right now, or I swear I'll come out there and join you."

His gaze shot to her, to where she now stood beside the hood of the car. When he didn't answer, she took another step toward him. And another.

She extended her hand to him. "Markos, you're my best friend, and I won't let you do this."

The open car door no longer protected her. She didn't look down the street, where another car's engine rumbled toward them, this one blaring party music. She strode toward him, keeping her eyes firmly on him.

"Don't," he begged. This was his failure. Not hers.

The car closed in on them. A clunk sounded on the sidewalk a few houses down as a passenger threw a can out the window. The occupants' yells and *whoops* carried over the pavement.

"No." She spread her fingers. "*You* don't. The only way you fail is if you give up, and I'm not going to let you do that."

The pavement under their feet vibrated.

Skoro. He grabbed her and bolted out of the road.

Hoots from the passing car sounded behind him. The wind gust helped propel them forward.

They landed on the hood of his car. Her soft body lay under his, and she stared up at him with wide eyes. So beautiful. So perfect. So pure.

His fingertips traced the curve of her cheek, and her smooth pink lips drew his eye, pulling him closer. His thumb stroked the corner of her mouth. He'd imagined this scene countless times, yet the reality was better than he could have dreamed.

And even more dangerous.

He growled and pushed off the car. He was tempted to bash his head on the metal. That might be the only way to knock sense and logic back into him.

Celia sat up, her fist clutching her jacket together and resting on her chest. "Thank you."

"Don't thank me." He paced back and forth in front of the car. "If you knew what I wanted to do to you right now, you *wouldn't* thank me."

If she knew, she'd run far away, and it still might not be far enough.

She released her jacket. "If you knew what I *wanted* you to do to me right now, maybe you'd do it."

He froze, staring at her in the reflected glow of the headlights. Curse the Maker and all her minions. Celia *couldn't* have meant what he thought she did.

"What are you talking about?"

She laughed and peered into the darkness. "You know it's sad when your sixteen-year-old sister knows more about guys than you do." She straightened her jacket over her shoulders. "Before we left my parents' house, before..." She inhaled and met his gaze. "Lisa told me that you weren't disgusted by my touch, but that you were terrified by it. I didn't believe her." She flipped her hand toward him. "Look at you—you shouldn't be terrified of anything."

She stood and faced him, her head upturned toward his.

"You don't need to be scared." She lifted her hand. "You don't need to hold yourself back."

Her hand slowly, tentatively, stretched up to him. His already wild heartbeat skittered and missed a beat. He held his breath, unable to give in and yet unable to resist.

"You don't have to push me away." Her fingers were near enough for him to feel her heat.

He was so close to giving in. To admitting everything.

To losing her forever when she learned the truth.

He stepped back several feet. "Yes, I do." He bent over and propped himself on his knees. "I can't let this happen."

"Can't?" She flinched and tucked her arms in front of her chest. "Oh God. This is related to the issue with my sister, isn't it? The whole 'religious belief against flirting' thing." Her head angled, and she caught his eye. "What are you? Like a priest or monk or something with a vow of chastity?"

"No, I said only that it was *like* a religious belief. This is not..."

He straightened and swallowed. She looked so close to crying he wanted to reassure her. Say something to let her know this was beyond their control.

"This is not something I chose. But it *is* a requirement of my people, so I must honor it."

"That's just great. The one guy who pays attention to me. The one guy I fall for..."

His heart did stop that time. *Fall for?* Was that slang for what he thought? Could she really have feelings like that for him?

When his heart restarted, it pumped harder than ever, like it had grown in size with her words. But along with that, his guilt redoubled as well.

"Is the one guy who *can't* do anything because of his job." Her arms swung in wild gestures. "Good Lord, it's like the universe wants me to stay a virgin my whole life."

Just as she cringed, as though embarrassed by her statement, an admission slipped from his mouth without thought. "Yes."

Ass. Were any of his secrets safe with her around to lure them from him?

"*Yes?* What the hell does that mean? Yes, the universe wants me to stay a virgin?"

He bowed his head, the better to avoid her eyes. "Ensuring you remain a virgin is part of my job responsibilities. Yes."

"No, no, no." She raised her hand, palm out toward him. "Why the holy hell would my virginity matter to you people? It's no one's business but mine."

His soul drained from him as he had to admit to himself what her destiny meant. That he'd condemned her with his impurity. That she'd surely die. But the other side of her destiny was that his tribe would all die if she was no longer the Virgin.

"Your"—he debated but decided to stick to the terminology of her mistaken impression—"*future* depends on you remaining a virgin."

"That..." She laughed and crossed her arms. "That's the most ridiculous thing I've ever heard in my life. Not to mention sexist. Why is my virginity such a big deal, and yet guys can go out and screw anyone they want?" She shook her head. "I don't believe you. It couldn't possibly be that impor—"

"I am also a virgin."

Her arms fell to her sides, and she took a step toward him. "You? Mr. Sexy Ass Bad Boy Extraordinaire. A virgin. And you expect me to believe *that*?"

Despite the danger of their confrontation, a grin threatened to curve his lips at her description. His chest burned at the thought of how she saw him.

Tantalized by the knowledge, he willingly played into her hands. "Never even kissed anyone." When her jaw slackened, he shrugged. "I told you. It is a belief of my people, and even though I did not make the rules, I must not disrespect them."

He'd expected her to be pleased by his confession. She wasn't.

"Well, screw you and your people. *I* have no reason to respect those beliefs. And I certainly don't want to stay a virgin for who-knows-how-long. I want what I want, and I want *you*, dammit. Do you not want *me*?"

His breath left him. Curse the Maker, that was the question of the evening. Of the past several months. That was the question that had haunted him since he'd first touched her.

"Yes." His mouth was dry. "But I can't have anyone, especially not you."

Her expression tightened. "Especially not me. Because I'm supposed to stay a virgin for 'the future.' Even though that makes no sense whatsoever."

She peered into the road, where more cars full of near-drunks had passed by them during their conversation, and she did a double take at something near the intersection down the block.

Her arms folded in front of her, which added to his distraction by lifting her breasts toward him. "And what if I'm determined to lose my virginity? What then?"

His gaze jumped from her chest to her face, and his insides sank deep enough to visit Hades. "No."

"No, what? No, I'd never be able to lose my virginity because 'the universe is against me'? Or no, you'd stop me? Where exactly do my rights end and your people's beliefs begin?"

His brain stumbled to a stop. She'd uncovered the core of his guilt.

Back when he had hope that the next Virgin would be the one to survive the ritual, he could rationalize what he put them through—that there was a possibility of a happy ending for both of them. But when he no longer had any hope, there was nothing left to rationalize. He didn't have an answer for himself, much less one to give her.

After a moment of his silence, she swallowed. "Right." She nodded to herself. "How about I save you the trouble of coming up with a lie by being honest with you. This future where I supposedly save a race from extinction doesn't look so great anymore, especially not if these people I'm saving think it's okay to control my life without giving me an *excellent* reason to let them do so. A scientific explanation for how my virginity could possibly affect my ability to save them would be a decent start. Do you have a reason to give me?"

Her brows rose as she waited for the answer that wouldn't come.

"Didn't think so." She uncrossed her arms and held open her palms. "So here's the deal—unscientific beliefs don't get to control my life. *I* am in charge of my life. *I* am in charge of my body. And no vague future and no controlling group of people and *no one* gets to tell me what I can and can't do with it. My virginity doesn't affect my ability to help others, and I'm going to prove it."

She strode around the side of the car and retrieved her purse.

"I'm going to go to a party that's happening down the block. I'm sure it will be filled with guys drunk enough to ignore whatever the universe's grand scheme against me happens to be. Maybe after I lose my virginity, my *friend* will be willing to treat me like a person instead of a pawn."

His hands clenched into fists, and his arms wrapped tightly around his chest. Her words sliced him open and left his emotions to bleed all over the street. She was right. She was right about everything.

He staggered over to her. "Please don't."

Her eyes still lit up with the fire of her justified anger. "Give me one good reason. Hell, give me *any* reason."

His mind raced through the possibilities, trying to come up with an excuse that would sound reasonable. Logical. Sympathetic.

Instead, warmth flooded his limbs, and his voice told her the truth. "Because I love you."

He hadn't consciously recognized that fact before, but now it was obvious. He loved her, and it was killing him that he couldn't make her happy.

Her lips parted, and the tightness around her eyes softened.

"Oh, Markos. I want to believe you. So much." She glanced away and then back up at him. "I want to believe you, because I love you too."

His knees threatened to buckle under him, and the warmth in his limbs now concentrated in his chest. She *loved* him.

Yet hope of any kind eluded him, dulling the joy he wanted to celebrate.

She closed her eyes, and her chin trembled. "I expect you to hate me for doing this, and I don't blame you. I would *much* rather be losing my virginity with you, but if you refuse, I have to do this. You might be okay with your people's beliefs holding you back, but I'm not. I have to prove that I don't need to be kept a pawn to do good in the world."

She stepped back, and tears now hung from her lashes.

"Stop me now if you've changed your mind. Please." Her lips pressed tight. "*Please.*"

He didn't—couldn't—move toward her. A cry choked her throat, and she covered her mouth.

Her hand dropped. "I'm so sorry to do this. But if you love me, you'll respect me and my rights just as much as you respect the beliefs of your people."

She hesitated again, silently begging him to stop her. He didn't.

Her eyelids pinched closed, sending several teardrops down her cheeks. "I'm sorry."

Her heels clacked down the sidewalk as she fled. And he let her go.

Because he *did* love her.

He loved her just as much as he was devoted to his tribe. And the coward's way out was to let her force the failure upon him.

The only thing she was wrong about was that he'd never hate her. She should hate *him.*

Chapter Twenty-Two

CELIA RUSHED DOWN THE SIDEWALK, RUNNING FROM THE FEAR that she'd just made the biggest mistake of her life. But every word she'd said was true, so she didn't have a choice. Right?

The more she heard about this future Markos came from, the more something about it sounded dark and foreboding. Especially as he hadn't chosen any of it.

She stumbled and wiped the tears from her eyes. In a way, she wanted to save Markos, break him free too. But he'd refused. Refused *her*.

Then the street sign for the road he'd parked on revealed her other option. All those cars were headed to the party the girls had been talking about in class. She could do it. She could lose her virginity, prove to them that they shouldn't use her or Markos as pawns, and...

Her steps halted on the sidewalk. Ahead of her, thumping music boomed from a large house. Lights were on in every room, silhouetting crowds of people inside. Dozens more partygoers spilled into the yard, yelling and singing and laughing. Everyone held clear plastic cups filled with different colored liquids.

Her knees locked, and she blinked. The place looked like every cliché of a frat party from every show she'd seen.

Was this really how she wanted to lose her virginity? To a

random drunk guy at a party she'd never go to under different circumstances?

Unable to help herself, she scanned the guys on the front lawn. Would she be picky and seek one out? Or just take whoever would talk to her? How desperate was she?

And more importantly, *why*?

Bile rose in her throat, and her legs wanted to carry her far, far away. Nothing about this felt right. Not when she didn't want this situation any more than she'd wanted her attacker's hands on her.

She gasped, desperate for air at the memory of that night. She plopped down in the middle of the sidewalk, her skirt making it difficult not to give everyone a show. Her head dropped into her palms, and she struggled to control her breathing.

Where was Markos when she needed him? Oh, that's right. Like an *idiot,* she'd told him that proving his people wrong by having sex with a random stranger was more important than their friendship. Her and her stupid scientific method, needing to prove her hypothesis this very minute.

She glanced back anyway, hoping to see his car. The curb along that spot was empty.

He'd left her.

It served her right. For all her claims about how he needed to respect her and how her beliefs didn't match up with those of his people, she'd disrespected him and his beliefs too.

Her chest clenched, every molecule crunching to a stop and freezing in place at once.

If part of his job was keeping her a virgin, wasn't this choice she'd made effectively calling his job irrelevant? Had he...?

She buried her head against her fists. She didn't want to think it, but now that the thought had occurred to her, she couldn't deny that it would make sense. If she wasn't a virgin anymore, did he still have a reason to stick around? Had he gone back to his own time, never to return?

The idea forced her to her feet. She ran back toward where his car had been. "Markos!"

Her shoe slipped off, and she hobbled back to pick it up.

She hopped on one foot, taking the other shoe off, and slipped her fingers through the straps to carry them. "Markos!"

Nothing. But she didn't let that stop her. She ran until she stood in front of the empty space along the curb.

She spun in a circle, searching for him lurking in the shadows, in the bushes, in the side yards. He'd been watching her for her whole life. He *had* to still be somewhere.

"Please, Markos. I'm sorry. I didn't mean it." A near-sob choked her for a moment. "I didn't mean it. I don't want to do this without you."

"And I don't want to do it without you either."

She twisted around at the voice. Not Markos's voice.

Another car, this one filled with jocks, had pulled into the empty parking space. One guy, biceps bulging, closed the car door behind him and crossed his arms.

"That's the whole idea of this party, blondie. That we won't leave alone."

If Markos were around, the blood wouldn't have fled her cheeks. No matter how big this guy was, Markos could chew him up and spit him out with his eyes closed and his arms tied behind him.

But Markos wasn't here.

She suppressed her sniffling and lifted her chin. "I wasn't talking to you. I was talking to my boyfriend."

That term was a stretch by any measure, even without the fact that he might be gone forever, but she didn't want to appear weak and alone either.

"Your boyfriend?" His brows rose, and he made a big show of peering up and down the sidewalk. "I don't see any boyfriend." He nodded toward his three friends over his shoulder and raised his voice. "Do any of you?"

They spouted their agreement and moved forward to stand at his side.

Her stomach dropped to somewhere around the vicinity of her toes. Gang rape had definitely *not* been on the agenda for the night.

He sauntered forward and cocked his head. "See, I'm thinking my boys and I could use a little warm up for the night. Take the edge off. What do you think? Think you could handle all of us?"

No, no, no. Not again.

Her limbs shook, panic electrifying her muscles. Then her ears caught the rumble of a bus approaching on the main street past the corner. Somewhere along that road, there was bound to be a bus stop.

She didn't take the time to think. She took off, running harder than she'd ever run before. Please, God, please let there be a bus stop soon.

Behind her, she heard them laugh and debate chasing her down. She shoved the thought from her mind and just ran, the pavement gouging the soles of her feet.

Oh thank God. A bus stop was just half a block ahead. Somehow she found another gear and ran faster, reaching the sign in time. The door of the bus opened in front of her, and she gratefully stepped on board.

After she flashed her student pass, the driver eyed her bare feet. She teetered from foot to foot and slid her heels back on, and then she scrambled into a seat as the door closed behind her.

Only after the bus pulled away did she gather her wits enough to check her surroundings. No sign of the jocks. No cars trailed the bus outside either.

More air than she thought her lungs could hold escaped her chest. Full-body trembles quickly followed, and she wrapped her arms around her ribs. The delayed gasps from her run started next. That had been too close.

The shaking didn't improve as the interrupted reaction to Markos's departure deepened. She shrank down into the bus seat and thumped her forehead against the window.

Oh God. He hadn't shown up to rescue her this time. He was really gone.

The world outside passed in a blur. She'd ruined everything. She'd been too demanding—and this time, Markos had fallen inside the scope of her curse.

What was wrong with her? Had she legitimately needed a *yes* or *no* answer at the spur of the moment? Hell, that attitude was as abysmal as those jocks, thinking she'd be eager just because the opportunity existed.

Would there have been anything wrong with knowing that he loved her—he frickin' *loved* her—and letting nature take its course?

Maybe he would have eventually changed his mind now that things were out in the open. Maybe he would have just needed a little foreplay for that matter, a little anticipation he couldn't resist. Maybe she could have even been happy with whatever they *could* do together.

But no. She'd had to push the issue. All because she'd thought science could fix everything in her life. And that if someone couldn't give her a scientific answer, she should ignore what they said.

She banged her head against the glass. Now... She sighed the sigh of someone taking their last breath on their deathbed. Now she had nothing.

She'd tasted friendship, she'd even tasted love—wonderful, heartbreaking, strength-giving love—but that hadn't been enough for her. And now Markos was as lost and dead to her as her family.

A fire engine passed, its siren blaring, drawing her eye to the outside world. The bus rounded a familiar corner.

Huh. This was *her* bus. They were just a few blocks from her stop. She vaguely recalled that the bus route continued down Skinker Boulevard after stopping at the university, so she must have picked it up going in the opposite direction. Well, one thing had gone right tonight.

So much for her dreams of a fun—and hopefully romantic—evening with Markos. So much for her dreams of anything.

Her stomach gurgled. Oh yeah, and she'd still never eaten dinner.

She trudged off the bus when it pulled up to her stop and started across the street.

Flashing lights swept across the road, and she lifted her gaze. Flames licked out of the windows at Auntie's house.

She broke out into a run. Her heels flung off. She left them behind.

She rushed through the line of neighbors milling behind the fire engine. "Auntie!" She grabbed an older woman she vaguely recognized by the collar of her bathrobe. "Have you seen Harriet? Where is she?"

The woman didn't answer.

Celia ran toward the house until a cop yanked her back.

"Auntie!"

"Miss, I have to ask you to stay back. Let the firefighters do their job."

"Where's Harriet? The woman who owns this house." Her arms pushed past him. "Where is she?"

She scanned the area. An ambulance was parked in front of the fire engine, its back doors open. The inside was empty.

"Please. There's an elderly woman inside. Her bedroom is on the first floor on the right. She's suffering from Alzheimer's. They have to get her out of there."

The cop considered her a moment. "If you promise to stay here, I'll check with them."

She nodded, and the cop started moving away. That's when she saw it—a sheet-covered stretcher being rolled down the driveway of the house next door. Her blood chilled to ice.

"No!" She barreled through the cop and skidded to a stop at the stretcher. Her hands lifted to her mouth. She couldn't breathe, couldn't think.

The paramedics halted. The one by the head of the stretcher spoke. "Do you know the owner?"

She forced herself to speak. "I rent the attic room from her."

The paramedics exchanged glances and folded the sheet back. Auntie lay there. One cheek swollen and blistered. Unmoving. Unseeing.

The world stopped. The crackles of the fire... The shouts of the firefighters as they unrolled more hose... The shattering of windows... All faded to silence.

In the void around her, the whisper of Celia's "no" blanketed the yard, the block, the city.

Her knees shook, and she grasped the bar of the stretcher. This couldn't be happening. This couldn't be real.

But the cold metal in her hand felt too solid. And then the world came rushing back.

A crash sounded from the house, its old timbers collapsing inside the brick walls. Water roared from the fire hose into the open windows. A blast covered her with heat.

And still Auntie lay unmoving.

Celia rolled her lips between her teeth, the emotions beyond her ability to contain. "No, Auntie." She bent over the stretcher. "I'm so sorry. I should have stayed with you."

She rested her head on the woman's chest and let the emptiness eat her alive.

Her confession came out in a whisper. "I should have been here with you."

A blanket draped her shoulders, and hands pulled her back.

Lights flashed, illuminating the firefighters losing against the blaze.

A mug of hot cocoa appeared in her hands.

Lights flashed, exposing tall flames dancing above the caved-in roof.

A cop guided her to sit in the front of his police car.

Lights flashed, revealing that the stretcher carrying Auntie had disappeared.

Lights flashed.

And in the same amount of time it took for the beams to sweep across the yard, her life changed forever. She had nothing. Nothing but the clothes on her body and the contents of her purse. All her artwork and worldly possessions were gone.

Her place to live—her home—was gone.

Auntie was gone.

Her family was gone.

Markos was gone.

She was alone. More alone than she'd ever felt as a child or teenager. Now she knew what it felt like to have a family, to care and be cared about, to be loved.

And now she knew what it felt like to lose it all.

Chapter Twenty-Three

MARKOS PULLED INTO HIS GARAGE, WHERE MOLLY WAITED for him. He opened the car door and let her lean against his leg.

"I know. I failed." He sighed and ran his fingers along her fur. "I failed with everything."

Celia thought who-knew-what about him, and the savior of his tribe was no more. But he couldn't begrudge her the decision she'd made. She deserved a happy, normal life, and he couldn't give that to her. He could only take it all away.

He bent over, emotions burying him in anguish once more. An aching hole grew in his heart and left an emptiness he'd never fill without her. His chest burned like he'd been gored. He loved her. And he'd lost her.

At least the Maker had blessed him by granting him the opportunity to know her. Even now, he wanted to be near her, keep her safe, make sure the man she chose was deserving of her and treated her with respect. That desire proved more than anything how much he loved her. But he needed to take the last sliver of honor he had left and face those he'd condemned.

Would they all die immediately? Or would they live until the Spring Equinox next month? Maybe Archimedes the historian would know.

He exited the car and closed the door. Molly cocked her head at him.

"I can't take you with me on this trip, and I don't know if I'll be back." If the council caught him, they might kill him on the spot. "If I don't come back, keep an eye on her for me."

Molly sat and nudged his knee. He'd never figured out how this dog understood his words so well, but he trusted Molly to watch over Celia. He gave her another pat and then formed the misty doorway to the Mythos plane with thoughts of Archimedes's quarters.

He stepped into the swirling mist and entered the old male's library. Shelves lined the walls, and lanterns reflected off a fine cloud of dust hanging on the air currents of the room. Markos coughed on the air particles. At the sound, Archimedes peeked out from between two cases of scrolls.

"Markos. What an unexpected surprise." The lean and wizened male glanced around and noted the closed door. "I take it the council doesn't know you're here."

Markos bowed, giving him the proper respect. "Greetings, Ancient One." He straightened. "You are correct. I..."

How did he tell someone that he'd just condemned them all to death?

"Come, come." The male waved him forward, his robes fluttering with the motion of his arms. "What's with the sour expression? Did your girl *not* like the present?"

Markos froze. How had Archimedes known? The notes he'd left for Hipdemos said only that he needed the case with the golden lid made, not who it was for.

"Rest easy, my boy. Your secret is safe with me."

"I don't know what you're referring to."

"No?" Archimedes gave Markos a sly smile, deepening the wrinkles on his face. "I must be thinking of a different Virgin you've had to befriend then, yes?"

He rubbed the back of his neck. "She is not *my girl*, but yes, she liked the present."

"Splendid." Archimedes clapped. "Now come tell me what's wrong."

He led Markos to his office in a back room. Something about the space struck him as odd, and he peered around the room until it dawned on him. No window openings.

Without the electricity of the Earthen plane, nearly everyone on the Mythos plane took advantage of openings in the walls for daytime illumination. However, open rooms allowed mist to flow, which created a potential security issue with those who could manipulate the magic of Mythos. The only other windowless locations he could think of were the council chamber and the prison. His estimation of the historian's cunning and forethought rose by several notches.

Archimedes lit a handful of sconces along the walls and closed the solid door. As he sat behind a large desk, he gestured to a generously sized chair. "Sit, sit. Tell me what brings you here against the strict orders of the council."

Markos took the indicated chair and gathered his thoughts. "I have a question about what will happen to our tribe if the Virgin loses her virginity before the ritual."

Archimedes's teasing expression fell from his face. He leaned back in his chair and steepled his bony fingers. "The magic Alkipsia distributes to the tribe from the spilled blood of sacrificed Virgins is not pure. The Maker did not design us to live off the *death* of Virgins. We are living on borrowed time already. If the bonds tying us to the Virgin's magic are shattered..." He opened his palms in a question no one could answer.

"What do you mean the magic isn't pure? I know it's not as strong, but are you saying it's tainted?"

"That is one theory."

"Why would Alkipsia risk offending the Maker with tainted magic?"

Archimedes leaned forward, his chair squeaking with his shifting weight. "The better question is—why wouldn't she? Don't forget the basis of the Civil War."

Had Alkipsia lied about how she'd learned that the spilled blood of a Virgin still contained enough magic to sustain them? Was that not a revelation from the Maker? If so, she'd deceived the entire tribe simply to gain enough support to overthrow his mother in the war.

"What other lies should I know about?"

"I know only rumors." Archimedes fiddled with piles of scrolls on his desk. "Some say she has sent unicorns to the faerie home-land"—he lifted his gaze to Markos—"not as an invading army, but to *work* for the faeries."

Markos sat back, dizzy. Faeries were their enemy from the days of ancient history. No unicorn should be turned over to the fae, especially not with the tribe already so weak.

Although—if the rumors were true—that weakness might be why Alkipsia would reach out to their enemies. What better way to maintain power than to befriend their foremost enemy?

Archimedes tapped his fist on his mouth and then stretched his arm toward Markos. "Why do you ask about the Virgin's magic? Has your relationship progressed so far that you're finding it hard to wait until after the ritual to consummate your feelings?"

Heat crept up Markos's ears, his impurities laid bare.

Archimedes raised a brow. "Is she *the one*? Do you love her and she you?"

The answer stalled in Markos's throat. The old male's questions held none of the censure he'd expect. None of the chastising for being *impure* that he'd hear from the council.

Knocks sounded on the door. A deep voice carried through the heavy wood. "Ancient One, are you in there? The council has summoned you."

Archimedes glanced at Markos, his eyes wide, and then he stood and raised his voice. "One moment, please. I have fragile documents exposed in here and must secure them before opening the door."

He scooted his chair loudly over the marble and leaned close to Markos, whispering, "You must be ready to leave as soon as I open the door."

Markos quietly moved behind the door. Near the wall, he formed a misty rectangle that would take him to the woods outside, where he could keep an eye on this "summons," but until Archimedes opened the door, the mist would have nowhere to go. He was just about to nod to Archimedes when he found his voice enough to ask the question swirling in his head.

"Would it make a difference if we did love each other?"

A smile incongruous to the danger outside the door formed on Archimedes's face.

"Ask yourself why the Maker would forbid matings."

With that incomprehensible statement, Archimedes placed his hand on the doorknob. As soon as the door opened a crack, the magic tying him to the Virgin gave a strong yank.

Threads of his spell connected them so he could always find her and know when she was in danger, and now they vibrated like the strings of a plucked instrument. He followed the threads, letting the magic redirect him and choose the destination for the doorway.

The last time he'd done this, he'd landed a block away from her, and he'd barely found her in time to kill her attacker and save her from bleeding to death. He hoped this time the magic would be more precise.

On the other side of the misty doorway, he walked into confusion. Flashing lights reflected off the houses in front of him. Where was he?

He spun around. This wasn't the street filled with large houses where he'd left Celia. This was Harriet's block. How had she ended up here so soon after he'd left?

A crowd formed a semicircle at the edge of the street, and he jostled his way to the front. A fire crew was working on putting out the flames inside a home. The collapsed roof and lawn full of people and equipment made it unidentifiable for a moment, but he finally realized where he was—Harriet's house.

Hades's crows! Celia was here? He glanced up at the house. Was she inside? Were the flames the danger he'd felt?

He rushed toward the house but slowed when he heard a voice. Her voice. Deadened.

"I don't know."

"And you said she suffered from Alzheimer's?"

Markos traced the second voice to a police officer standing by Celia with a notepad while she sat sideways in the front of an open police car.

"Yes." She had a blanket wrapped around her, yet when it slipped from her shoulders, she seemed unaware of this fact, or of anything for that matter.

"Do you have a place to stay tonight—a friend's house, relatives in the area?"

"No, I don't have—"

Markos strode forward and answered without thinking. "She'll stay with me."

Celia startled, standing up and dropping the mug in her hands. Her face crumpled, and she took a step toward him and then hesitated.

He closed the distance between them and folded her into his arms. She collapsed against him and started sliding down his front, her legs giving out. He scooped her into his arms and held her tight.

She clutched his shirt. "You're here. You're here. You're here."

"Shh. I'm here. And I'm never letting you go again."

At that, she cried and buried her face into his chest.

Because of his failings, he hadn't been here for her, and he wouldn't make that mistake again. Markos lifted his head to hold off the drops filling his own eyes and met the gaze of the policeman.

The officer cleared his throat and positioned his pencil over the notepad. "And you are?"

"Markos Ambrostead."

"Did you also live with the deceased?"

Deceased. That answered his question.

He squeezed Celia tighter. "No. I'm a friend of Celia's and knew Harriet only through her."

"Did you see Harriet earlier tonight?"

"Yes, Celia and I left here together."

"Notice anything unusual before you left? Any smells, any activity?"

"No. Harriet said she had a headache and was going to warm up some milk before going to sleep."

The policeman tapped his pencil against the metal spirals of his notepad. "We won't have the official report from the fire investigator for a while, but the initial belief of the captain is that the fire started in the kitchen. Neighbors reported hearing an explosion." The officer gestured toward Celia, who still clutched him as if afraid he was a figment of her imagination. "She mentioned something about Alzheimer's. Is it possible that Mrs. Williams did something odd or forgetful in the kitchen after you left?"

Markos slowly closed his eyes. Celia would blame herself. He knew it.

He silently nodded to the policeman.

"Does Mrs. Williams have any family we should notify?"

"Her son, Dr. Roger Williams." He bounced his knee against Celia's purse, which he felt hanging down along his leg. "You can find his number in her cell phone."

The police officer jotted down the number and replaced her phone in her purse. "Thanks. We'll update the immediate family, and they can pass on the information if they wish."

The man seemed to be done with them, so Markos started walking away, still with Celia shuddering in his arms. Then he realized he didn't have a way to get her to his house. His car was back in the garage, and he didn't want to upset her fragile state even further by transporting her directly.

He turned back to the policeman. "Could we get a ride to my house? I don't have my car here."

"Uh, sure. How far away is it?" The officer opened his back door, where there was room for both Markos and Celia.

"Just across from the university. Lindell Boulevard."

"Oh." His voice rose in surprise. "Beautiful homes along there. Give me a minute to check in with the fire captain, and we'll be on our way."

After the officer walked away, Markos gazed down at Celia. She'd stopped crying, and now she looked withdrawn, her eyes blank and unseeing.

He recognized the expression. That's all he'd seen from her for the past month and a half until this afternoon—and then everything had gone so horribly wrong.

He wasn't going to make the same mistake this time. Last time, he'd stayed distant, let her stare out the window in silence for their whole ride home from Iowa and suffer a lonely depression inside her head.

This time, he'd be there for her. He'd hold her close and never let her go.

"Celia, I'm here for you now. Always."

The words held a promise he couldn't keep, but his heart wanted to make it anyway.

"Thank you." She lifted her gaze to his. "I still can't believe you're here. I thought you'd left me."

"Never." He squeezed her, emphasizing his promise. "I'm not going anywhere."

Her focus drifted away. "You're the only thing I have left. I have no place to live, no clothes, no school books." She swallowed. "All my art is gone. Auntie..."

"I wish I could fix everything and bring Harriet back. But I can't. However, there are some things you shouldn't worry about, so wipe them from your mind. My house is now your home too. I'll buy you all new clothes, all new school books, all new art supplies."

She gasped and leaned forward in his arms, straining to catch a glimpse of the house. "The box you gave me."

"I'll look for it in the morning."

She settled back against him. "What would I ever do without you?"

"You'll never need to find out."

She bit her lip and looked down. "I didn't do it, you know. I couldn't hurt you more than I already had. I never even made it up to the house where the party was."

"I know." Her smell had let him know her status instantly, not to mention that his magic had called him here because his spell tying him to the Virgin remained unbroken. "I'm sorry I drove you to think you needed to do that."

"I'm sorry too." She snuggled into him. "I'm sorry too."

He slid into the back of the police car and struggled to make sense of his thoughts. Now that he held her in his arms, he could never go back to the way things were before.

What did it say about him that he'd almost been disappointed to discover she was still a virgin? That fact meant the hopes of his tribe were still alive. That fact meant he still had to face the temptation...

And the choice.

Chapter Twenty-Four

AFTER THE OFFICER DROPPED THEM OFF AT THE HOUSE, CELIA still seemed numb, so Markos carried her upstairs, Molly at his heels. He nearly entered his bedroom without thinking of the implications, but stopped himself and instead took her to a guest bedroom down the hall. He bumped his elbow against the light switch and surveyed the room, a small lamp on the nightstand providing soft illumination. He wasn't sure he'd ever paid attention to this bedroom before.

Where the master bedroom was dramatic and contemporary, this bedroom projected old-world classical elegance, much like Celia herself. The thick white rug covering most of the floor silenced his footsteps. Molly, brilliant dog that she was, hopped on the bed and gripped the fluffy covers with her teeth, tugging them down, as he had his hands full.

He laid Celia down on the bed, and she promptly curled into a ball on her side.

When he reached for the bedspread, Celia stopped him, her voice raw and muffled. "Please don't leave me."

Donkey's balls. He was supposed to get into bed with her? The possibility seemed like a bad idea on every level, but how could he deny her? Rather than being the siren song of a temptress, it was the plea of a friend who needed him.

He couldn't muster any resistance. He wasn't sure if he even wanted to.

He removed his boots and climbed into the bed behind her. As he pulled the covers up, Molly spun in a circle and settled herself on the front side of Celia. He lay on his side along her back and wrapped his arms around her. She uncurled herself and scooted back against his chest—and groin. He held in a groan. This night obviously wouldn't allow him any sleep.

Her tears resumed, proving her thoughts weren't in the same place as his. "I can't believe she's gone."

He tucked her in tight against him. "I'm sorry. I know how much she meant to you."

Molly leaned her weight along Celia's stomach, and Celia stretched to hold her. They made a strange little gathering of bed-fellows, the three of them.

"It's all my fault, you know." She gave a sigh broken by leftover hitches from her crying. "I should have stayed with her. I shouldn't have been selfish."

"Don't think that." He stroked her hair behind her ear. "You have your own life, your schooling, your dreams. You couldn't give that all up to stay with her all day, every day. Neither she nor Roger ever asked that of you."

His words echoed uncomfortably in his head. The recognition of how much he and his tribe expected her to give up to be their savior turned sour on his tongue.

"I know, but I still can't help thinking—"

"Don't. There will be time enough for that after we learn more. Right now, you need sleep."

She nodded, and her hair tickled the triangle of his exposed chest at his open collar. Her body moved against his with her deep inhalation, and then she let the air out slowly.

Her head tipped down, and she kissed the back of his hand, where he held her high across her shoulders to avoid coming into contact with her breasts. "Thank you. For being here, for being you. For everything."

He closed his eyes at the touch of her soft lips. She was so much more than he'd ever imagined. He could lose himself with her, in her, and be happy for the rest of his life. However long that may be.

Holding her like this was better than his most private dreams, and he could no longer worry about what his impure thoughts meant for the ritual or his tribe. Now he could feel only regret that he wasn't worthy of her.

Once he sensed that she'd fallen asleep, he dozed on and off until the sun lightened the sky beyond the edges of the curtains. He wanted to check the status of her things at the house before she woke and before anyone else went scavenging. Anything he could do to make up for the fact that he hadn't been there for her earlier.

He slowly pulled himself away from her. It was like crawling away from his own limbs. Molly squinted at him with one sleepy eye.

"I'll be back," he whispered. "I want to salvage anything of hers I can. Stay with her."

Molly settled, apparently deciding that was a legitimate excuse. He grabbed his boots and slipped to the garage so he'd have the car to bring back any clothes or art supplies he found.

Harriet's neighborhood was quiet in the pre-dawn light, the fire trucks and ambulance long gone. If anything, the remains of the house looked in worse shape now than they had in last night's darkness. Brick walls stood along the edges, but the front door and windows were all burned out, and the roof was caved in, exposing the inside to the foggy morning.

As soon as he opened his car door, the thick stench of smoke choked him. Drips sounded from inside the house, whether from the fog's heavy dew, the soaking the house had received last night, or a combination of the two, he couldn't say.

Yellow caution tape blocked the front entrance, and he ducked under it to let himself inside. Charred remains of the hardwood floor creaked under his feet. Fire usually traveled up, so he hoped the boards were undamaged enough to hold his weight. While he could heal from falling through to the basement, leaving his blood around for humans to analyze would be unwise. Above him, gaps in the ceiling opened to the gray sky.

The kitchen to his left was gone. A massive hole in the wall behind the mangled stove explained why the fire captain had made his guess before the investigation even started. On his right, undamaged streaks of wallpaper in the living room gave evidence to the random nature of flames. The couch he and Celia had spent so much time on was burned to its springs, but Harriet's chair in the corner farthest from the kitchen seemed soggy, but otherwise undamaged.

Markos snatched the quilt she'd made from the arm of the chair and set the damp patchwork by the entrance. Roger might want to keep that remembrance.

Celia's room was at the back end of the attic, and he hoped it was far enough away from the kitchen to have survived. Or to have a floor at least.

At the top of the stairs, brightening sky illuminated his way, as only a few partial rafters were left of the roof. The front wall of her room had burned through and collapsed, allowing him to see inside. The left side of her room had caved, and her bed and the cabinet that had held her clothes were down below, burned to blackened lumps. At least clothes were easy enough to replace.

His gaze scanned the rest of the room—past the busted-out window where the main roof beam at the gable had collapsed through the center of the house—and stopped at her desk on the right. Roof shingles covered it, but he could make out the material of her backpack below the pile of asphalt rectangles.

He took a step, and his foot punched through the floor. *Mugarok!*

He threw his weight back and yanked his foot from the hole. How could he salvage the items in her desk without a floor to stand on?

A glint of sunlight shone through the house's back wall, the sun now cresting the horizon. Even where the brick exterior remained, its structural integrity was broken, with chinks in the mortar and pieces of bricks missing. Maybe he could *relocate* the desk.

He braced his feet against the base of what remained of the wall behind him, squatted down, and stretched out his arms. A massive thrust against the wall propelled him forward with a strength and speed no human could match. His palms hit the side of the desk, and he shoved the whole mess through the back wall of the house.

The desk smashed through the bricks and toppled to the backyard a story below with a tremendous crash. His momentum carried him through the new hole, and he curled and rolled across the lawn with the impact.

He stood and brushed brick dust and grass clippings off his clothes. Mule's piss. That had been louder than expected. Given his luck, a police car would probably show up in a few minutes at a neighbor's complaint.

The desk now lay in a heap of shingles, broken bricks, and charred wood next to the back porch. He uncovered her soggy backpack and rummaged through the rest of the pile. The gold lid of the box Celia had been so concerned about was near the top, but the rest of the box was burned and splintered like everything else.

He brushed off the roof fragments and flipped the lid upright. Some of the metal had partially melted in the fire. His hand stopped mid-stroke of wiping away the soot.

The faces of the Virgin and the unicorn remained, but the near side must have been closer to the burning timber of the rafter. The lower half of the lid, where the bodies of the two figures were, had melded into one solid swirl of silver. The two had become one.

He closed his eyes and inhaled. The damage to the box made it even more valuable in his mind. His heartbeat thumped against the lid as he held it close.

The Virgin on the lid had survived death. If only Celia could be granted the same miracle.

Chapter Twenty-Five

B Y THE TIME MARKOS FINISHED PAWING THROUGH THE PILE OF her smashed desk, he'd uncovered several sketchbooks— thoroughly soaked and blackened, but Celia might want them anyway—and some melted art supplies. He carried the golden lid, her backpack, and his other discoveries to the car.

He went back inside to collect the quilt but decided to check Harriet's room too. The furniture was upturned and half-burned, and he didn't have a clue what might be worth keeping in there. He checked the time and dialed Roger's number. It was still early for a Saturday morning call, but North Carolina was an hour ahead, so it might not be too early.

"Dr. Williams." Roger's voice sounded tired and subdued.

"Roger, this is Celia's friend Markos. I assume the police reached you last night with the news."

"Yes, I'm on my way out there in a few hours."

"I'm sorry for your loss."

"Thank you. How is Celia holding up?"

"Not well. She blames herself because we weren't here when it happened."

"She couldn't be there twenty-four seven. As a matter of fact, I'm glad no one else was around to get hurt. You tell her that."

"I will. I'm calling because I came out to the house this morning to see if any of Celia's things survived. The house is in bad shape, but some of the contents are still in one piece. While I'm here, is there anything of your mother's you'd like me to search for?"

The man on the other end of the line sighed. "I can't think of— No, wait. Can you get to her room?"

"I'm looking into it right now."

"She had a jewelry box on her dresser, just costume jewelry, but she had one ring from her mother that I'd like to keep."

Markos picked his way through the room and made it to the overturned dresser. A small wooden case had tumbled off the top and spilled its contents under the bed. Sparkles reflected in the dim light, and he shoved the blackened bedsprings across the floor to expose them.

"I see the jewelry box. Everything is scattered around. I'd take the whole box, but I don't want to miss it if the ring has rolled away."

"The ring is—um, let's see—a diamond surrounded by those blue stones. Sapphires?"

Markos bent down to pick through the jewelry. A creak in the hall brought his head up.

A policeman aimed a gun at him from between the bare wall studs. "Hold it right there. Put your hands where I can see them. This is the scene of an ongoing investigation and is under the protection of the St. Louis Police Department."

Markos stood and raised his hands while switching his cell to speakerphone mode. "I'm Markos Ambrostead. Check the report filed by the officer on scene last night, and you'll know I'm authorized to be here. The owner's son is on the line here if you'd like to confirm that."

The officer glanced at the phone right as Roger spoke up through the phone's speaker. "This is Dr. Roger Williams, son of Harriet Williams. What information do you need from me to verify that fact?"

The policeman activated his radio. "Dispatch, this is Davis. Can you confirm for me the name of the owner of the house that caught fire on Enright last night?"

Squawks sounded over the speaker that Markos couldn't make out, but apparently the officer was satisfied with the answer. Markos lowered his hands when the man holstered his weapon.

The policeman shook his head. "This house is still subject to an ongoing investigation. The fire inspector hasn't completed his report."

"I didn't go into the kitchen or do anything that would interfere with an investigation." Not counting the new hole along the back wall. "I'm just here to try to salvage some items for the renter and the owner."

Roger piped in. "Markos is retrieving an item at my request."

"Then you won't mind if I stick around and keep an eye on things."

Markos knelt on the floor. "Just be careful where you walk. Some of the flooring isn't stable." He left his cell on speakerphone and set it on the remains of the bed. "All right, Roger, I'm searching for the ring now."

He rummaged through the jewelry. The one real piece among the pile caught his eye right away. A gold band with diamonds and sapphires, just as Roger had said.

"Found it. It seems to be in fine shape. Anything else you'd like me to get? I did grab your mother's latest completed quilt already."

"Really? She always seemed to give those things away as fast as she made them."

"I think she hadn't decided who to give this one to yet."

Roger chuckled, and his voice now sounded slightly less deadened. "Thank you, Markos. You're a good man. My mother adored you, mentioning you every phone call. I'm glad you were part of her life. And Celia is lucky to have you in hers as well."

Skoro and ass. The man's words, while meant kindly, punched a hole in Markos's gut, renewing his guilt for what he was expected to do. "No, I'm the one lucky enough to know both of them."

"Spoken like a true gentleman. I can't think of anything else, and I'll be in town by this evening anyway. I'll give you a call after I'm settled, and we'll get together."

"I look forward to it."

After hanging up the call, Markos tucked the ring and his phone into his pocket and eyed the officer. "I'm ready to go, unless you need to do something else here."

The policeman waved his hand along the hall. "After you."

Markos headed toward the front, avoiding the damaged

floorboards parallel to the kitchen on the right. He was just about to pass on the advice when a crash sounded behind him. He whirled around.

The officer had veered too close to the kitchen and fallen through the floor up to his waist. An angled piece of jagged wood had impaled his lower back and was sticking out through his upper abdomen, but blood hadn't started spreading.

The man might not have even realized yet how severely he was injured. He looked more shocked than anything, his mouth wide open, and his arms outstretched. Regardless, the officer would die here if Markos didn't get him out.

Markos dropped to his knee for better leverage. "Give me your hand. I'll pull you out."

"I—" He flailed his arms. "I'm stuck."

Markos seized the officer's wrist mid-flail and gave a horizontal pull beyond the strength of men. They tumbled together onto the floor of the living room. The policeman opened his mouth, like he was about to thank Markos, when pain registered on his face. He put his hand to his abdomen and started shaking, the spot of red rapidly growing under his palm.

Skoro. Massive internal bleeding.

Markos knocked the man's hand away and tugged up the uniform's shirt. He placed his palm on the bare skin and started the healing process without a second thought.

He locked onto the officer's eyes. "The blood looks worse than the injury. I'm going to keep pressure on it, and you're going to call for an ambulance."

The officer wordlessly nodded, activated his radio, and followed the instructions. Markos surreptitiously used his magic to heal the internal injuries and seal up most of the external wound. The gash was no longer critical, much less fatal, but it might be enough to explain the presence of bloodstains. The hospital would likely think it odd that the officer had matching wounds, front and back, with no injuries connecting them, but that couldn't be helped. Maybe the jagged nature of the wounds would make that fact less obvious.

The only reason the man was here was because he was following up on Markos's exploits. So Markos didn't argue with the obligation he felt to save him.

A few minutes later, the ambulance arrived and took over the officer's care. Before they wheeled the stretcher away, the policeman clutched his forearm.

"That guy on the phone was right. You *are* a good man. Thank you."

Markos's chest tightened, and his throat thickened until he couldn't swallow. During the whole drive home, after he double-checked he had everything, his throat remained constricted and painful.

By the time he stood alongside Celia's bed, his stomach had twisted into a bigger mess than Harriet's destroyed house.

Celia still slept peacefully, but while he was gone, the sun had begun to heat up this eastern-facing room, and she'd kicked off some of the covers. Her skirt had worked its way up to her behind, exposing her luscious thighs. Her jacket and blouse had likewise bunched up during the night, and her abdomen lay bare and tempting.

Son of a mule. His cock hardened. He longed to crawl into bed with her, but unlike last night, if he did, he wouldn't be doing so out of concern for her. His hands itched to slide her skirt further up to her waist or to fill his palms with her breasts.

He could so easily wake her. Convince her. Make her his. Condemn himself and his whole tribe.

He wasn't "a good man." He was a horrible man *and* a horrible male. A man who would save the life of a stranger just a half-hour ago, but who couldn't do what it would take to save the woman he loved. A male who had resisted the temptations so far, but who couldn't control his traitorous desires and fulfill the commandment of purity necessary to truly heal his tribe.

He was a failure on both ends. He didn't deserve to have these thoughts about her.

He didn't deserve *her.*

Chapter Twenty-Six

CELIA WOKE TO SOMETHING TUGGING ON HER ARM. SHE OPENED her eyes, thick with the sticky sleep of dried tears. Molly gently pulled the sleeve of her jacket.

Molly? The events of last night came rushing back—the argument she'd had with Markos, the frat guys, the fire, Auntie, and then Markos's return. Markos?

She sat up and surveyed the huge bedroom, decorated in white and subtle grays. Intricately carved crown molding ringed the ceiling, and delicate curves shaped the silver posts of the canopy bed.

This was Markos's house? The room looked like something out of an interior decorating magazine.

Celia slipped out of her jacket and started exploring the room. The stench of smoke followed, trailing from her hair and clothes. Her melted backpack and blackened sketchbooks sat beside the bed. She crouched down and touched them, unsure if she were dreaming. Dampness met her fingertips. That meant she hadn't dreamed up the fire, and that he'd already visited the house to retrieve what he could.

In fact, the golden lid of her box was on the dresser by the door. Before her fingers touched the swirls of silver, Molly nudged her leg.

Celia let Molly lead her to the door and then into the hall, where another shock awaited her. The hallway was longer than

Auntie's entire house and lined with fine artwork.

This place was a mansion.

Molly didn't give her time to absorb the artistic details, nudging her down the hall to the next open door. This bedroom was dark and sumptuous, with chocolate-brown silk sheets and furniture set off by stunning free-hanging sculptures made up of faceted glass beads strung from ceiling to floor at either end of the velvet headboard.

Noise like loud static from the partially open door on the opposite wall got her attention just as Molly's shoving in that direction got more insistent. Was Markos in trouble?

That thought got her to open the door, even though she suspected it led to a bathroom. A blast of freezing cold air caused chill bumps to sprout over her body.

The room was a bathroom all right, with a luxury tub centered under a window overlooking a sprawling yard, but the rushing sound was coming from a glass-enclosed shower on the left. Water droplets coated the inside of the glass, making it impossible to see inside. Markos's tall form didn't shadow the inside of the walk-in-closet-sized shower, and that gave her the confidence to check out the situation. Maybe he'd left the water running.

She opened the door to the shower and was hit with an even colder wave of air. The faucet was set to the coldest level, and at this time of year, that meant the water was just a few degrees above freezing. She started to reach inside to shut the water off, and splashes from the multiple shower heads quickly dampened the front of her shirt, setting her teeth chattering.

Clicks echoing her chatter made her look down. Markos sat hugging his knees on the floor of the shower, the target of all the showerheads.

"What the heck are you *doing*?" She plunged her hand through the spray and adjusted the temperature to set the water to lukewarm. Too hot, and it might be dangerous for him.

He squinted up at her, but seemed to have trouble focusing. "Cold shower good. Help. Control."

His words were slurred, and his constant shivering didn't help. His head nodded down again, drowsiness overwhelming him.

Oh crap. She ran through everything she knew about

hypothermia from various books and movies. Layers and skin-to-skin contact. Hopefully, they'd been at least semi-accurate.

She slipped off her wet blouse and skirt. Her bra was damp and cold too, so she removed that as well, leaving on only her underwear. She grabbed a whole stack of towels from the counter behind her and then joined him in the shower, making sure to close the door to keep the heat inside. He wasn't even aware of her presence.

She sat behind him, draped several towels over his front and a couple over her back for insulation, and then pulled him to lean against her bare chest. His cold skin shocked hers, and she shivered along with him. The shower's glass wall supported her back, and she wrapped her arms and legs around him to provide as much skin-to-skin contact as possible. The water was just warm enough to not make her colder, so she hoped it was the right temperature to help him.

"Oh Markos, why did you do this to yourself?" She figured she was talking to herself, given his condition, but she didn't know if it would be dangerous for him to fall asleep, so she babbled to keep him awake. "I'm beginning to sense a pattern of self-destructive behavior here. What does that say about you? What does that say about *me* that I love you anyway?"

He surprised her by answering. "Love you too much. And not enough. You deserve better."

At least, that's what she thought he said. His slurring made his words near-incomprehensible. For as unclear as his words were, he might as well have said that she deserved *butter*, but that made even less sense than his completely inaccurate statement about not deserving her.

"Don't kid yourself. I'm no saint. Besides, I saw that you'd already gone to the house and saved some of my things." She didn't mention that the sketchbooks were probably beyond help. This was one time the thought definitely counted. "Thank you."

She snaked her hands under his arms, between his knees and chest, so she could bring more heat to his core. With her worry, the fact that she was touching his bare, muscled chest for the first time almost escaped her.

Almost. But not quite.

She resumed her senseless patter of words to keep him conscious. "Tell me about the house. Is it as bad as it seemed last night?"

His head lifted and leaned against her temple. The towels were now thoroughly soaked and clinging to their skin to wrap them in a warm cocoon. Already, he didn't feel as cold to the touch. She moved her arms and hands lower on his chest to heat up a new area.

"Mostly gone. Clothes gone. Talked to..." A giant shudder overtook his body in what she hoped was one of the last gasps of the cold. "Roger. He'll be here tonight."

Okay, so that was about what she expected. But something must have happened to bring on the latest display of self-loathing.

"Thank you for taking care of all that. You're so good to me."

He shook his head, and his dreadlocks rubbed against her cold-erect nipples. "Not good. Roger wrong. Officer wrong."

What delusions went on in his head? "Why are they wrong?"

"Because I'm not strong."

A wry smile curved her lips. How could she resist that opening? She caressed his muscled chest. "You feel strong to me."

Her gentle strokes discovered cold skin on his abdomen, where the water couldn't reach with his legs propped up, and she spread her hands over the spot. His back and chest were so broad she couldn't wrap her arms around his front at this angle. She needed longer arms.

"Not strong. Not inside." He leaned further against her, creating more room between his chest and thighs and giving her better access. The towels now sagged between his shoulders and knees, which would help his upper body retain the warmth she'd given him. "Not strong enough to let you go. Not strong enough to resist you."

At his words—especially in that husky tone—tingles that had nothing to do with the cold sent a shiver through her body. He wasn't strong enough to resist her. What woman didn't long to hear that?

Of their own volition, her hands slid over his skin and soaked up the feel of his body, the ripples of his muscles. His knees separated an inch or two. Her fingers roamed lower and lower, seeking out any remaining cold areas. They stopped when short, springy hair met her fingertips.

Holy crap. He was naked under the towels. He was naked, and she was nearly naked. They were virtually naked—in the shower—together. She hadn't even noticed because his knees were pulled up.

Her heartbeat sounded over the splashing of the water around them, and she held her breath. He stiffened but made no move to stop her. Did she dare?

Was this what he'd hinted at with his "not strong enough to resist you" confession? Did he *want* her to overcome his resistance?

She had to be sure. Just because she didn't share his beliefs didn't mean she wanted to push *him* to dishonor them. She cared about him too much to take advantage of his uncertainty.

"Markos, I don't want to do anything you don't want to do, but..." She swallowed, working up the courage to be forward. Considering all the other times she'd had to make the first moves in their friendship, she should be used to it. "I think there's a lot we can explore without..." She struggled for the right phrase. "Crossing the line."

His head twitched against her cheek, and then he nodded, slowly, hesitantly.

Her fingertips inched forward from either side, taking their time, giving him plenty of chances to stop her. She swirled her fingers in the short hair, and his head tipped back as he groaned. The sound brought a smile to her face, and she pressed onward.

She slid her arms down his sides so she could stretch farther. Her fingers almost met in the middle when they encountered warm skin. His breaths quickened, his ribs pressing against her chest in a panting rhythm.

Her fingertips flitted up the hard rod from its base, and then she circled her hand around his thickness. He melted against her, his knees separating and loosening, his arms falling to his sides. The towels divided, one draping from his shoulders down his chest and another draping from his knees down his thighs. Around the side of his shoulder, she had a perfect view of him and all his very *large* maleness.

She stroked gently. Given how cold he was earlier, she didn't want to traumatize his skin. But oh boy, was his skin ever not-cold around here now.

He grunted with each slow pump of her hand. She couldn't explain why, but she felt more powerful than she ever had in her life. She had a man a foot taller than her, a man so intimidating-looking that most people would expect to see him on a *Most Wanted* list, a man who had resisted her so thoroughly that she hadn't even known he was interested, reduced to a pile of goo from just her touch. She controlled his body like a marionette.

With her other hand, she caressed his chest without the tentativeness of before. Her palm soaked up the sensations of his skin, the sparse hairs on his pecs, the lines of his muscles.

Again, he didn't stop her. And she knew: He didn't want her to stop.

His grunts became louder, sharper. His rod hardened more than she thought possible. Liquid seeped from the tip of the head, and she used its slipperiness to increase her pressure and speed.

Her oversized marionette responded. His arms and legs tensed, ropes of muscle standing out under his skin, bracing for impact.

She flicked her thumb over the head to gather more liquid, and the impact hit. He gave a guttural yell, and white cream shot from the head and landed on his abdomen. She continued pumping him until he fell against her, all tension gone from his limbs. Her lips lifted into a curve. She'd call that a success.

Never had she expected to be a seductress. To be the one taking control. To be the one pushing a man for more. But damn, did it feel good.

For once, she'd gotten exactly the reaction from someone that she'd wanted.

Chapter Twenty-Seven

MARKOS BREATHED AS HEAVILY AS HE DID AFTER ONE OF HIS marathon runs in Ireland. His lungs needed more of the warm, moist air inside the shower than he could inhale, and the earlier cold wasn't the problem. The struggle to get his breathing under control echoed his struggle to put the pieces of his mind back together.

The gift Celia had given him was even more amazing than he could have imagined. If just her hand was that enjoyable, what would sex itself be like? He couldn't conceive of it.

So why—as Archimedes had asked—would the Maker forbid matings?

The standard line was that they needed to avoid passing on their degraded genetics, with some unable to shapeshift. But now that Archimedes had pointed out the question, the usual answer no longer made sense in Markos's mind.

Before his mother's death, she'd asked the tribe to support her in the war, to be patient, to trust that if a Virgin accepted a Guardian at the ritual, everyone would be healed by her magic.

Everyone—children of matings or otherwise.

Even Alkipsia hadn't denied that fact. She'd only incited the tribe to feel desperate enough to accept the lesser magic available from the blood spilled at Virgin deaths.

So why would the Maker reveal to Alkipsia that all matings

were suddenly forbidden? As long as the Virgin remained pure until the ceremony, the Maker had never decreed rules about purity and matings for the tribe as a whole before.

And nothing that felt so incredible could possibly be immoral anyway. The experience had been miraculous, enlightening, sacred. Definitely not impure.

He tried to make sense of it while the water spray washed his torso clean. He had no words to express to Celia what that gift meant to him. Somehow, he had to find a way, had to make her understand.

"How can I ever thank you for that?" His voice was rough.

Her answer sounded soft and tempting in his ear. "Kiss me."

He sat up and twisted toward her. She was nearly naked from head to toe, and every inch of her was perfection.

A towel slid from his shoulders, and he tossed it away. Her wet hair hung down around her face, and water droplets clung to her eyelashes as she peered up at him.

As he watched, a drop fell from her lashes and landed on her cheek. From there, the bead of water wove down to her lips. Her tongue flicked out and licked it away.

Another drip followed. He waited for this one to track its twin to her lips, and then he caught it on his tongue before she did. Her inhale turned into a whimper. The next one he kissed away while it was still on her cheek.

He proceeded to kiss every inch of her face, her eyelids, her forehead, the tip of her nose. Only when he'd covered every spot *except* her lips did he allow himself the indulgence.

He met her heated gaze for a second and then closed on her mouth. Slow, gentle, nibbles and licks. Her lips were as soft and delicate as the most exquisite flower. He might never stop kissing her.

Her hands found his shoulders and pulled him nearer. He braced himself on the tile floor with one hand and sank the other into the damp tendrils of her hair. He cradled her head and deepened his kisses. Their tongues stroked and caressed together. Their lips danced in a harmony of pliant and yielding and hard and demanding. This was better than the Afterlife could ever be.

He sensed her breathing quicken and her nipples harden

against his chest. He wanted to do for her what she'd done for him. And she'd given him the perfect excuse by asking for a kiss—as he intended to kiss her *everywhere*.

Water pelted his back and splashed around them. The effect added to the feeling that he was drowning in her, and he wanted to swim deeper.

He pulled away from her mouth and trailed kisses down her neck, first on one side and then on the other. While he was doing that, he lifted one of her arms. When he brought her hand to his mouth, her brows raised, and then a slow smile built on her face as he traced kisses up her arm. He repeated with her other arm and finished with a path across her collarbone.

She frowned when he sat back, but he used the towel still pinned between her back and the shower enclosure to scoot her behind along the tile and slide her onto her back. The towel beneath her provided some cushioning from the hard surface. A necessary comfort, as he planned on keeping her here a while.

His back still blocked most of the spray, and mist bounced around her like a veil of magic. He gave each leg a turn, leaving a line of kisses from her toes to her hips. Her eyes were now wide and questioning.

He knelt between her legs and propped himself on one hand next to her ribs. Her hands had crossed over her abdomen, and he tugged them out of the way. He followed the curve on the underside of each breast in turn, placing kisses in a circle. Her breaths came as quick pants, and her eyes closed.

He bent down and licked one nipple and then the other. The nearest breast called him again, and he drew the softness into his mouth. He groaned with pleasure at the malleable flesh. With his free hand, he caressed her other breast and rolled his knuckles against the nipple. She gasped with each suck and flick.

This was the promised land. He could stay here forever, live here, sleep here, love here. Or according to the old myths of the Earthen plane, this was how he would die.

He could accept that. Happily.

Only the desire to bring her the same ecstasy she'd given to him lured him away. He continued his kisses down her belly, where the water droplets danced with her ticklish skitters.

When he reached the top of her underwear, he sat back on his heels and removed the lone piece of cloth, guiding her legs from the fabric. He bent down between her legs and spread her thighs.

Her body trembled, and she lifted her head. "Uh, Markos?"

He gave her a wink. "You *did* say that you wanted me to kiss you, did you not?"

She flushed. "Oh. Um, yes. I guess I did."

He licked along her opening. "You guess?" He deepened his next lick. "Do you want me to stop?"

"No." Her answer came quickly and confidently. When he swirled his tongue, her head dropped back to the tile. "Definitely not."

He smiled and increased his play. He sucked her juices and pressed his tongue against her sensitive nub. Selfishness drove him to drag out her pleasure, slow and deliberate. He had centuries' worth of waiting saved up to share with her. This was a banquet to be savored.

His hand's caresses stretched up her wet, slick body until he reached her soft breast, his long arm able to knead and tease one nipple as he feasted below. Her body jerked at the extra sensation.

Pink spread across her skin as she neared her release. She brought her knees up and tilted her hips, the angle allowing him to plunge deeper into her glorious nectar. As he continued his licks and sucks, her legs began to shake beside his shoulders.

Her breath suddenly stopped, and her muscles tensed. He increased the pressure of his tongue and lightly pinched both her nub and her nipple, rolling them between his lips and fingertips.

The sexiest sound he'd ever heard escaped her, and she rhythmically shuddered against him. Moments later, her legs slid flat, and her body drooped on the tile.

He'd succeeded. Only after his accomplishment did he realize that a part of him had worried about not knowing how to satisfy her. But she'd made it easy, her body's reactions guiding him on how best to give her pleasure.

Not bad for a virgin. Two, in fact.

He rinsed in the shower spray and then leaned over her. "I like this *exploring* idea of yours."

"Me too." Her grin stretched wide, and she stroked his face.

Tingles followed her fingertips, and flutters scrambled his stomach. He *loved* her, and that meant he *loved* the Virgin...

Who had only a bit over a month until the Spring Equinox's ceremony.

The flutters turned to roiling dread.

After she recovered, he turned off the water, and they dried off from their very long shower. Thank the Maker this house had a large hot water heater and her turn hadn't been interrupted by the unwelcome return of cold water. He grabbed a shirt from his closet for her to wear and escorted her down to the kitchen to find food. Molly tagged along, happily scampering around their legs.

Celia peered through all the open doors they passed. "I think I'm going to need a map or else I'll get lost."

"I'll take you on a tour once we get some food in you." He directed her to sit at the raised countertop on the kitchen island. "When did you say was the last time you'd eaten?"

"Yesterday. Lunch." She took a seat on the stool.

He opened the refrigerator and grunted. "I should have made you eat last night."

Her arm stretched across the countertop, and she laid her head down on her shoulder. "Last night, I wasn't up for doing anything but crawling into a hole. Or a comfortable warm bed with two snuggle partners." Her lips twisted into a pained smile. She sat up and sighed. "Honestly, I'm not feeling hungry now either, but I know I should eat."

His housekeeper kept his refrigerator stocked with prepared meals, despite the fact that he'd eaten most dinners with Celia and Harriet. His mood drooped at the thought of Harriet. The woman had been a great cook. He selected a few possibilities and closed the refrigerator door.

Celia eyed him. "What? I said I'd eat."

"No, I was just thinking about all our dinners together with Harriet." He opened the various containers and brought down two plates from the cupboard. "I'm going to miss her too."

Her smile turned even sadder. "Thank you for understanding."

She picked out a selection of foods to reheat while he filled Molly's food dish. Once their plates were ready, he lifted his water glass for a toast, imitating the way he'd seen humans do it.

"To Harriet."

She clinked his glass. "To Auntie."

Molly barked, chiming in with the sentiment.

After Celia had eaten her fill, she set down her fork. Her brows pulled down to what he recognized as her *serious* expression.

"Okay, so what's the deal with this mansion? You never even hinted that you had *this* kind of money. And while some girls would be ga-ga over the idea of being with a rich guy, I see this and wonder what else you're keeping from me."

He nearly choked on his sip of water. He quickly swallowed, ready to protest that it wasn't anything to worry about, but his mouth refused to form the words.

Given everything they'd been through together—their admission of love, their *expression* of love—he didn't want lies to stand between them anymore. *Piss.* No, it was more than that. He *couldn't* lie to her anymore.

Lying to her would render the sacred experience they'd shared as irrelevant. Lying to her would destroy any remaining fragments of his soul. Lying to her would kill him.

Chapter Twenty-Eight

CELIA WATCHED THE CONFLICT PLAY OUT ON MARKOS'S FEATURES. With his sunglasses off, his eyes gave away his thoughts. Clearly, her gut instinct had been correct. He *was* hiding things from her. Things that were beyond anything to do with the secrets of her future.

Instead of answering, he gathered their dishes and left them in the sink. "Ready for that tour of the house?"

Oh, so that was the game he was going to play. Called "change the subject." She'd let him get away with that for now—patience was virtue and all that—but she'd get her answers.

He led her outside to the front yard, insisting she get the full experience. Good thing the shirt he'd loaned her fell past her mid-thigh, living up to the term *shirtdress.*

The sun was already headed toward late afternoon. How long had she slept? However long it was, apparently she'd needed it.

The front of the house faced Lindell Boulevard, famous in St. Louis because the expansive Forest Park—St. Louis's version of New York City's Central Park—lay right across the street. These were the luxury houses that tourists, and oftentimes locals, would drive by to *ooo* and *ahh* over and imagine what it would be like to live in one. And now here she was.

The idea was crazy. The last twenty-four hours felt more like a surrealistic dream than her life.

The Tudor-style brick house was probably close to a century old, and she tried not to think about how she was standing in the front yard of this fancy house clad only in a shirt, as her underwear was sopping wet and hanging over the shower door.

She nudged him back inside as soon as she'd gotten her fill of the view. As Markos took her into each room, she made him wait while she appreciated all the old-world details, like leaded glass windows and the original chandeliers. And as if the three stories weren't enough square footage, the house had a full walkout basement too.

"What do you do with all this space?" Every room appeared to be professionally decorated, and most of them struck her as not Markos's style.

"Nothing. I've never even been in some of these rooms."

She ran her hand across the back of a leather chair situated in front of a fireplace in what he said the Realtor called the *hearth room*. Well, lah-dee-dah. "Yet you had them all furnished and decorated?"

"I bought the house fully furnished."

"Oh." Because the millions of dollars just the house would cost on its own wasn't expensive enough? She picked up her finger and pretended to check for dust. "I hope you didn't invite me to live here simply because you needed help cleaning the place."

He met her teasing smile with confused furrows. "I have a full-time housekeeper for that."

She plopped into the chair. "Of course you do." She leaned forward. "Markos, do you have any idea how *bizarre* this all seems to me? I mean, for most of the time I've known you, you've acted as if you're a poor, public-transportation-using, crappy-neighborhood-living peer. Like we're in the same situation."

Unable to sit still, she stood by the fireplace and checked out the bronze sculpture on the mantle. Yep, a Remington. She sighed.

"But no, first you show up in that car. Okay, I let that slide. I can see how time-travel could create investment opportunities, and it's not like it was a three-hundred-thousand dollar Ferrari. So it didn't feel like a major deception."

She pointed to the Remington sculpture. "Now I find out that you're in a multi-million dollar mansion with a maid and museum-quality art and that you *could* afford that Ferrari. Possibly several." She crossed her arms. "And I have to ask myself. Do I even know who you are? Or has *everything* been a lie?"

He twisted away and peered out the window, where the setting sun threw dark shadows over the yard. "I wish you wouldn't ask me these questions."

"Why? After everything between us, don't you think I deserve to know if *any* of it has been real? For all I know, you're just faking your feelings for me. Maybe that's all part of the grand plan the people of your future have for manipulating me. Maybe tricking me is part of your mission too." Chills broke out over her skin, and her voice lowered to a whisper. "Maybe you don't love me at all."

He strode over and seized the back of her head. "Do not ever doubt my feelings for you."

With that, he plundered her lips with a kiss that spoke of desperation and desire. Her surprised gasp turned into a moan, echoing his yearning. She dove into the sensations just as eagerly and held on to his shoulders for support.

His facial hair was so much softer than she'd expected before today's experience. Her knees turned to jelly at the memory of how the prickles had added to the sensations that had driven her wild earlier. She pressed her body against his, and like her, he was obviously ready for another round.

And... He was changing the subject again. Damn.

She reluctantly pulled away and stepped back. She drew in a shaky breath and ignored the pounding of her heart. "Okay, but you still haven't answered the other questions."

He wiped a hand over his mustache and goatee. "Can't you let this go?"

"Did you ever think that I might want to know who I've fallen in love with? That I want to understand *you* better because you're important to me?"

His slackened jaw answered that question.

She caressed his cheek. "No one has ever cared about *you* as a person before, have they? It's always been about your job or your responsibilities, but never about *you*." She held his face in her palms. "Well, guess what? I love you. And that means I care about you. I want to know you. I want to know how to bring you happiness. I want to know what our future can be."

Muscles clenched along his jawline. Something she'd said had upset him. Big time.

"I don't believe we have a future."

Chapter Twenty-Nine

MARKOS'S DECLARATION LANDED LIKE AN ANVIL BETWEEN them, and Celia dropped her hand from his cheek.

"You don't mean that." A confusing thought crept into her mind. "Unless you're trying to tell me that you know in my future I end up with someone else?"

"No, that's not what I mean."

Cracks formed along the edges of her heart, which suddenly felt as heavy as that metaphorical anvil. Her voice came out a whisper, begging him to say the right words, to make things better. "Then what did you mean?"

He spun around and walked out of the room. He *frickin'* walked out of the room.

"Hey!" She chased after him, jogging toward the back of the house. "Do you *want* me to think the worst possible things about you?"

He marched onto the back patio and kept going, deep into the neighborhood-block-sized backyard. Molly followed both of them, her bounding subdued to a low slink. Shadows now completely blanketed the yard in darkness, especially as tall trees lined the fences, which obstructed the last of the sun's rays and created a pocket of night.

When he ran out of room at the back of the lot, he finally faced her and took her hands in his. Trembles shook along his fingers.

"I'm sorry I can't be the man I *want* to be for you. If I could change the circumstances, I would. But you deserve to know the truth—all of the truth."

Time slowed, each heartbeat separate and distinct as she tried to understand his words. Whatever he was about to tell her would destroy her, she knew.

A childish voice in the back of her mind protested. She didn't want everything to change between them. She just wanted to know him. That voice nearly took control of her mouth and begged him to forget all the questions, leave everything the way it was.

But the rest of her, the more mature side of her, realized that things were already changed, already broken. They'd been that way from the beginning. The only difference now was that she'd lose her ignorance. Her scientific mind wouldn't let her go back to the *old* way when the old way had never existed. Not really.

He squeezed her hands. "I *do* love you, and I can't lie to you anymore." He dropped his gaze. "I'm not the man I've let you believe me to be. I'm not from the future."

"Not from the future?"

Her thoughts veered out of control. Rather than anger, confusion swirled in her head. Didn't the evidence contradict him?

She pulled from his grasp and rubbed her forehead. "No, that's the only way things make sense. How could you have witnessed my childhood otherwise?" She waved up and down, indicating his body. "You're what? Twenty-seven. Twenty-eight. That would mean you would have had to start your job at sixteen—at the latest."

"I started my job when I turned twenty-eight, and I was beside your crib the night you were born. I'm currently 468 years old."

She rolled her eyes and laughed. "You're pulling my leg, right?"

He didn't crack a smile.

"Markos, you can't be serious." She glanced at Molly beside them. "He's joking, right?"

Molly laid her head on her paws and whimpered. Oh, that wasn't good. She rubbed her arms. Her chill bumps had nothing to do with the dropping temperature of sunset.

"Oh. My. God." What could she say to that?

Time travel was science, and who was to say what would and

wouldn't be possible in the distant future. If he wasn't from the future, however, this situation smacked up against what science was capable of in the here and now. And lifetimes of that length weren't possible with today's knowledge of human biology.

"What about your disappearing act?"

"When I disappear, I'm not jumping between times."

She blinked at his non-answer. "Then where are you going?"

"To another place here on Earth, or to the Mythos plane. A parallel plane of existence to this one, the Earthen plane."

"Mythos. Like myths?" Each concept was more bizarre than the last. Her head felt fuzzy, and she wondered if she was hyperventilating without realizing it. That was entirely possible.

"Yes. The Mythos plane is the source of all Earthen myths, from faeries and dragons to water spirits and unicorns."

Even though none of his claims conformed to science, she still tried to think through the situation logically. A mental *click* sounded as her brain started piecing together the puzzle.

Vague memories of medieval mythology floated to the forefront. According to the ancient tales, only virgins could tame and capture unicorns.

"Unicorns. You work for unicorns. That's why they want you to keep me a virgin."

"No, Celia. I am not employed by unicorns."

He stepped back and nodded to Molly, directing his words to her. "I think she'll be safe because there's no ritual magic here, but keep an eye on her. I'm trusting you to keep her safe."

Safe? From what?

Molly whimpered and took up a guard position in front of Markos. Fog condensed out of clear air, gathering around Markos as if he had a separate gravitational field. He seemed to absorb the clouds and grow bigger. The mists swirled, becoming denser, and she couldn't make out his body behind the vapor.

Her knees didn't want to hold her up anymore, but she couldn't take her eyes off the billowing shape. This definitely wasn't good.

A loud thump shook the ground beneath her feet, like an elephant had parachuted into the yard, and the haze scattered into wisps. In the empty space—in the space where Markos had just been—was a beast. A beast over ten feet tall and three feet broad.

A beast with legs thicker than both of her thighs put together. A beast with a golden horn.

Celia's legs gave out, and she fell onto her butt. She tried to swallow but was quite sure her heart had decided to make a run for it by escaping up her throat.

The beast pawed the lawn and bobbed its head, but otherwise remained still. It—he—was waiting for her to process the information. She knew that. Could recognize that. But comprehending what her eyes were telling her was beyond her ability right now.

Molly and the he-beast thing touched noses, even though the creature was at least twenty-four hands high at the shoulders, and then Molly turned to her, as though in invitation.

Unable to make anything fit into the scientific theories of the world, she mentally chucked the textbook over her shoulder. No aspect of science applied to this. Obviously, *they*—whoever they were—hadn't known what the hell they were talking about.

Unicorns weren't the rainbow-and-glitter creatures little girls imagined and displayed on posters and decorations. They weren't the small, goat-like creatures of the ancient myths either.

Oh sure, they were horse-shaped, with a mane and tail and four legs and horse-like head. But they were like the prehistoric version of a horse. The difference between a little lizard and a tyrannosaurus rex.

The horn was the closest thing the clueless *they* had gotten right. Golden and spiraled, the horn sat upon the middle of his forehead, bright against the blinding white of his body.

A white horse.

She finally found her voice. "I saw you. The night of my attack. Between moments of unconsciousness, I..." She reprocessed her memories with the new information. "I felt the thunder of your hooves as you ran past, I saw the white of your body, and I saw..." She glanced at his horn. The very sharp and pointy horn. "I saw his blood streaking down your neck after you'd gored him."

"Yes." His voice was nearly the same, deep and booming, but with an added hint of musicality.

"You can speak in this form. Good. It makes you seem more like..." She stood and brushed off Markos's shirt at her bottom. "You." She scanned the lawn around him. "No shredded clothes left behind when you shifted. How's that work?"

"All races of the Mythos plane—those who can shift anyway—retain their clothes with their human form. When I shift back, my clothes will reappear. That is simply how the magic works."

"That's too bad."

His head reared back, and she gave him a smile. "The clothes thing, I mean. It'd be more fun to see naked-Markos."

His ears pivoted toward her. "You *accept* this?"

"Like I have a choice?" She shrugged. "Either I accept what I'm seeing or decide I'm going crazy. I'd rather it not be that second option." She lifted her hand and then drew it back. "May I touch you?"

His nostrils flared, and his eyes widened to show a white ring around his large amber pupils. "Are you feeling an urge to impale yourself on my horn?"

She laughed. "No, I'd just like to touch you. Are we back to the no-touching rule?"

He snorted. "I think we lost that last night."

Markos lowered his head, and Celia moved closer and stroked along his jaw. They both gave a deep sigh, almost like a hum. Tingles danced on every part of her skin in contact with him.

She brought her other hand up to the other side of his head. The tingles intensified, multiplying in power. "Is this your magic I feel?"

He blew out a puff of air, and his tail swished. "You feel it too?"

"Mmm. Yes." Her hands moved up his head, skating over the short, soft hair.

He stretched his neck lower so she could reach him. Under his neck, along the top of his muzzle, up to the base of the golden horn. Her fingers curved around his horn, barely able to encircle its diameter.

As though his legs gave out at her touch of his horn, he folded his legs under him and lay down. Even while he was flat on the ground, his back was level with her waist, but their heads were close to the same height now.

She continued her exploration, sliding her fingers up to his forelock. One bead from his dreadlocks remained, the blue bead. The same one she'd found in her bedroom so long ago.

The beaded lock rolled across her palm. "Is this one special?"

"It is a symbol of my birthright."

"Birthright?" No wonder it had been so important for him to get it back from her months ago.

"My mother was the noble ruler of our tribe. She had no female heir, so the bead fell to me."

"Noble? Like a queen?"

"Yes. I am not usually recognized as such—we are a matriarchal society—but I am technically a prince."

She sank her hands into his ridiculously long mane. The strands almost reached the ground, especially at the base of his neck. Their texture was a cross between silk and angora, sinfully luxurious.

"Mmm. I always knew you were special. I just didn't know *how* special."

She understood now. This explained so much. His dismissal of her father's racist comments. His Christmas gift to her. His ability to heal her. His fear of his attraction to her. Even the design of the flowing mane on the side of his car.

She ran her palms along his neck, and they both sighed in unison again. Whatever magic connected them was strong and intoxicatingly pleasurable.

It wasn't sexual. Not quite. However, the pleasure she felt—and apparently he felt it too—when she touched him was oddly similar.

When her hands got to his back, his thick voice revealed that he'd had the same thought she had. "Climb on. I want to feel more of your skin on mine."

Without needing further invitation, she hiked his shirt up to her waist, exposing her bare bottom, and awkwardly hoisted one leg over his broad back. As soon as her private parts touched him, they both moaned aloud. Tingles spread through her body, up from her core and down her legs, where she was spread-eagled on top of him. His ultra-soft hair prickled all over the sensitive skin.

At the same time she started lifting his shirt over her head, he grunted and added his agreement. "The shirt. Now. I have to feel all of you."

She tossed the shirt behind her and wrapped her arms around his neck. His scent was the same, but a touch of wildness flavored the sunshine aroma. The long silky hair of his mane buried her naked breasts and face.

As her bare skin made full contact, the tingles exploded and spread delicious heat through her body. They both shuddered, unable to contain the pleasurable sensations.

The motion of his body under hers—his skin contracting, nearly vibrating—set her nerve endings ablaze. She rocked against him, rubbing all her sensitive parts on the soft prickles and silken strands of his hair. Added together with the tingles of the magic and the heat of their contact, the passion growing inside made her lose any concern for whether she should be embarrassed by her behavior.

He quivered under her in rhythm with her quickening movements. Almost there. The peak was within reach, the physical sensations quickly building. The magic flowing between them had already pushed her body to level eleven.

The dam broke and pleasure shot through her limbs from her core. She rode it for all she could, holding tightly onto Markos. All her nerve endings felt alive, plugged into the magic of the universe. His drawn-out grunt harmonized with her moan, as they shared every sensation. They were one.

After a moment, her heartbeat and breathing slowed. She didn't know what the heck had just happened, but she couldn't be bothered to feel weirded out about it. Whatever magic connected them was more important to this experience than the physical sensations. Those had just pushed her over the edge.

No wonder unicorn mythology was popular. If there was such a thing as a collective unconscious across humanity, the magic created an instinctive attraction to unicorns that hinted at this experience. This sex without the sex.

So much for whatever he'd apologized for and seemed so upset about. Sure, others probably wouldn't have been as accepting, so she could understand his fear. But she could handle the fact that the man she loved wasn't a man at all. No problem. Especially since the truth came with some interesting side effects.

Markos got his voice back first, still husky and winded, but something about his tone indicated seriousness. "I am yours."

She stroked the underside of his neck. "And I am yours."

Chapter Thirty

FTER THE EMOTIONAL MOMENT PASSED, CELIA FELT EVERY inch of her nakedness and slid off Markos's back. Sure, they were at the back of his tree-shielded backyard and concealed by the dark, but she still felt a bit too exposed. She grabbed his shirt from the tree branch that had snagged it mid-toss and slipped it over her head.

Sometime during their not-sex joining, Molly had taken off. She couldn't blame the dog. Their behavior hadn't been anywhere close to normal.

Fog gathered around Markos again, condensing from the clear night air. The cloud covered him and pulled tighter, thickening into a smaller shape. Although *small* was relative.

The mist dissipated and revealed Markos, once again in his normal oversized human form and leather clothes. He rolled onto his back, arms outstretched and looking utterly spent.

His voice still sounded shaky. "I don't know what—I didn't know that was even possible."

She knelt beside him and rested her hand on his chest. "That's some powerful magic."

"More powerful than anything I've ever felt before. More powerful than the magic I used the night you were born." He stared at the night sky overhead, seeming too shocked to meet her gaze.

That was the second time he'd mentioned being around right after she was born. And while it was odd to think that he'd lived through the same passage of time as her whole life, even odder was the concept that her birth might have been special in some way.

"Why me? I mean, I'm guessing you don't feel this connection to every virgin in the world."

"Only you. I'm aware of only one virgin in each generation."

"But why *me*? It's not like I was born to a special family or anything."

"Every twenty-one years, the magic chooses one Virgin, a girl born at the exact moment of the Spring Equinox. At midnight, the magic leads me to the chosen Virgin of that generation. You are the twenty-first Virgin I have watched over."

"How close were you to the others?"

"Not at all." Under her palm, his ribs shifted with his shrug. "I couldn't even tell you their names."

"So for twenty years, you keep them safe, and when they turn twenty-one, a new one is chosen?"

He finally met her gaze, and his body trembled. "Yes."

Maybe this was why he didn't believe they had a future. That when she turned twenty-one, he'd be pulled to the next chosen virgin who-knew-where on the planet.

They could work around that though. He could still do his disappearing act to travel wherever he wanted, and depending on where he ended up, she might even be able to do her graduate school nearby. Their future didn't have to be set in stone.

If they wanted to be together, they would find a way. Unless...

Could something in the magic prevent him from being close to her once her time was passed?

"What happens to the chosen virgin when they turn twenty-one?"

He closed his eyes and shuddered. "They're brought to my homeland, where their magic helps my tribe. If not for the ritual that gathers and shares the magic of the Virgin at the Spring Equinox ceremony, all unicorns would die."

Something about his explanation didn't add up. "How could you watch over twenty other Virgins—who went and helped your tribe—and *not* know their names?"

His eyes opened, sad and pleading. "They all died at their ritual."

Icy cold encased her chest, and then a burst of adrenaline flooded her veins, her fight-or-flight instincts kicking in. "What?" Her voice came out as croak, and she pressed her fingers against her breastbone, but nothing could help her swallow.

The significance of the circumstances of the ritual, what he hadn't specified, trickled into her thoughts. Her adrenaline turned into anger. She scampered backward until she stood several feet away.

"You mean they were all frickin' *virgin sacrifices*?" Her voice rose to a near-shriek. "*That's* my purpose in life? *That's* why you've kept me safe? *That's* why you've kept me a virgin? You said I had a future. That I would save a race from extinction."

Another thought occurred to her. So horrible, so devastating, that she didn't want to believe it, but her gut suspected it was true. Her blood pounded in her ears, her muscles ready to beat the out crap of someone. Maybe him.

"It's all your fault, isn't it? My life and the way people treat me." She paced, almost stomping as her legs shook hard. "You said you did magic on me the night I was born. That magic makes people ignore me, dismiss me, forget I exist, doesn't it?" She didn't wait for his answer. "Of course. Because if guys noticed me, I might not stay a virgin for your precious little ritual. And heaven forbid I be allowed to live my normal life and interrupt this system you have."

Bile rose up her throat, and she stood over him. He'd covered his face with his hands, so she couldn't even see his reaction. But he wasn't denying her guess.

She kicked him, and she wasn't gentle about it. "So you're responsible for screwing up my life. Do you even realize how awful most of my life has been?"

His voice, anguished and shaky, finally emerged from behind his hands. "I'm sorry."

"*I'm sorry?* Over twenty years of emotional neglect from virtually everyone, and all you can say is 'I'm sorry'? Well, *I'm* sorry, but that doesn't cut it. You *owe* me." When he lowered his hands and gave her a questioning look, she jabbed a finger down at him. "You're going to tell me every detail about this ritual of yours and help me put a stop to it. I *won't* be a sacrifice."

He nodded, clearly content to go along with her plan. "There are large knives in the kitchen. Aim for the heart to prevent healing." He pushed himself to his feet, squarely caught her gaze, and spread his arms wide. "Kill me, and there will be no ritual."

Her limbs dropped, and her muscles lost their angry strength. A whisper was all she could manage. "You." The bigger picture of his life came into focus. His job was about more than just *watching* over her. "You killed all the others."

"Yes." Her statement hadn't been a question, but he'd answered it anyway, acting eager to earn her hatred.

She bent over and wrapped her arms around her waist, her insides threatening to retch. Even though the very thought disgusted her on a primal level, she had to put words to the horror.

"You killed twenty young women, after making their entire life a living hell, all so that your kind could survive."

Her heart thrashed against her ribs, aching with sympathy for all those other lives. She hadn't known him at all. Hadn't known the first thing about him.

He was worse than a beast. He was a monster.

"Screw you." A roar built in her head, filling her ears, and she lunged at him and pounded his chest. "The lives of your kind are *not* more important than all those women. Not more important than mine. Why should I die just so you can do this to another girl? That's not the life of an innocent I want to help. That's the life of a predator."

Her hands grew sore with her pounding—and of course her weak blows did nothing to him—but she didn't stop. Couldn't stop.

"I hate you. I hate you." She slid to the ground, her limbs weighed down by the emotions burying her. Drowning her. "I. Hate. You."

Shudders wracked her body, pulling her muscles into painful contortions, and sourness rose from her throat. Loud breaths heaved in and out of her lungs, but nothing would quench the black hole eating her heart. Her chest was an empty cavern, void of every sensation but nausea and heartache.

Pure Sacrifice

Her whole life had been a lie. She was never going to make an incredible scientific discovery. She was never going to help people. She was special only for the circumstances of her birth. Her only value was to die.

Her life had been as meaningless as Auntie's death.

And she would have even less to show for it.

Chapter Thirty-One

MARKOS WANTED TO HOLD CELIA, EASE HER PAIN. BUT HE was the last person she wanted near her now. Or ever again.

All he could do was watch her curl over her knees on the lawn and pour her anguish over his betrayal into her tears. He'd broken her, just as he feared he would. Knew he would.

She *hated* him.

He hadn't realized how ugly the English language could sound until he'd heard those words from her mouth. Yet they were all true, and he deserved every one of them.

If he could fix this by carving out his insides and presenting them to her, he would.

He headed back to the house. He could think of only one thing that would make up for everything that he'd done to her, done to the rest of the Virgins. His stomach churned, recognition of her accusations about the others burning hot and true.

His whole life, he'd pulled away from others out of fear. His fear of being shunned for his mistakes had kept him distant from his tribe. His fear of Celia's grief after Christmas had kept him from helping her through the pain. His fear of experiencing guilt when yet another Virgin died due to his failures had kept him so distant from them that he hadn't seen them as individuals to respect.

Celia had changed everything, opened his eyes to the truth. Their lives mattered, and their deaths *should* cause heartache.

The recognition of how much his tribe had stolen from the Virgins had only grown in the months since her revelation at Thanksgiving. Even before all the deaths during his Guardianship, they'd taken away the Virgins' lives on the Earthen plane to fulfill their needs.

How was that different from slavery? His tribe didn't deserve to survive at all.

Inside his kitchen, he selected the biggest chef knife in the wood block. Molly entered the room and cocked her head at him.

"I have to do something to fix this. Besides, I promised her brother and father that I would protect her—and her heart—for as long as she resided on Earth. I've lost count of how many times I've broken that promise in the past twenty-four hours."

Molly whimpered and nudged his leg.

"I know." He scratched her ears. "But she deserves to live, and I deserve to die."

Even faster than he thought it would happen, the blade shook out of his grasp as soon as the *idea* of aiming the tip at his heart formed in his mind. The magic prevented a Guardian from killing himself, ensuring he would always fulfill his oh-so-important duty. He needed help.

He eyed the black and white animal that seemed so much more than a mere dog. "I don't suppose you could hold a knife for me?"

Molly backed away and lowered her head. Thought not.

She followed him back out to Celia's spot in the yard. She still sat on the grass, hugging her knees, her head buried between them. Molly snuggled against her, doing what he couldn't.

Celia's crying had quieted. He couldn't imagine how emotionally drained she must feel. Had it been only last night that he'd brought her home from Harriet's house? That was too many emotional hits for anyone.

He sat next to her but didn't attempt to touch her, even though the urge to comfort her twitched through his nerves. "You're right about everything. I deserve your hatred." He scooted closer. "Yet no matter how strong your hatred, you couldn't hate me more than I hate myself. I hate that I didn't recognize it before. That I allowed myself to believe I was doing a service for my tribe. That I didn't see the part I played in our exploitation of the Virgins."

Before she could respond or run away, he grabbed her right wrist. Her head jerked up, and she yanked her arm back, but her strength was no match for his. He uncurled her fingers and placed the knife handle in her palm, and then he wrapped his hand around hers, forcing her to grasp the weapon. With one hand still on hers, he lay down on her side and tugged her wrist to aim the knife tip over his heart.

"Kill me."

Her eyes widened, and her jaw dropped open. "What?"

"I want you to kill me. I want to die. I deserve to die. And when I die, you'll be free. I'm the last of the unicorn Guardians. Only the Guardians can shift into human form on the Earthen plane, so the others can't come here anymore without attracting attention. Only the Guardians can collect the Virgin's magic for the tribe. Only the Guardians can track the Virgin."

He tipped his chin toward the knife. "Kill me, and my whole tribe will die. You and every Virgin after you will be safe from my kind forever."

She recoiled and shook her head, her lip curling. "What if I don't want to be a mass murderer? What if I don't want to become like you?"

His hand dropped off from holding hers over his chest. Mule's piss. He hadn't even thought of that issue. Had he become so emotionless, so heartless, so distanced from others that he couldn't think in terms of right and wrong anymore?

"I'm sorry, I just want you to be safe. You were angry, and I thought you might want this opportunity for revenge."

"I don't understand. If you don't *want* to kill me, then why not just *not* kill me? It's not like there's a crazy axe murderer chasing me. *You're* the one responsible for killing the others, so just don't do it. Shouldn't I be safe already?"

He waved toward the patch of grass where his life had changed so dramatically that he didn't yet understand all the implications. "You've experienced this magic. It's powerful. It creates compulsions. If I still live, it will compel me to bring you to my homeland on the Spring Equinox. And then..."

He had to explain his failures, let her know just how unworthy he was.

"I have never *tried* to kill a Virgin. During the ceremony, our high priestess, Alkipsia, invites the Virgin to embrace me while I'm in unicorn form to show that she wants to become part of our tribe. The magic of the ritual compels me to my knees. And every time, the Virgin impales herself on my horn rather than joining us."

The skin around Celia's eyes tightened. "How is that your fault?"

"Because I'm not virtuous enough, I'm not pure enough. They'd rather die than accept my offer, and I don't blame them. My tribe has only *taken* from the Virgins. Even in their death, we still take from them, gathering enough magic from their spilled blood to survive another generation. I'm ashamed of what we've become, and I'm ashamed of my role in it. I wish I could blame my failures on someone or something else. But I can't."

His fingers dug between the blades of grass and sought the touch of the earth. The reassurance from the connection wasn't enough, but he wouldn't call Molly from her side. Celia needed comforting more than he did.

"When I was five, the tribe was weak because several generations of Virgins in a row had refused the invitation and returned to the Earthen plane. Then Alkipsia revealed how the ritual could prevent the Virgins from escaping, that their choice would be to join or die. She argued that the Maker wanted us to change, that we should salvage at least some magic from them. More were losing their ability to shift every day, and many were desperate enough to go along with her plan over my mother's calls for patience—especially because no one believed any Virgin would choose death. The tribe was thrown into chaos and war over the debate."

He shuddered at the memories of how many had been lost in the war. His mother, father, siblings, cousins, aunts, uncles. The deaths had decimated the already weakened tribe. And as a male child, he'd been as impotent as a gelding to call for a halt to the bloodshed.

"By the time the dust settled three years later, most of the warriors had died in battle, and Alkipsia had claimed the council's throne as high priestess. As the only surviving member of the royal family, I was the last threat to her rule—the last one the holdouts rallied around. I had to swear allegiance to her, or she'd hunt down the rebels. Although I didn't agree with her, her methods, or her decisions, I cooperated for the good of the tribe. I couldn't be responsible for any more deaths."

He pulled his fingers from the dirt, where he'd ripped clumps of sod from the ground during the telling of his tale. He rubbed his fingers on his palm and brushed the granules off his hands.

"I was kept under house arrest so I wouldn't accidentally reignite the fighting. When I was twenty-eight, something re-triggered the hostilities. I don't even know what, as anyone who spoke about it disappeared. Alkipsia summoned me to the council chamber and told me that the last official Guardian had died, but that my royal bloodline would be pure enough to perform the magic necessary for our survival. I didn't care about her promise to release me from house arrest if I agreed, but she convinced me with the explanation of how I was the only one who could save the tribe from extinction."

Hipdemos had been a council attendant at the time, in charge of Markos's house arrest. Ever since he'd witnessed the agreement, the male had been the closest thing Markos had to a loyal friend.

Celia spoke for the first time since he'd begun sharing his past. "You agreed because you wanted to undo the damage of the war that cost you your family."

"Yes, I'd felt like a burden to the tribe—the cause of so much bloodshed—that I longed to do something to make me worthy of those who'd fought for me, to prevent their deaths from being meaningless. But it didn't work. My failures to convince a Virgin to join us have meant that our magic *still* isn't fully healed. And worse, instead of fixing things, I brought the damage here. I can't express how sorry I am for that. In the years since my agreement, I've done horrible things to you and those other Virgins. And all their families.

"I thought I was doing the right thing for my tribe, but that doesn't excuse my actions. I wish I could take a lot of things back. Instead, all I can do is think of the future. Our oldest historian doesn't know how soon we'd die if you lost your virginity. If my tribe didn't die immediately, another Virgin would be born next month, and I would be called to her." He nodded down to the knife she still gripped in her hand. "That's why I asked you to kill me. The magic makes it impossible for me—a Guardian—to kill myself. But if you kill me, you can go and live your life the way you deserve."

A grimace crossed her face. A second later, she scrambled to her feet and tossed the knife aside. By the time he sat up and exchanged a glance with Molly, Celia had almost made it to the house. A moment after that, a glow shone through the curtains of her bedroom.

He sighed and pushed himself to his feet. Now what? Molly trotted off and barked when she found the knife. He picked up the blade and trudged toward the house, his faithful companion at his heels.

He'd failed Celia again. He never should have asked her to ruin her purity and goodness by becoming a murderer.

He left the knife in the sink and headed upstairs. The sound of gasps, quite probably accompanying tears, carried though her bedroom door, but he didn't dare disturb her. How could he fix this if she didn't want anything to do with him?

Maybe he should find that semi-truck he wanted from last night.

At the thought, he stumbled, his mind and body rebelling at the idea. He caught himself on the frame of the door to his room and shook his head. Was *everything* turning against him now?

In his bathroom, her clothes were still draped over the shower enclosure to dry off. In the past few hours, she'd brought him to ecstasy by her hands twice, and now she wasn't even talking to him. He'd almost feel sorry for himself except that he knew Celia's situation was so much worse.

He washed the rest of the dirt off his hands at the sink. His reflection in the mirror drew his eye.

What the piss was *that*? He leaned toward the mirror and yanked open his shirt. A black design in his skin wove along the front of his neck. He twisted and lifted his dreadlocks. The tattoo-like stripe continued around the back.

The three braided lines formed a virtual rope around his neck. A collar.

His mind flashed back to their magical joining on the lawn. He'd never before felt so close to her, so connected to her, so much a part of her. They'd become one entity, just like on the gold and silver lid.

Somehow, through the magic, she'd *claimed* him. The Virgin had claimed the unicorn for her own.

The urge he'd had to promise her, "I am yours," now made sense. She owned him. She owned his life. He *couldn't* kill himself.

Did this magic mean she would accept the invitation at the ritual? Possibly. But he didn't want to trust it—the risk was too great. And he couldn't take a chance on visiting Archimedes again to ask, given his narrow escape last time.

Maybe he could explore the limits of his magic here though. See what he could change. Attempt to undo some of the damage.

He stroked down his neck and stood straight and tall. His lungs expanded, filling to capacity, and he lifted his chin. He was *hers*.

His weight rolled to the balls of his feet, and his heels rose off the tile. A small smile curved the tips of his lips. He was *hers*.

The idea triggered unfamiliar emotions, like serenity and hope. His muscles relaxed, and his breathing settled as his smile grew broader. He was *hers*.

Trying to kill himself was the coward's way out. He belonged to the most amazing female, from either plane. His duty now was to fix things for her. Somehow.

Chapter Thirty-Two

A KNOCK SOUNDED ON CELIA'S DOOR. WAS THAT THE lunchtime knock or the dinnertime knock? She couldn't remember anymore, her days and nights of secluding herself in this bedroom at Markos's house running together in a blur of uncertainty.

The housekeeper entered, as she'd probably learned Celia had no intention of answering the door. "Good morning, Miss Hawkins."

Oh, breakfast time. She'd forgotten about that one.

The older woman set the tray of food on the side table, right where Celia could see it from her pillow. "I see you're still in bed. Mr. Ambrose says I'm to be nothing but kind to you, but I think you need a bit of a kick in the pants. Today of all days, you need to be getting showered and dressed." She yanked the curtains open, sending bright morning light streaking across the bedspread, and then gasped. "Would you look at yourself? You've been wearing that same shirt for days—at least four days that I know of—"

Huh. So that's how long it'd been.

"—and that means you haven't taken a shower during that whole time either. Mr. Ambrose bought you a whole wardrobe of beautiful new clothes to wear. Even if you insist on skipping the service today, there's no reason to lay there like a slugabug, unshowered and in a dirty shirt. So why are you still wearing it?"

Why *was* she still wearing Markos's shirt? Sure, at first she'd had the excuse that she didn't have any other clothes. After all, that little problem had held her back from leaving this place however many nights ago when she'd learned the truth. She might have wanted to run away, but she wasn't stupid. Striking out on her own with no money, no place to live, and no clothes was too many *no* issues for her practical side to overcome.

But Markos had sent a personal shopper to her room a couple of days ago with enough designer-label clothes to last a month. So what was her excuse now?

She hadn't even let Molly into the room because she didn't want the reminder of Markos, so why had she kept—and worn— one of the biggest reminders of all?

The housekeeper rummaged through the closet and laid out clothes on the foot of the bed. Celia didn't look too closely, but they seemed too dark to be her style. She leaned toward the tray and picked at the food. Her gaze once more landed on the clothes at the foot of the bed. In fact, they were black. All black.

Oh God. The housekeeper had mentioned "the service." Today was Auntie's funeral.

She sat up in bed. "How long do I have?"

A smug smile peeked through the woman's brusque exterior. "Long enough. Especially if I help you with your hair." She snapped her fingers in a hurry-up gesture. "Eat up. I'll give you two minutes while the shower heats up."

Celia shoveled a few forkfuls of eggs into her mouth and attacked the bowl of grapes and clementine slices.

The housekeeper nodded approvingly at the sight when she reemerged from the bathroom. "I'll check on you in twenty minutes. No dawdling."

Celia stopped the woman before she left, one thought nagging at her. "If today's the funeral, that means I missed all the visitations."

A sad expression crossed her face. "Yes, dear, you did. So make sure you don't miss today."

At that, the woman left her alone. Celia munched on sourdough toast and checked the water temperature. How could she have been so wrapped up in her own problems that she'd withdrawn from life itself?

When the water was warm enough, she stepped under the spray. Along with the lather of the high-end shampoo and body wash, the shroud of her fatalism and anger washed down the drain. The body left behind was not only clean, but also determined to face the problem.

Okay, she didn't want to be responsible for the genocide of a whole race. That was a given. But she had no intention of becoming the next sacrifice either.

Somewhere in her scientific brain, there had to be an answer.

The housekeeper—Martha, she finally figured out—stuck to her word and dried and curled her hair in record time. Martha also continued her earlier chastising while helping her get dressed. "I'm very sorry for your loss, but we have to go on living. I'm sure Mrs. Williams would want that for you."

Martha's well-meaning words plucked at the self-pity Celia was barely keeping under control. "That's the problem. On Saturday, I learned that I might have only a month to live."

The woman stopped in the middle of zipping up the back of Celia's tailored dress. "I'm so sorry. I didn't know. Mr. Ambrose didn't mention that to me. I apologize if I was too harsh, Miss Hawkins."

Of course he wouldn't mention it. He hadn't even told Martha his real name, as she always called him Mr. Ambrose instead of Mr. Ambrostead.

"No, you were right. I *did* need a kick in the pants. I've decided to fight that fate in every way I can."

"I admire that attitude." Martha finished with the zipper and helped Celia slip into the matching jacket. "I'd like to say some prayers for you tonight, if you wouldn't mind."

Celia's eyes stung and filled with tears. "Thank you. That's the sort of thing Auntie—Mrs. Williams—would do for me."

Impulsively, she gave the woman a hug.

Martha returned the embrace. "Okay, get going. Mr. Ambrose is waiting for you downstairs."

Celia's chest tightened, and she hesitated. She hadn't thought about how she'd be getting to the funeral, but logically, he was her ride. Was she ready to face him again?

Her thoughts were still too tangled to know how she felt about his involvement with the past sacrifices, but she inhaled deeply, shoving the tension inside her ribs away, and headed out the door. Whether she was ready or not, she had to go through with this. Missing the funeral wasn't an option.

Molly nearly tackled her as she entered the hallway. Celia bent down and gave her a pet. "I know. I'm sorry. I'm feeling better now."

At least until she got downstairs.

Markos stood in the kitchen, and her heart—her silly heart that hadn't gotten the memo that everything had changed—gave a leap at seeing him after so long an absence. He didn't turn from the window to look at her, but in profile, she could see that he'd dressed up, leaving his sunglasses behind and wearing a collared black silk shirt under his leather jacket.

"The weather isn't cooperating today. I'll get your coat." And with that, he left the room.

Oh-kay. Apparently, he was even more nervous about facing her than she was about him. In a way, his uncertainty gave her more confidence.

A moment later, he returned with a beautiful, full-length black wool dress coat edged in faux fur and laid it on the counter in front of her. Between her tangled emotions and her smidgen of courage, she had the urge to tease.

"Tut tut. What would Auntie say?"

He still didn't face her, but the tip of his lips she could see in profile twitched up. "Quite right. My mistake."

He slipped the long coat over her outfit, arranged the cashmere scarf around her neck, and handed her black leather dress gloves. She almost protested how all that was overkill, but then a dark cloud dimmed the light in the kitchen, stealing from the previously sunny day.

Snow flurries started during their drive to Auntie's church, and the slick walkway into the building didn't play nice with her no-traction-whatsoever dress shoes. Misogynists must design the things. Her foot slid out from under her, but before her arms could even wheel around to regain her balance, Markos's hand steadied her.

She got her balance again. "Thank you."

He removed his hand as soon as possible. Were they back to *that* rule? She really hadn't missed it. But inside the vestibule, he helped her shrug off her coat without being prompted, so maybe the no-touching thing wasn't as serious as before.

She saw Auntie's son and his family by the entrance, and she grabbed Markos's hand to lead him over to them. He didn't flinch then either, another good sign.

Dr. Williams's eyes lit in recognition as she approached, which struck her as odd for some reason she couldn't put her finger on.

She gave him a hug. "I'm so sorry for your loss."

"Celia, I'm so glad you were able to make it. I was tempted to delay the funeral when Markos told me you were bedridden. You're feeling better, I hope?"

"Yes, thank you. I'm sorry I missed the visitation at the funeral home." She gave hugs to the rest of his family too, his wife and their kids.

"We understand. It's been a rough few days. Everyone asked about you, so they'll be happy to see you up and feeling better."

She swung back to Dr. Williams. "Everyone asked about *me*?"

"Yes, all of Mom's friends and neighbors."

What? Since when did anyone remember she existed?

Dr. Williams held her hands. "They told me about everything you'd done to take care of her, the errands, the grocery shopping, last Thanksgiving when I couldn't come for a visit." He squeezed her hands. "My mom couldn't have asked for a better friend this last year and a half. Thank you."

"Uh, you're welcome." She pulled from Dr. Williams's grasp. "I still wish things had ended differently."

"No, the coroner said she had several massive strokes, and one was instantly fatal. The fire didn't kill her. The firefighters found her lying peacefully in her bed. And maybe that was kinder than what she was facing."

She peered at Markos. "She'd said she had a headache that night, right?"

"Yes, and she was limping and seemed to struggle for words." He glanced at Celia out of the corner of his eye. "This was before you came down, so you never knew."

Celia gave his arm a squeeze—which still didn't elicit a cringe—and then turned to Dr. Williams. "Did they figure out what caused the fire?"

"That old gas stove of hers. They think she turned on the oven instead of the burner. Then the old wiring of the house sparked the cloud of gas. I'm just glad neither of you were there to be caught in the explosion."

She released her guilt the best she could. "Thank you, Dr. Williams."

"Please, call me Roger. We're practically family."

She managed a smile. "Thank you, Roger."

Roger's wife waved at someone behind them, and he leaned toward Celia and Markos. "I need to meet up with these people, but you two take care of each other."

Markos clapped Roger on the shoulder before he walked away. "I intend to."

As soon as Celia entered the church, Auntie's friends and neighbors surrounded her with hugs and condolences. The attention made her shudder. No longer did her pale skin go unnoticed among the crowd. Rather, she overheard several references to "that nice white girl."

She escaped to the pew the usher indicated as soon as possible and bowed her head so they'd leave her alone. She'd lived her whole life as an outsider, but never as an outsider that others paid attention to. Markos wordlessly took a seat next to her.

His presence was oddly comforting and distracting at the same time. His scent—which had been her solace through the nightmares—enveloped her in peacefulness now. Throughout the service, she found herself wanting to hold his hand several times. And earlier, she'd wanted to test his reaction to her touch.

Why? What insight was that urge providing into the emotions tangled in her head?

During the last few days, she'd had plenty of time to review the facts. How his tragic childhood had not only led to his lack of family and friends, but also given him understandable motivations for his decisions. How his self-destructive behaviors gave proof to his deep and complete remorse for the role he'd played. How she wasn't convinced he should be blamed for the other Virgins' deaths anyway.

Despite all the magic inherent in the situation, she couldn't help applying her scientific mind to the facts, and no logic could explain why twenty women would all decide they'd rather *die* than live with unicorns. Unicorns! Even if some of them over the centuries had freaked out and thought they were possessed by demons or going to hell, that didn't explain all of them.

No, something else—something Markos was likely unaware of— had caused their deaths. His horn was just the tool.

Not that he was completely innocent. He *was* guilty of going along with his society's expectations—casting the spell that warped the Virgins' lives and participating in the ritual. Yet she couldn't find enough anger to hold that against him either.

He'd been manipulated, his desire to heal his tribe used against him in a no-win situation. She, of all people, understood the importance of feeling helpful to society.

Back when she'd thought she'd save lives with her discoveries, that empowerment had been the best feeling in the world. So when the ruler of his people—tribe, whatever they called themselves— offered him the chance to do something helpful, he'd understandably been eager for the opportunity.

He'd then spent the next four-hundred-some years trying to prove that those who'd died in his family's defense hadn't died in vain. That he could help the tribe, heal the damage. Over four-hundred years, and all he had to show for it was more guilt.

She felt sorry for him, for how he was being used and exploited just as much as the other Virgins had been. But what did that mean? What was she supposed to do with that feeling?

Chapter Thirty-Three

U P AT THE CHURCH PODIUM, THE MINISTER SPOKE ABOUT
Auntie going home to heaven, where she would be embraced by God's forgiveness. Forgiveness.

Celia's heartbeat sped up, the beginning of a solution coalescing in her mind. The details still eluded her, but one certainty stuck out among the vague thoughts—fixing the situation for herself *and* future Virgins *and* Markos's tribe required forgiveness.

She sat straighter and rolled her shoulders back. As the congregation lifted their voices in a stirring gospel tune, her whisper was low and steady. "I forgive him."

She let her hand do what it had wanted to do since he sat beside her. Her fingers wrapped around his.

He jerked at the contact. Not a flinch, more like surprise. He kept his gaze on the altar at the front of the church, but she'd swear his shoulders relaxed by several inches.

When Roger trudged up to give the final eulogy, she dropped her head and let her hair drape around her face. The tears started almost immediately, with his stories of his mother's struggle with single parenthood after the death of his father. Celia had known some of Auntie's history but not all of it. And she'd known her only after the Alzheimer's diagnosis, so she'd missed experiencing the woman's strength over the years.

One of her tears fell onto Markos's hand in her grasp. Without hesitation, he switched hands in hers and used his closer hand to tuck her under his arm. Snug against his side, she grieved.

She grieved for the loss of Auntie, the first person who had treated her like family. For the loss of her innocence about Markos's background. For the loss of the Virgins who had died for nothing.

She grieved for it all. But unlike the tears of the past few days, these tears were cleansing. The last recognition of things she couldn't change. From this moment on, she would move forward.

No one noticed the change in her heart. Certainly not when she was surrounded by shouts and exclamations by the congregation celebrating Auntie's life. But she knew.

When it was her turn to pay her respects to Auntie, she gathered the shreds of her strength and placed a goodbye kiss on the top of the closed coffin. She rubbed the glossy wood in an inadequate attempt to embrace the woman's spirit.

"Thank you for being the first person to see me as I am."

As she straightened, she covered her mouth with her hand. Just when she thought she was done with the tears, more threatened to follow. Markos drew her into his arms and gave her a kiss on her forehead before turning his attention to the coffin.

He rested one palm on the lid and spoke in a hoarse and emotional voice. "Thank you for everything you did for Celia."

He then led her back to the car for the funeral procession. The snow had picked up while they were inside. She hunkered down in her coat and stumbled through the cemetery portion of the service. Her determination to remain strong faded as the day wore on, and the gray sky stole her energy.

Back at the church parking lot, Markos opened her door, ready to escort her to the church basement for the post-ceremony meal. She sighed, more from exhaustion than feeling whiny.

"Do we have to go?"

He squeezed her shoulder. "You don't have to do anything you don't want to do. However, I need to drop off some things with Roger that I salvaged from the house for him. You could come with me and say your goodbyes to the family."

She nodded and stood from the car. He grabbed something from the trunk and then guided her across the increasingly slippery pavement. Once they safely reached the church basement, she looked up from plotting each careful step and noticed what he held in his other hand. Auntie's quilt, the last one she'd made. The last one she'd ever make.

"Her quilt survived." A weak smile crossed her face. "That almost makes me feel better."

At Roger's table in the cramped basement, Markos set the quilt on the tabletop and pulled out a small jewelry box from an inner pocket of his jacket. "I had a restoration company remove the smoke from the quilt, and a jeweler cleaned the ring and checked it for damage."

Roger opened the box and checked the ring inside. "Thank you, Markos. You didn't have to do that." He waved to Celia. "Sit down. You look tired."

"I am tired," she admitted, "so we're not able to stay. I just wanted to say goodbye before we left."

"Of course." He snapped the box closed and pocketed it. "I'm glad you came by so I could give this to you personally." He slid the quilt toward her.

"Me? But this is the last one she made." She stroked one of the seams where Auntie had carefully joined the fabric squares. "You don't want it?"

"I have plenty." He gave her a wry grin. "She gave me one for Christmas—for each of the past five years. And if the one she gave you last year burned in the fire, I'm certain she'd want you to have this."

A lump formed in her throat. She hadn't let her brain do the mental inventory of everything she'd lost yet. Her mind had enough other losses to deal with.

She hugged the quilt to her chest. "Thank you."

Markos shook Roger's hand. "Thank you. I know how much this means to her."

As Markos pivoted toward her to help navigate through the crowd, she saw thick black lines scrawled across the sliver of his neck exposed by his collared shirt. "You got a tattoo?"

When had he had time for that?

He sighed so deeply she heard it over the clamor around them. "No."

"Then what is it?"

He didn't answer. At the top of the stairs, she towed him into the now-empty church and opened his collar. Three woven black lines encircled his neck.

"Markos, this didn't used to be there. If it's not a tattoo, where did it come from?"

"Magic." For the first time all day, he met her eyes. "The other day, you *rode* me." His choice of the word *rode* implied all the subtextual meanings of the experience. "And when a Virgin gains a unicorn's trust enough to approach and ride him, he is captured. You own me now. I am yours."

Her jaw slackened, and she shuddered. "Oh no. I'm so sorry. I didn't know."

The magic had treated him like a *pet* rather than a person.

He draped the quilt over a pew and took her hands in his large ones, stroking his thumbs over her knuckles. "No, don't be sorry. Please don't be sorry. Belonging to you is the best thing that's ever happened to me. I am honored to be yours."

"Oh, Markos." Dryness in her mouth kept her from saying anything more, which was probably a good thing because she didn't know how she felt about this development.

She brought his fingers to her lips. "The magic has messed with both of us, hasn't it?"

He squeezed her hands. "But I figured out how to remove my spell over you. You saw today. You're not invisible anymore."

Yes, she'd noticed. And gotten freaked out by the attention.

"So that's not just a change for today, or for this place?"

"No, I broke the magic—for that aspect anyway. Others will treat you normally from now on." His head dipped, and he swallowed. "This means you can live the life you want. Forget all about me and my tribe."

"*What?*" Her question reverberated through the empty church, and she silently made apologies to God. Despite her focus on science, nothing could erase the comfortable traditions of her religious upbringing.

She tugged her hands from his. He *wanted* her to condemn his tribe?

He'd repeatedly put her needs above his own, and she loved

him for it. Really and truly loved him. As in, she-couldn't-imagine-ever-being-with-someone-else loved him.

She looked into those amazing eyes and stroked his cheek. "The life I want is with you."

Conflicting emotions flickered across his face. Love, concern, fear, denial, and then back to love.

He shook his head. "No, I want you to be safe. You have to leave me. Let me die."

The fuzzy ideas that had been swirling in her mind since Auntie's homegoing ceremony snapped into focus. She'd *already* accepted Markos. Hell, he had the not-tattoo to prove it. So out of all of the Virgins, she shouldn't die at the ritual—especially now that she'd forgiven him.

She *did* have the opportunity to save his race, but not through her death. If the mythology of his tribe was right, she could be the one who would live and fully heal their magic. Not that she felt in any way magical.

But even if they were wrong and she had no magic inside her, she could still help his tribe after surviving the ritual. Maybe there was a compound in her blood that reacted with something in his world. Or maybe there was something in their genetics, their food, water, or air. Solve that, and they wouldn't need a ritual that needlessly risked women's lives.

She wouldn't make the positive difference in human lives as she'd planned, but she could help his kind instead. The chance to save a race from extinction was something worth doing, even if they weren't human.

He might want her to leave him and let him die, but she didn't have to go along with his plan. She took control of her destiny with one word.

"No."

Chapter Thirty-Four

MARKOS'S HEARTBEAT RACED SO FAST HE FELT DIZZY, AND his limbs shook with weakness. He must have heard her wrong. Or must have misunderstood her. She couldn't possibly mean that she was going to risk death.

She held his jaw between her palms. "If I went along with your plan, I'd be responsible for the death of a whole race. I could never enjoy my life with that on my conscience. I'm going to stay a virgin and go through the ritual. I believe I'm going to survive, and that I can help your tribe."

His heartbeat went from speeding to slogging. Awkward and heavy. Time itself seemed to slow, every blink of her eyelashes cajoling him to catch up. His brain struggled to make sense of her plans—and then quickly regretted figuring out the truth.

She *wanted* to risk her life.

Pain burst through his chest. He couldn't let her die.

Skoro! No, it was worse than that. Fulfilling her wish would mean he'd be *responsible* for her death. He'd have to watch the brilliant sparkle of her personality fade from her eyes. He'd have to feel her blood flowing down his forehead. He'd have to know that his life—and the lives of his whole tribe—came at the cost of hers.

His stomach twisted in one direction while his heart twisted in another. His breathing quickened to desperate gulps. He sent the

world's loudest silent prayer to the Maker that Celia wouldn't realize she could now order him to do this and force him to obey.

He drew her against his chest. "Come home with me." His voice
was rough. "I want to show you something before you make this
decision."

Her head slid along his shirt with her nod. He gathered the
quilt, scooped her into his arms, and carried both to the car. She
said something about him being gentlemanly and saving her from
walking over the slippery ground again, but really he wanted—
needed—to feel that he could keep her safe in his arms.

Back at the house, he let her walk only after she demanded that
he put her down. He kept his arms around her though, steering her
to his office, where his plans of these past few days had kept him
busy. Molly started to follow but stopped when he nearly growled
his frustration.

"Okay, I'm here." Celia huffed from the chair he'd aimed her
toward. "But unless you found a way to avoid your tribe's extinction without me, nothing you can say will change my mind."

He didn't let himself think about what her words meant, what
his chances were. He had to try. His hands shook as he spread the
papers across the table in front of her.

"What is this?" She picked up the first stack and sucked in a
breath. "Markos, this is the deed to this house, and it has *my* name
on it. Why?"

He didn't look at her. He couldn't take seeing whether or not
this was having an effect.

"The same reason this private gold mint in London has your
name on it." He pushed that pile toward her. "And why this estate
in Ireland has your name on it." He shoved another stack across
the table. "And why this title to the car, and these bank accounts,
and this manufacturing company all have your name on them."
With each item, he thrust another collection of papers at her, desperate to make her see, make her understand.

"I don't understand. Why are you doing this?"

"The question should be—why *didn't* I do this as soon as I realized I loved you? Why didn't I spoil you with clothes, a car, and a
place to live? Why didn't I do more to show you how much you
mean to me?" He paced to the far end of the office and back, his

limbs too full of nerves to remain still. "And my only excuse is that I've never experienced this before. I've never loved anyone. Not like this."

How could this day have gone from fear of her rejection, to his utter joy at her forgiveness, to now this—these threats against everything that mattered to him?

"Markos..." Her voice was quiet and calm. "I never expected you to do any of that. When I told you how crazy it was that you had all this money, that wasn't a complaint about you not sharing it with me."

"But I had no business asking you to kill me when I hadn't done the first thing to make sure you'd be taken care of after I was gone. So I fixed that." He waved to the scattered pages covering the table. "You're now worth about two billion dollars, depending on the gold market."

Her mouth parted, and the color left her face. "Two billion..." She shook her head. "Markos, that's insane. You can't do that."

"Yes, I can. And I did." He lunged toward her so fast she flinched, and he knelt, bringing him to her eye level while she sat in the chair. He grasped her biceps, barely restraining the urge to shake sense into her. "What's mine is yours. You are me and I am you, don't you see?"

He knew he wasn't making any sense, but he couldn't get past the panic to think clearly. He couldn't let her risk this. He just couldn't.

An expression he never wanted to see from her shaped her features. Pity.

"The magic made you do this, didn't it?" She stroked her fingertips lightly along his hairline. "I'm so sorry. I don't care if the magic says you're supposed to *belong* to me—that doesn't mean all your possessions should belong to me too."

His gut clenched like she'd punched him. "*Skoro*, no!" He pounded the arms of her chair and stood. "This isn't about the magic. This is about me and you and how much I love you." He pressed on his temples. "Don't let my failure to do all this earlier lead you to think that my motives aren't real. If you would have me, I'd marry you and add your name to everything the normal way, but I didn't think you'd agree to that—given your hatred of me—so I went this route." His wild gesture over the stacks of paper sent a few skittering in the breeze. "Don't ever think this isn't *real.*"

She tilted her head, slowly and deliberately. "Wait. Did you just propose to marry me?"

His heart thudded powerfully against his ribs. He'd gotten her attention. Maybe he could convince her after all.

He took a deep breath to silence his anxiety and knelt once more in front of her. He took her hands in his and let himself fall into her gaze.

"Celia Hawkins, I love you more than life itself. I'd protect you, give you anything you desired. I'd show you the wonders of the world on a—what's the word—a honeymoon fit for a queen. I'd prove my love a thousand times every day. Yes, I want to marry you. I'm already *yours* in every way possible, not due to magic, but to love, and my question for you is, will you be *mine*?"

As she met his gaze and didn't look away, weight fell from his shoulders and limbs, and the tension around his chest loosened. Floating from the back of his mind, the hope buried under his panic peeked forward and outshone his fears. Could she be *the one*? Could she survive the ritual?

Should he allow himself to *hope*?

A ticklish sensation fluttered in his stomach. And he let himself dream of spending days doing nothing but staring into her eyes. And even more days making sweet, passionate love to her. Bringing her to ecstasy over and over. He grew hard at the thought.

Maker above, please let her say yes.

THAT HAD TO BE THE MOST ROMANTIC PROPOSAL IN THE HISTORY OF mankind. The answer of *yes* sat on the tip of Celia's tongue and pounded on her lips, urging her to say the word. She just had to verify two things first.

Her gaze drifted over the tattoo-like marking on his neck. What power did it hold over him? Or what power did it mean *she* held over him?

"If you promised me something, would you honor that promise?"

He stiffened, and his nose flared. Obviously, her response wasn't what he'd hoped for.

"Yes." The word was clipped.

"Then I ask you to promise me two things. One, I want every Virgin from now on to be given her freedom. No more cutting her off from her family. No more using whatever spell was used on me. And two, when they're old enough, they'll be told about the opportunity they have to help your race. If they're not interested, don't bring them to your plane for the ritual. Don't expose them to that risk. Will you promise me both of those things?"

A deep sigh released the tension from his body. "Yes, I promise."

He almost seemed relieved compared to his earlier stress. Maybe her requested promises weren't as terrible as he feared.

"Thank you." She lifted their interlocked hands and stroked his jaw with her knuckle. The motion brought her left ring finger—the spot an engagement ring would fit—front and center. "I do want to marry you, but to do this—to have the chance to heal your tribe—I have to stay a virgin until the ritual, so we'd have to put off sex for a while." The blunt statement made her mouth dry, and she peeked at him through her lashes. "Agreed?"

His eyes closed, and his head tilted back, exposing the lines across his neck. No matter how he felt about the markings, she still wished the magic hadn't created them. He deserved the same amount of free will she did. She ran her fingertip over the lines.

At her touch, he opened his eyes and stared at her with a hungry longing that stole her heart. "I would marry you if *breathing* weren't allowed."

"Oh..." The air in her chest took flight at his declaration, and she was as breathless as the situation he described. Lordy, did she love this man.

"Then I say *yes*—on one condition." She paused and gave him a saucy grin. When curiosity lifted his brow to a sharp angle, she straddled his lap and placed her hands on his shoulders. "That we make the most of the next month here on Earth before we leave."

He gave her a sidelong glance and a sexy smile. "Are you referring to world travel and spoiling galore, or to as many endless pleasures of the flesh as we're capable of without crossing the line?"

She laughed. "Both!"

"Then you shall have both, my love."

She studied his face, memorizing this moment. "Yes, I will be yours. I'll marry you."

Her lips sought his like a woman rushing into freedom after being released from death row. She pressed herself against his chest, wanting to devour him. He captured her mouth and invited her deeper. He stroked her desire with plundering sweeps that reminded her just how talented he was with his tongue.

His hands slid from her hips to her spine, following the zipper of her dress. His fingers reached the pull, and she whimpered against his mouth. But he didn't move, and the curve of his lips gave away his plan to torture her.

She squirmed on his lap. Two could play that game.

Auntie's homegoing ceremony that morning had made one thing clear—life was to be celebrated. And before she left, she intended to enjoy *everything* the Earthen plane had to offer.

Starting with this...

Chapter Thirty-Five

C ELIA CLOSED THE DOOR TO THE BEDROOM AND PRAYED
Markos would remain asleep. His deep breathing was
usually a good sign that he would be out of it for another
hour or so. He claimed he'd never slept well before they'd shared a
bed, and it was quite possible that he was making up for centuries
of being short of sleep.

She crept into the study of their hotel suite, which served more
as a makeshift closet for the clothes-filled shopping bags he'd
insisted on purchasing. Apparently he'd decided that Australia's
early fall weather required an entirely different wardrobe from the
early spring clothes he'd gotten her for the European, North
African, and Asian stops of their around-the-world tour.

Early morning sun filled the room with a rosy glow bright
enough to serve her needs. The blue waves of Sydney Harbor
glistened far below. She set up the camera and, once she was in
position on the sofa, pressed *record* on the remote.

"We're leaving for home this afternoon, and this might be the
last of these recordings I get to make for you." She pressed her fingertips to her lips and blew a kiss to the camera. "I want to thank
you for this past month. You've exceeded my dreams in every way.
Never think 'if only.' It was all utterly perfect."

She gazed out the window and buried her worries. For all the
confidence she'd exhibited over the past month that she'd survive

the ritual, the truth was more questionable.

The other Virgins had died because something had happened to them on Mythos. Something dreadful and possibly underhanded. If she wasn't careful, the same thing could happen to her. These secret recordings were her gift to Markos in case she failed.

The suite provided a poster-worthy view of both the Harbor Bridge and the Sydney Opera House. But this wasn't her favorite memory.

A smile curved deep into her cheeks, and she turned back to the camera. "You know what my favorite memory is? Our wedding. Simple, but a beautiful reflection of our love."

Markos had arranged for them to marry under the Gateway Arch in downtown St. Louis the morning after she'd said yes. Along with Martha, his housekeeper, Roger and his family had been happy to witness the event before they flew back to North Carolina. All of them together hadn't quite added up to having Auntie there with her, but it had been close.

"The best part was when you pointed out that the two sides of the arch seem independent until you look up, and then—"

A deeper voice joined her own for the words, "The two become one."

She whirled around. Markos, breathtaking in his nakedness, leaned against the doorframe.

"You were supposed to be sleeping."

"Hmm." He stepped behind her and kissed her neck. "Why would I waste time sleeping when I could spend it with you?"

Electrifying tingles traveled through her body at his touch. She arched her neck, encouraging him to continue. He swept her hair out of the way and nibbled up to her earlobe.

Such an accommodating man.

"I was trying to make a surprise for you."

In the mirrored wall behind the camera, she saw him lift his head from her neck and nod to the device. "Is it still recording?"

"Yes." She reached for the remote.

He knocked it off the arm of the couch. "Oops."

"Markos, what are you doing?" Her voice was breathy, and her skin tightened with the suspicion of what he had in mind.

"I'm making myself a present."

He pulled her nightie tight across her breasts. Her nipples were visible through the thin fabric. He ran his fingers over the tiny beads and watched them pebble in the mirrored wall across the room.

She laughed, needing a release of her embarrassment. "You mean you're making a sex tape."

"Mmm, a *present* sounds better, don't you think?" He straightened and met her gaze in the reflection. "Stand up."

She didn't want to discourage his plans, and she certainly didn't want to argue semantics. She stood and crossed her arms in front of her chest.

He checked out the camera and adjusted the zoom. He probably wanted a wider field of view than just focusing on her from the waist up when she was sitting. When he was satisfied, he sat on the sofa behind her and took a classic alpha-male pose of legs spread and arms outstretched on the back of the couch.

Her legs wobbled under her as one of his feet stroked the back of her calf. Somehow, watching him in the mirror added to his sexiness. Maybe because he was so big that she rarely got a wide-angled glimpse of him, much less getting this view while still in contact with him.

His gaze similarly appraised her reflection. "Turn around. Slowly."

She lowered her arms and followed his instructions. When she faced away from the camera, he held up his hand for her to stop. He slid to sit in front of her on the couch and leaned around her waist, probably watching in the mirror behind her.

His broad hands covered her bottom and slid her nightie up to her waist. "Did I ever tell you that your behind was the first thing that attracted me to you?"

"My butt?" She laughed so hard she rested her hand on his shoulder for support. "Um, no, you've never mentioned that before."

He looked up at her. The skin had tightened around his eyes, appearing disappointed in her reaction. "Yes, that's how I knew I was doomed."

She traced his lips and tried to make up for interrupting his *present.* "Tell me."

His brow lifted in a dare. "Take them off first."

"My underwear?"

At his nod, she hooked the waistband and slid them down her legs, slowly, like she knew he wanted. She refused to think about how she was pointing her ass at the camera as she bent over, but he made appreciative noises at the scene. After she straightened, he gathered the satiny fabric of her nightie at her bellybutton and directed her to hold it in place.

His chest hair tickled the tops of her thighs as he leaned forward and around her waist again. He brushed the skin of her bottom and playfully squeezed.

"On the night I brought you home unconscious, I had to heal you, which meant I had to touch you. Skin to skin."

Even though he wasn't watching her face, she nodded anyway, thanking him for getting over his touching aversion to save her life.

"The man had..." He faltered. "Damaged your behind. The cuts were deep and bleeding heavily." He placed a kiss above her hip. "So the first place I ever touched you was here." He gave her bottom another squeeze. "I remember thinking that I'd never felt anything so luscious in my hands. I caught myself caressing you by accident." At those words, he stroked her skin, slow and sensual, emphasizing how far they'd come.

His confession explained so many things about his outright panic about touching her. Thank goodness they'd moved beyond that.

At the thought, she trailed one hand down his neck. "Really?"

"Yes. And I was doomed since that moment."

She knew he must be teasing but asked anyway. "Do you regret anything?"

He sat back and met her eyes. "Only that I resisted your seduction for so long."

"My *seduction*?"

"Everything about you is seductive. I wore those sunglasses in an attempt to protect myself from looking directly at your enchanting beauty." His features broke into a smile. "It didn't help."

She released her nightgown and pressed his shoulders back against the couch. She murmured at his lips. "You say the sweetest things."

He allowed her one kiss before pushing her away. "This is *my* present, remember?" He scooted back into the cushion, adjusted himself so his manhood wasn't sticking straight up, and brought his legs together. "Turn around and sit on my lap."

She did as he asked. He grabbed the hem of her nightie so her bare bottom landed on his thighs.

The camera and mirrored wall caught her eye. She'd almost forgotten about those while she'd faced the other direction.

"All the way back," he directed. "Up against my chest."

Her thighs were shorter, so to scoot back she had to separate her knees and straddle his legs. His height also meant that he could easily see over her shoulder and gaze into the mirror.

He started nibbling on her neck again, and he pinned her arms as he reached forward to hold her breasts in his palms. She melted against him. He rubbed the satin fabric of her nightie around her nipples, and her skin tingled at the sensation. He inched the fabric higher and higher until it barely hid her breasts from view.

Then he pushed her forward enough to release the material between them. With a quick flick of his arm, he disrobed her in front of the camera and mirror. She'd never felt so exposed. Before she could cover herself, he pinned her biceps again and rolled his hands over her breasts.

"Watch us in the mirror." His tone was a strict order to be obeyed. "Watch and see how much I love you. Watch what I'm going to see when I play this recording." He gave her a wicked grin. "Maybe I should install a large-screen TV over the bed."

Her thighs clenched together at the thought.

"No cheating. Hook your toes behind my calves." Then he brought her attention back to the mirror. "See how your nipples come to a point when I stroke them?"

On command, her nipples rose and hardened at his playful pinches. He rubbed his thumbs over the nubs and let the curves of her breasts rest in his palms. He squeezed gently and deliberately, as though measuring and weighing, watching how their shape changed in his hands.

Seeing the concentration on his face as he fondled her made her feel better about the visual aid. She got over her shyness and relaxed into him.

"That's right, love. Notice how your skin flushes as you get excited. The pink of a perfect blooming rose—that's how I always think of you." His finger came up and traced her lips. "And these are the soft petals I want to see open."

She kissed his finger and ran her tongue along its length. When he groaned, she sucked his finger into her mouth. In and out, imitating another gift she'd given to him several times over the past month.

He didn't let her keep control this time. He separated his knees. Her legs—on the outside of his and hooked into place—spread wide open in front of the mirror.

"See how you glisten dark pink down here. I love these petals too." He slipped his finger from her mouth and used the moisture to rub her opening. "Watch how you writhe in pleasure when I do this."

Oh Lord, it was true. He pressed and rolled his fingertip over her nub, and she couldn't remain still. She wiggled and slid down the front of his abs.

Her opening, wet and wanting, lowered until the length of him rubbed against her. She reached down with her pinned arm and found his hard rod beneath her. Her hand held him in place while she rocked her hips. Her lips spread moisture along the top side of his length, and her palm coated his head with his own liquid.

He twisted her nipple, and she couldn't help speeding up her rocking motion. Back and forth along his length. His head rubbed the bottom end of her apex, and his fingers twirled the top end. So many sensations. She was going to lose it big time. And soon.

She pressed him harder against the outside of her opening. Faster and faster.

Her wild movements caught the tip of his head against the front wall of her entrance. She froze.

They locked on each other's wide-eyed gazes in the mirror. Half a centimeter and he'd slip inside her. Her hand held him against her opening. If she rocked backward, her slick channel would sweep him inside. If she rocked forward, his tip would veer away from the opening.

The muscles of her walls squeezed, begging her to fill their emptiness. It would be so easy.

He finally spoke in a voice that matched his pained expression. "Please do it. Don't take the risk of going through with the ritual."

For her sake, he'd kept his fears under control over the past month. Never bringing up the issue. Never pressuring her. But now...

The beat of her heart seemed to slow even though she knew it must be racing. Two paths unrolled in front of her, sharpened and defined by the camera's presence.

If she chose the route he asked her to, he would die—maybe immediately—and this recording would forever stand as a cautionary tale. If she stuck to her plan and failed to survive, he would be the one tortured by his inability to convince her.

The seconds ticked by, yet she needed to communicate her decision before the moment was lost. She stared at the camera, directing her explanation to his future self in an attempt to prevent the torment waiting for him on each viewing if the worst came to pass.

"I want you more than you can imagine. A part of me wishes I could be selfish and take what we both desire." She rocked forward, releasing his head from its precarious position, and gazed at the camera lens with as earnest an expression as she could manage. "But I love you too much to be selfish. And I can't wish that I loved you less."

She resumed her rocking, slow and gentle, just enough to prevent the mood from escaping. She reached up with her other hand and caressed his face. To add to the distraction, she arched back and bit her lip in a blatant sexual pose. Like the fine male he was, he responded, his hands resuming their motion over her breasts and core of her nerve endings below.

"Watch me." She grinned at taking control from him. "Recognize my love for you. Recognize my soul." She stroked his length more forcefully, and he hardened to perfection again. "I give it to you to own and hold forever. Just as I am yours, so is my soul."

Even across the distance of the room, she saw his eyes melt into rich gold at her words. His breathing quickened, and he squeezed her against his chest. "Then you have already given me the best part of you."

Her fingers drifted down his neck. "It's what you deserve."

Their movements soon became heated and focused solely on pleasure once more. He stared at her in the mirror, enraptured. A glint of possessiveness she'd never seen before glowed in his eyes.

Beyond just the turn-on of knowing he desired her as much as she desired him, she wanted him to claim her. She wanted to belong to him. Forever.

Her legs opened further, and she gave herself over to him. She leaned back and arched her neck, exposing herself to him in every way. Her pulse throbbed in her elongated throat.

His length glided beneath her slick skin, and his fingers expertly sent twangs of bliss to her core. Heat coursed through her body and joined with his. Sensations washed over her and through her. Energy tingled on every nerve ending, danced with him, and warmed her from the inside out.

"Take my heart, take my soul." Her voice was low and breathy. "I'm yours."

A growl rumbled low in his chest, vibrating against her back. His eyes flashed in the reflection, and at the same time, his expression changed.

Became hungry and beastly. And very, very possessive.

The spectacle brought her to the edge of ecstasy, teetering. He gripped her torso hard, and the rumble escaped up his throat in a roar. His mouth clamped onto her neck, muffling his yell.

His barely restrained aggression pushed her over the edge. She screamed at the force of her orgasm. His release came at the same time, coating her hand as she pumped him against her.

Energy seemed to bind them together—even though he wasn't in his unicorn form—and the wave of ecstasy rolled on and on. She reached higher with her free hand and anchored herself by holding his head above his ear, forcing him to stay just as he was, biting down on her neck above and sliding in a pool of pleasure below.

He similarly seemed to be in no mood to let go. His tongue flicked over her skin, and one hand twirled her nipple and the other continued to swirl around the nub of her core.

He shuddered beneath her, and his teeth scraped her neck. His trembles built until energy burst through them in another orgasmic blast. Her consciousness seemed to be blown out of her body and hovered just above her skin. For a second, she thought she touched his mind, but the feeling disappeared with the sensation of falling back into herself.

When the energy faded, she was utterly spent, and his arms likewise flopped onto the cushions. Together they listed to the side and landed lengthwise on the couch in a huddle of warm fuzzies. She rolled to face him and snuggled into his embrace. For several moments, they just inhaled each other's scent and caught their breath.

Finally, her gasps slowed enough to speak. "That was..."

"Amazing."

"Yes, that's exactly what I was going to say." The fact that the camera was still recording dimly registered in her mind. "Should we turn off the camera?"

"There's nothing wrong with more footage of your behind." He playfully patted her bottom.

She laughed. She'd have never guessed he was such an *ass* man.

Her hand trailed down from his jaw and stopped at the lines across his neck. Gold now swirled among the black.

"Are these new?"

He shot up and strode to the mirror. He lifted his dreadlocks and examined the design that no longer looked like a tattoo up close. Shimmers of gold—not just gold pigment, but actual reflective gold loops and spirals—would never be found on a regular tattoo.

She sat up on the couch and watched his expression as she cleaned her hand on the discarded nightie. After a moment of confusion, a look of pure, unadulterated joy formed on his face. He bounded back to the sofa and gave her a deep kiss.

When he pulled back, he held her cheeks in his palms. "Thank you." He kissed her again. "Thank you." And again. "Thank you."

She giggled. "Are you going to tell me what you're thanking me for?"

"I don't know what the gold is—I've never even heard of it from our own mythology—but if I had to take a guess..." His chin dipped for a moment. When he looked up again, she noticed the gold flecks in his eyes had increased in size and number. His voice came out more husky than normal. "I think you gave me a piece of your soul."

Any other woman would probably have been concerned about *missing* a piece of her soul, but Celia could think of only one response. "Good. If the black signifies that I have power over you in some way, then it's only right that I give you something in return. Maybe the threads between my soul and yours are stronger now, strong enough to survive anything."

"You don't regret it?"

"Not at all, especially if it brings us closer. I meant everything I said earlier. I'm yours—heart and soul."

She didn't mention the part about how she loved seeing him so happy—happier than she'd ever seen him, and certainly happier than he'd been since her decision to go through with the ritual. If this would give him hope, would make him believe he wouldn't lose her, she'd gladly give up a piece of herself to him.

To have and to hold. Forever.

Whatever price she had to pay would be worth it.

Chapter Thirty-Six

MARKOS GLANCED UP AT THE SOUND OF MOLLY'S BARK. Several hundred feet away, Celia strolled onto the patio and headed toward him in the private-most back corner of the yard.

Mugarok. He wiped a hand over his mouth and hid his expression. She was perfection. Maybe it had been a mistake to buy her that outfit.

Her pure white dress draped over her shoulders and gathered with the material around her hips, emphasizing her figure before softly curving to the ground. Her pale hair fell around her face in gentle waves, and her lips and cheeks were the ideal shade of pink. Moonlight shone on her, emanated from her, became her. She was a goddess.

His hand dropped from his face. No, even though seeing her like this was torture, he was right to introduce her this way. She was the first Virgin to walk knowingly into a ritual, and by the Maker, if he had any say in the matter, they all would worship her for that fact.

Of course, if all went as he hoped, the ritual wouldn't happen at all. That irrational belief was the only thing keeping him from crawling out of his skin with worry.

The surprise appearance of gold threading through his collar the other day had given him hope. Between the fact that she'd made—and meant—the offer of her soul, that the magic had joined them again, and that when his teeth had scratched her neck during their passion, he'd ingested half a drop of her blood, he clung to his belief that he'd guessed right about the meaning behind the gold: They were *already* joined as one in the magic.

He deeply inhaled, tempering his optimism as she crossed the lawn toward him. At least, he *hoped* all that added up to the magical equivalent of marriage.

Only Archimedes would be able to tell him for sure, and now that Markos was *supposed* to be back on the Mythos plane, a visit to the ancient historian shouldn't raise an alarm with the council. Hopefully the old male would give him a straight answer this time.

Too much had been going on lately for Markos to figure out if there were multiple meanings to the male's last words to him: *Ask yourself why the Maker would forbid matings.*

As Archimedes had pointed out, the commandment made no sense. After all, two of their not-quite matings had strengthened his magic, not destroyed it. So was Archimedes just implying that Alkipsia had lied about yet another thing? Or was there another layer to the question?

As Celia approached, Markos held out his hand for his bride. She slipped her fingers into his grasp, and he bowed and kissed her hand. "You are the loveliest creature ever to walk on either plane."

Her blush added more pink to her cheeks, increasing her beauty.

A tremor of uncertainty tickled the back of his skull. "What's wrong?"

Her gaze shot up to his. "When did you get so skilled at reading my moods?" Before he could process her question, she nibbled her lip. "All this white..." She swept the fabric of her dress wide. "I *feel* like a virgin sacrifice."

Even though he knew she was joking, the urge to retch pressed on his throat. He glanced at the bare branches of the trees around them. Every one reminded him of his deadly horn, and he bowed forward, gagging on a swallow.

She enfolded him in an embrace. "I'm sorry. Don't worry. I'm not planning on dying."

He forced himself to stand upright. *She* was the one volunteering for the ritual, yet she was consoling *him.*

"No, I apologize. I'm the one who picked out the dress after all."

He'd selected the dress for exactly that impression on the tribe. He needed them to see how their methods were wrong, and inciting a little guilt never hurt.

She released him and held his hands. "Okay, so what happens now?"

"In the past, the Virgins have been—"

He shook his head and interrupted himself to take responsibility. He must not lie to her, no matter how much he wished to spare her from the details.

"In the past, *I* abducted the Virgins and brought them—unconscious—to the Mythos plane the midnight before the Spring Equinox. Attendants then took them to be cleansed and await the ritual in the temple arena. They were restrained in the center of the arena until the high priestess asked her question, at which point, they were released to make their choice."

And impaled themselves on his horn...

His chin dipped to his chest, and his fingers curled around hers. He wanted to hold on to her. Protect her. Love her.

"But this time is entirely different. In fact, we're not quite done with our honeymoon travel. I want to show you a bit of my homeland before we have to report to Alkipsia at midnight."

"We're not going to run into any scary creatures like dragons or anything, are we?"

"You're not too scared to risk death, but you're worried about dragons?"

This woman was amazing. And inscrutable.

He didn't wait for her to come up with a logical answer to an illogical fear. "The dragons lost a war with the faeries and were kicked out of the Mythos plane millennia ago." A wry smile curved across his face. "So they all live here on the Earthen plane."

"Dragons are real? And they're on *Earth*?" Her brows pulled down. "You're joking, right?"

"Not at all. They live in mountain caves in Europe and Asia and mostly stay far away from humans." He shrugged. "Except for the one living in Chicago."

"*Chicago?*"

"They're also shapeshifters. If some have learned to control their violent nature, you wouldn't know they were around." He squeezed her hands. "Regardless, I will keep you safe."

At her nod, he formed the doorway of mist in front of them. Molly sidled closer, obviously wanting to go on the trip.

"Sorry, Molly." He glanced down at the dog. "This one isn't for you."

She barked and nudged harder.

Celia laughed. "I think she begs to differ."

The last thing he wanted was for something to distract his attention from focusing on Celia. He bent down to give Molly a stern refusal. But just as he opened his mouth, Molly's eyes glinted with a hint of gold and then went back to their normal dark brown color.

He jerked upright and closed his mouth. Had he just seen that?

He'd always suspected there was more to her than met the eye. There were rumors that some of the fae could speak to animals and used them as—what was the word faeries used?—*familiars*.

He didn't know any faeries personally, so he had no idea if one could create a familiar for the Earthen plane. But if that was the case, it explained a few things about her behavior.

Normally, he wouldn't trust anything to do with the faeries, but Molly had proved her loyalty several times over. More often than not, she'd acted like a matchmaker for him and Celia, and he was grateful for that.

"Okay, you can come." He scooped Molly into his right arm and tucked Celia in close on his left side. "Hold on to me," he told her. "We're just walking through a doorway."

Celia wrapped her arms around him, and they all stepped into the rectangle of mist. Her gasp at the scene let him know that she'd managed the transition fine. He set Molly down and enjoyed the sense of wonder on Celia's face.

She took in the vast, deep blue sea below them beyond the cliff. The waves sparkled in the moonlight, and glowing shapes swam beneath the surface, dodging rocks as the surf crashed into the shore. She looked up and squinted, focusing on the stars moving in the sky. Then she completed a slow circle, noticing the white marble of Council Hall on the distant hilltop beyond the forest. Her wide-eyed gaze finally settled on him.

"This? This is your homeland?"

"Yes."

He took a deep breath. Instead of a sense of relief at returning home, a pang stabbed his chest, twisting and digging, leaving shredded dreams in its wake. He'd thought he'd been adrift and lonely before. That would be nothing compared to his despair if he lost her. Everything depended on her surviving the ritual.

He felt more at home with Celia—no matter where they'd traveled during the past month. Home was with her.

She twined her fingers between his and grinned. "Thank you for inviting me, and yes, I'd love to stay with you. It's beautiful here."

Her words, reinforcing a successful end for the ritual, calmed the pains in his chest. Molly had wandered in the direction of Archimedes's home and seemed to be waiting at the edge of the trees for them to follow.

"Molly, do you know Archimedes?"

The dog's attention veered toward a tree trunk. She nosed the bark, maybe trying to tickle the hamadryad inside. He took her obvious avoidance as a yes.

Archimedes had been next on his list of things to do anyway. Especially if the Ancient One was at the center of this mystery of Molly as well.

The dog bounded ahead, not needing to be shown the way, and Celia's eyes stayed wide, taking in every aspect of his homeland. She seemed to understand without being told that nature was truly alive here. Everything, from the stars in the sky to the stream they crossed, had a spirit connected to the rest of the world. Even the moonlight chose to follow her through the trees, keeping her in glowing beauty despite the thick foliage above.

When they reached the clearing around Archimedes's pond, Markos steered her toward the house. The front door was open, but he knocked anyway. "Archimedes?"

Molly sniffed and whimpered before running toward the back office. That door was open as well. Archimedes wasn't there.

But his scrolls—the same scrolls he'd been fiddling with and stacking as Markos had asked his questions over a month ago—remained stacked in the same shape in the same place on his desk.

Markos's memory flashed back to that evening.

His meeting with Archimedes had been interrupted when someone had come to summon him to the council. Markos had assumed the attendant was searching for him due to his unapproved visit, but what if the council had been after Archimedes instead?

Son of a mule. Was Archimedes in trouble? Had he been imprisoned this whole time?

There was no question of *who* would have done this. Alkipsia was the only one with the authority. But he had a hard time understanding how even she could justify *arresting* their most revered male, the Ancient One.

Molly stared up at him. Her tail hung low, and her ears pressed back. Her fear reflected his own.

Chills crept through his limbs, and a sour taste rose up his throat. Instinctively, he tucked Celia into his arms. Something was seriously wrong.

Something that recalled the dark days of war and rebellion of centuries ago.

"Celia."

She squinted up at him, likely surprised by his rare use of her name.

"I have a bad feeling about this. Things on this plane are not as they were when I left. Something has changed. Something malicious." He put all his persuasive powers he could into his voice. "I should take you home."

Before she could respond, clouds of mist formed all around them.

Skoro and ass. Armed attendants, clad in the purple-hemmed robes of the council, surrounded them and gripped their spears. They did a double take at Celia at his side, and frowns formed on many of their faces. Every one of his muscles tensed.

One stepped forward. "Guardian Markos. You have not delivered the Virgin to the council."

"I had questions for Archimedes." That was the truth. Only now he had several more questions than before. "We were heading to the council next. It is not yet midnight."

The leader tipped his spear toward the door. "We'll escort you to the council and ensure you're not late."

More likely, they meant to ensure he and Celia wouldn't leave the Mythos plane, now that he knew Archimedes had been taken. Although he could summon a doorway to the Earthen plane, he couldn't do it so quickly that the guards would be unable to use their spears. He wouldn't risk Celia's life like that. He didn't mean for her to die by his horn—or by rash escape attempts.

Markos kept his arm around her and allowed them to be herded outside and onto the paths that would take them to Council Hall. Sometime during the confrontation, Molly had slunk off unnoticed. Hopefully, she'd be all right.

More worrisome was an impression of Celia's fear, nibbling at the back of his mind. Was he somehow sensing her emotions or just attuned to her moods? Either way, he wished he could reassure her, but any placating statements would be a lie.

Instead, he offered, "At least you'll get to see more of my homeland."

She looked up at him and swallowed. He kept his gaze steady and full of concern for her. Especially as they passed the temple arena, the place where she would face her fate.

The marble building caught her eye. "I think I liked our tour of the Roman Coliseum better."

He squeezed her shoulders. Her comment proved she'd figured out the purpose of the oval building. "I don't blame you."

He hated himself more with every step. He should have done more to argue with her, convince her, force her to choose her own life over those of his and his tribe.

All evidence pointed toward Alkipsia enacting another major crackdown, and who knew what lies she'd tell, what magic she'd twist and ruin. And every change endangered Celia's life more than they'd dreamed.

His stomach worked its way into tangles tighter than his dreadlocks. The golden gift she'd given him weighed heavy around his neck. His lungs refused to fill with air.

He'd failed her.

Chapter Thirty-Seven

THE ATTENDANTS FELL INTO LINE ON EITHER SIDE OF THEM AS they climbed the stairs to Council Hall. Markos kept Celia close with one arm and held her hands with his other one. He probably should have been spending this time planning his strategy for dealing with Alkipsia, but too much had changed since last fall for him to guess at the right approach.

Two of the attendants held back the curtains for them to pass into the council chamber. The day of the ceremony was the one time others were allowed before the council in their human form. The guards needed hands to hold the spears they used to avoid contact with the Virgin. A stretcher-like litter leaned against the back wall. Normally, the unconscious Virgin would be rolled onto the sling to carry her to the holding area.

Alkipsia's gaze burned into them as she took in the scene. The lower priestesses just looked confused. Not only was Celia *not* being dropped, unconscious, onto the marble floor at the earliest opportunity to end the necessity of touching the Virgin, but he was also being protective of her.

Alkipsia tipped her chin. "The Virgin is *conscious.*"

"Yes, she is." He let go of Celia's hands long enough to gesture. "Celia, this is our high priestess and ruler, Alkipsia. Alkipsia, this is Celia." He met the priestess's gaze. "My *wife.*"

One of the lower priestesses fainted and slipped off her throne.

Grunts traveled around the semicircle of attendants behind them. Alkipsia's eyes narrowed, her lids twitching. Then she snapped her fingers and beckoned one of the attendants forward to assist her fallen cohort.

"Whatever you think the point of your lie is, it won't work. We can all smell that she's still the Virgin, and you will be punished for your attempt at insurrection."

"Yes, she is still the Virgin. She made the choice to remain a virgin so she could heal our tribe."

A wicked smile spread across Alkipsia's face, a smile of greed and power. "She knows why she is here and has chosen to participate in the ritual?"

Celia spoke up for the first time. "Yes. Markos is worth the risk, and even if the rest of you added together are only half as worthy as he is, I still make that choice."

Alkipsia's smile drooped for a second, but she quickly recovered. "Well done, Markos. No one can claim we're going against the Maker's wishes under these circumstances."

His attention perked up at the implications of her comment. Someone *had* claimed that their way of life went against the Maker's wishes.

His instincts immediately suspected Archimedes. Was that the reason for her latest crackdown and his disappearance? Had he questioned her about the truth of the ritual and commandment against matings?

He worded his rebuttal carefully to knock Alkipsia off balance from her smug posturing. "Regardless of the state of her virginity, Celia is indeed my wife. We are wed both according to the traditions of the Earthen plane and in the magic."

He opened the collar of his shirt and displayed the black lines of Celia's claim on him.

Alkipsia sucked in a breath, sharpening her cheekbones. "What *is* that?"

"To be honest, I don't know." He made his play, counting on her curiosity to take over. "Only Archimedes would be able to say for certain what kind of magic this is. That's why I was attempting to visit with him before coming here."

She sat back and considered him. Her head tilted, and she

interlaced her fingers and tapped her lips in a slow rhythm. Just when he thought she wouldn't take the bait, she gestured to the leader of her guards.

"Bring him here."

Markos kept his face blank. Inside, his nerves quivered. May the Maker reveal the solution through Archimedes. He'd be willing to become a devout believer in the Maker's true revelations if this worked.

The attendant took two of the other guards out to the hallway with him. A few minutes later, they reentered the council chamber, dragging a pale and thin Archimedes between them.

The male's appearance left no doubt in Markos's mind that Alkipsia had kept him imprisoned the past five weeks. Archimedes's hair hung down in strings, his robes were dirty and ripped at the hems, and his feet were bare and cracked.

Curse the Maker. Markos's throat clenched, and his hands twitched, longing to curl into fists. How dare they treat the Ancient One so disrespectfully.

The guards dropped Archimedes into a heap before Alkipsia's throne. She leaned forward, her eyes thin slits. "You are here for one purpose only. Tell me about the magic that created the marking around the Guardian's neck."

Archimedes's shoulders squared beneath his grayed robe.

"Do you understand?" She gripped the top edge of the half wall between the throne level and the main floor. "You'll be returned to where you came from immediately if you deviate from that answer."

Markos understood her warning for the threat it was. Archimedes *had* gotten in trouble for undermining Alkipsia in some way, and she didn't want him saying anything that would turn others to his cause. Regardless of the restriction, the ancient male nodded his compliance.

The guards took one half-step back, allowing him room to struggle to his feet. Markos restrained himself from assisting Archimedes. Interfering with how he hoped this would play out would only cause problems.

Celia had no such reluctance. She left Markos's hold before he could stop her and helped Archimedes stand. The guards gasped and staggered back to protect themselves from her touch.

Archimedes's eyes lit up with some of his former vigor, his gaze taking in his assistant. His fingertips stroked her simple wedding ring.

He straightened and attempted a bow. "I am glad to meet you at last, my queen."

Alkipsia shot to her feet. "What did you call the Virgin?"

"My queen." His expression turned innocent, almost child-like with a faked dementia. "Shouldn't we honor the savior of our tribe?"

Innocent? Hardly. The implications of Archimedes's falsely doddering words sent icy shards through Markos's veins.

In calling Celia *queen*, the implication was that her husband would be—or should be—*king*. If news spread of Archimedes's choice of honorific, some would pick up on that subtext. Piss. The male was trying to reignite the war. As if they hadn't all endured enough suffering.

"The markings. Around Markos's neck. Now." Alkipsia returned to her throne with an exaggerated calm, taking her time with arranging the folds of her dress. "I'm growing impatient."

Celia helped Archimedes limp back to Markos. A twinkle flickered in the old male's eye, his gaze drawn to the magical symbol around Markos's neck.

"Hmm."

He clicked his tongue, as if trying to remember the meaning of the marks. More likely he was weighing his answer.

"Black." A half-smile curved his lips, and he gave Markos a wink. "Oh... Very interesting. Gold too." He glanced at Celia. "You are a most generous person." He arched his brow at Markos. "And you are able to feel her emotions now, yes?"

The adrenaline racing through Markos's body stopped, every part of him focusing on the comment. Those little tingles in the back of his mind weren't just experienced guesses of her feelings. He actually had a connection to her emotional thoughts now.

He finally gave a slow nod. Bless the Maker for such magic.

Alkipsia snapped her fingers. "You know what this means?"

"Indeed." Archimedes faced the high priestess. "It means that she owns his life, and he owns her soul. There's no need for a ritual, as the magic tying these two together is already the strongest we've seen in millennia. The tribe will be fully healed if they consummate their relationship before the next midnight, ideally around noon, the height of the Spring Equinox." He focused on Markos, ignoring the clicking of Alkipsia's fingers as she gestured to her attendants. "It makes you wonder why—"

The guards dragged him toward the doorway.

"—matings were forbidden."

Markos couldn't hide his reaction from Alkipsia that time. His head jerked back in a double take. The Ancient One's defiance of their ruler not only was leading him to be punished, as they roughly yanked him from the room, but his cryptic message also triggered Markos's memory of the male's previous statement: *Ask yourself why the Maker would forbid matings.*

Celia whirled on Alkipsia. "Why *are* matings forbidden now?"

"It is a commandment from our Maker." Alkipsia's willingness to answer surprised him, but perhaps she was just as helpless against the Virgin's magic as he was. "Matings of *any* kind are not allowed, including touching." She locked onto him. "Which is why Markos will face charges of treason tomorrow."

"No, he won't." Celia emphasized her position with a shake of her head.

Gasps sounded from the remaining guards. *No one* defied Alkipsia so brazenly.

Celia held his hand and winked at him. "A... I seduced him." She glanced at Alkipsia and laughed. "Believe me, he resisted plenty, but I *am* the Virgin." She waggled her fingers toward an attendant, who stumbled back and paled. "I have magical powers of my own."

Maker's blessings, did he love this woman.

Alkipsia blanched, her eyes wide. If she disputed Celia's assertion, he wouldn't put it past his wife to turn her charms to the guards in a more blatant demonstration.

"And B..." Celia's jaw shifted into a serious expression. "Don't give me that 'commandment from our Maker' crap. It's just a rule—a *temporary* rule. It didn't exist before and won't exist after I heal the tribe. He shouldn't be punished for something that's irrelevant."

Yes. It *was* irrelevant. How had he never seen it before? The

Pure Sacrifice

lies. The misinformation. The trickery. Alkipsia's word meant nothing.

The truth gathered in his chest, aching with the heavy realization of how he'd been manipulated. His vision blurred, and the floor seemed to shift under his feet.

The Maker had never revealed *anything* to Alkipsia. The Maker hadn't instructed her to change the ritual to survive. Alkipsia had lied to the tribe, giving them false hope with a ritual that offered only tainted magic, all to manipulate the balance of power and win the war.

The Maker hadn't commanded her to ban matings for their genetic purity. Healing magic made their genetic weaknesses irrelevant. The truth was that matings were forbidden because of Alkipsia's insatiable hunger for power. She'd outlawed them for everyone, all to prevent *one* of them from having a child.

Him.

If the last of the royal family had a daughter, the line of succession would be restored. And she would lose her easy claim to the throne.

That's why there were no other Guardians. While Markos was under house arrest, she must have killed them off because they refused to conform to her version of the ritual.

She'd kept him alive only because he had the necessary magic and had been a child at the time of the war, unable to question her edicts from a position of knowledge or experience. He'd been easily lied to and manipulated. And he'd fallen for it.

Alkipsia peered down from her perch, her eyes blacker than usual. "Separate them."

Three spear tips aimed at his heart. Yesterday, he would have been happy for the opportunity to die in a way the collar couldn't prevent, if only it would save Celia. Now, though, he had to stay alive.

If he died, Celia would be trapped here with Alkipsia, and who knew what would happen then. The possibilities were too horrible to contemplate.

He dropped Celia's hand, even though it felt like the worst kind of betrayal, and played innocent—whatever it took to stay alive. "Archimedes stated there would be no ritual today. Shouldn't I take Celia home?"

"Archimedes's ramblings are nothing more than the delusions of a feeble mind. We will complete the ceremony." Alkipsia motioned to her guards. "Escort her to the holding area."

His stomach hardened, filling his chest with tension, and his muscles vibrated with anger and dread. The truth sent ice crackling through his limbs. Alkipsia had a plan to ensure Celia's death.

They'd been set up.

And he'd been set up every time, with every Virgin. Alkipsia had orchestrated their deaths to prevent any from accepting him and being willing to mate with him.

He grasped for any opening to impede her plan. "Celia's a volunteer. She needn't be locked up like the others." The *holding area* was a cell in a special wing of the prison, and the whole building was inescapable. "I thought you wanted to show off the fact that she offered to do this for our tribe."

"She'll be well taken care of there." A smile twisted her face into a cruel expression. "It is for her safety. Others might not restrain themselves around her as you have done."

Prickles of unease poked at the back of his mind. Rape. Fear rolled off Celia and spread from the back of his skull through his body. She recognized Alkipsia's statement for the threat it was.

"It's fine, Markos." Her eyes were tight, asking him to go along with the plan, to trust that she'd be okay.

"At least allow me to say goodbye to my wife."

"I allow it."

The consent came not from Alkipsia, but from Charisia, the lower priestess who hadn't fainted earlier. He usually didn't pay attention to them because Alkipsia alone ruled the land, the two lower priestesses mere puppets to make her appear less like a dictator. But now, Charisia ignored Alkipsia's glare. Faceted lantern light reflected off her overly shiny eyes.

He bowed within bounds of the spear tips surrounding him. "Thank you."

He didn't wait for Alkipsia to countermand the official approval. He shoved the spears aside and pulled Celia into his arms, seeking her lips for a desperate kiss. Hunger for her touch drove his heartbeat into a galloping rhythm, and his chest ached like he was about to sprout additional arms to hold her tighter.

She melted against him, her soft curves pressing into him. His fingers buried themselves in her hair, and he slipped his tongue past her lips. He needed to touch her, needed to connect them as much as possible, needed to be *in* her the only way allowed.

She matched his desire, passion igniting through their connection. Sensing her emotions enflamed his craving for her even more. He *would* find a way to save her.

When the commotion around him reached a crescendo, he broke away and whispered in her ear, "We'll make this work. I love you."

He didn't know what his plan was yet, but he knew he'd never give up trying. And he needed her to be ready for whatever he figured out.

Sharp points forced him back. He let them lead her away only because fighting now—without a plan—would get them both killed.

A pop sounded from his jaw, his teeth grinding hard against each other. Blood rushed through his limbs, ready to attack, and his throat dried with his harsh breaths. But now wasn't the time.

Not yet. Soon. Time itself was the enemy. He needed a plan before the ritual. He had until noon.

He hoped it would be long enough.

Chapter Thirty-Eight

ONLY AFTER MARKOS COULD NO LONGER HEAR CELIA'S GROUP down the hall did he turn to the council. Emotions had left all their cheeks flushed, but their body language couldn't be more different. Charisia looked embarrassed, glancing to anywhere but him. The priestess who'd fainted earlier crossed and uncrossed her arms repeatedly. And Alkipsia didn't disappoint— her fingers curled into claws and shook in front of her.

"How dare you defile the council chamber with that–that *display*."

He gave them a sheepish smile and touched the black lines at his neck. "I'm sorry, I couldn't help myself. The magic between us is too strong to resist."

Alkipsia wouldn't believe his exaggeration, but Charisia finally met his eye and touched her fingers to her lips. A romantic who still believed in matings. He filed the information away. He would need all the allies he could get.

Alkipsia angled her chin to one of the remaining guards. "Summon Hipdemos."

Interesting. The summoning of Hipdemos meant only one thing—a return to house arrest.

Of course, Alkipsia didn't know that in the centuries since he was last under house arrest, Hipdemos had revealed himself to be loyal to Markos, not her. He buried the smug smile threatening to give him away and instead let his anger rise to the surface. The stupid donkey would expect nothing less, and he couldn't let her suspect that Hipdemos wouldn't fulfill his duty.

"You're placing me under *arrest* again?" He stormed up to her perch. "Over four centuries of keeping my word and serving your rule, and this is how you thank me?"

"The risks are too great. You admitted you cannot control yourself when it comes to this Virgin."

"But she *volunteered* to be here. If anything, you should trust me more, as her wishes align with yours."

"Regardless. A few hours to ensure the safety of the tribe should not be too much to ask of you."

"It's not the hours. It's the lack of respect for me, for my centuries of dedication, and for the fact that Celia volunteered."

Alkipsia waved her hand, dismissing his complaint. "It's a shame you've chosen to see it that way."

His muscles burned. Her haughtiness knew no bounds, and he longed to leap over the wall and teach her a lesson about humility. However, now that Celia wasn't in the room, the remaining guards had closed ranks between him and Alkipsia.

If he wanted to stay alive for Celia's sake, keeping his mouth shut was safer.

Luckily, the other guard returned with Hipdemos a moment later, saving Markos from having to bite through his tongue with the effort to stay silent. In the time since he'd last seen his friend, the male had started wearing his hair in beaded dreadlocks. Was that symbolic of his loyalty to Markos or just coincidence?

Hipdemos startled at seeing Markos in the council chamber. Markos kept his face passive. He didn't want to trigger Hipdemos into defending him.

Alkipsia grabbed Hipdemos's attention. "Escort Markos to his quarters, and ensure he remains there until it's time for the ceremony. Then bring him to the temple arena."

Curious. Other than tradition, she could have assigned one of her attendants to the job rather than placing him under Hipdemos's watch. Did she trust Hipdemos to meet her expectations better than a random guard, or did she need her attendants elsewhere?

To Hipdemos's credit, he played along, bowing without hesitation. "I hear and obey."

Markos inclined his head to Alkipsia. "I will do what is best for the tribe."

A true statement, but vague enough to seem that he was following her wishes.

Hipdemos gestured, and Markos fell into step beside him. They remained silent until the darkened forest surrounded them.

"So are you going to tell me what you did to earn her ire this time, or do you want me to guess?"

Markos snorted. As if his friend could ever guess the truth. "Where do you want me to start? With the fact that I married the Virgin and all we have to do is have sex sometime before midnight to fully heal the tribe, or that Archimedes is trying to reignite the war."

Hipdemos stopped and faced him. "You *married* the Virgin?"

Markos chuckled at Hipdemos's surprise, and the twists of his stomach unwound a bit in the company of his friend. He spent the next several minutes sharing stories of Celia, his collar, and what he'd learned from Archimedes and Alkipsia's exchange. All the while, Markos led them not toward his quarters, but toward the prison. As expected, Hipdemos made no move to carry out Alkipsia's orders.

They paused at the edge of the trees below the prison building. Despite the soft moonlight and the fact that a majority of the enclosure was built into a flower-covered hill, the windowless stone wall at the entrance looked intimidating. Only one way in or out, so when closed tightly, the structure prevented access to the mists of his kind's magical transportation abilities.

Hipdemos squared his shoulders, and his eyes glinted in the low light. "What are your orders, my prince?"

"I'm not asking you to risk yourself for me."

"That's beside the point. I'm here, and I *will* help."

Did he really want to involve his friend? He glanced at the dark shadows near the prison entrance. Guards. Did he have a choice?

"I need to get Celia out of there. And I'd like to get Archimedes out too." He lifted his hands in a silent request for insights. "However, my lack of time here has made me the least qualified of our kind to know how to accomplish either of those tasks. Do you have any ideas?"

"That depends. Why do you want to get Archimedes out?"

He answered from his heart. "Because it's wrong for our Ancient One to be imprisoned at all. Because he alone knows—and can probably prove—the extent of Alkipsia's lies." His jaw hardened. "Because Alkipsia needs to be stopped."

A slow smile built across Hipdemos's features. "I've been waiting for you to rise to the crown for centuries." He tilted his head toward the prison, bouncing his dreadlocks across his shoulders. "When I heard the rumors about Archimedes's arrest, I hoped that was a sign of change. I've spent the last few weeks reaching out to those I believed to be like-minded. You'll know those who have pledged their loyalty to the royal line by their hair."

"The dreadlocks." They *were* symbolic, just as he'd guessed. But he'd never have thought others would follow Hipdemos's example.

All members of his tribe, male and female alike, wore their hair long in their human form. Every few centuries, trends converged to make certain hairstyles popular. Dreadlocks had been fashionable less than a half-century before—the perfect amount of time so that his kind wouldn't wear them just because they saw others with the style but also so that the knotted locks wouldn't draw suspicion either.

"Does that mean you have suggestions for how to get them out?"

Hipdemos grinned. "Leave it to me."

He gripped Markos's arms and shoved him toward the prison entrance. Markos followed his lead, acting angry but compliant.

One guard at the doorway aimed his spear at them. "Halt. Report."

Hipdemos yanked Markos forward. "The high priestess told me to keep Guardian Markos under house arrest until the ceremony, but he's being troublesome. I ask for your help by holding him here while I clarify my orders."

Another guard, this one with dreadlocks, approached. "I'll take him in."

Hipdemos bowed. "I appreciate the assistance. However, I prefer to see him secured before I relinquish my duty."

Jami Gold

The dreadlocked guard nodded. "Come with me."

He led them through the thick door and stopped at the front desk. The guard there looked up at their approach.

"Not *another* one."

Their escort gave a shrug. "Alkipsia's orders."

"I don't know where we're supposed to keep all these prisoners." He shook his head and consulted a scroll. His fingertip skated down a list of cells, each with several names beside them. More evidence of a major crackdown in progress.

With their tribe's small population, the prison was often completely empty. There had never been more than a handful of occupants since the war ended with Markos's surrender. So much for that decision bringing peace to his kind. In human terms, if his agreement was akin to a peace treaty, she'd apparently been breaking the terms of their arrangement for a while.

The more he learned, the more he realized that his urge to confront Alkipsia went beyond just his desire to keep Celia safe. His sense of responsibility for his kind now weighed on him with a desire to free them from her tyranny.

Just what he needed—a more complicated to-do list.

The male drummed his fingers and sighed. "Every cell is already stuffed like a sky full of stars. I don't know where we should put him."

Their escort pointed to one line. "This cell has only one occupant."

"Yes, but that's..." The guard glanced at Markos, finally noticing who he was committing to imprisonment, and raised a brow. "I see what you mean." He reached into the desk and handed their escort a key. "You'll need this one. The normal key won't open that door."

Hipdemos bowed. "My apologies for bringing you trouble."

"I don't want apologies. I want Alkipsia to stop sending anyone here. All the extra attendants she's sending as guards don't help if we don't have the room."

Hipdemos bowed again. "I shall pass on the message."

"You do that."

Their escort opened the inner door, and Hipdemos dragged Markos into the main prison hallway. Massive wooden doors lined both sides of the hundred-foot long passageway. Stone formed the walls between the doors. Guards stood at attention every ten feet. Was half their population now working as guards while the other half was locked up?

Beside Markos, Hipdemos muttered under his breath at the sight.

Mule's piss. Getting out might not be as easy as getting in.

Chapter Thirty-Nine

THE OCCUPANTS OF THE FIRST PRISON CELL TO THEIR RIGHT rushed to the small cutout inset in the thick door. Markos could make out only several eyes filling the opening.

"It's Prince Markos!" The call from a prisoner traveled down the hallway.

"Prince Markos! Prince Markos!"

The guards lining the dark passage thumped on the doors closest to them. "Quiet in there."

However, the fire was too big to extinguish. Fingers reached through the cutouts, and wails echoed through the stone hallway.

"That donkey is locking up the prince!"

"Curse us all!"

"May the Maker save the prince!"

Warmth filled his heart and expanded through his ribs. These were his people, his tribe. He owed them a better life.

He drew himself taller and thumped his chest in a salute to their loyalty. If they weren't already locked up, their brave words would probably have put them here again. Never before had he been exposed to those who supported him. Never before had he realized how much some *wanted* him to take up the fight. Never before had he wanted to be the leader they longed for.

The nearest guard glared at their group. "We don't need anyone riling up these prisoners."

Their escort tipped his head. "That's why I'm taking him to solitary confinement. His presence is too disruptive out here."

"That's the smartest idea I've heard all night." The guard stepped back against the stone, clearing the path to allow them through, and away from the other prisoners, faster.

Markos continued saluting and meeting the gazes of all those he passed. If he seemed to fight his arrest, guards would storm to his side, so he couldn't react the way he wanted, but he would recognize and thank his supporters as much as he could.

Two thick doors sat at the end of the hall. He guessed one led to the Virgin's wing and one led to the solitary confinement wing. This end of the prison lay deep into the hill, secluded and utterly impossible to travel into or out of by magic. Two guards stood along the back wall.

One eyed their escort. "This is even worse than when the Virgin was paraded through here."

Markos stiffened, and Hipdemos tightened the grip on his arm, warning him. But so help him, if anyone had hurt her, he'd kill them all before they could scream.

Hipdemos chuckled. "What were they yelling then?"

"When that old fool came through here, he told them to make way for the queen." The guard rolled his eyes. "These idiots believed him and kept calling out for the queen as the Virgin walked through. Curse the *skoro* who thought it was a good idea to have her conscious this time."

Yes! These *were* his people. His responsibility.

He was far more connected to his tribe than he'd ever guessed, and perhaps those who knew or suspected Alkipsia's lies didn't blame him for his failures over the centuries.

Their escort unlocked the door to the left, and Hipdemos nudged them toward the doorway.

Markos couldn't help himself. Before he left the main hall, he yelled, "Long live the queen!"

His cry carried down the passageway, and the guards shoved him into the hall for the separate wing. The door slammed shut behind him, but not before he heard the prisoners turn his words into a chant. "Long live the queen! Long live the queen! Long live the queen!"

He pumped his fist and smiled. His admission of Celia as his queen—and his wish for her to live long—would get across the idea that the deadly rituals belonged in the past. Change was coming.

The hall for the solitary confinement wing was short and empty of guards. Only one door lay ahead of them. Like the others in the main hall, this door had a cutout so guards could check on the prisoner inside, but the door behind them was solid, isolating this cell from the rest of the building.

Alone now, Hipdemos released Markos. "Well done."

Their escort unlocked the door ahead of them and laughed. "I'd say that Alkipsia might send more guards if she hears of the disruption, but I don't know that she has any more to send."

Inside, Archimedes rose. "Good to see you, my boy." He waved toward the ruckus beyond the solid door behind them and winked. "That's a fine start to the revolution."

"Is that what I'm doing here?" Markos crossed his arms. "Reigniting the war?"

"What makes you think the war ever ended?" Archimedes tilted his chin. "You saw what she's doing out there. She restarted hostilities long before you returned. Your presence is simply giving them hope." He beckoned to something in the corner. "A friend wants to say hello to you."

Markos caught a black and white ball of fur in his arms. "Molly! I should have known you were involved." He scanned the cell. Solid stone and twenty-plus feet of packed dirt from the surrounding hill encircled them on all sides. "How did you get in here, girl?"

"Molly, is she?" Archimedes lifted his robes off the floor. "When the guards transported me back to the entrance, she dashed from the shadows and hid at my feet under here as we walked down the hall. She's a smart girl."

"Yes, she is." Markos set her down and ruffled her fur. "Is she yours?"

"Hardly. I'm not sure she belongs to anyone."

Markos scrutinized the Ancient One's expression. "But she knows you, and while on the Earthen plane, I thought I saw..." It sounded stupid to say it aloud when he wasn't sure, but he had to know. "I'm probably wrong, but for a second, I thought I saw gold in her eyes."

"Ah-ha, so we have a spy in our midst." Despite the threatening words, the old male chuckled. "Only a faerie would have the magic to create a familiar to coordinate with you. So it seems that one of the faerie clans wishes to help you. Perhaps Alkipsia's behavior has concerned some of them as well."

Worrying about Archimedes, then the rest of his tribe, and now faeries. The web of complications to the situation kept growing.

The guard who'd escorted them to the cell strode forward. "Forgive me, my prince, but we must make our move soon. One of those guards is bound to check on us any moment."

Markos stood and took command. "Do you have the key to the Virgin's wing?"

Their escort handed him the key that he'd used to unlock this wing. "This should work on that door as well."

"Thank you...?" he prompted.

"Kosmas, my prince." The dreadlocks of their escort swung forward off his shoulders with his bow. "I am pleased to serve you and your queen."

"Thank you, Kosmas. I'll release Celia, but we need a distraction so Hipdemos can open the other doors. I want this whole building emptied."

Molly yipped at his feet.

Markos patted her head. "Good idea, girl." He indicated the key ring on Kosmas's belt. "Hand the necessary keys to free the others to Hipdemos, and give the rest of the key ring to Molly. Let her be the distraction."

Kosmas removed several keys from the large ring. "Some of the guards in the hallway are with us. I take it my job is to get those who aren't to follow the dog?"

It still felt odd to give orders and ask others to risk themselves. "Are you willing?"

"Of course, my prince." Kosmas held his hand in front of Molly. "Can she bite me to make the story more convincing?"

Molly whimpered.

Markos crouched to look her in the eye. "I know you're not a biting kind of dog, but Kosmas is right. If the guards see an injury, your distraction will work better."

Molly slunk over to Kosmas and gave his hand a lick. Then she stared up at the male, as if to double check what he wanted.

Kosmas ran his hand over her head. "It doesn't have to be a big bite, but it does need to bleed."

Molly gave him another lick and then chomped down on his hand.

Kosmas winced at the impact, and blood leaked through his skin. "Good girl. Quick, Hipdemos with me."

Kosmas shut the cell door just enough to make it look closed, but not enough to engage the lock. The inside of the door didn't have a keyhole, and it wouldn't do them any good to be locked inside with the key.

Markos joined Archimedes at the cutout in the cell's door to watch. Kosmas gave Molly the rest of his key ring and then opened the door at the end of the short hall.

"Yowch!"

Kosmas yanked his hand back, faking a bigger injury, and Molly took off down the main hall, the key ring jangling in her teeth. Kosmas held his hand, faking pain, and displayed the blood dripping down his forearm.

"Stop that dog! She stole my keys!"

The guards standing between the secluded wings didn't move.

Kosmas gave a pained moan and shoved them. "Go! Go! We can't let the keys to the prison fall into the wrong hands!"

This time, the guards took off down the hall, and shouts echoed from around the corner. Hipdemos gave Markos and Archimedes a nod from the far doorway and headed after Kosmas.

Markos opened the door to the cell and crept down the short hall. He glanced down the main passageway from the doorway Hipdemos and Kosmas had just left.

Molly's distraction had done the trick. The guards were clustered at the far end of the hall, scrambling after the dog. Someone—either a guard on their side or one who was clueless—opened the door to the front office. The door to the outside was open a second after that. The pile of guards chased the black and white troublemaker out into the night.

Archimedes waved for Markos. "Get your queen and meet us at the sea cave."

With that, the old male helped Hipdemos direct the remaining dreadlocked guards—who had been smart enough to recognize a distraction from one of their own when they saw one—to unlock the cells. Now that the prison was open, many magically transported to freedom. Others guided each other into the night.

Markos shook his head. Did the Maker herself even know who was really in charge of this plan?

He slipped the key from Kosmas into the door to the Virgin's wing and pushed the door open. Like the wing on the other side, a short hall led to another door, but this one didn't have a cutout for guards to peer inside. The better to keep the Virgin's temptations isolated, most likely. He twisted the key into the second door and cracked it open, attempting to be prepared for whoever might be holding Celia captive on the other side.

A high-pitched scream rent the air, and he burst inside, stumbling into a sitting room. A female attendant lunged for a spear and thrust it in his direction. Adrenaline sped up his reactions, and he instinctively stepped aside and batted the spear, breaking it in two. She screamed again and broke for the door.

He twisted to stop her, but she ducked under his arm. The attendant made it to the short hall for this wing. She slammed the door before he could get his arm out to catch it.

The lock clicked into place.

Chapter Forty

ASS, ASS, AND MORE ASS. MARKOS CHECKED THE INSIDE OF the cell door, but like in the other wing, there was no keyhole on this side. These secure wings were designed to be opened only from the outside. He was locked inside this room, and only the Maker knew if anyone else had a key.

"Markos?"

He spun toward Celia, who was struggling to untie herself from a chair. At least after that colossal failure, she *was* in here with him.

He assisted her in loosening the ties. "Are you all right?"

The pallor of her face sent chills down his limbs, and his fingers fumbled over the knots.

She spit on the ground, enlarging a wet spot beside her. "You got here just in time. That woman was trying to force some sort of tea down my throat, claiming it would help me relax. I think Alkipsia's been *drugging* the Virgins to manipulate their deaths."

As she rubbed her freed wrists, he wiped his palm over his mustache and goatee, soothing muscles that didn't know whether to relax in relief or tense up in anger. Had *all* the guilt he'd carried inside for centuries been based on a lie?

"Nothing surprises me anymore. Did you swallow any of it?"

"Some." She stood and swayed. "Hopefully not too—"

Pounding on the door from the hall interrupted them. Had

Hipdemos or Kosmas come back for him?

He held up a finger and sprinted to the door. "We're locked in here!" He yelled against the thick wood. "Find a key!"

He laid his ear on the door to make out their reply.

"The attendant was right." The voice didn't belong to anyone he knew. "There *is* a male in there with her. Find another key. Quickly. Before he can defile her."

Hades's crows. Markos stepped back from the door. Ice filled his limbs, cracking his hope into tiny splinters. Reinforcements had already arrived.

He couldn't count on Hipdemos or Kosmas to come to their rescue, and now that the guards knew he was in here, they'd be prepared. When they opened the door, the entire guard force would stand between them and the freedom outside.

Only one thing would keep Celia safe now...

If she was no longer a virgin by the time the guards found another key.

CELIA KICKED OFF HER SHOES AND LAY DOWN ON THE BED. NAUSEA rolled through her, and cotton twisted around her thoughts.

Should she force herself to move around, keep her blood circulating? Or try to vomit and get rid of whatever amount of the drug she'd ingested? Or did the fact that she was already feeling the effects mean it was too late for that?

She closed her eyes and moaned. Her brain wasn't working, wasn't providing an answer.

Heavy boots sounded on the stone floor of the room. The thumps were followed by the jangling of buckles. A leather jacket slumped onto the stone, metal clanging against the rock.

She knew the sounds but couldn't understand the context. Were they far away, or right beside her?

The bed indented on both sides of her, and she opened her eyes. Markos leaned over her, his forehead glistening with a thin sheen. His jaw clenched, and his eyelids tightened, like he was in pain.

"I'm sorry. This isn't how I wanted our first time to go, but we have to do this now."

Her eyes couldn't focus on him. He looked far away, and yet someone's hands pulled her dress up to her waist.

"Markos..." She flailed against the unseen assailant and pushed her dress down.

"This is the only way. I'm sorry." The hand that couldn't belong to Markos, couldn't belong to her husband in the distance, yanked her underwear out of the way.

"Markos!" She shoved the invisible chest, but it was too big and strong for her to move.

She was trapped.

Powerless.

Vulnerable.

"It will be okay, and then we'll be together."

Helpless under the solid mass of the unseen attacker, ringing sounded in her ears, and panic over-sensitized her nerves. The weight engulfed her.

Tears sprang into her eyes. "Markos, please help me."

Why wasn't he saving her? Rescuing her?

Despite his constant murmurings to remain calm, flashbacks filled her mind of a dark, cold night with her face smashed onto broken glass. Too much weight. Too much not under her control. Too much not what she wanted.

"Don't worry. I'll keep you safe." Bare skin—too soft to be anything other than the head of a shaft—pressed against her opening.

Her fear burst out in a shriek. "No!"

Markos made a strangled noise and flew off the bed. She sat up at the sudden release of pressure, and her vision cleared for a moment. He sank to the floor against the wall, and his fingers clawed at his throat, as though he couldn't breathe.

Oh God. It *had* been Markos the whole time, and the collar was punishing him for going against her wishes.

"I forgive you!" She crawled toward him across the bed, kicking off her half-removed underwear as she went, un-hobbling her movement. "I didn't know—"

The door in the front room broke open, and over a dozen attendants poured into the room. Like Markos and the other unicorns she'd seen, their brown skin tone would pass for black on Earth, but unlike him, their hair flowed loose around their heads, similar to the others she'd met in the council room.

They surrounded Markos, spears extended. One poked him with a tip hard enough that he flinched while curled in a ball on the floor.

"Markos Ambrostead, you've been found guilty of high treason, consorting with enemies of the tribe, encouraging a rebellion, enacting a prison break, and attempting to defile the Virgin."

"What? No!" She stumbled off the bed and elbowed her way through the spears to stand in front of Markos.

Markos straightened behind her, squeaks of leather indicating he was fastening his pants before facing the attendants. The effect of the drugs washed over her again, and her legs wobbled. The weight of Markos's hands on her shoulders didn't help.

He gave her a squeeze. "Am I to be put to death?"

Dizziness swirled in her head. Although whether that was due to fear for him or a symptom of the drugs, she couldn't be sure. She hoped to God that she'd recover fast enough to help him.

"Your sentencing is delayed until such time that our high priestess can determine the suitable punishment. Come with us. Our high priestess will begin the ritual as soon as we arrive at the temple arena."

"*Now?*" She and Markos echoed each other's thoughts.

The ritual was supposed to be at noon, right? Something about the height of the magic matching the height of the Mythos sun?

"It is past midnight on the day of the Spring Equinox, close enough to the height of the Virgin's power to meet our needs. Our high priestess doesn't want to take any more chances."

The attendant emphasized his point by motioning for the others to clear the path to the door. Their instructions clear, she and Markos headed to the doorway. Markos reached out and tried to take her hand, but they forced him away with their spear points.

They might be able to threaten Markos, but they couldn't threaten her. As they passed the now-empty cells in the main hallway, she moved toward him instead. Unwilling to spill her blood, the attendants were helpless to stop her.

She squeezed his hand. "I'm sorry."

"You have nothing to apologize for. I didn't realize the drugs had taken effect already, and I forgot how the situation could scare you, and that's inexcusable. I'm sorry. Besides, I haven't given up yet."

The evidence around her confirmed that he'd organized a prison break. All the cell doors stood wide open, wood pieces littered the ground, and glass shards from smashed lanterns forced her to ignore the hallucinatory effects of the drugs and watch her step, her still-bare feet vulnerable to injuries. Not a prisoner was in sight.

Why would he release prisoners? She hoped that meant he had a plan.

Outside, the cool night air chilled her arms, and dew dampened the soles of her feet. Bells rang through the darkness. She didn't have to be told what they signified. They called the tribe to the ceremony.

To her death.

Chapter Forty-One

HALLUCINATIONS SCRAMBLED THE SENSORY INFORMATION from her nerves, and Celia's steps faltered over the grass. Markos held her up and gave her a small smile.

"Now we know for certain that the magic won't let me do anything you don't want me to do."

She took a calming breath. He was right. She still had power in this confrontation to come.

Like before, the attendants didn't want to touch her, so they walked rather than use magic to travel from the prison. Silvery paths cut through the trees, becoming broader and more crowded as they neared their destination. Nothing in Markos's homeland could be termed a downtown area, but the collection of marble buildings in this clearing came the closest.

Others of his tribe emerged from the surrounding forest and joined them in the journey to the oval arena. Like their guards, the others' hair was loose around their heads. Many stared at her with open curiosity, sharing widened eyes and whispered comments. A couple of them stomped along the path in their unicorn form. None was as big or tall as Markos, in either form. Together with his magic abilities, he truly was one of a kind, even among his tribe.

And he's my husband.

Warmth filled her chest. In every way, he was special.

Then the oval-shaped building of her destiny rose before them, glowing in white marble like something out of Ancient Greece or Rome, and the warmth crackled into ice chips stabbing her ribs. Only her trust in the man beside her and the magic between them kept her from fainting on the spot.

The crowd jostled them, the path narrowing at the entrance. The attendants encircled her as close as they dared without touching her. Darkness surrounded them, the tunnel under the stands blocking the light from the moon. A sharp rock pierced the sole of her foot, and a yelp squeaked through her lips.

Markos gave a loud grunt beside her, and his hand slipped from her grasp.

"Markos?" Blackness concealed the bodies around her, and she couldn't make out his shape among the faint shadows.

Sharp points nudged her forward, and she shuffled into the open. Soft light from the moon illuminated an arena very much like the Roman Coliseum of old, where gladiators, slaves, and lions had battled to the death. But Markos was nowhere to be seen.

Horizontal spear lengths boxed her in from all sides and shoved her toward the center of the field. Two poles stood upright on a raised platform in the middle of the arena.

Her heartbeat raced, and the press of attendants and spears around her felt too constricting. She gasped in desperate breaths. Where was Markos?

Her legs stopped moving with any coordination, and the attendants became more aggressive, bruising her with whacks from their spears, forcing her forward.

"Markos!"

Her vision telescoped again, and she couldn't tell what was near and what was far. If it weren't for the spears pressing her forward, she'd guess she could escape from the guards that appeared to be in the distance. Between their heads, she glimpsed stands at one end of the oval, filling with others of Markos's tribe. But no Markos.

Bang, bang, bang. Several guards pounded a stake as long and thick as her leg into the ground in front of the raised dais.

All too quickly, she stood on the elevated platform with the poles. Her breaths accelerated.

Fast. Too fast. Black spots formed on the edge of her vision, and her throat ached from hyperventilating.

What had they done to Markos? Had they found another way to kill her and take her magic? One that allowed them to carry out a death sentence on him after all? Oh God, was Markos dead already?

Spear rods crushed her ribs from all sides, making her gasps even shallower. She thrashed but couldn't move. Twenty guards, each carrying two-inch-thick spears, surrounded her with the wooden bars, imprisoning her and her limbs, moving her like a puppet.

Spears caught under her arms. Crossed in a triangle, the wooden rods slid and forced her hand up. She tried to slump and pull her arm from their grip, but other spears held her in place. Her gaze tracked to where they were leading her hand.

A shackle high on the pole glinted in the moonlight.

Oh God. She twisted but couldn't free herself, especially with the drugs sending her false information. And no matter what, her strength was no match for twenty large guards determined to keep her still and prevent her from touching them. Several held rods on either side of her legs so she couldn't even kick.

They knew what they were doing. They'd done this many times before. At least twenty times before, in fact.

Alkipsia probably had an excuse for this treatment—to prevent the Virgins from freaking out and hurting themselves upon their first sight of Markos, most likely—but the truth was that everything was designed to induce their panic. She wanted to keep the Virgins deep under the effects of the drugs.

Clunk. The manacle clamped around her wrist and bit into her skin.

A matching shackle on the other pole caught her eye. They were going to string her up. Helpless. Exposed. Alone.

She was going to be murdered, and who knew what they'd already done to Markos. If he was alive, if he was all right, he'd be here with her right now. He'd make everything okay.

But he wasn't here. He wasn't all right.

Her struggles didn't prevent the capture of her other wrist in the second manacle. *Clunk.*

Her shoulders burned, but if she fought her predicament now, she'd just dislocate her shoulders. The wide metal bands on her wrists extended several inches up her forearms, taking away any hope of yanking her hands through the loops. These weren't skinny handcuffs she could slide her hands through to escape. Sure, the shackles were lightly padded with a thin strip of leather, but that was probably just so she couldn't cut herself on the metal and *waste* any of her blood.

Similar manacles, but attached to chains secured to the platform, locked around her ankles. The chains didn't spread her legs too much, but they did prevent her from kicking.

The guards stepped back, all except one. A scar slashed his thick eyebrow in half, and unlike Markos's neat mustache and goatee, this man's facial hair was wild and unruly. He moved closer and sneered.

"You've made our last Guardian impure. You *deserve* to die."

He bent down and slipped the tip of his spear under the hem of her dress. Ice shot through her limbs, and she didn't dare move. Misjudging the hallucinatory effects now might kill her.

Darkness gleamed from deep inside his eyes. "The high priestess let me volunteer to make you suffer."

The cold metal tip slid up the front of her dress like a rigid snake. She held her breath, and the triangular lump under the fabric passed over her stomach and chest. She tried not to show fear, but she flinched when the point poked the curve of her neck.

Just like the rapist's knife in the alley.

He kept one hand on the bottom of the spear and half-stood, grabbing the top end with his other hand. "We can't lose any of your precious blood in your clothes now, can we?"

Oh shit. Her stomach hollowed out and made her want to vomit. He was going to strip her, making her truly exposed in front of this crowd. She didn't even have her underwear on anymore, as she'd kicked them off in her haste to release Markos from his collar. Her skin crawled at the thought of being naked in front of everyone.

She swirled her tongue in her mouth, gathering saliva, and spit in his face. "Markos would kill you for doing this."

He recoiled and snapped his teeth at her. "I'd defile you with this spear if I could."

He angled the spear and pressed the rod between the tops of her spread legs in demonstration. The binding fabric of her dress pulled at her back and neck, and the pole jammed against her groin. She rose up on tiptoes to relieve the pressure, but he kept pushing, bruising her pelvic bone and prickling the sensitive skin with splintery wood.

He shoved the bottom of the spear back at such an angle that stitches ripped at her dress's neckline and his hand lay between her separated thighs. She squeezed her knees together, trapping his hand and forcing her skin against his. He screamed like her touch burned him.

"*Skoro!*" He released the end of the spear and flattened his hand, sliding it out from between her thighs. "You donkey."

He grasped the bottom of the pole again and yanked both ends hard enough to pull her off her feet. She fell forward until the manacles caught her weight and cut into the heel of her palms. Her dress ripped off her body at the sharp tug and slid down the spear over his hands.

Chill bumps rose over her skin at the sudden exposure. If the crowd's gasps at her complete nudity were causing her to blush, she couldn't tell. The cold air sucked every bit of heat from her body, including her cheeks. The guard spit back into her face and left her hanging there, shivering in her nakedness.

He twisted his spear and flung the fabric toward the other guards fifteen feet away. They jumped out of the way of the parachuting material. Her beautiful dress fluttered to the ground, where the guards stomped it into the dirt until no white remained.

Laughter brought her gaze back to the scar-marked guard. He smirked and hopped off the chest-high platform and then joined the others in heading toward the front of the arena.

She dug her toes into the wooden floor and rocked her weight backward. After two swings, she finally got her balance again and straightened, relieving the manacles' grip on her wrists.

While the other guards gathered near an exit, her tormentor stood below a viewing box built at the front of the arena opposite the stands. Alkipsia and the other two women sat in thrones on the elevated platform.

Alkipsia bared her teeth at the guard, and her voice carried over the flat dirt field. "You weren't supposed to remove *all* her clothes."

"I didn't. The Guardian must have removed the rest in his attempt to defile her."

Alkipsia waved. "Bring out the traitor."

The traitor? Markos was still *alive.*

Chapter Forty-Two

THE GUARDS LEFT THE ARENA AND REENTERED A MOMENT later, dragging something between them. A dust cloud hung in the air behind their path, swirling in her hallucinatory vision.

Testing a hypothesis, Celia blinked and concentrated on slowing her breathing and heartbeat. If Alkipsia had designed the platform and restraints to make the Virgins panicky, then being calm might lessen the effects of the drugs. Another slow blink and inhalation. Her vision cleared, and as the guards neared, she finally made out their burden.

The guards had split into four groups, each lugging a length of chain as thick as her leg. The four chains each attached to a limb. The leather-pants and huge-biceps limbs of Markos. They towed him, spread-eagle and face down, over the dirt. A dark trail she suspected was blood marked his passage over the ground.

"Markos..." Every ounce of pain and guilt she felt for getting them into this situation came out in her whisper.

He didn't look up, didn't move. How injured was he? Was it too much for him to recover from?

The guards locked his chains to the loop at the top of the stake that had been driven into the ground a few feet in front of her. Unlike her shackles that kept her open and exposed, his chains forced him to stay hunched over on the ground.

No. Not hunched over.

If he was in his unicorn form, the chains would keep all four legs on the ground, but leave his head—and his horn—free to kill her.

Okay, think. What was Alkipsia's plan?

Celia analyzed the situation and the physical setup of the center of the arena. Maybe by understanding the past, she could see weaknesses in the present.

All the other times, the Virgins would have been fully drugged and terrified, seeing hallucinations everywhere they turned. Unaware of Alkipsia's trickery, Markos would have changed to unicorn form and knelt at the front of the platform to offer himself, which would place his horn chest-high with Virgin. When Alkipsia gave the invitation—which might have even used trigger words to enhance the power of suggestion—and released the Virgins, their telescoping vision and panic would make them run off the platform—and onto Markos's horn.

That hypothesis made sense, right? Close enough anyway. So how could she beat it?

For one thing, she'd spit out most of the drugs and knew how to fight their effects.

For another thing, Markos wasn't in his unicorn form, so Alkipsia must have a plan to force him to change. What that plan might be was a big question mark.

The guards stepped back from him and took their place in front of Alkipsia's viewing stage. She stood and rang a bell.

The crowd in the stands behind Celia, which had gotten louder at Markos's entrance, silenced. In fact, from what she could see over her shoulders, the arena was almost full now, populated by latecomers who had arrived during her and Markos's ordeals.

"Greetings, my subjects. I am afraid today is a sad day. Guardian Markos has failed in his duty. He brought the Virgin to us, but then committed treason by releasing the prison population to terrorize us all."

Shocked murmurs swept through the audience in the arena.

"And worse, he attempted to defile the Virgin before the ceremony."

Some in the arena shot to their feet, words of hate on their lips.

She held up a hand. "Just as our Maker is merciful, so am I. Guardian Markos has fallen under the spell of this Virgin, and he must be given the opportunity to make up for his mistakes."

Boos echoed through the stands. *Plunk.* A puff of dirt marked where a rock landed beside the platform.

"Guardian Markos refuses to shift forms and start the ritual, but the Maker has provided a way to *force* him to change. If the Virgin orders him to shift, the magic will compel him to obey."

Quiet pressed over the arena until Celia could hear her pulse in her ears. The collar. She theoretically *could* order Markos to change to his unicorn form, but why would she do anything Alkipsia wanted?

She lifted her chin and faced Alkipsia at her viewing stage. "I voluntarily came here because I love Markos and wanted to help him heal his tribe. But we both know this ritual isn't needed at all. I've *already* accepted him. You just want me dead, and you think if Markos changes form that I'll fling myself off this platform like all the other Virgins you drugged and murdered."

Grumbles spread out around her. The bell rang out again, and Alkipsia whispered to the guards. A few disappeared under the stadium and returned a moment later, one of them carrying a dark loop of something.

The guard who'd tormented her earlier approached. He unwound the loop to reveal a whip, its frayed tail threaded with... Things. Metal, rock, or bone, she couldn't tell, but this whip was designed for cruel and agonizing punishment. He didn't come up to her—the Virgin whose blood must be preserved—but stopped at Markos's still form.

Oh God, no.

The whip whistled through the air and landed on Markos bare back with a crack.

"No!"

Markos woke and staggered to his knees. The chains around his wrists prevented him from righting himself further.

Her guilt burst out in a rush. "Oh, Markos, I'm so sorry. I love you. I never wanted you to be hurt."

He spun toward her, his eyes widening at her nudity displayed on the poles.

He scrambled toward the guard near him. "You animal!"

The chains yanked him back to the spike in the ground, and he landed on his face. The guard laughed, his scar twisting with his expression.

Markos knelt up again and spat at the man, splattering him with blood. "I swear on my mother's soul, I will *kill* you for treating Celia like this."

The guard sneered and swaggered closer, just out of reach of Markos. He leaned close and whispered so low only she and Markos could hear his threat. "I'll make you watch when I *katepelso* her dead body."

She had no idea what the untranslatable word meant, but Markos lowered his arms, creating more slack in the chains, and jumped. The top of his skull caught the man's face.

The guard staggered back and held his hand to his nose. Blood dripped down his forearm. Alkipsia thumped the arm of her throne and called him back to her side.

Markos scanned the crowds and knelt as upright as he could. "I am *Prince* Markos, and my duty has been, and always will be, to do what is right for my tribe. I take the responsibility granted by my heritage seriously. For a long time, I thought capitulating to Alkipsia was the best thing for all of us. I didn't want to cause more deaths in a never-ending war."

Up on her stage, Alkipsia shouted orders to the guards.

"But everything she's told us is a lie. The Maker does *not* want us to force Virgins into this ritual. The Maker does *not* want us to survive off the tainted magic of a Virgin's death. The magic of the Maker placed this mark around my neck." He arched his head, showing off the tattoo-like lines. "The magic of the Maker bound me to my wife. The Maker wants us to mate and have babies, to live and love, to grow old and die, like we did before the war. Alkipsia wants us to deny that magic, deny the Maker."

The scarred torturer rushed toward Markos, whip in hand. *Crack.* The whip landed across Markos's back. He flinched but didn't yield.

"The high priestess lied to us all." *Crack.* "She outlawed matings for everyone so I would never have a female child and reestablish the line of succession." *Crack.* "She enacted these rituals to twist the magic so the Virgins' deaths would sustain her everlasting life." *Crack.* "This is not the Maker's way."

His voice broke on the last word, but the guard unleashed his cruelty, continuing to punish the now-silent, hunched-over Markos. *Crack. Crack. Crack.*

Celia bit back the tears gathering in her eyes. Markos sat with his knees pointed out, feet tucked close to him, and he curled forward over his toes. His back took the full brunt of each impact, and he jerked with each strike. How much more could he take?

He was a hero in every respect. Her hero. Her love. Her husband.

She'd rarely had the guts to stand up to anyone other than Markos before, much less a whole mob, but he needed her to be strong. She took up where he'd left off. "Is this the behavior of a virtuous and merciful ruler? She punishes Markos for telling the truth."

She did her best to ignore the cracks from the whip, now punishing Markos for *her* protests. Each one scored her heart, tempting her to doubt herself. But she trusted Markos enough to follow his lead.

"There is *no* commandment from the Maker against matings. Don't you want to love? To find your true mate? To know boundless joy in the arms of someone who loves you unconditionally? Don't you long to raise children and see them grow?"

She didn't know if she was convincing them, but the murmurs rolling through the audience sounded better than their earlier shouts of anger.

"I *love* Markos. I love him so much I gave him my soul. I would gladly die to protect him from the cruelty of Alkipsia and her lapdog, but that's not what Markos wants. He *knows* how she's imprisoned you all with her lies, and he wants you to be free, to live your life the way your Maker meant for you to live. My death won't bring that about. My death will only make her stronger."

Markos screamed in agony, choking the next words in her throat.

Oh no. Her chest stiffened, tension slicing deep into her core, and she couldn't draw a breath. She'd never learned how to be good with people, how to relate to them, and now she'd made

Jami Gold

Markos suffer for that flaw.

The bell rang out again, and Alkipsia stood at the edge of her stage. "You speak as though we don't know love. We know love very well. The love of a tribe for their Maker. A Maker who wants to shield us from making mistakes—"

"Liar!" Markos's strangled yell emerged from his huddled form, where he still bent over his hands and feet. He didn't move his shredded back to sit up, but he lifted his head. "Celia and I have shared"—he panted—"incredible experiences because of our love." He gasped for another breath. "The Maker would never forbid us from knowing that kind of pure goodness." He grimaced and panted again. "*You're* the one making a mistake, Alkipsia."

Maybe it was wishful thinking, but the crowd seemed to be turning their way. Alkipsia seemed to come to the same conclusion. She recalled the guard with the whip and sent a different one to the center of the arena.

Celia almost felt hopeful until noticing this one brandished an axe. Dismemberment? That seemed rather...

Permanent.

She swallowed the panic bubbling up her throat. She couldn't lose her head to the drugs again. "Markos, how can I help?"

He glanced at the new weapon and smiled. "Stall for as long as you can, and then get ready for a ride."

What?

He winked, hiding the now-brilliant gold of his eyes for a second. "Trust me."

"Always."

The new guard took position over Markos and held the axe above his head. No, not dismemberment.

Beheading.

Chapter Forty-Three

CELIA'S HEART LODGED IN HER THROAT, BLOCKING AIR FROM reaching her lungs. The pulse at the base of her neck pounded so hard she feared the throbbing mass would burst through her skin.

She forced calm back into her mind. Unless Alkipsia planned to condemn the whole tribe, this was a bluff. It had to be.

Alkipsia rang the bell up on her platform, silencing the growing rabble from the assembly in the stadium. "Order Markos to take his unicorn shape and kill you, or I'll kill him. Let's see if your love is really as strong as you say. Do you wish for him to live or not?"

Her instructions no longer pretended that this ritual was anything but a deadly sacrifice. Markos's face was blank, giving her no indication of how she should answer.

Movement in the shadows on either side of the viewing stage caught her eye. The old man from the council room stood to one side of the low wall around Alkipsia's stage. Another man in dreadlocks stood next to the wall on the other side of the platform. Friends of Markos's?

The old man bent down and picked up a black and white dog. Molly...

Markos's gaze settled on hers and glowed for a second, like he knew what she'd seen. What had the old man said in the council room? That Markos could read her emotions?

Could she send him a message that way?

Alkipsia raised her hand, and the axeman hefted his weapon higher in preparation for a strike. "Your answer. Now."

"I wish for him to live."

She filled her mind with images of her and Markos escaping from the arena and living happily ever after. She closed her eyes and pictured their children scampering around their feet. She stoked the warmth in her heart with thoughts of many passionate nights in each other's arms. She imagined what she'd do to him to bring him pleasure.

When she'd formed an image so solid in her mind of what she wanted their future to be that she almost forgot about the chill on her naked body and the threats around them, she opened her eyes and gave him a smile.

"Markos Ambrostead, I love you more than life itself. I order you to give me what I want. Make it happen."

The axeman stepped back and loosened his grip on the weapon.

Markos grinned and whispered, "With pleasure."

He sprang up, free of his chains—but oh God, the skin of his hands and feet was ragged and coated with blood, like he'd forcefully yanked them through the cuffs—and grappled the axe from the unsuspecting guard. He twisted in a smooth motion and smacked the guard with the blunt edge of the weapon.

The guard flew into the air and fell to the ground like a hay bale dropped from a barn loft. Markos was at her side by the time the crowd rose to its feet. Four powerful strokes of the axe released her shackles.

He handed her the weapon and stepped to the side. The blade thumped to the platform, her strained shoulders unable to hold up its weight.

He yelled into the shocked arena. "Join me, and experience true magic—life and love!"

She glanced at him to ask him the plan, but mist already surrounded him as he transformed. The other guards rushed the platform from their place in front of Alkipsia, and she couldn't help whispering, "Hurry."

As though her wish was made reality, he solidified in his unicorn form, his back still shredded from the whipping even in this form, and he lay down next to her. She figured he wanted her to ride him and wield the heavy axe, but she had no strength for a one-handed climb.

Yet as soon as she touched him, his strength and power flowed into her body. His magic, her magic, and the magic between them combined to make them a single entity. She scrambled onto his back, and he leaped off the platform and faced the oncoming horde.

Like she and Markos were one and the same, she swung the axe and connected with the onrushing guards with the skill of a warrior. She incapacitated them with the blunt face, but didn't kill. Despite their loyalty to Alkipsia, they were still his people.

A spear whizzed toward them, and she tossed the axe into her left hand. She snatched the spear out of mid-air with her right hand and spun it like a baton, knocking several guards off their feet. She hardly had time to marvel at her borrowed skill.

Most of the guards came at them from the sides, avoiding Markos's deadly horn. The long rod of the spear twirled in her hands, shielding them from most of the spears thrown their way. A few nicks, but no piercing injuries.

Ahead, Alkipsia crouched behind her throne and dragged it with her as she shrank against the back wall of her viewing stage. Markos burst through the guards surrounding them and galloped toward her perch.

A unicorn, nearly as big as Markos, stamped in front of their path to Alkipsia. A jagged scar cut across its forehead. The torturer.

She didn't need to ask Markos's plan. The magic joined them so completely that they were one being. One mind. One heart.

Like a mythological version of the game of chicken, Markos aimed straight for the fast-approaching unicorn. At the last second, Markos veered to the side and aimed his horn at the male's chest.

The scarred unicorn did the same, but she was ready. The mighty axe whacked into the other beast's horn. The blade cleaved the golden point from his forehead.

He shrieked with an unearthly cry, and Markos's horn found its target. The other male's vulnerable heart.

His screech cut off. Markos dipped his head and let the other unicorn slip from his horn. The beast's body slumped to the ground.

As one, she and Markos sought Alkipsia. The two men, whom she knew from Markos's mind to be Archimedes and Hipdemos, held Alkipsia's arms against the back wall of the viewing stage, preventing her from drawing a magical doorway and escaping.

For a second, Celia sensed Markos hesitate, wondering if he should kill her. Then memories flashed between them of the other Virgins. The other lives Alkipsia had made him take. The way she'd turned him into a murderer for her selfishness.

He gathered his speed again and leapt onto the elevated dais. He aimed his horn for her heart behind the throne.

When they were mid-air, her expression changed. Fear turned to smugness. Defeat turned to contempt. A flash burst from her body just as his horn pierced the throne.

The wood cracked and split in half, but his horn met only air on the other side.

Alkipsia wasn't there.

Chapter Forty-Four

MARKOS SKIDDED TO A STOP AND TUGGED THE POINT OF HIS horn from the wooden back wall. *Hades's curse.* How had she escaped?

Before dealing with the mystery, he checked the scene on the arena floor to see if they needed to rejoin the battle. Some of the guards were still unconscious. Some had thrown down their weapons with Alkipsia's disappearance. And some were surrounded by clusters of tribe members with dreadlocks.

In the corner of the platform, the two lower priestesses were cowering and telling anyone who would listen that they surrendered.

Was the war really over?

He slid Celia off his back and changed back to his human shape. Molly sniffed around the empty space where Alkipsia had been while he re-solidified.

He ignored the stings on his back from the still-healing slashes and tucked Celia's nakedness against his body. "Someone bring me a robe."

A wad of fabric was pressed into his hands, and he helped Celia slip her arms into the holes. Her body shook, probably a combination of the cold, leftover shock and fear, and blood circulation issues from being strung up. He wrapped the cloth across her front and tightened the sash.

"It's all right." He drew her into his arms, determined to never let her go again. "I've got you."

Molly barked and pawed at Archimedes. He sniffed the spot on the wall she indicated. If Markos wasn't mistaken, the location was where one of Alkipsia's hands had touched the wall while they'd restrained her.

Archimedes looked at him. "See if you recognize that scent."

He bent and smelled the wood along the wall. Singed. Like ozone.

Donkey's balls. Right as Alkipsia disappeared, there had been a flash. Unicorns didn't use magic like that, but he knew who did. And their magic left behind the scent of ozone.

"Faeries."

"Faeries," Archimedes confirmed. He glanced at Molly by their feet. "So at least one of the faerie clans wants to help you, and at least one clan has been helping Alkipsia. Rather directly."

A world of difference separated an animal-familiar with limited power and a faerie with strong enough magic to pierce the borders of his homeland. Penetrating their temple arena, no less. If enough faeries had that ability, invasion was a real possibility.

His chest tightened, and chills coated his skin in a cold sweat. "This isn't over, is it?"

Archimedes gave him a sad smile. "The battle for your crown is over, but I fear the war for the Mythos plane has just begun."

Hipdemos tapped him on the shoulder and gestured to the arena, where his tribe sat in shocked silence. "I think you should make an address."

Probably a good idea. If only he knew what to say.

Beside him, Celia seemed to be settling from the trauma. A murmur floated to his ears. "We did it. We survived."

"Yes, we did." He longed to kiss her, to comfort her, to make love to his wife for the first time, but celebrations would have to wait.

She met his eyes, and determination shone in her gaze. She understood.

Together, they walked to the edge of the platform. Markos took a deep breath and decided to honor the vow he'd made to always tell Celia the truth. Only this time, he'd apply it to his subjects.

"Alkipsia has disappeared." He let their outburst quiet down before adding, "She escaped with the help of faerie magic."

Anger rippled through the arena. Despite the passage of millennia since the last hostilities between the homelands, distrust still ran high.

One of her guards limped forward. "Was that the flash of light?"

"Yes."

Markos scanned the crowd. A few dreadlocked tribe members dotted the stands here and there, but most showed no evidence of being on his side. Ass. From their perspective, he had a lot of explaining to do.

"Over four hundred and sixty years ago, Alkipsia changed our world. We replaced a royal ruler who had a sense of responsibility to her subjects with one who perverted our religion to claim her superiority and justify her selfishness. Things weren't perfect under the old way, but things haven't been perfect the last few centuries either."

No one spoke up in Alkipsia's defense. Whether his earlier words or her faerie-assisted escape had done more to decimate her reputation, he didn't know, but they weren't clamoring to have her back in either case. Hopefully that would make the next step easier.

"I'd like to try a better way. A path where we can honor the traditions of our past and work together for our future."

He checked the faces of those around him. Archimedes and Hipdemos looked about to burst with pride, and Celia gave him a supportive smile.

"Alkipsia kept me under house arrest until she needed my magic for her schemes, and I've since spent most of my life on the Earthen plane. Most of you don't know me at all. Or maybe you merely know my name. After living for centuries under Alkipsia's lies, I hardly know who I am myself. But let me tell you what I *do* know."

He squeezed his wife against his side. "I know I love Celia beyond description. We're married by Earthen plane traditions and bound by magic. Alkipsia tried to tell us matings were forbidden, but to believe that, we'd have to deny our Maker's magic." He touched his neck, reminding them of his collar. "I refuse to do that. I plan on having many children with my wife. And if we should be so fortunate as to have a female heir..."

He swept his hand in front of him to indicate everyone in the arena.

"I'll leave it up to you to determine whether my daughters will rule or not. Regardless, I will raise them to believe that the will of their subjects must be respected."

He gestured to the splintered throne behind him and then out to the posts on the center mound.

"I don't want another like Alkipsia to rise to power." He let his gaze linger on those without dreadlocks now. He needed them to understand. "I know many of you supported her in the war centuries ago. I'm not interested in keeping track." He repeated the observation he'd given to Hipdemos long ago. "A tribe divided is no tribe at all."

He surveyed the crowd again. "Some of you might have agreed with her methods of gathering magic to sustain us—even though it meant the death of Virgins—but we're closer to extinction now than before the changes. If she hadn't been drugging and killing Virgins to prevent matings, we probably would have been healed long ago. Celia is proof of the true possibilities of mutual respect between our kinds."

He extended his arm in the direction of the lightening horizon.

"In a couple of hours, the sun will rise on a new day in our homeland. I ask you to set aside our differences so it will also rise on the birth of a stronger, fairer, and happier tribe. Will you greet the dawn with me?"

For a moment, no one responded. Then from the depths of the stands, someone shouted, "I greet the dawn! Long live the king! Long live the queen!"

In the next moment, others took up the cry. Soon, the arena echoed with hundreds of voices, chanting the same words.

He thumped his fist to his chest in a salute of respect. Beside him, Celia charmed the crowd by waving and blowing kisses.

This was more than he'd ever imagined. No longer the outcast with barely a friend to his name, he now had a whole tribe, many friends and allies—a wife. All thanks to Celia. Warmth filled his heart until it overflowed, expanding through his ribs, spreading through his limbs.

He let the moment sink deep into his soul, patching the holes of self-doubt and stitching the shreds of false failures. He *belonged*. Here. Now. He felt healed already.

They spent the rest of the night greeting their subjects. Several couples approached them, thanking Markos and Celia for ridding the tribe of the law against mating. The love those couples shared, even after centuries of being forced apart, filled him with a sense of certainty. They'd fixed the wrongs and made things right.

When the sky lightened enough, the entire tribe walked to the sea cliff together. As one, they watched the sun rise over the water.

Chapter Forty-Five

THE RISING SUN WARMED CELIA'S SKIN AND BANISHED THE LAST of her chill. The new day brought new questions, however. Markos's words had been grand and inspiring but left a huge *now what?* question mark over their future together.

Becoming queen to a unicorn tribe hadn't been part of her plan to do something positive and good with her life. His homeland was magical and beautiful, and maybe they even farted glitter and pooped rainbows like the jokes about unicorns claimed, but this was his dream, not hers.

She'd come to *heal* the tribe. The politics of being the dutiful wife of a ruler in a foreign land were beyond her qualifications. She'd spent her whole life as an outsider, and just like in Auntie's neighborhood, her looks marked her as an outsider here.

She tried to put a bright face on the situation for his sake, but her smile faltered more often than not as the sun's disk fully formed in the sky. She hadn't slept all night, she'd frozen her ass off, and every single person around her had seen that ass, along with every other part of her, not that long ago. To say she was *effing* exhausted was putting it mildly.

Hell, she was even using profanity, and that wasn't like her at all.

Mentally, emotionally, and physically, she was done. She just wanted to curl under the covers at home. Wherever that was.

Pure Sacrifice

Yet the conversations around her dragged on. After strategies were discussed for how to deal with the faerie entanglement, plans were outlined to appoint Hipdemos as regent, whatever that meant, Archimedes as chief adviser, someone named Parimenos as chief attendant, and someone called Kosmas as head of the security force. The gathering seemed to take these developments in stride, but something about them bugged her.

Maybe it was the feminist in her who noticed the lack of females in the mix—which struck her as odd for a supposedly matriarchal society. Or maybe it was her American upbringing that chafed at the lack of democracy. Regardless, she found herself slipping away from Markos's inner circle before she bit through her tongue.

She stood near the edge of the cliff and let the warming breeze blow her troubled mood away. Songs drifted on the wind from the waves below. Did they have sirens here? Or singing mermaids? There was so much she didn't know. This wasn't her home.

She turned toward the forest so the sun could warm her back. Most of the tribe was grouped around Markos, but one clump stuck together near the trees. No surprise. Politics were the same no matter where you went. They were probably already planning a rebellion against the revolution.

Like her, Molly was outside the main clump of people. Instead, she nosed around various rocks and flowers near the smaller group.

Celia decided to wander in that direction and visit with Molly, the one familiar creature other than Markos here. And if she happened to overhear the rebels' grumblings, that'd be a bonus.

She sat on the grass next to Molly and stroked the dog's fur. As she suspected, the solitary group wasn't happy.

"But what are we to do about a high priestess in the meantime?"

"Markos has never been a believer."

"He keeps talking about a ruler, but the high priestess does more than just rule."

"He—"

The voices cut off, and she followed the flight of a butterfly as an excuse to look in their direction. They all stared at her. After a lifetime of being ignored, being the target of so many gazes still struck her as odd.

And small talk wasn't one of her strengths. "Er, nice morning, isn't it?"

One woman bowed. "Greetings, my queen. Yes, it is a lovely morning."

They continued staring. Probably hoping she would leave. The one who'd spoken shuffled her feet.

Ugh. She was going to have to get involved.

She patted Molly's head one last time before standing and approaching them. "If you have questions or concerns about all these changes, I'm sure Markos will listen to what you have to say."

The woman who'd greeted her glanced down. "The king has no reason to listen to us."

"Sure he does." Her lips curved at the memory. "If you had any idea how much he resisted me, you'd *know* he takes your tribe's beliefs very seriously."

Another female voice from the back of the group piped up. "Is it true you seduced him?"

A blush heated her cheeks. "That's probably the best description for it, yes." She winced. "Sorry."

The first woman shook her head. "Don't be. We respect strong females who go after what they want." She scanned the faces of those around her. "Your presence, your strength of will, your ability to take control—that is what allowed Markos to claim the throne. No solitary male would be allowed to rule."

The others nodded their agreement.

"So..." A suspicion built in the back of her mind. "If Markos wasn't married, there would already be a rebellion against him?"

"If Markos wasn't married, the battle in the temple arena would still be ongoing."

Her shoulders slumped. The dissidents would rather have a female—any female, even one who wasn't a unicorn or a member of the tribe—in a position of power than have a male in charge. And although the two who had spoken up so far were female, at least half of this group were males.

Just as most of the guards were male, the tribe was content to let males do whatever work they wanted. That's why they were all going along with his male-dominated inner circle. But when it came to who was truly in control, only females counted.

Markos needed her if he was to maintain the peace.

"Would you like for me to take your concerns to Markos and ensure he listens and addresses them?"

Smiles lit across their faces. The woman who'd taken the lead bowed. "We are honored by your understanding, my queen."

The group chattered at her for a moment, ensuring she understood they weren't looking for a high priestess to rule or overthrow the crown—they hadn't been happy with Alkipsia either—but they wanted someone who could perform the religious aspects of the position.

"Do you have someone in mind for a high priestess?"

The group split and let one older woman step forward. "Greetings, my queen." Her voice was that of the second female who'd asked about the rumored seduction. She gave a quick bow. "I am Charisia. I have been a priestess for centuries. The beliefs of our tribe are sacred to me, and I long to return to the purity of the Maker's wishes." She looked down and crossed her hands at her collarbone. "However, I am tainted because I performed my duty alongside Alkipsia. I remained in that position because I hoped some influence of purity was better than none at all, but I'm not sure others will see things that way."

Celia gave her a grin. "Let's find out."

She led the group through the crowd to where Markos stood in the center. His brow rose at the procession, his expression one of curiosity.

"Hi." She dove into the issue. Regardless of the others' fears, she knew he'd be perfectly reasonable. "Some of"—she struggled with the right word, but decided to use the same term he had—"our subjects have concerns about the changes, and I think we should listen to them."

She'd expected his "of course." What she wasn't prepared for was the reaction from the crowd. Like a wave, they sank to one knee and bowed their heads. Those in unicorn form lay down. Soon, only she, Markos, and the dissident group remained standing. After a second, even the dissidents sank to one knee. The breeze blew loud in her ears at their sudden silence.

Oh-kay. That made things awkward.

Markos quietly chuckled. "I think they're eager for a few words from their queen."

Crap. This had been a mistake. How had she gone from nearly invisible to someone who commanded hundreds without even trying? She was *so* not the right person for this job.

"Um, hi. I'm Celia."

She had so much she wanted to say about democracy and equality, but those concepts would fly over their heads. Instead, she had to approach this from a perspective they'd understand.

"You should know that Markos and I are a team. He is my equal, and I am his. We respect each other. We listen to each other. We solve problems together."

A subtle *chuffing* sound floated through the air, the crowd squirming in their clothes. She glanced at Markos to see if she was screwing this all up. He gave her a supportive nod.

"We want the same for all of you. No matter which side you supported during the war, we respect all of you. We'll listen to your concerns, and we'll work together to find a solution."

A few exchanged confused looks. A society without a history of democracy probably had no idea what that *working together* would look like. Maybe she was being arrogant for thinking democracy was the "best" way for them, especially when she hardly understood their culture at all, but if she was going to have to live here and be part of their society, she figured she should get some say in the matter.

"For example, some have already come to me with their concerns about the lack of a high priestess, even one who doesn't rule. Yes, Markos and I plan to have children, but a daughter isn't guaranteed, and infants take a while to grow up." She raised her hand high above her head. "Raise your hand"—she noted those in their unicorn form—"or lift your horn, if you'd like to have a high priestess who doesn't rule but who can teach the beliefs of the Maker's wishes."

No one moved. Not even the dissidents. Democracy 101 lesson needed—stat.

"Okay, I'm going to ask two questions—do you want a high priestess or do you *not* want a high priestess? There's no wrong answer, and everyone should raise their hand or horn and vote for one question or the other. We can't make the decisions that are best for everyone unless we figure out what we want." She waved her hand. "So let's try that again. Do you want a non-ruling high priestess for now?"

Slowly, a few hands and horns crept up, and then more, and even more.

"Okay, put your hands down. Now raise your hand or horn if you *don't* want a high priestess at all." Again, no one moved, but she'd expected that. Some probably worried about disagreeing with what they thought she wanted, even though *she* certainly didn't care one way or another. "Remember, there's no wrong answer. Everyone's opinion is respected."

A few dozen people raised their hands, fewer than before. And it seemed like everyone in the crowd had raised their hand or horn for one or the other, so maybe they'd listened to her instructions.

"More people raised their hands and horns to say they *wanted* a high priestess, so we'll have a high priestess. See how easy it is to have your voice heard? And when you have concerns about how things are run, you can come to Markos"—she hated to involve herself even more, but apparently this was part of the job description—"or me, with your concerns. If we can't fix it ourselves, we'll ask everyone their thoughts in a vote like we just had to determine the best way to handle the situation. Any questions?"

A man's voice spoke up from the edges. "Will you be our high priestess?"

"Good question, and no."

When many in the crowd groaned, she stifled an eye roll. After being subjugated for so long, they were too willing to have a stranger dictate their lives.

"I'm not familiar with your beliefs. Believe me, I'm the wrong person for that job." She extended her arm toward the woman she'd met earlier. "But Charisia says she knows how to be a priestess, and she'd like the opportunity to teach the true beliefs of the Maker and not the lies Alkipsia taught."

She beckoned the woman to stand. As Charisia stood, Markos sucked in a breath. Celia cut off her next words. Maybe he knew this woman to be an enemy.

But he thumped his chest in a salute to her and whispered so low only Celia could hear. "That's the priestess who gave us permission to kiss in the council chamber."

"I like her already." Celia gave the woman a nod. "Charisia, would you introduce yourself?"

Charisia shyly glanced at Archimedes and then looked down. "A long time ago, I loved a male. He spoke of a Virgin who would heal our tribe, return strength to our magic. When our king told Alkipsia about the strengths and awareness of *this* Virgin, months ago, I hoped she would be the one. I was the priestess who suggested to Alkipsia that perhaps our king should watch this Virgin more closely to keep her safe. Alkipsia never listened to us, and I was not able to have as much positive influence as I hoped throughout the centuries, but thanks to the Maker, she did listen—just that once—out of fear. And we are blessed indeed."

Archimedes strode forward and grasped Charisia's hands. "Even when I despaired that you had gone to work with Alkipsia, I could never stop loving you. You were there to influence her when it most counted, and for that, I am grateful and forgiving." He kissed her hand.

Celia swallowed and blinked away the moisture in her eyes. They had to be the cutest couple she'd ever seen. Beside her, Markos's lips twitched, fighting a smile.

She returned her attention to the crowd. "Now we can vote on whether we think Charisia should be the high priestess for the interim."

Charisia was quickly voted into the position, and little by little, Celia led the tribe through the process of democracy and ensuring everyone had a say.

After the issues died down, Markos raised his hand.

Bemused, she laughed. "Yes?"

"What do you think about the idea of me making my wife no longer a virgin and finally healing the tribe?"

The gathering gasped and then broke out into giggles and elbow nudges.

A huge grin burst onto her face. "I think that's a perfect idea, and no"—she eyed the crowd—"I'm not putting that up for a vote."

The tribe laughed, filling her with warmth. Maybe she could do this after all.

If only she didn't have to give up electricity, this future might not be too terrible.

Chapter Forty-Six

AFTER MARKOS DREW A RECTANGLE IN THE AIR AND FORMED a doorway, Celia stepped into his embrace and walked into the mist with him. But instead of white marble or whatever his place on the Mythos plane looked like, the dark colors and dramatically lit glass sculptures of their bedroom in St. Louis met her gaze.

"We're here? We don't have to stay in your homeland all the time?"

His mouth curled teasingly. "We can go back if you want."

"No. Here is fine. Better than fine." A hot shower sounded luxurious, especially compared to the quick dip they'd taken in the sea earlier to rinse off the dirt from the arena.

"I can transport us anywhere, so why not go where you most want to be? I checked with Archimedes, and there's nothing in the history that indicates the magic cares where we are." He pointed to his collar. "In fact, we already know the magic can find us here. So I figured we could split our time between here and there, just like any working couple."

"Markos..." Her breath left her. "That's perfect."

The cell phone she'd left on the dresser buzzed, reiterating the idea that she really *was* on Earth. Markos eyed the device and grinned. "You can even reconnect with your family."

Ever since the funeral—when Markos had permanently

removed his spell—her mother had been trying to get a hold of her. Celia had ignored the calls during their honeymoon, not wanting to open those emotional wounds before she had to leave them. But now...

They needed to plan another wedding.

Her family—the real family she knew from Christmas—would never forgive her if they missed her wedding. And now that she knew she could keep them, she wanted her family to be there with her.

She ran her hand over Markos's bare chest, needing to ensure this vision wasn't a dream. In the low light, her hand nearly glowed against his dark skin. But he was real. *This* was real.

"Handy stuff—that magic. You're already healed."

He held up his hands. Red marks tinged his skin from forearms to fingers. "Mostly. I broke nearly every bone in my hands and feet to pull them through the shackles. Your delay gave me the time I needed to be able to move again while I was huddled over the chains so no one could see what I was doing."

Holy cow. He'd inflicted that pain on himself at the same time he'd endured the agony of being whipped. And then he'd *smiled* about it. "You're amazing."

"Only half as amazing as you. You've already saved my tribe. I gave them words about unification and peace. You made it happen." His gaze held hers, his eyes shining like molten gold. "Thank you."

She stretched on tiptoe and kissed his nose. "So are you only full of *words* about this 'making your wife not a virgin' thing too? Or are you going to make it *happen*?"

He roared with laughter. "Trust me. It'll happen."

With that, he yanked the belt from her robe and pushed the fabric off her shoulders. The material puddled at her feet, and she was once again completely naked. This time, she didn't mind in the least.

His fingertips dove into her hair, and he captured her lips in a sizzling kiss. She moaned against his mouth. This was heaven, especially compared to the hell of a few hours ago.

While his tongue plundered her mouth, he carried her to the bed. His hands moved across her body—arms to wrists, across her ribs and hips, and down to her legs and feet. His healing warmth removed the tenderness from the shackles and the nicks from the spear tips.

He pulled back from their kiss. "All better?"

"All better." But she couldn't help giving him a sly smile. "Except for this tingle deep inside me that might be hard to reach with your hands."

"Mmm-hmm. I have a special trick for reaching that spot."

"Do you now?" She batted her eyelashes in faux innocence. "Will you demonstrate it for me?"

He laid her back on the mattress and pressed his hips against hers. "Over and over and over."

She sucked in a breath. "Can you do it soon? Because I *really* think we've waited long enough."

He chuckled and ran his tongue over her nipple. "Are you sure? I could torture you for a bit longer. We could consider it my birthday present to you."

Oh God. She wanted him so much.

Her fingers shoved between their bodies, and she undid his pants. "No, I'm thinking now."

He leaned away and removed his remaining clothes. Then he lay on his side next to her and skated his fingertip around her breasts and down to the tops of her thighs.

"Too bad. I use only my fingers for the first step of the trick. The magic in them makes you wet, which is needed for the next step." His fingers slipped easily into her opening and started a slow rhythm.

She bit her lip and tried not to rock her hips. He didn't need the encouragement to torture her longer.

"See? Already wet." She gripped his hips and pulled. "Time for phase two."

His eyes glinted, and he didn't move on top of her. "The tool I use for the next step is big. You need to be really wet. *I'll* say when you're ready."

She couldn't argue with his point about being big. He was *huge*, in fact.

His thumb joined in his rhythm below, and her hips gave up their resistance. She rocked into his hand, encouraging the electric sensations building in her core.

He gazed down at her, mischievousness sparkling in his eyes. "Do you know what Archimedes told me about Virgins of the past and all the ways we'll heal the tribe today?"

Archimedes? Who the hell cared about Archimedes at a time like this?

"Um..." She rocked harder, but he didn't increase his rhythm. "No."

"The Guardians' ability to collect magic from a Virgin's spilled blood was meant to keep her alive if anything damaging happened to her. Everything was about connecting the two."

"Fascinating." And it was. But that didn't stop her from stretching and nibbling on his neck to drive him as crazy as he was driving her.

"But you're one of the few Virgins in Archimedes's very long memory who have married into the tribe."

"Mmm." She swirled her tongue on the sensitive spot below his ear. "Maybe that's because unicorns have been too much into torture lately. Like a certain husband I know."

"I tell you all this because I want you to know just how much you mean to me. What we're doing here, today, will at least create additional Guardians and restore the tribe's magic so all can shapeshift again. And because you're marrying into the royal line, there might be other benefits as well." He pulled away, his lips twitching in a teasing curve. "I don't know if you're aware, but a Virgin marrying into the royal line may as well be a goddess."

She stopped her efforts and stared at him, speechless. A *goddess?*

Between the reaction of the crowd on the cliff and the goddess idea, she almost felt powerful. After all her years of being invisible—a *nobody*—she could get used to this sense of being someone worth listening to, someone worth caring about, someone worthwhile.

A *somebody.*

A wicked grin broke across his face. "And now my goddess is going to come for me."

He sped up the rhythm of his fingers and bent down his head. His lips closed over her breast, and his tongue caressed her nipple.

She panted, silently begging for more. His fingers beckoned her to a frenzied peak. Tension swelled, her muscles taut.

Yes. Her hips lifted off the bed. She was so close now.

His teeth lightly clamped down on her nipple, and shocks traveled straight to her core. Her body responded, and she clutched his shoulders, hanging on for the ride. Wave after wave of ecstasy broke over her and shot through her limbs. He'd become an expert at how to pleasure her, no doubt about that.

After her body fell limp, he gave her a kiss. "And now you're ready for step two."

She nodded as enthusiastically as she could against the mattress. "Yes, I am."

He rose above her and settled between her thighs. It wasn't close enough.

She bent her knees, molding herself around him, holding him against her most sensitive spots. He slid his shaft along her, spreading her moisture across his length. His head came close to her opening many times, but never slipped in.

More torture, or was he simply letting her take the lead for her first time?

Didn't matter. She maneuvered her fingers between them and encircled his rod. "I choose this. I choose you."

She pressed the head of his shaft past the lips below and grabbed his hips to ease him inside.

"Oh *God...*"

"By the *Maker...*"

Yes, he was huge, but she loved the sense of fullness, of holding him inside her, of feeling his skin inside hers. Electric tingles vibrated in every cell. So much better than just fingers.

They remained still for a moment, enjoying the sensations. She sank into the pools of his molten eyes and swam in the love between them. Then he lifted his hips, sliding himself nearly out, before pressing back down again.

"*Yes...*"

The connection between their bodies built like when she'd first ridden him. Magic thrummed through their touch. She didn't feel pain. Only him.

The motion of his hips sped up, and she pulled him harder,

encouraging him to fill her, make her complete. He obliged, strengthening his thrusts.

"More." She begged and slid her arms and legs around him.

Tighter. Harder. Faster.

Magic coiled between them, daring the dam to break and let it escape. Almost.

Tension hardened her muscles, and she strained to reach the release waiting for her. His thrusts stroked the spot where the tingles and the tension and the magic all gathered. Nothing could feel this amazing. And yet it did.

His eyes glowed. The gold overpowered all other colors in his gaze, reflecting the magic strengthening between them. Making them one.

She clutched him hard enough to force his whole body to sink into hers. In rhythm with the clock bonging twelve-noon out in the hallway, she moaned a *yes, yes, yes...*

The wall holding back the power between them shattered—and took her with it. She was crashing, flying, out of control. Her muscles shook, trembling waves drowning her in pleasure. If the sensations from her nerves weren't so incredible, she'd completely forget she had a body. *This* was what she'd wanted.

Magic shot through them, connecting them, filling them, completing them.

The powerful forces carried him along as well. He stiffened into her and held on like his life depended on it.

He grunted something that sounded vaguely like a worshipful "Maker's blessings."

They seized each other in the face of the magic binding them. Swirling energy resonated in every molecule and drove the sensations to something beyond description. Beyond imagination. She'd swear they levitated off the mattress.

The binding energy wrapped tighter and tighter, squeezing pleasure into every pore. Forcing them to live, breathe, and remain in the bubble of ecstasy. Until finally—after some measure of time that had lost all meaning—the magic coalesced into a cloud of mist.

The cloud circled like a tornado above them, glowing with its power. The column of mist swirled faster and faster, tightening into a beam of light, and then shot up past the ceiling, delivering the healing power to the unicorn homeland.

Together, they collapsed against the bed. That had been everything she needed, plus a bonus near-religious experience. For several minutes, their breathing sounded ragged and gasping.

Slowly, the pieces of her mind fell back into place, but this experience had changed her. She was stronger, more powerful, more confident in her ability to meet expectations.

And she knew—could feel—with absolute certainty that Markos felt the same.

"Did I hurt you?" He stroked her hair back from her face.

"Not at all." Probably more doings of the magic. That wonderful magic. "Do you think the magic will always make it like that?"

"I don't know." He grinned. "But maybe we should try again and find out."

"Already?"

He kissed along her neck and pressed his hips against her, proving his readiness. "Maybe another side effect of the magic is that I could do this all day."

All day. And they would have a lifetime of days like this.

She kissed him back. "I like the sound of that."

In fact, it sounded...

Magical.

Be part of all
the love stories found in the...

Thank you for reading *Pure Sacrifice*! I hope you enjoyed meeting Markos and Celia. The next book in the Mythos Legacy series is also available. Read on to learn more!

~ Jami

- If you enjoyed being part of the Mythos world, sign up for Jami's email list at *jamigold.com/mail*. Learn when her new books become available and **take advantage of her pre-order-only sale prices**!
- At *jamigold.com*, find information for all of Jami's books, including extra content for this book, and connect with her on social media.
- Reviews help other readers discover new books! If you have a moment, please leave a review on Goodreads, Amazon, and/or your favorite online retailer.

Ironclad Devotion, the third novel-length story
in the Mythos Legacy series, features
a **motorcycle-riding faerie princess**.
Go to *jamigold.com/id* to order!

IRONCLAD DEVOTION

**Safeguarding her freedom,
a faerie princess locks down her heart,
but a blacksmith forges the key...**

A faerie princess evading her fate...

Earth is no place for a faerie, but Kira can't go home without dooming her people. Desperate to avoid the pull of her homeland, she fosters an abandoned girl, the child's joy a source of much-needed energy.

A blacksmith with something to prove...

When Zachary Chase discovers he has a daughter, he's determined to be part of his child's life and not repeat his mother's neglect. But to open the little girl's heart, he must earn her foster mother's trust.

One night is never enough...

Despite their rivalry, Kira and Zac's desires tempt them into one no-consequences night. Yet the more passion flares between them, the more Kira risks destroying the life she's carved out on Earth—and endangering those she cares about in both worlds.

For more about *Ironclad Devotion*,
go to *jamigold.com/id* to read an excerpt
and **order your copy**!

About the Author

After capturing a unicorn and braiding its tail, Jami Gold moved to Arizona and decided to become a writer, where she could put her talent for making up stuff to good use. Fortunately, her muse, an arrogant male who delights in causing her to sound as insane as possible, rewards her with unique and rich story ideas.

Fueled by chocolate, she writes paranormal romance and urban fantasy tales that range from dark to humorous, but one thing remains the same: Normal need not apply. Just ask her family—and zombie cat.

Sign up for news on upcoming releases, find preview excerpts, and connect with Jami on social media by visiting *jamigold.com*.

Acknowledgements

I keep waiting for the process of writing a book to get easier. In some ways, it has—I've streamlined my beta reading and editing processes anyway. But in other ways, each book is so different that we never know what challenges we're going to encounter.

This was my "How the heck am I supposed to make a serial killer sympathetic and relatable?" book. The word challenge doesn't even start to describe how I struggled.

Once again, I couldn't have completed this book without the support of my family. They listened to my brainstorming rambles and tolerated me venting my frustrations.

I send hugs and thanks to my best beta buddies: Angela, Buffy, and Jay. You are better friends than I deserve. *listens to mental whispers* And Markos and Celia thank you too—you all helped me brainstorm my way through the *challenge* that is Markos.

Thanks to my editor Jessa who gave me insightful and detailed ideas for how to fix the story. And thanks to my other editors—Marcy, Erynn, and Julie—who made sure Humpty Dumpty was put together again after I smashed the story into bits. Thanks again to Laird for the wonderful cover. All of you helped me make this book even better than the vision in my head.

Thanks also to the amazing writing community, including the awesomeness that is NaNo (National Novel Writing Month). You all helped me finish this story faster than I thought possible. And my Twitter and Facebook friends—thank you for making my corner of the world a little brighter and happier.

And most of all, to my readers, the joy of writing wouldn't be the same without you!